PRAISE FOR CRIME WRITER

Sheppard writes with verve... revealing a deep knowledge
of detective-novel conventions and a keen understanding of
human behaviour to boot... engaging through all its twists and
turns... [a] gripping postmodern crime novel.

Kirkus

...a thrilling, more-ish novel... Sheppard masterfully depicts
her characters with a sense of real-worldliness. Her characters'
insecurities go hand in hand with their action-packed lives,
ultimately making them more honest and authentic. Add in
some well-placed wit, romance and a plot twist, and I devoured
this story in two days.

Others Magazine

This is a breathlessly fast-paced book... terrifically written with
great quotes scattered throughout... An excellent read.

Sydney Arts Guide

Such an original and absorbing novel...
A wonderful debut; an absolute pleasure to read.

City Hub Sydney

Fresh and original... one of my favourite new authors.

The Record

PRAISE FOR CRIME WRITER

Equal parts detective thriller and meta giggle-fest... impeccably
literary; beautifully written and self-aware. I've never
read anything like it. This is an extraordinarily good and
challenging debut.

3D Radio

...had me captured from the moment I turned the first page...
This novel was a refreshing change that kept me guessing from
start to finish... Sheppard writes her characters with a quirky
realism that makes the reader feel part of the story and the
characters come to life. One of my favourite new authors.

1079Life Radio

...will explode away the cobwebs of other formulaic offerings
and detonate a desire to play around in their world with a
second reading.

Reviews By Judith

I couldn't put it down!

98Five FM

CRIME WRITER SERIES

CRIME WRITER

DIME SHEPPARD

RUBY BOOKS
Brisbane, Australia

First published in Australia
in 2021 by Ruby Books
ABN: 60656353376

Copyright © Dime Sheppard 2022

Editor: Glenda Downing
Cover Design: Samantha Brown
Interior Design: Samantha Brown
@hello.samanthabrown

ISBN: 978-0-6488770-4-2
eBook ISBN: 978-0-6488770-1-1

A catalogue record for this work is available from the National Library of Australia

For Dad,
who loved to read.

DRAFT: Book Sixteen
By Evie Howland

Chapter One

Detective Carolyn Harding narrowed her blue eyes and crunched her second antacid for the morning, resisting indigestion. The source of discomfort was, as usual, someone nice. Recently, nice people made her feel depressed and queasy, and today's example was no exception.

Edgar Polton, a gentle South African with one leg in a large cast. He reminded her of a marshmallow, despite the hard edges of his accent. White, soft, sweet. The personal charisma of steamed rice. In fact the only cheering thing about him was the large black plastic bag of human body parts that had been leaking fluid through the iron slats of the fire escape outside his living room window. No amount of sugared niceness could explain that away.

But sadly, Harding didn't think he was the murder suspect, and now she scowled across miles of open-concept loft space to where Polton was standing limply in his own kitchen, giving his statement to Davits. Davits looked bored. Polton was leaning on crutches, white plaster stretching from foot to thigh on his right leg, and wearing a tailored button-up shirt that was literally the colour of cotton candy. Ugh.

'We done here?' She fired this at Detective Jay Ryan as he stepped back into the room from the foyer, slipping his notebook into the pocket of his navy sports coat. 'Rivas wants to deal with the scene before it degrades any further.' Rivas was head of the CS team, who had been here when they arrived. Harding glanced over at the CS photographer, who was collecting up his numbered markers, and a woman from forensics who was dusting the final surfaces.

Ryan acknowledged her words with a nod, his blue eyes sweeping the hardwood floors, luxury fixtures and high ceilings yet again. No detail escaped Jay Ryan.

'Neighbours got nothing,' he said. 'Some beat cops out of the First are talking to the apartments across the street.' He eyed the window where the drooling, ruptured bag had been, and where the artistic cast-iron facades of the facing buildings were visible.

'Something tells me they won't get anything.' Harding snapped a latex glove from her right hand and shoved it into the pocket of her skirt.

Ryan nodded. 'Looks like the bag was dumped from the roof and not from inside. Juice every-where. You get anything from the papers?'

He meant the newspapers. There had been a stack of five or six newspapers under the bag, like padding. Until recently they had protected the street four storeys below from the dribbling contents. Weird that whoever dumped the bag had thought to put newspapers down first.

Or not weird.

Harding waited for Ryan to turn from the window before she answered.

'Copies of *The Voice*. Back issues. At least one from 1997.'

Ryan's eyes jumped to hers. She knew they both had the same name in their minds, so she didn't bother voicing it.

Tillman.

Ryan nodded as if she had spoken it aloud and said, 'If it's him, he hung a sign on it.'

Tillman. Tillman and his newspaper obsession. But why would he make it so obvious? And what did he have to do with sappy Edgar Polton?

Harding stepped closer to the wide, wood-framed window and cast her eyes over the smudgy early morning view of downtown SoHo. The scattering of boutique stores on the cobbled street below were just opening for the day. This was a nice apartment. It was a shame to see it ruined with forensic powder. Nothing like organic charcoal to stick in the crevices of reclaimed hardwood furniture forever. She supposed Edgar Polton might even tear up about it, like he had when the rookie cop responding to a routine 10-64 that morning had knocked on his door and pointed out that Polton's unlawful garbage was dripping onto the pavement below. The hapless Polton took him willingly to the window and together they made the discovery of the pre-bagged DOA.

'We taking him with us?' Ryan angled his sober gaze towards Polton, his voice low and careful. Harding huffed and shook her head.

'No. I don't see him sawing that body into half a dozen pieces.' She glanced back into the kitchen to

Polton in his pink shirt. Marshmallow. Polton was nodding earnestly at Davits, and wobbling on his crutches. His eyes kept darting to the place where the bag had been with a kind of horrified confusion. The cast was from a skiing injury, supposedly.

Moneyed, coddled marshmallow.

'You don't like him.' A statement of fact from Ryan, though Harding had given no indication of this. She certainly hadn't mentioned indigestion. Ryan shrugged. 'Maybe we take him back with us and stew him for awhile.'

'No.' She grimaced. That would likely lead to full-blown heartburn. 'I don't think we need to break him. He looks broken already.' This drew a faint look of amusement from Ryan. Harding added, 'He might start crying or need help getting out of the elevator.'

Ryan had the nerve to roll his eyes. 'You're all heart, Harding.'

She turned from the window and stalked toward the door.

'I don't need one.'

1

They say you should write from the heart. You know? Write what's inside, write what's true. But I've always thought that was kind of dumb. I mean, what do writers have in their hearts, really, except for a bunch of stuff they've imagined while sitting at a desk? If I wrote from the heart it would be about...

Well, it wouldn't be very interesting.

I shift in my chair and eye the mug of cold tea next to my computer. People walk through personal trials or whatever but the only walking I've been doing recently is pacing the room. I add *cardio* to my list of achievements for the day and mentally congratulate myself. Maybe I could try a visualisation technique? Like those athletes who imagine themselves winning a race. They see it in their mind—crossing the line first, and then jumping and pumping their arms in the air. I could visualise myself...er, typing at my computer. Never mind.

Write from the heart. Ha. The fact is, sometimes the things in people's hearts are best left unsaid. Sometimes they're a bit grim and unsightly. Or if they're not, they might get *stuck* on the way out. Not *blocked*. No one's saying the b-word here. I pick up a Q-tip and skate it around my keyboard, making sure to scrub at all the liquorice-smudges.

Have I become a cliché? This whole staring-blankly-at-the-cursor scene feels pretty old, as far as plots go. If my life was a plot, that is. But a cliché isn't the worst thing to be, is it? Clichés are part of the human experience. They're easy to understand. They're safe and familiar.

I love safe and familiar things!

I throw the Q-tip into my full wastepaper basket and do an awkward, stagy laugh to no one in particular, since I'm completely alone here in my writing room, except for a profound lack of inspiration and the empty first page of Chapter Three.

I gulp a mouthful of stagnant tea, flick off Chopin and increase the volume on the *Meditation for Creativity* series playing through my speakers, something I was desperate enough to pay actual money for this morning. So far it has been mostly ocean sounds, which isn't helpful when I'm on my seventh cup.

The truth is, this has never happened to me before. Never. Not in fifteen books. I glance over at the mocking row of them lined up on my shelves. The most recent paperback printing has a chic black cover, with my name printed boldly down the spine, *Evie Howland*. The books dominate the room, identical, like vertebrae.

Hmm. *Vertebrae*, I muse. *Spines*.

A broken back? Interesting way to go. *Vertebral compression fracture*. Maybe a push off a high cliff? I see it immediately, the breathless drop, grey waves making a grisly mess of the shore below, a hole cut crudely in the wire safety fence. In my mind's eye something white goes swooping on the wind. A seabird?

The ocean sounds recede.

'I am creative.' A numbing voice booms gently out of them.

'I am creative,' I repeat obediently, pulling my eye mask back down. *Focus, Evie*. There is no point inventing random killings. I need to solve the stakeout. Today.

'Inspiration is flowing through me,' the meditation track enthuses, if mellowly.

'Inspiration is flowing through me,' I mumble.

Blegh. I bite my lip and press my fingers into my covered eyes. This feels like rock bottom. Why can't I seem to get through this fictional stakeout? Book Sixteen. What is wrong with Book Sixteen?

Outside my window, the distant scattered sounds of leafy, sunlit suburbia—kids walking home from school, neighbours' voices, garage doors, dogs—are faintly audible. I love this part of New York. It's only thirty minutes from the heart of the city but the Village of Pelham is like the safe, storybook version of living in Manhattan. It reminds me of England.

'Now write, as the creativity bursts from your fingertips.'

Ugh. I push my eye mask up and glance around the room, as if seeking salvation from my pile of weapons encyclopaedias and the length of rope I've been practicing tying nooses on. Who am I kidding? This *is* rock bottom. I punch off my speaker and grab a new pair of earplugs from the industrial-sized tub under my desk.

'Bursting from my fingertips,' I mutter.

I can feel Harding's boredom seeping off the page like hydrogen cyanide.

A gas at room temperature, I think. Interesting way to go. *Ingestion of as little as 270 ppm is sufficient to cause death within minutes.*

Ack. *Focus.* I've written fifteen books. There is *no reason* I can't write a sixteenth.

I blink at the screen, fingers poised.

Chapter Three

Harding slouched in the car, glaring at the house. Its bland brick squareness and bare lawn screamed textbook emotional detachment.

She felt like she had been on this stakeout for months, and she hated waiting. But if this was

Tillman's house, and she felt in her gut that it was, then nothing was going to stop her from seeing him dragged out of it and cuffed on the curb. She picked up the binoculars again. She had already spent half an hour imagining a gas leak that suddenly blew Tillman and his pointy little face to smithereens.

The passenger door opened and Ryan slid into his seat, bringing the smell of coffee with him.

'Donut?'

She shuddered and didn't answer as he obligingly put the coffee into her reaching fingers. She scowled through the lenses.

'WHAT is Tillman doing in there?'

I stop typing and thunk my head on the desk. Okay, fail.

Harding's unhealthy rage is disquieting. And donuts? Really?

Detectives plus donuts equals *cliché*. And Jay *knows* Carolyn has stopped eating donuts, or anything sweet for that matter. She's had a permanent case of indigestion after meeting Edgar Polton. She's also feeling old at the moment, and at some level she's taken to fighting a battle to keep her bombshell looks, even if it means giving up things she enjoys.

The fact that Jay offered her one tells me something, at least. That he's almost as bored and annoyed about being stuck in that car as she is.

My forehead senses a vibration through the desk, and I look up. I keep my phone in a big glass vase full of shredded paper while I'm working—I like to manage distractions in this room—and now the glow of the screen is just visible through its papery shroud. The caller ID says *Jenna*.

'Gah.' I pluck it out, palm a handful of liquorice allsorts from the bowl next to my computer, and tweak out an earplug.

'Are you dressed?' Jenna never bothers with preamble. I can hear the clatter of the city in the background of the call, so she must be leaving work. She's probably on her way somewhere fashionable, wearing something unashamedly low-cut, and eyeing up an attractive broker or hedge fund manager as we speak. I thunk my head back down on the desk again.

'I don't know what to wear.'

'Please. He hasn't stopped buying you clothes,' she says. In my mind's eye I can see the flick of her black bob and the expression on her red lips as she narrows her eyes at me, and I brace myself for her next question. I swallow my liquorice, hoping the sugar rush will ease the niggle of impotence I feel. It doesn't. 'Pages?'

The only reason Jenna can ask me so bluntly about how many pages I've done is because she's been my agent for ten years. If I were a bold, confident person, I might tell her about the cardio and the visualisation technique I almost did today. Instead I make a kind of whimpering noise and slide down my chair until I'm effectively hiding under my desk.

'Fine.' She has taken my silence as discouragement, which it is. 'Are we talking fractions here?' She hasn't had to ask after my pages before. This is new ground for us.

'Um.' I clear my throat. 'A third?' I can't bring myself to say *of a page.*

There's a second's pause on the other end where I hear that cluttered noise of life in motion again. I eye my writing room. One wall is all bookshelves, and the brown leather reading chair that used to be my father's is in the far corner. There's only one window, and the noise from outside is muted by the heavy fabric blind. It's cave-like, and quiet. Safe.

'What about reflexology?' she drills. 'Have you tried apple cider vinegar?'

'Ugh.'

'What about wheatgrass, or kombucha? Ginseng? Tumeric? Freaking, I don't know, matcha? Did you have a massage like I told you to?' I scrunch my face, and make the whimpering noise again. I didn't have a massage. I did consume a lot of liquorice, though. 'A *week*, Evie,' she continues. 'A week past deadline. At least do publicity tonight and pacify me.'

'My personal life is not publicity,' I say. 'It's a dinner party. Not a media event.'

'Any place full of the rich and influential is a media event.'

'Jenna—'

'Do the interview, then.' I can practically hear her put a hand on her hip. 'They're going to call you "the sassiest voice in crime fiction". They want to put you on the cover, Evie. The *cover*. And you're actually hot enough to rock it, too. Do you know when a writer gets this much attention?' She doesn't wait for my reply. 'They *don't. Ever.*'

I close my eyes. I'm one hundred per cent sure the *Vogue* writer has wildly exaggerated my chances of getting on the cover, but it wouldn't have made a difference. 'No interviews,' I say.

'Wrong. No interviews *recently.*'

Three years is stretching *recently*, even for Jenna. I feel a pang of guilt. Getting me into *Vogue* would have made her really happy. I haven't exactly made her job easy in the last three years. But she hasn't given up, even if it means poking at me like this. It's actually what I like about her, this bold New-York-ness she has. The hard-and-fast gritty fearlessness the city perfects in people. I glance at the photo above my desk.

'I have a dress,' I say, giving in. 'It's not that I don't want to go out tonight. It's...'

'It's that you don't want to go out *ever.*' I frown. 'Well,' she says, as though consoling herself, 'maybe I can get them to do the piece anyway because you've turned into a hermit. Like Dickinson or

Harper Lee. Reclusive but enigmatic. It could sell.' She pauses. 'But it's not *normal*, Evie. Now obey me. Get dressed immediately. You don't want to disappoint his parents. You love his parents. And take some freaking vitamins or something.'

I hang up and notice that I have two missed calls from Uncle Allan. It gives me a little warm glow, but it's unusual. He or Aunt Jo often call, but twice in one day?

Then I see the time.

Fastest shower ever. The dress *is* pretty, since the personal stylist Daniel's mother hired for me has impeccable taste, but I don't have time to do my hair properly, or paint my nails, or spend a portion of time breathing deeply and preparing myself for a glittering Gatsby-esque mansion full of senators and philanthropists and Major League baseball players.

My face in the mirror has a fight-or-flight look about it. Am I a disaster? The dress is silk, the right shade of green to match my eyes and elegant; the pumps make my legs look longer and force me to straighten my posture. Generally, I go for quirky. I grimace at myself.

I grab my engagement ring off the dresser on my way out the door, flying down the stairs and trying to put it on at the same time. It's a huge thing, too flashy to write with, the diamond too dazzling and distracting. Five carats, I mean, geez. I poke my head out the front door to see if Daniel has arrived...and come face to face with Detective Carolyn Harding.

'Well that was a productive day,' she says sarcastically as she pushes past me.

I drop the ring in surprise. *Not now. I can't do this right now.*

Jay is right behind her. His holstered gun slips into view as he bends down to scoop up the diamond.

'Donuts?' he says. He's referring to the stakeout, of course. He quirks an eyebrow at me. 'You hate clichés.'

'Her *life* is a cliché.' Carolyn throws this over her shoulder as she barges past the living room. Jay hands me the ring and there's a second where his eyes flick over what I'm wearing. Usually I wear a baggy grey sweater when I'm writing, like a uniform, kind of the writer's equivalent of a painter's smock. It's ugly but comfortable. Right now this dress is hugging places Jay probably never knew existed on me.

I look up and meet his eyes. Detective Jay Ryan. He's tall and broad-shouldered, and all the things fictional heroes should be. He's also sharp as a flick knife in a dark alley, with eyes like heat. He's the reason my books do so well among my female demographic. He has this searing glance that can liquefy just about anyone, though generally he's too focused and serious about his work to notice the effect he has on people. Women especially.

Carolyn is one of the smartest people in the NYPD and she's also stunning: long-legged, blue-eyed and smooth-skinned, like a Charlie's Angel, and with a will of solid steel. The two of them are electric, as far as the books go. Together they're the kind of partners who function like finely-tuned machinery. My readers love them. She never holds back, a heady mix of sass and cool class. He's all physical strength held still until the right moment. She exudes chic aggression. He's comfortable in the background watching, seeing everything that no one else sees. Together they've been solving cases for five years, in book time. And they bicker like brother and sister. But they trust each other, and they have the other's back. They're a force of nature, and probably the real reason I've managed more than a book a year for so long.

'I knew it. She's got a crazy-wall in here.'

Carolyn has breached the sanctity of my writing room, and I hustle after her. Okay, so yes, I have some newspaper articles and other items up on the far wall. Covering the wall. Sure, I connected some of them up with string, just for convenience sake.

Red seemed the obvious colour choice at the time.

'You realise this is a cliché, don't you?' Carolyn points at it. 'And what the hell is the rest of this stuff?'

Most of my notes are handwritten and piled on my desk in a tall, precarious hump, and there is crime detritus everywhere: anatomy posters, medical journals, maps, police reports, ID sketches, post-mortem textbooks, poisons information.

It's kind of dark in there, now that I look at it from the doorway. I keep the blinds closed to block the noise out, because the kids from next door often sneak past that window into my yard. I like to feel the cosy safety of the heavy material between me and all their...adventure-seeking. I think possibly they believe I'm some kind of crazy Boo Radley person.

I glance over to where there's a fake human skull on my third shelf, holding up a large hardcover book on Jack the Ripper. Well.

And then there's that photo above my desk of my dad and I, with him in his uniform and me all gangly and pre-teen and proud.

'What, did you drink like fifteen cups of tea today?' Carolyn has her arms folded, her shoulder-length blonde hair looking effortlessly messy-chic in a way I can never achieve. She's staring down the seven mugs beside my computer. They're surrounded by an Olympic network of permanent rings, and I squirm. This desk is something I inherited, along with my father's chair. It's French carved oak, and antique. I should have taken better care of it. I just get so *involved* when I'm working.

Jay is lounging against the doorframe. 'You left evidence?' There's mild accusation in his tone.

'I thought I should maybe start counting cups,' I say. 'For my health.'

'Oh yeah? Did you eat anything today?' Jay takes me in with that hot gaze. 'Candy doesn't count.' I glance involuntarily at the empty liquorice bowl, trying to remember. I'm pretty sure there's nothing in my fridge except milk and carrots. Old carrots. So possibly not.

'I'm doing a cleanse,' I say.

'Oh yeah?'

'Yes. Flushing all the nutrients and vitamins out of my body.'

'That must feel great.' Jay's tone is one hundred per cent deadpan.

I match it. 'It does.'

He cracks a smile, and I feel like I've won something. Jay's smiles are rare, and therefore precious. He has straight teeth, thanks to a couple of years in braces when he was thirteen or so, and also when he smiles it emphasises the fact that his jawline is...well, if I were writing something a bit more trashy I might say *chiselled*. But I don't write Jay like that.

In any case the smile is short lived, as all Jay's smiles are.

'An apple a day wouldn't hurt, you know.' His eyes are knowing.

'Apple seeds are full of cyanoglycosides,' I say.

'Right. Remind me how many seeds you gotta eat to get cyanide poisoning?'

'About two hundred,' I mutter. I sidle my eyes away from his. 'Finely crushed.'

'You know,' says Carolyn conversationally, 'I would have liked about this many cups of coffee today. Or just better coffee. Instead of hours of a sore butt and *no progress*. And I would have liked a good massage, instead of *donuts*.' She cuts her eyes pointedly to Jay, before they land back on me and narrow. 'Are you planning to do something with your face?'

My hands go to my cheeks with a little intake of breath. I forgot makeup.

Whenever these two show up it's like the practical part of my brain just shuts down. I run for the mirror near my front door and scrabble through my purse. Carolyn yells after me, 'How much longer are we going to be there, Evie?'

She means *at the stakeout*. They have a habit of referring to their life in the books as 'work', as if floating around with me in the real world is some kind of holiday. Or worse yet, calling it 'inside', for example, 'Do we really have to go back inside?' As if their time spent advancing the story under my pen is a prison sentence.

'Easy, Harding.' Jay's tone is pacifying. He has followed me as far as the wide entryway to the living room. He's still wearing the same clothes he had on for the stakeout, and his leather jacket, olive skin and dark jeans make him look like a shot of technicolour against the neutral tones of my interior design. My living room especially is a little bland. Beige sofa, beige walls and carpet. I never really bothered decorating it. It's not like I ever have anyone over. Anyone real, that is. And I never spend any time in it myself.

'Three weeks.' Carolyn says this to the back of Jay's head as she stomps down the hall toward us but I know she's really talking to me. 'Three weeks we've been sitting in that car. Staring at that same house, drinking the same coffee.' I quail under the blanching glare of her ice-blue eyes. Carolyn is the kind of beautiful that only fictional heroines can be, the kind that defies logic. But right now her dewy complexion is contorted, her slender limbs are twitchy and tense, her fists clenched, her movements jerky. It's so unlike her. She stomps all the way into the living room and over to my sideboard, pulls open the door and rummages inside like she'll find the answer to the stakeout there. I wish I knew. She doesn't need to remind *me* that her life is at a dead standstill. I'm the one writing it. But every day I sit at my computer and... nothing.

'She's been busy.' Jay never gets ruffled by Carolyn.

'She's *not* busy. Mr Perfect has hired a stupid-expensive wedding planner. *She's* busy.' Carolyn's razor expression takes in the prepared, untouched stacks of wedding magazines, linen swatches and card samples on my beige coffee table, all tied up with white bridal ribbons and cute little notes from the long-suffering Magdeline. I open my mouth to rebuke Carolyn for calling Daniel 'Mr Perfect', mascara half on, when the front door opens behind me and Tillman walks in. Great.

'Hello Tillman,' I say politely. This greeting is more habit than anything else. He doesn't acknowledge me. Morton Tillman: thirty-something high-functioning criminal with technically only a handful of misdemeanours on his rap sheet, and an unaccountable soft-spot in my readers' hearts. He's been around for a long time, so it's possibly longevity rather than personality that makes them gush about him in their fan mail.

His shirt is buttoned to the neck on his reedy frame and he has a vacant, almost childlike expression. He wanders into the living room and sits awkwardly into a corner of the sofa just as Carolyn yanks a bottle of expensive red wine out of my sideboard. She spies him and turns back to me.

'Tillman?' she says, dismayed. 'Oh, that's just great. I'm busting my ass trying to put him in prison and now I have to see him during my down time? I'm drinking this wine.' She storms back down the hall into the kitchen and I throw an anxious look to Jay.

'She's not...I mean, she won't...?'

'Was it a gift?'

It was actually. Daniel's father gave it to me when Book Fifteen came out. It's probably one of those rare bottles that cost about a zillion dollars. 'Yes, but I mean, she's not actually going to...she can't *drink* it?'

Jay shakes his head. 'She just likes to hold the glass in her hand.'

I feel a flutter of dismay. I've never seen Carolyn like this. 'She's so...' *Bitter.* I fumble for a kinder word. 'Different, these days.' I'm feeling slightly bewildered. Sure, Carolyn has always been assertive, incisively honest and articulate. It comes with the territory. But not brutal. Not with that tinge of hopelessness I've just seen. Like she's on the edge of giving in.

Jay is still standing on my beige carpet with his hands in his pockets, as if sitting down isn't an option. It's typical Jay. His 'relaxed' is someone else's 'poised and ready'.

'Yeah, but remember she only got divorced two books ago. We've been busy since then. It's gonna take time to process.'

'I guess that's my fault.' I sigh.

'I guess so.' A gentle pause. 'And you made her ex-husband a real asshole.'

'Please,' I say. 'He already was one. I just let him into the story.' There's a crash from the kitchen. Jay shakes his head.

'She's tired. She's lost her focus. She's been chasing the same guy for over a dozen books, and he's still just a shadow. And Tillman is a major pain in her ass.'

'No offence,' I say to Tillman, who is busy putting weird greasy fingerprints on the antique carriage clock Daniel's parents gave me for my last birthday.

'None taken,' he murmurs, to the clock. He never looks at me.

Carolyn returns with the uncorked bottle and a full wineglass. Tillman puts a shy hand up like he might want some.

'Forget it, Tillman,' she snarls. 'It's enough that I have to look at you.' She turns to me. 'Is the Blade coming too? Because you know having two psychopaths in the room together would just be the perfect end to my day.'

'You know the Blade never comes,' Jay reproves mildly. His eyes flick my way. 'He disturbs her.'

Carolyn huffs and smells her wine. 'What time does Mr Perfect arrive?'

'About now,' I say. I feel nervous. 'Do I look alright?'

Carolyn shrugs. Jay's eyes are hooded. *Great response, team.* I feel self-conscious, like this whole thing isn't me—these bare arms aren't me, my hair all loose and swingy isn't me. 'Anyway, he's not perfect,' I say, trying to self-inject some confidence. *He's just regular, like me.* Okay, there's no way I can argue that. Daniel Bradley is not regular.

'Please,' Carolyn scoffs. 'He's pure fantasy. He's literally as far from reality as a person can get. You need to spend some time in the real world, Evie.'

The irony of this statement is not lost on me.

'Reality's a scary place,' Tillman pipes up suddenly. He's staring off into the corner of the ceiling like he isn't paying attention to the conversation. 'Real scary,' he adds, and we all look at him. And then he drops his gaze, and looks right at me. 'You should be scared.'

Er, creepy. I frown.

The doorbell sounds, startling all of us, except Jay. It must be Daniel. *Maybe I have time to change into jeans and a hoodie. Maybe I can sprain my ankle on the way to the door.* Carolyn snaps past me in her high heels, which she is never without and can basically run a six-minute mile in, and clomps loudly up the stairs.

'I'm going to soak in your tub. By the way, you forgot lipstick.'

I make a little noise of horror but Jay is standing behind me and helping me on with my coat.

'You're fine,' he says in a low voice. Like Daniel is going to hear him from the other side of the door. Like Daniel could ever hear him, period. Jay is careful not to touch me, not that he could. 'Put it on in the car.' Jay has three sisters. He's comfortable with women, comfortable being brotherly.

'Right.' I don't turn to look at him but stay facing the door. I grit my teeth, close my eyes, and try to centre myself. It's not that easy today. I breathe a couple of times, clearing my mind, getting my head-space back.

When I open the door I don't need to look behind me to know that all traces of them are gone, like they were never there. But I do glance behind me—*just to check*—and let out a little sigh. The living room is spotless and bland as ever, Carolyn gone from the stairs, even Tillman's creepy smudges gone from my carriage clock. I stoop to sweep up my ring from the floor and grab my coat and throw it on.

On the front step stands Daniel Bradley in an impeccable tux, as smoothly pressed and sharply finished as new-minted money. Behind him a sleek black limousine waits at the curb. He is gorgeous, gleaming, confident, and smiling like I'm exactly what he always wanted.

'Hey.'

I smile back. 'Hey yourself.'

2

Daniel Bradley came into my life like a hot knife into butter. And I mean hot. He has this brown-eyed, beach tan, biceps thing going that sets him apart from the rest of the nerdy Silicon Valley kids, pasty games designers and jaded playboy heirs on the Forbes list of young billionaires. Daniel is special. It's been kind of a whirlwind. We met six months ago and his family is lovely. I'm very happy.

The wealth thing is an issue. Yachts and private jets are nice in theory, but in practice I find them rather garish, and I'm not exactly anxious for the attention they bring. Generally I try not to spend a lot of time thinking about how being an American billionaire is a cliché. It makes me squirm at the too-white-teeth New-York-nobility prosaicism of it all.

Only last week I signed the pre-nup. Daniel's lovely mother, Eileen, was concerned about the awkwardness but really, they could have done it without the lawyers. I'm not fussed about the money. Next year Daniel's father, James Bradley, will sign over the majority of his shares to his two children, Daniel and his sister Juliana, and Daniel will take over as CEO of the company. It will mean his net worth becomes something doubly hair-raising, so I could understand Eileen's motherly concern wanting to safeguard the bedazzling family birthright.

But I'm not exactly poor myself. I own my own home, I have

my own car and I can keep food in my fridge and be generous to my aunt and uncle. My books sell and I'm pretty proud of my accomplishments, even if they don't get written about in Forbes Magazine.

'You look like James Bond,' I say. I pull the door closed and step into him. He puts two warm hands onto my waist and kisses me, making me glad I forgot lipstick. He's a great kisser. Then he pulls back, looking at me.

'Bad day?' My smile falters. Daniel always notices how I'm feeling. He's very perceptive. It makes him a good businessman.

'It's nothing.'

'Liar.' He smiles, and I smile back. I'm not going to lament over my problems with Chapter Three. Daniel is working sixty-hour weeks and feeling the pressure of running his father's multinational company. My worries over a little fictional crime-solving don't really compare. 'And, you're nervous.'

'It's you,' I say. 'You're very tall and handsome. I'm much more confident with shorter, ugly people.' I sober. 'You can tell?' He gives me a tiny squeeze.

'I can tell. It's cute.' He has a gorgeous smile, and I soak it up before he kisses me again. 'Come on. I know exactly what you need to make you feel better.'

'A formal dinner with your parents?'

He laughs. 'I was going to say a Pimm's.'

I let him lead me to the limo, and deliberately put Jay and Carolyn out of my mind. Daniel doesn't quite get the whole writer's thing. I tried explaining how it is for me, why I talk about Carolyn and Jay as if they're real people. Writers have less control than people think, I told him. Writing characters often feels like sitting back and watching something happen, rather than creating or deciding. The story appears, either wholly or in its elements, like it came out of the ether. And the characters themselves show up without permission, mostly. They're just there, unavoidable.

'Characters are people,' I explained, 'and the only way to figure out who they are and how they behave is to spend time with them. Otherwise they do things that surprise the pants off you.' And potentially derail the story in a big way.

'But they're not there,' he argued. 'They don't exist.' Daniel is very practical.

'They do exist,' I argued back. 'Just not here, exactly.'

'Like another dimension?' He was smiling by then, humouring me.

'No,' I smiled back. 'But they exist to me, and when people read my books they exist to them, too. Sort of. They have existence, just maybe not substance.'

Well. It's hard to explain at the best of times. And Daniel spends his days taking risks with millions of dollars and managing a fleet of ships that support the lives of thousands of people. Whimsy and the metaphysical aren't exactly high on his list of priorities.

These days he talks about my 'creative process' and 'spending time with my characters' with those air quotes you make with your hands. I don't mind. It's just the circle he moves in. He's concerned with cold hard reality, and frankly, I can't see that as a bad thing. It's people like him who change the world.

Thankfully he doesn't press me about it tonight after we've made it into the Bradleys' helicopter, an all-black Eurocopter EC145. I'm pretty savvy with civil and military helicopters, thanks to research I did for Book Nine, where the Blade managed to steal a nice AgustaWestland that he stashed in a barn somewhere in West Virginia.

Daniel likes to use the chopper on Friday nights. He gets impatient in traffic, especially the gridlock on the Montauk Highway heading to Southampton for the weekend. The fact that he met me with the limo was very sweet considering it must have taken forever to drive up to the burbs from Manhattan. So I don't begrudge him the airtime, though flying is my least favourite form of travel. Totally unnecessary danger, in my opinion. But the interior is all spacious luxury—creamy Italian leather and wood panelling appointed in 24-carat gold, with soft ambient lighting—so it doesn't feel terribly dangerous.

We don't speak. Daniel is working on his laptop, and I'm quiet and processing, still a little dazed after the episode with Carolyn. She shocked me by how out of control she was—how loose and volatile.

It's out of character.

'How's the planning coming?' Daniel's voice comes through my headset. It might be stately and insulated in here but it's still a helicopter. The sunset is in full swing through the tinted windows but Daniel has been looking at his laptop. Now he's looking at me.

'Good,' I say, confused. Did he mean my plot twists?

'Magdeline said you have a fitting tomorrow.'

Oh, right. The wedding. Wedding planning. I clear my throat.

'Er, yes.'

'I'll send the car for you. You got my message about Hong Kong?'

'Uh...' I rifle the indecipherable pages of my memory from today. Since I almost never answer my phone, it's safe to assume I don't know anything about Hong Kong.

'Hong Kong?' he says patiently. 'The meeting I have there tomorrow morning, my late flight tonight...?'

'Oh.' I really need to check my messages more often.

'You need to check your messages more often, Jane.' This makes me smile. He calls me Jane every now and then with a little twist of irony, usually when I've been absentminded, caught up in the books. As in, Jane Austen. Ha ha. He knows that what I write is about as far removed from period romance as possible. Maybe if Elizabeth Bennet had a gun and a nasty breakup behind her. And a much shorter skirt.

'You're adorable,' he says. He scoops me in, pulls off his headset and my own in a way that is both theatrical and romantic, and kisses me as I laugh and try not to crumple his gorgeous tux. *This is not a fantasy*, I think dreamily, as I enjoy every slow second of it. The startling streaks of pink and orange outside are cooling into purples and blues.

Not a fairytale. This is real.

3

The Bradley mansion looks every inch the fairytale palace, however, when we arrive a half hour later. It's a sprawling twelve-bedroom home set on ten acres with a tennis court, heated swimming pool, green house, separate staff quarters, and two four-car garages. Tonight the sculpted lawn is strung with lights, the glass-enclosed pool is reflecting starlight, and the main house is ablaze from within. There's an extravagant number of guests spilling through French doors thrown open for the occasion, mingling in the scented breeze with crystal glasses of champagne.

Crickets chirp softly and Daniel's hand rests lightly on my back as we walk up through the gardens from the helipad. The house was designed with entertaining in mind, and three wide steps give access directly from the grounds to what the Bradleys call 'the Ballroom'. It's a grand room with oak-panelled floors and gold leaf trim, and I feel Daniel stiffen as we cross the threshold. He dislikes this, all the high society stuff. He prefers the business world. But I'm glad he's by my side because he couldn't possibly be as nervous and overwhelmed as I am. There's so much glittering and sparkling and chiming laughter. Uniformed waiters are serving drinks and there's even a champagne tower in one corner. I briefly wish I'd never come, and then Daniel's mother appears and captures my hand.

'Here's my favourite daughter-in-law!' Eileen Bradley hugs me, all elegance, warmth and motherliness. The pale cinnamon shade and artistic drapes of her gown match her complexion and her slim figure perfectly. I relax a fraction.

'To-be!' says Magdeline, smiling sweetly, who I hadn't seen there behind Eileen, and who apparently doesn't want anyone to forget that the wedding hasn't happened yet, and that she's the one with the brand-new daddy-bought company that's planning it.

Magdeline is an heiress in her own right, and fits in perfectly here. She's slightly younger than me, and one of those women who seem to be all legs, and all tan. She has a long straight ponytail, which she doesn't flick or swing, but ignores carefully in a way that says she is intelligent, professional and gracious.

Yet as I smile a greeting, I see her eyes slide from me to slant a little look at Daniel, as if she would eat him alive if she could, and I remember that she's also wired for shark-like social snobbery, like the rest of the women at this party. I experience a moment of paralysing anxiety. I know I'm not considered a satisfying reason for Daniel Bradley to stop appearing on the GQ Hottest Bachelors list. A fiction writer, who hasn't done any modelling and has no money to speak of, old or new. I may not have grown up sipping elitist social cues like single malt, but I'm sensitive enough to notice the age-old art of subtle condescension. Which is exactly the look Magdeline is giving me now.

And then I give myself a shake. No. I'm glad someone toothy is tackling the wedding. The last thing I want to think about is how many hundreds of people are going to be at the church, or the reception, or the dress I'll be wearing while they all stare at me.

'Hello, Mother,' Daniel says beside me. 'Magdeline.'

'Darling, you're late,' Eileen reproves, a comment to which Daniel replies by removing a glass of wine from the tray of a nearby waiter, sipping a mouthful and raising roguish eyebrows at her. This gesture tells me that he made sure we were late on purpose, and I give him a grateful look. 'It's almost dinner, and we wanted more time with Evie,' Eileen adds. She squeezes my hand again. 'Sweetheart, Daniel tells me you turned down an interview with *Vogue?*'

'Oh!' I say, feeling awkward. Is she disappointed? Perhaps I should apologise. Eileen recently retired from a long Art History professorship at Yale. I suppose I hadn't counted on the tickling of her vanity by an *haute couture* women's magazine superseding her commitment to highbrow scholarliness.

'Mother, you promised you wouldn't bring it up.' Daniel rolls his eyes, sounding both resigned and indulgent at the same time. 'Evie is famous and successful enough. It's the books that count.' He winks at me. He knows he's quoting my words back to me.

'Sweetheart,' Eileen shakes her head in kindly disagreement, 'you owe it to writers everywhere to be as visible as possible. The written word is all but lost—*lost!*—as an art form.'

'That's nothing,' Daniel says. 'Wait till you hear what she told *The New Yorker.*'

Eileen's beautiful lips part in shock at this heresy, and I gasp, because I can't believe he would drop that bomb, and I have no idea how to diffuse it. But I'm saved from replying by a bejewelled matron who sidles up and puts a possessive hand under my elbow.

'Is this her, Eileen? It is a thrill to meet you, my dear,' she says, turning to me, and I sag in relief. She's a lady of solid proportions, gathered into a concoction of many turquoise sequins. 'My husband is such a fan, and so am I. I absolutely love your characters.'

I smile. 'Thank you. So do I.'

'You must be so proud, Eileen, having this girl under your wing.'

'I would be more proud if you could talk some sense into her, Rachel. She has just turned down *another* interview.' But Mrs

Bradley does sound proud. I realise this has more to do with tickling family vanity than endangerment to the written word, after all. It isn't really about doing the interview, but that it can get talked about at dinner parties like this. I relax. I may be an odd choice for Daniel, but at least I'm moderately famous. Eileen glances at me with a kind of conspiratorial affection, and I relax a little more.

'Another...!' Rachel is shocked.

'Last month it was for that talk show on NBC.'

Rachel looks like the robust state of her health has been rocked by this revelation. 'Why, Eileen?'

I turn to share a smile with Daniel over how entertaining this is, Rachel asking Mrs Bradley about my motives when I'm standing right there, but Daniel has moved away, caught by a conversation with a skinny little whiskered man with drooping black circles under his eyes like a ferret. The man looks at me and then his eyes slide away as if I'm not important. I suppose he's a business acquaintance. I'm still getting to know who's who in Daniel's life.

Daniel's sister joins the group and there are general air-kisses. Juliana is a couple of years older than me and regally beautiful, with sheets of long dark hair and imposing posture. She has the kind of pale, porcelain skin that shows up the delicate traceries of her veins, giving real meaning to the term blue-blooded, and unlike Daniel, whose warm brown eyes are my favourite feature, Juliana's eyes are darker and rather withering. She has been in charge of planning this party, though I believe the extent of her involvement has been to hire and then repeatedly badger the event planners. I take a better look around me. There seems to be the usual curated, deliberately diverse range of people here, though I'm still not sure what the party is for. They host so many.

'Hello, Evie.'

'Hello, Jules,' I say, trying for warmth. Jules is the name Daniel affectionately calls his sister, though she drives him crazy. She has a habit of looking at me like I'm a baby bird that's been pushed out of the nest, all fluttering and lost and young, so we haven't exactly become BFFs since I started dating Daniel. As far as I can tell Juliana mostly passed her affluent formative years nurturing an obsession for expensive thoroughbreds and a rather rabid competitive streak. In her early twenties she pursued a place on the Olympic showjumping team but her career pinnacled disappointingly at the limited yearly celebrity of the Hampton Classic, and mostly in the social rather than equestrian events.

She married an Italian count last summer. Now she divides her time between her horses in Tuscany and her horses in the Catskills. Daniel prefers it when she's in Italy.

'Hello, darling,' Eileen says. 'You look very well tonight.'

Juliana is apparently so moved by this affection that she turns a cold gaze back to me and says, 'I see you've discovered the new spring season, Evie.' She's staring at my dress, so I suppose I must be wearing something fashionable. 'You look the part...finally.' She says this a little smugly.

'Is she shy, Eileen? One of those Creative Types?' Rachel's unnaturally stiff coiffure makes wide arcs as she shakes her head. She obviously can't let this conversation go, and I suspect she has equally manicured daughters who went to expensive places like Harvard or Princeton but who now specialise in shopping and lunching with friends.

'You must help me talk sense into her, Rachel.' Mrs Bradley's tone is amused and kind.

'Well,' Rachel regains her composure, 'there are so many people who are anxious to meet you, dear, and there's no escaping interviews here. Tonight is all about you, after all.' She twinkles at me, and my stomach drops.

'What do you mean?' I ask lightly. I look to Mrs Bradley, and realise the expression on her face is faintly pensive. Juliana is giving me the baby-bird look again. Oh no. Could this be some kind of Get to Know Daniel's Fiancée night? Our engagement party a few weeks ago had been a family-only affair, because I had asked for it to be that way. I guess I knew I'd have to be formally introduced to their social circle at some point, but not all in one flashy, centre-of-attention situation. I feel a rush of affection for Daniel, who obviously tried to shield me from the worst of this by getting us here late. But...am I not going to be able to hide in a corner with him, whispering and enjoying his nearness, but rather led around on Mrs Bradley's arm to be showcased like a valuable, literary prize?

I feel both an unexpected tickle of warmth and a rush of terror at the same time. Mostly terror.

'Darling,' Mrs Bradley has dropped a hand to mine, 'I should warn you. I think James is going to make a speech.'

No. No.

'Eileen...' I gulp. *I am shy. I am a creative type. Please let me go home and hide under my desk?*

'Ah, here she is!'

James Bradley appears at my side. He's a portly but ruggedly active man with a good sense of humour. He's also someone who, despite graduating top of his class from Harvard Business School and becoming a formidable, flint-hearted businessman in the forty years since, has an entirely healthy dose of whimsy. In addition to the twelve bathrooms and six fireplaces in this house there's a special gallery devoted to his antique pipe collection.

He wraps me in a warm bear hug. I hug him back, clinging to his fatherly solidness. 'You're looking very pretty tonight, dear girl. And just as well, since everyone's going to be looking at you.' He gives me a conspiratorial look. 'I'm going to make a speech.'

I gulp, and glance around for Daniel in the hope he might rescue me but he's still talking to the whiskered man and it's too late, in any case. Dinner is being announced, and James Bradley puts a gentle hand on my elbow and leads me into the Bradleys' formal dining room, which is the kind of ostentatious space whose tall ceilings and baroque décor would be enough to distract anyone from being scared. And the food, of course, is delicious.

It's at the end of the third course that I hear the sound of crystal being tapped like a priceless percussion instrument. James Bradley, shipping magnate, businessman, tennis player, and frankly, a very handsome sixty-five-year-old example of 'old money', stands at the head of the long table. We all turn our heads that way, except for me. I close my eyes and try not to sink down in my chair.

'I would like to make a toast,' he announces cheerfully. 'To my favourite, soon-to-be daughter-in-law. Hopefully you've all met her by now, she's the pretty one over there.' He slants his champagne in my direction. There is a gentle laugh from the table, and my cheeks explode with heat. I glance at Daniel but he's looking at his plate. I take another gulp of my third Pimm's.

'Don't mind her accent. As most of you know, she's an import,' he continues, to another, smaller titter. This is an exaggeration, since I think I hardly have an accent any more. I've been here for almost half my life. And even though my aunt Jo still speaks like the Wiltshire girl she was when she married and moved over here, my uncle Allan is Brooklyn born and bred.

'England is one of my favourite countries.' James Bradley's smile reminds the company that his ancestors were British nobility, and that he's been to most countries in the world, more than once. 'The food is improving, and the poets and writers have always been astonishingly good. You may have heard of our little acquisition here, she has published a couple of books.' The tittering continues. Mr Bradley is playing to the crowd, and everyone has downed enough Bollinger to enjoy his jokes, regardless of how pink my cheeks are.

'In fact Evie is currently working on her sixteenth book in one of the most successful crime series ever written. I'm still hoping she'll name a character after me.' He sends an affectionate grin my way, which warms me in a way that stops my squirming. I realise, in quite a wonderful rush, that this celebration—the inclusion, even the embarrassment—well, it feels like *family*. I remember Mrs Bradley's proud tone as she talked about my interviews with Rachel. As if I'm already one of them, a daughter whose achievements she can celebrate. I look around at the guests and elegant place settings with new eyes. The Bradleys did this for me, because that's what families do. I look at Daniel again, wanting to share the glow of this with him, but he doesn't look up. I notice Juliana is watching him too.

James continues. 'She's the only girl my wife and I ever enjoyed the company of enough to suggest to Daniel he might want to take the Black Card and spend the family money. Eileen suggested he spend more rather than less, which is the first time *that's* ever happened. Honey, thank you for making my son so happy. He's a different man with you, a better man.' This time Daniel's brightest smile is perfectly in place, for me and the rest of the table. 'I only wish your own mother and father could be here to celebrate with us tonight. Welcome to the family.'

This has me feeling the press of sudden tears, so after the toast has ended I get up and move toward the bathroom. Once there I hold a corner of one of the linen hand towels to the bottom of my eyes so I won't smudge anything, and will myself not to cry more. It's been a long time since I cried about my parents. All the warmth and realisation I've experienced about the Bradleys tonight is mixing with the deeper wish that my mother and father were here too. I can feel an unwelcome tight feeling in my chest creeping up my throat, when Magdeline glides in.

'Evie! Are you alright?' She is full of concern. I think.

'Of course,' I say, trying for a smile. 'It's a lovely dinner.'

Magdeline leans forward to the mirror and examines her impeccable makeup. I reflect briefly on the fact that having perfect skin can often distract people from six or seven major character flaws.

Seeing our two reflections side by side isn't terribly flattering. Magdeline is like a tall, golden tigress. I'm not short, but I have a kind of pale, indoors look about me. My grandparents on my mother's side were French, and it shows: I have dark hair and light eyes, and the kind of defined features that look good with bold lipstick shades and smokey eyes, both of which I wish I had applied before I left this afternoon. My reflection looks slightly unkempt and fragile. I pat my hair, wishing it would sit with some sort of order instead of kinking into tousled licks and snarls that defy logic. 'It's nice to have a moment alone, though,' I say.

'Well, you should enjoy it while you can.' Magdeline is touching up her lip gloss.

'Oh.' I blink. 'What do you mean?'

She meets my eyes in the mirror, surprised.

'I mean, it's going to get way harder after you marry Danny. You can forget the quiet life.' This sounds so exactly like what I've experienced tonight that I stare at her. And now I remember getting snapped by a lone photographer as we were moving between the limo and chopper at the 6N5 heliport tonight. At the time I'd been focused on not getting my head hacked off by the blades (*Violent decapitation: interesting way to go*). Now I imagine the photographer's low-res images turning up in the society pages of *People*, and Jenna wetting her pants with joy. I feel slightly ill. I *like* the quiet life.

'That reminds me.' Magdeline turns from our reflections to face me. 'I've been thinking about your honeymoon.'

'Oh. You have?' A host of improbable reasons why Magdeline would be thinking about my honeymoon rush through my mind.

'Well, yeah, it's a lot to plan, you know? A lot of flights. Obviously you'll take the jet. But still. Three weeks in Europe...'

'Europe.' I stare at her. Daniel has asked Magdeline to plan our honeymoon. In Europe.

'Obviously Daniel gave me some details but I wanted to get your—'

'Excuse me. So sorry, I just...' I have to get out of here.

'Don't forget your fitting tomorrow!' she calls after me.

4

'I thought you'd be pleased.' Daniel's voice in my headset is tinged with frustration.

The lights of the city below us are only dimly visible through the Eurocopter's tinted glass. Of course he assumed I would be pleased. Who wouldn't want a tour of Europe's most beautiful cities? I can picture the exquisite, exclusive line-up of hotels, restaurants and elegant soirees with the *nobiltà italiana* that is Daniel's 'normal' in Europe. I stare out the window. It's late, and Daniel has turned the lights off inside the cabin at my request. I needed the safety of the dark.

I wish now that I had explained to him about the state the book is in. It's been going downhill for months, but I haven't been able to tell him. Talking about it has felt dangerously like cementing a disaster in place.

'Daniel, I need space. I need quiet.'

'Honey, that's exactly what a hotel suite is for.' I begin to argue, but he says, 'I know, I know, "creative process". "Spending time with your characters".'

'Don't!' I stop him from doing the air quotes thing. 'We talked about this. A week in Australia. One week. One.'

'And I said I'd been there before.'

'You've been to Europe too. Multiple times.' I can understand why he wants to go there. He has about a hundred obscenely wealthy 'close' friends there. It's a comfortable destination for him. 'I was hoping for, I don't know, horses. Nature. Parachutes even. I don't want to look at old buildings.'

'Evie, you're afraid of heights. Remember? Parachutes? You'd never go through with it.'

'I—'

'Anyway, you *live* in that room. Three weeks would be good for you. You need to see Europe.' I frown. Doesn't he remember who I am? I grew up a train ride away from Europe. Sure, Wiltshire isn't exactly the Amalfi Coast, and two short family holidays on the Isle of Wight when I was aged ten and eleven don't quite qualify as European vacations. But it's close enough to England, geographically, to make me uncomfortable. I don't want to go back there. And I don't have a strong desire to analyse my reasons why.

But over the sound of the rotors I can hear the irritated under-current that burns off the corners of Daniel's words when things don't go his way, and I pause. Daniel lives the life of someone who never waits in queues, who never flies commercial, who always gets to choose exactly what he wants and have it brought to him immediately. This doesn't exactly make for a soul of deep patience. And what am I complaining about? That he's going to whisk me away to Paris and other exquisite cities, and coerce me into having a cultured, fabulous time?

'You don't understand,' I say. 'I...I'm not writing well at the moment. I haven't been for a while. I'm behind on my deadline.'

'Well, I'm glad you didn't tell my father that. I can't believe he's still nudging you about naming a character after him.' There's still that impatient flare in his words. 'Evie.' He puts his phone down, so his face is no longer lit with the glow and his voice, coming out of the dark, tells me he's really exasperated. 'So you have writer's b—?'

'Don't say it! Don't say the b-word. It's not a medical condition, it's not even a real thing. I'm just stuck, is all.'

'So doesn't that happen to everyone at some point?'

'Not to me.' There's a pause here, and I sense him shifting into problem-solving mode. I sigh inwardly. This isn't something that can be fixed with money.

'What have you tried?'

I grimace. I haven't tried anything really. I haven't wanted to admit the truth. I definitely haven't tried apple cider vinegar.

'You don't understand,' I say. 'This isn't something you can just fix.'

'Well, does it really matter? I mean, the wedding's only weeks away.'

'That's all the more reason it should be finished already.'

'But, realistically, it isn't like you need to finish it at all, is it? I assumed you wouldn't sign for another book after this deadline passed anyway.'

I gape at him in the dark. 'No, I...*no*. That is definitely not what I had planned. Daniel, how could you *think* that? It makes me feel like you...' My words trail away. I've shocked myself with my anger. We never argue. I mean, we've never had so much as a heated discussion before. Daniel always makes an effort to be accommodating and take my opinions into consideration. He isn't usually this tense and assertive with me. Is he stressed about something? He did have that look about him at dinner.

I feel the rattle of his impatience reach a peak, and then be forced down. The heat of irritation smoothes from his tone. He clears his throat, as if beginning the conversation afresh.

'Well. Of course, I understand. I'm sorry.' He pauses again, as if gathering his thoughts. 'Honey, you've supported yourself writing crime fiction for the last ten years, and I love that about you. I just wanted to take you travelling, and give you a proper vacation. You work so much. And I guess I imagined you would want to redecorate the apartment, and that sort of thing. I thought it might be good for you to...take a break. For a while. You know, no more deadlines, no more getting tormented by your characters. But not if it's going to make you unhappy. You know I only want you to be happy.'

His tone is so reasonable and inoffensive it's almost wooden. I feel touched and I'm very glad we aren't going to argue but also I feel oddly uneasy. I give myself a shake. He's being kind, and it isn't his fault that I hadn't thought through what it would really mean to marry into the Bradleys—to 'forget the quiet life.' We've landed at this point in our relationship with the same surprising velocity as a blind leap, and I realise that in a way, I have been blind. I need to open my eyes to reality and remember that being part of the Bradley family won't be perfect. Nothing is.

I feel his long, soft fingers reaching for mine and I let him take my hand.

'Thank you. I want you to be happy too,' I say. 'But I...I really would rather not go to Europe,' I say.

Again I sense him think this through and take my feelings into consideration.

'Okay. No Europe. We'll go to Australia. I'll get Magdeline to find us some horses.'

'Thank you,' I say again, though I wish he would find someone other than Magdeline to plan our honeymoon.

His hand closes into a fist and pulls out of mine, and I would notice this more except that he says, 'I adore you, Evie.'

I stare at the dark silhouette of his handsome face. And then he takes my hand again and kisses it, all knightly, and I feel relieved. He does adore me.

5

It's late by the time I get home. Daniel went straight to the airport, which meant saying goodbye to him at the heliport and then letting his second driver bring me the rest of the way alone. It's after midnight by the time I fall into bed.

But I can't sleep. Instead I restlessly fidget through my strong reaction to the idea of going to Europe. Of course it's not old buildings I'm worried about seeing. It's England. Ironically, I'm afraid of going to Australia too, with its teeming plethora of bitey, toxic wildlife. What was I thinking?

At about 4 a.m. I give up and pad downstairs to make some tea. As I near the kitchen I see the Blade, standing next to my kitchen counter and holding a knife as if he's about to make food.

I stop in shock, and my heart thuds.

He's wearing a baggy brown suit like a dodgy, small-town mortgage broker, and the assured, charming light in his eyes is stronger than usual. The knife is one of my own. I recognise it.

'I let myself in,' he murmurs, and gives me a half-shy smile that is both menacing and creepily intimate.

My breath freezes.

Next thing, I am sitting bolt upright in bed, yellow sunlight streaming through my window.

Holy. It's morning. I fall back against the pillow and run a hand over my eyes. *A dream.* My pounding heart hammers inside my ribcage. It's okay. It was only a dream.

The Blade is a character I never spend time with. Jay is right—he disturbs me. When I write about him, I do it from a distance, like the literary equivalent of using a ten-foot pole. His personality makes me uncomfortable because of its icy lack of normal human feeling and blank, mechanistic reasoning processes. He's someone who is untrustworthy and unsafe. Broken. And since I know exactly what it is that shattered his mind so badly, and exactly what he has done as a result of it, I keep as far away from him as I can.

The only other time I ever dreamed about him was when he first turned up in the shadows of Book Four, and I learned how his parents had died. He'd carefully locked them, along with all his childhood pets, into their family home and set fire to it. He was sixteen at the time, but so catastrophically brilliant that he was able, with unnatural dexterity, to clean out their bank accounts, assume the identity of the son of their reclusive neighbour, and disappear. I remember waking in a cold sweat that night.

That was when I realised Carolyn was going to need help to stop him. It was when I started looking for Jay.

My phone's urgent ring sounds from beside the bed, giving me a fright. My hand shakes slightly as I put it to my ear. 'Hello?'

'Oh, honey, I finally got you. What, did you answer the phone by accident or something?'

'Oh. Hey, Uncle Allan.' His warm voice and familiar, unpolished accent are very welcome. I get up and wander down to the kitchen to make a cup of calming tea. Or maybe a pot of tea. A large pot.

When I get there my eyes sweep over the wooden block where my knives are, and I find myself counting them. They're all there. Orderly and in place. *Just a dream.*

'What are you up to, sweetie?'

'Oh, you know.' I yawn. 'I'm wishing I...had food.' The tea canister is empty. I rifle the large box on my bench ("De Luca & Sons Delivered Groceries—Never Leave Home!"), but it's also basically finished, except for a pre-apocalyptic supply of liquorice allsorts.

'Hey listen, I had those people from *The New Yorker* on the phone again, looking for you.'

'I hope you told them I was dead this time,' I huff. How weird that they kept calling back when I'd turned them down so recently.

'Well, they were pretty persistent. Real persistent.' I can tell from Uncle Allan's voice that they got his hackles up. He didn't spend twenty-five years working a Brooklyn precinct without learning how to stand his ground. 'But,' and now I can hear the pride in his tone, 'they want to interview you, baby girl, and why wouldn't they?' I smile. From this I understand that he blew them off like a boss but was tickled they called. He adds, 'Your dad would be very proud.'

I still. 'Thanks, Uncle Allan.'

'And probably word's gotten out that you're hard to track down. I guess those journalists like a challenge, huh?'

'I suppose so. Hey, that reminds me, I need to ask you about the protocol for a detective third grade when—'

'No way! You want to ask me work questions, you come over and have some dinner with us. We've almost forgotten what you look like.'

I smile. 'Okay.' The doorbell rings. 'I have to go.'

'Alright, honey. Come visit us. Your aunt Jo is worried you're turning into a hermit.'

I laugh, and we hang up.

Hermit? How silly! On second thought...I pad stealthily down the hall and into the living room in my bare feet so I can peer unobtrusively through my front window. Through the chink in my curtains my next-door neighbour is visible, standing on my doorstep. She's a cheerful, stay-at-home mum, Leslie, who likes to invite me to stuff, or politely ask me when I'm going to clean up my yard. I mean, my yard is clean. Clean-ish. I just forget to call the guy sometimes. And obviously I can't do it myself. I'm busy. Inside.

I decide to creep into my writing room and pretend I'm not home.

6

'WHAT is Tillman doing in there?'

The curser blinks at me, mocking. I groan. I've been sitting here, impotent, for at least an hour. *Just write something. Anything.* The liquorice bowl is full. I adjust an earplug.

Harding dropped the binoculars onto her lap, then shoved her coffee into the car's cup holder, crossed her arms and snapped her gum like a pouty teenager. SHE WAS SO UNCOMFORTABLE. She flicked her eyes over to Ryan, who was slouched too, but looking relaxed, as always. He was staring straight ahead, watching the street.

'So what about the new one then, the skinny one?' She glared at him while she said this. It saved her glaring at the house. Prodding him about his dating life always annoyed him, which was exactly why she was doing it.

'Karen.'

'Ooh. You know her name. That's a good sign. She's pretty.'

Ryan's eyes didn't move from the windshield.

'I know her name because I helped her pick up

the files she dropped after you yelled at her last week. She's not an option. I don't date people I work with.'

'Huh. That's why we've never dated, right?'

That got a reaction, if a subtle one.

'Oh, come on,' she pressed. 'You've never thought about it?'

She leaned closer. He could have glanced straight down her shirt if he chose to—she made sure of it—and she was only half playing. Ryan paused less than a second.

'I'm gonna get us some more donuts.'

I pull the discoloured sleeves of my writer's smock over my hands and slump my face into them. Blasted donuts. And where did Carolyn get gum from, anyway? Chapter Three is officially a catastrophe. I'm going to have to delete that whole paragraph.

What a waste of time, I think. And then, *Holy. The time.*

I'm late for my dress fitting. I contemplate this as the scruffy, graffitied scenery on the Metro North line blurs in my peripheral vision. In particular I can foresee Magdeline's subtle eye roll, a bored blend of pity and disdain.

Poor Magdeline. Of course she wants her new business to be a success. Her family are old friends of the Bradleys, and I was an obvious choice for her first customer. It isn't her fault I've been... well, a teensy bit unhelpful.

But now I'm stuck taking the train into the city, having cancelled Daniel's car earlier this morning. A limo seemed like overkill, and I was feeling needled by his 'you live in that room' comment. I mean, I leave home. I mingle with humanity. Meanwhile I hold *The Daily News* right up in front of my face so that it blocks off the rest of the train carriage and makes a nice little protected nook for me next to the window.

And then I see it.

Woman Found Dead in Abandoned Taxi

A small square of print on page fourteen. An odd prickle creeps over me. The story is about Sally Carston, twenty-six, Brooklyn schoolteacher, dead. I scan the rest of the article, and take a deep breath. Um. That's *my* Sally Carston. And she's dead in the exact specific way I had planned to kill her. Strangled. Purple scarf. The taxi abandoned in a lane behind Mei's Hardware. Every detail is there.

I drop the paper in shock. Because the really chilling thing, the thing that sends a bolt of hot, irrational fear down my spine, is the third paragraph. 'Possible eighth victim.' Because she is the eighth. Which means they know.

They know about the others.

And then I shriek. Jay is sitting right in front of me.

He's still in his leather jacket and jeans and he looks sour, like he just got a parking ticket. I cover my mouth with my hand, recovering. We are not alone in the carriage; across the way is a girl in her early twenties with a child who looks about four. They're sitting side by side with the air of an *au pair* and charge, and until now they've been pouring over a picture book together. The *au pair* is pretending she doesn't notice me but the child, a small, well-dressed girl with a cloud of dark hair, has looked up from her book and is staring straight at me with big dark eyes. Or at Jay. I'm not sure which.

I mumble through the article like a stuttering speed-reader.

'The body has been identified as twenty-six-year-old...strangled...Chinatown...small cuts on upper neck...it's not possible...'

'You knew her?'

'She's...That is exactly...' I try to keep my voice low.

'Exactly what?' I see him take all of a millisecond to read my face. 'Some kind of copycat? Like a tribute?'

I gulp for air. Okay. This is a possibility. A copycat. Someone who's read my books and is acting out the horrors of my worst criminal mastermind. The idea of a real-world criminal doing psychopathic things partially calms my racing heart—about the third paragraph, at least. *Eighth victim.*

But it doesn't explain Sally Carston. I have to call Uncle Allan.

I register Jay's attitude. He's watching me with hard eyes. They are dark blue, the kind of blue from the deepest part of the Mediterranean, but without any of its warmth. His full mouth is set firm.

'Are you okay?' I ask.

'So what was that?'

I blink. 'What was what?'

'All that weird innuendo in the car between me and Harding.'

Oh. I huff, exasperated. Seriously? Can't he see that I'm desperate? I'm clutching at straws with Chapter Three, and the awkwardness from Carolyn just came out of nowhere. I frown. She had surprised me with that, actually.

'What, you don't find Carolyn attractive?' I retort.

'Should I?'

'Well, I get about a hundred fan-messages a day asking why you two aren't together yet. Maybe you've been in love with her the whole time. Maybe there's been sexual tension brewing for ages and I haven't noticed.'

'You wouldn't notice.'

'And that was a stupid excuse for not asking Karen out,' I add. 'What's wrong with you going on a date with her? She'd be great for you.'

'How do I know she'd be great for me? She's nobody. She's a stick figure.'

'Huh.' That's true, I realise. 'I haven't really thought about her much.'

I notice the little girl is still watching us, wide-eyed. I'm still not quite sure if she can see Jay as well. Kids are pretty intuitive. If she can't then that means I've become one of those crazy people who talk to themselves on the train. Brilliant. I look out the window, trying to see her *au pair*'s expression in its reflection, and whether her face reads 'psycho-alert,' and get another mini-scare when I turn back. Tillman is sitting beside me.

'Argh!' I yank my body away from his spindly frame, too close beside me on the seat, my skin crawling. But I can't feel him, thank goodness. I examine his expression. He's got that look on his face when he's pleased with himself. I narrow my gaze. 'Where have you been?'

'Around,' he says pleasantly. He waves at the little girl. It's been a long time since I was this close to him and I notice that his thin face is looking drawn, as if he's lost weight or had trouble sleeping recently, and he has a tiny patch of fine hair on the side of his jaw that he missed while shaving. I sniff him. He smells gross.

'What did you have for breakfast this morning?' I accuse.

'Oatmeal,' he offers. His tone is bland but he's still staring at the girl, and it's creepy. I frown at him as he pulls a tiny cheese knife out of his trouser pocket and begins puncturing the red naugahyde seat. It makes a repetitive *pock* noise, like he's responding to an unconscious urge for destruction, but trying to keep it in check.

'You're scaring the kid,' Jay says.

'Yes, that's right, Tillman,' I say.

'No—' Jay pauses. He's looking at me. '*You're* scaring the kid.'

7

I manage to get rid of Tillman before we reach Grand Central, but Jay sticks stubbornly close. As we step off the train, an eccentrically dressed old lady loses her balance, her walking stick flailing as she struggles to get her second foot down from the carriage. Jay, quicker than me, reaches to steady her, before reason kicks in and he halts halfway. But the action is enough to snap in my own reflexes, and I thrust a hand under her elbow to take her weight, before helping her into the greasy half-light of the underground platform.

Train tracks, I think, as I climb the ramp from the lower concourse and am poured into the turbulent crush of people in the echoey hall of the main concourse, with its vaulted ceiling of trumpeting turquoise curves. *An unexpected fall, the blast of a horn. A messy dismemberment.* Interesting way to go.

'You're going to be late,' Jay points out as I'm jostled by the crowd. Shoot. I've come the wrong way. I always get so lost in here, with the confusing abundance of creamy limestone columns and the rosy marble exits in every direction.

'Go away,' I say, changing course.

'Are you wearing a disguise?'

'No!' I sound defensive. It's just a baseball cap and sunglasses. And not a great moment for Jay to remind me that I like to wear them when I come to the city because it makes me feel safer—a tiny barrier against the tide of humanity I supposedly enjoy mingling with so much.

Someone jostles me again and I throw a semi-aggressive look to Jay, who of course is completely immune to all this—people just naturally stream around him like a rock in a river. He's sauntering along, head and shoulders above most people, and they all look straight through him as though he isn't there. Which he isn't.

The thing is, I like Jay. I always have. Sure, he never laughs at my jokes, and his intensity and focus border on scary, but I like the patience and integrity he has, and how much he loves his city, and being a cop. That's not to say I want him following me all the way to a sniffy wedding dress boutique in the heart of the Garment District, while I clutch a bag of La Perla lingerie under my arm.

I stomp towards the 42nd Street exit and thrust open one of the quaint paned-glass doors. The street outside is just as busy, the pavement a chaotic spillway of strolling tourists, brisk office workers and the jumbled rainbow of humans that make New York City the mosaic that it is. The day is sunny, the sky bright blue— at least the fraction I can see when I glance directly upwards past the painted iron ribs of the Park Avenue Viaduct—and clear light is glinting off the windows of the skyscrapers towering above. The road is zinging with yellow taxis and bike messengers, and the red fabric awnings of the shops nearby are stirring in a spring breeze.

I yank the brim of my hat down and make a left. There's a subway station on the corner of Lexington, where I can catch a 7 train.

'You don't seem very excited about this whole wedding dress thing,' Jay says, still behind me. 'Don't women usually take their friends and get all gushy and drink champagne?'

This touches a nerve. I'm not gushy. Should I be? I'm just so caught up in the book right now. It's no wonder I can't focus on anything else. Also, I don't really have any friends. Well, I do—I *did*. The last three years I just seemed to lose touch and...well.

I'm about to politely explain to him what I happen to know for a fact: that what Jay Ryan knows about brides and weddings wouldn't fill a pinhead, which is exactly what he's being at the moment, when I notice how tense he looks. He's not sauntering, but pensive, the broad line of his shoulders hunched. I stop in my tracks and pull off my sunglasses.

'Look, I'm sorry. About the Carolyn thing.' Our eyes meet. 'I just...I'm desperate.'

He stops too. His eyes warm up a fraction.

'Excuse me dear, are ye talking to yourself?' A lilting accent. I turn.

'Mrs Andrews!' There she is, totally out of place in the busy street. Mrs Andrews is about seventy-five, white-haired, bright-eyed, Scottish and spry. I first met her at my writers' group about seven years ago.

'Ye need to be a little more careful about character development in public, dear.' She smiles.

'Oh,' I say. Oops. 'Yes, you're right. I'm just a bit...on edge at the moment. I get careless sometimes. I forget how crazy it makes me look. What on earth are you doing here?' I'm so fond of Mrs Andrews. She's like a literary grandmother to me, and she looks so incongruous here in the thick of Midtown in her knitted cardigan, and those clumpy shoes old people wear because they have more support.

'Och, my wee boy works here, ye know. Away down there.' She points, as if she's directing the way to a juvenile detention centre instead of a top-tier law firm. I happen to know her son is a handsome forty-five-year-old attorney who would definitely make the 'Successful Children' list of any remotely shallow parent.

'You've come to bring him lunch?'

She holds up a brown bag. 'Aye. I've come to remind him that love is more important than money.'

No shallowness here, apparently. I smile. She's such a breath of fresh air, and so proper and motherly, and she tilts her body slightly left then, which in any ordinary situation would be a subtle opening for an introduction, so without thinking I say, 'This is Jay.'

I feel Jay tense beside me, and I realise what a silly thing I've done. Then, unexpectedly, Mrs Andrews sees him. She looks up and meets his eyes.

'Ah, there ye are, dear,' she says. 'Yes, of course, you're Detective Ryan. I recognise ye from Evie's books.'

Holy. My mouth drops open and Mrs Andrews turns to give me a brief but very measured look. My eyes flick to the nearest bystanders. Can everyone see him, or just her? I can't tell for sure.

I say, with automated politeness, 'Mrs Andrews runs my writers' group. She writes historical fiction. At least, she used to.' Mrs Andrews proceeds to twinkle at Jay, who is tense but apparently fascinated.

'Weel, I'm retired. I only write my online blog now.' She winks. 'What a shame ye never bring this laddie to the meetings, Evie. We could do with some characters like you, dear,' she adds to Jay. 'And there's a meeting tonight, too.'

I stifle an urge to laugh. Jay looks flabbergasted, and seeing such an expression on his face is like hearing music for the first time. 'May I ask why ye're bringing your characters into town, dearie? Not that I've never done the same myself, but I would have thought ye didn't need this young man around so much. I would think ye'd figured him out by now. He's been with you for what, twelve or thirteen books, has he not?'

'I don't know if anyone could ever really say they've figured Jay out,' I say.

Mrs Andrews takes Jay's measure. 'Mmm.'

I blurt, 'Actually Mrs Andrews, I'm having a bit of a crisis.' I want to explain to her about the newspaper and the eight people dead and Sally Carston and ask her if she thinks that isn't the craziest coincidence she's ever heard of.

Because it is a coincidence. There is no other explanation.

'Oh dear. You're stuck, are you? I thought ye had that look about ye.'

I think wildly, *What look?*

'Ye know there are ever so many books on writer's block, dear. We were talking about one at the meeting last month. *Free Flow.* Ye remember it? Very helpful. Ye could go and get it from Jeanie.'

Mrs Andrews points her neat little chin in the opposite direction to the one I'm heading, toward Sixth. Jeanie also goes to my writers' group and she has a bookstore about five blocks from here. It would be on the way, if I was walking.

'That's a good idea,' I say. It is a good idea. It's time to accept I have a problem. And what do New Yorkers do when they're grappling with an inner psychological issue? Okay, they see their therapist. But I'm English. At least, I grew up there until I moved at sixteen. So seeing a therapist is not an option for me. A book is surely a decent second best.

'That's alright, dearie. I'm looking forward to Book Sixteen. Perhaps...' her glance shifts back to Jay for a moment, 'ye should come over and have tea with me one day. Ye could bring this dear boy with ye. Shall I be seeing ye tonight?'

'Maybe. Thank you.'

'Best of luck, dearie!'

Jay and I turn to walk.

'She saw me pretty easily,' he says in a low voice.

I clear my throat. 'Well, she's a writer. She has characters of her own.' I'm not about to admit to the weird jolt it gave me. I increase my speed. If I'm going to walk to Jeanie's I need to hurry. Sure, authors drag their characters out to examine at writers' groups and conferences, and generally, when the writer chooses to reveal them, they can be seen by other writers. In context. But I didn't think it happened out of context. Not in plain view on a city street and half by accident. 'There are visible characters at my writers' group meetings,' I add, casual. 'Sometimes.'

'Yeah? You interact with them? Ask them how they are, pass the time of day?'

'It's a special group,' I say.

'Yeah. A bunch of frustrated middle-aged women who've been working on the same unpublished story for the last eighteen years.'

I *tsk*. 'And me.'

He raises his eyebrows in a look that's all the more offensive for how straight it is.

'And you,' he says.

8

'So you're saying you have no books on writer's block?'

I tamp down a little impatience. Jeanie's bookstore is crammed to overflowing. There's a sandwich board at the front door that announces 'Energy Readings Here' and a bunch of coloured healing stones set up along the front counter with the books. Jeanie giggles vacantly at my question, picks up what appears to be a homemade seed-ball and takes a bite.

She's sitting at the counter, and it seems I have interrupted her partway through *The Thinking Fruitarian*. I don't wish to be judgy about Jeanie but I'd forgotten how sleepy and blank she can be. Her characters are fantasy novel types who wear a lot of strategically placed leaves. Jeanie herself is in all-natural fabrics and might not have washed her hair very recently.

'Oh, no! I'm saying there are newer, more holistic ideas. Natural solutions.' I find myself distracted by a seed in her teeth. 'Apple cider vinegar is a great option,' she adds. 'Get your creative juices flowing.'

'Ah.'

'Yes! I used to have trouble remembering which day to go to work, but now I'm on this all-organic diet, I never forget.' She beams.

This isn't helping. My gaze wanders a little, and I feel it pulled down to the books lined up against the counter. There's a big hardcover edition there, *A History of Cults and Sects*. Frowning, I run a finger across it. It's thick, and there's a montage of old photographs on the front cover, men with long hairstyles and big glasses, and a grainy shot of the Waco compound in 1993. I pick it up and stare at it. Something vibrates inside me.

'You know,' Jeanie picks at the seed in her teeth as she continues, 'I always wanted to ask you how you name your characters?' Jay, who has been standing to the side listening, perks up.

'Uh, they already have names when they come into the story,' I say, distracted. Jeanie looks confused at this so I try to explain. 'I mean, they are who they are. I just write about them.'

'Oh. Right.' She smiles.

'Sometimes I go searching for a name, but I'm only looking for the name that was already theirs to begin with. You know what I mean?'

'Oh, yes!' A pause. 'Me too.'

'Um, so you mentioned natural foods or something?'

'Well,' Jeanie has the seed out at last, 'have you tried any herbal supplements? Or Chinese medicine? There's a place right across the road—Mr Woo does that kind of thing. You could get an evaluation of your *qi*.' I peer through the window. Sixth Avenue is a wide, unvarnished thoroughfare clogged with buses and other mid-morning traffic, and the section of stores directly on the other side are partially obscured by the scaffolding so common on New York streets. Through the metal latticework I can make out a café, a hair salon, and one store painted a smart black, with big windows full of bottles that might be vitamins or herbal supplements. Well. That doesn't look too scary. Am I finally desperate enough for herbal supplements?

I turn back to Jeanie, only to notice that she's squinting into the corner where Jay is standing, as if there's something there that caught her attention. She frowns.

Yes, I decide suddenly, *I'm desperate enough.*

Twenty minutes later, Jay and I cross Seventh Avenue and head into the dingy chaos of delivery vehicles, fabric retailers and construction scaffolding on West 38th Street. I'm very late. *So* late. I'm power walking, aware of what a disaster I've created this morning, and I have a giant packet of Chinese medicine and a hardcover book on cults tucked under my arm, along with my lingerie.

'Those herbs look like weed, you know.'

'Quiet please,' I say. 'My *qi* is flowing.' Mr Woo talked me into ten minutes of acupuncture.

'*Just Say No.*' Jay sounds annoyingly as if he wants to laugh, which I would be more gratified by if it wasn't at my expense. 'I don't think you need Chinese medicine,' he says. 'I think you should go do something you've never done before, something that scares you.'

I huff. 'Like what? I already know how to shoot a gun.'

'You already know how to do a lot of things. You just never do any of them.'

I scowl. He's right. I know how to hot-wire a car, lift wallets, pick locks, and drive a fishing trawler. To name a few. My conversational Swedish isn't bad either. But I never actually do any of it. Obviously. I just learn as much as I need to know to be competent, and therefore realistic in writing about it.

'What about skiing,' he says, 'or skydiving?'

I roll my eyes. Skiing only reminds me of soppy Edgar Polton, anyway.

'What about parasailing?'

'Wrong type of sailing. Daniel likes cruising on the Riviera.'

'Scared? I'd come with you.'

'Great idea,' I say, deadpan. 'Maybe we can go tandem skydiving together. You could pull the cord.'

His gaze flattens out and I expect a smart response but instead he glances over my left shoulder and frowns. I turn to look at whatever has caught his attention and to my surprise I see Daniel. He's hurrying along the other side of the road with a huge bunch of flowers. Roses actually. Red roses. I open my mouth to call out to him, some part of my brain thrilled to see him, recognising his profile and shooting off an automatic squeeze of happy chemicals. But he's heading the other way and is too far away to hear me if I did call out. And reality comes flooding in, in any case. I swing back to Jay, confused. *Daniel is in Hong Kong. Isn't he? Daniel, who never goes anywhere on foot if he can help it. Daniel, who knows I think red roses are a cliché.*

I gulp down some air, and see that Jay's eyes are full of concern. Not confusion. Jay is not confused. I stare at him for too long, absorbing this.

'Let's go.' I put my head down and keep walking.

'Evie, wait. You're not gonna go talk to him?'

'There's no need to,' I say. 'There'll be an explanation. And... and I'm late.'

Magdeline's chosen *haute couture* bridal designer, Cintia Lareu, is the latest hot name for New York brides, and therefore, a Must Have for me. Despite her prestige Cintia isn't snobby or pretentious; she's a kind, talented lady with startling cherry-red hair and an Argentine accent. It's Magdeline who's made the big-white-dress experience uncomfortable. Perhaps my tastes really are too ordinary.

I make it to the glistening bronze-and-glass atelier in a kind of numb daze. On the third floor an assistant ushers me to the main salon, where frothy dresses hang on racks like an art installation entitled *Vanilla Milkshakes Trapped in Time*. Magdeline is on the phone.

'Wait, she's here! Yes, she's here. Yes, everything's fine now. Okay, I'll call them.' She hangs up and stalks over to me. 'Evie! Where have you been?'

'I...' I look behind me for Jay, as if an invisible person will provide a rational excuse for my ridiculous lateness. His expression is closed.

'You're so late! Nearly forty minutes late, Evie! I tried calling you. Why don't you ever answer your phone? Cintia's schedule is really upset.' She pauses. 'Is that weed?'

I glance at the pillow-sized bag of herbs in my hand. 'Yes,' I announce. 'It is.'

'Evie, Daniel has been frantic.'

Has he? I think. *He didn't look frantic when I saw him a couple of blocks from here.*

'You called him?' I ask, ignoring the lump in my throat. 'In Hong Kong?'

'Just then. He was between meetings.' She turns to the assistant. 'Morgan, we're going to need to reschedule, I think. You understand. You don't want to try on your dress now, do you Evie?'

I manage a wobbly smile.

'No.'

9

'I think we should investigate him,' Carolyn says.

She's pacing my kitchen, with an overfull glass of wine in her hand. I'm brewing hot water for the Chinese herbs, and I try to block her out. Jay leans against the counter, his arms folded, watching me. We didn't talk on the way back. I took a cab, and Jay sat beside me in the back seat and said nothing. He knows how to be silent, and he knows how to wait. Carolyn, on the other hand, was somehow already here when we got home, and creating havoc. She was like a shark with the smell of fresh meat when she found out I'd seen Daniel.

I narrow my gaze at her. 'Are you wearing my shirt?' She's wearing an exquisite sheer silk top I know is from the personal-stylist collection stashed in my wardrobe. And I'm pretty sure the beautiful black lace bra clearly visible beneath it is one of mine as well. She ignores me, sloshing her wineglass.

'He was carrying flowers?'

'Harding.' Jay's voice is quiet, but his tone speaks volumes.

'There's an explanation,' I say. I turn back to the herbs. *There is an explanation.*

'You tried calling him?' Carolyn prods.

I purse my lips. Jay answers for me.

'He didn't pick up.'

I pour the water while Jay and Carolyn have a silent argument almost, but not quite, out of my line of sight. The mixture turns a revolting black. Am I really supposed to drink this?

'He said to let it steep for ten minutes,' I murmur.

'Ugh.' Carolyn shudders.

I call my voicemail and put it on speaker. Magdeline's chirpy voice pipes out.

'Hi Evie, just making sure you're okay since you left quite suddenly today. Oh, and I got that embossed card for the table plaques, which I thought you might prefer, since they'll look great with the snowdrop sprays on the sculptures I chose.'

I pound the delete button before the message finishes.

'Snowdrops?' Carolyn shudders again and sniffs her wine. 'You know, she doesn't sound that excited to be planning your wedding. Aren't you, like, her first business client or something? You'd think she'd be more grateful.' She throws herself against the counter next to Jay. 'Come on Evie, you have elite mystery-solving minds here in the room with you. Don't you want to investigate him just a little bit? What did he say to you at dinner last night?'

'Nothing,' I say. 'That he was going away for a couple of days.' Daniel often has to travel. It wasn't unusual.

'Classic.' She snorts. I see Jay shoot her a look. 'Fine! I'm going to drink in solitude.' This is worrying but Jay shakes his head at me. Carolyn stalks out.

'Are you okay?' he asks.

I can't meet his eyes. It's funny, the thing that's uppermost in my mind is how disappointed Daniel's parents would be if he was having an affair. I can picture their indignation and their compassion. I don't know if I find it comforting or painful. Because of course, if we ever broke up, they would have to side with Daniel. They're not *my* parents, after all.

'I'm pretty sure Carolyn's wearing my shirt,' I say. 'And my underwear.'

A beat.

'That's *your*...?'

'That isn't normal, is it? I can't tell anymore. Jay...' I see Jay move a few centimetres toward me and then stop. I purse my lips. 'I just want to finish this book.'

'How do you feel? *Qi* flowing?'

'I feel weird. Mr Woo did say I was blocked. I feel like something is...' *Wrong.*

'Unblocking?' He gives a half-grin. 'Do you need the bathroom?'

'Toilet humour. Nice.' I smile, and his eyes smile back.

'Are you two flirting?' Carolyn yells from the other room.

'Wear your own clothes!' I yell back. I stir the mixture. 'I think this is ready.'

'I can tell it's ready.' Jay's face is all primmed up adorably.

I cough a laugh. I really can't believe I'm doing this.

'I hope it doesn't taste as bad as it smells,' I say. I extract the gunge of undissolved powder, add cold water and put the cup to my lips.

'Maybe just drink the whole thing as fast as you can.'

'He said to sip it.' There's a strange oily sheen on the surface. 'Okay, I'm not sipping it.' I hold my nose.

Jay looks unconvinced. 'Are you really this desperate?'

'Yes,' I say. But it's too pungent, too ghastly, and I only manage a single mouthful, nearly spitting it back into the sink in the process. 'Oh...oh no...ooooh, that tasted sooo much worse than it smelled.'

'That's not possible.'

'Blegh,' I cough. 'You're supposed to be the toughest cop in the city.'

'I am the toughest cop in the city.'

'You must be allergic to Chinese food. That's too many nights coming home to your empty apartment and Chinese takeout. It's given you an intolerance.'

Jay is thoughtful while I lean over the sink and wonder if eating liquorice will change the taste in my mouth.

'You know,' he says, 'we could go and stake Daniel out. Even if you don't find out anything, it might help.' His blue eyes are unreadable. 'Sixteen,' he adds. 'Give you some ideas.'

'No way.' I shake my head. 'It would be too weird. And wrong.'

'Evie?' Carolyn's voice calls apologetically from the living room. 'I think I just spilled wine on your shirt.'

Jay's eyes meet mine. I press my lips together.

'Okay, fine. Let's do it.'

10

I avoid driving in Manhattan, as a rule. Too crazy. But though the afternoon traffic is unpleasant, by some miracle I manage to find a park not too far from Daniel's penthouse on Park Avenue. I'm still not sure doing a stakeout is a good iea, but we settle in to wait.

His apartment sits atop an extravagant pre-war mid-rise. It's the kind of stately jewel that makes ordinary people like me self-consciously brush lint from their clothing as they enter. But I like the sculpted safety of Park Avenue, the pristine sidewalks, the clean-cut solidity of the limestone buildings, the small glistening gardens and crisp awnings.

And Daniel likes the city, of course. He grew up here, and now he works so much it makes sense to live here. The 'Bradley Incorporated'—real name Amiton Corp.—offices are in the Financial District and James and Eileen's beautiful townhouse is only three blocks away.

For some reason though, the penthouse always reminds me that I grew up far away from here, amid the quirky quaintness of a small English village, where my father was the local constable and we lived in a whitewashed cottage across the Green. I used to work in the local pub some nights pulling pints, despite being underage, and when my dad was alive there was nothing I liked more than taking him a packed lunch on the weekends. Being transplanted to a tiny clapboard house in Brooklyn, more or less against my will when I was sixteen, didn't change where home was. But it did change everything else.

'I can't believe I'm doing a stakeout in the real world as well.' Carolyn has her arms crossed in the backseat, pouting. 'Geez. It's like my life is one continuous freaking stakeout. Everyone...literally the whole world passing me by, while I just sit here.'

The park I found is a few cars away from the entrance to Daniel's building, which works perfectly since I drive a peach Mini. It's a great car, but not exactly blend-in material. There are at least three black Escalades wedged between me and Daniel's marble entryway behind us, and I'm hoping the celebrity sheen of them will shield his potential gaze.

Jay sits beside me in the front, as we both peer into my rear-view mirrors.

'Carolyn, that was my favourite shirt,' I say. She is slumped and adolescent among the helpful safety items—fire blanket, first-aid kit—I have on my backseat. She's wearing a lovely designer printed tank. 'And now, you're wearing my second favourite shirt.'

'His Porsche is here.' She ignores me. 'How did he get a park right in front? Nobody ever gets a park right in front.'

She's right. Daniel's silver Porsche 911 Speedster is nestled directly in front of the navy blue entrance awning, four or five cars back from us.

'He would've taken the limo to the airport,' I argue.

'Except that he clearly didn't go to the airport. Anyway, why would he park it out front if he was going away?'

She's right. Daniel would never leave his car on the street and risk getting towed during street-sweeping hours.

'Maybe his flight got pushed back,' I say. 'Maybe he got delayed.'

'Maybe he's having an affair,' Carolyn mutters.

'Don't you have a key?' Jay asks quietly.

'Of course,' I mumble. 'But what if he's there? He'll think I don't trust him.'

Carolyn guffaws.

'Talk to the doorman,' Jay suggests.

I shake my head. I know Reynaldo pretty well. He's about a hundred and five years old, and both his respectable grey uniform and his skin hang loosely on his kindly frame. I picture him answering the awkward private eye-style questions I could potentially ask him. Stuff that I should definitely know if I'm Daniel's fiancée.

I can't ask him.

'Call him again,' Carolyn demands. But I can't do that either. Three messages is my limit. I'm not a psycho.

'I could go in there,' Jay says. I start to shake my head but he continues. 'Reynaldo can't see me, right? So I could go in and see if Daniel's there.'

The thought of Jay walking right up to Daniel's apartment is—

'Way too weird,' I say. 'And anyway, how would you do it? You can't change anything here, remember? You can't alter reality. You can't just let yourself in. And I wouldn't want you to even if you could.'

'I could listen at the door.'

This makes me uncomfortable, but he has a point. And it might save some time.

'Key?' He puts his palm out and I hand it to him. He gets out of the car, slips past good stoic Reynaldo, and heads inside. Carolyn and I both watch him go, his leather jacket gleaming in the sunshine. He's all smooth movement and well-proportioned muscle. It's kind of mesmerising.

Carolyn climbs over into the front seat beside me.

'Why do you like him, anyway?' She still sounds grumpy.

'I mean, what's not to like? He's so...solid. And good. He's completely trustworthy.'

'Not Ryan. *Obviously.* Daniel.'

'Oh.' I blink several times.

'How did you guys meet, anyway?'

I clear my throat. 'His parents called my publisher. They really love the books.' They had called my books 'intelligent and stylish', which had been awfully flattering, and been warmly persistent about meeting me. 'They took me out to lunch. They were so nice. Then they wanted to introduce me to Daniel.' We clicked together right away, the Bradleys and I, and Daniel had just seemed a natural extension of that.

'What would your dad think of him?'

I purse my lips.

But Carolyn isn't really interested in my response. 'This is. *So. Frustrating,*' she growls. 'I can't stand it anymore. I want to *do* something for a change. I want to break something!'

Suddenly Daniel walks out onto the street, *sans* suitcase and looking nonchalant. He's dressed for the office, crisp and handsome. He heads straight for his car, and Reynaldo skips forward to open the door.

'Where's Jay?' I say. 'What do we do?'

Unexpectedly Carolyn jumps out of the car. I swivel my body to watch through the rear window as she runs back to where Daniel is standing and gives the bumper of the Escalade in front of his Porsche a good kick. The alarm goes off, loudly. I clap my hand over my mouth. Both Daniel and Reynaldo stop and look, and as they do Carolyn runs to kick the car parked directly behind the Porsche. Lights are flashing. A girl walking past with a posse of dogs pauses. Jay slips from the building, giving me momentary relief, as Carolyn bounces up and down, thrilled with her mayhem, before adding some inappropriate dance moves.

And then I watch, in a kind of surreal slow motion, as the

dog-walker and all four dogs snap their heads toward Carolyn as if they just saw her. I gasp. And a woman with a stroller pulls out her phone and points the camera.

They can see her.

'Oooh no,' I say into my hand. Something is very wrong.

Daniel looks in my direction, possibly catching sight of my bright car in the mid-distance. I dive out of sight. A peek reveals Jay dragging Carolyn toward my rear door. He opens it.

'Get in the car, Harding. Evie, go.' He jumps in after Carolyn and I crash into gear. I swerve out into traffic, then screech around the corner and onto East 72nd Street.

What just happened?

'We're leaving?' Carolyn whines.

'Yes, we are!' I shriek. I slam my foot onto the accelerator and blow through an orange light to spin a breakneck right onto Madison.

'We can't just let Daniel skulk off somewhere. We have to keep following him!'

'We have to go home, Carolyn!' The shock is singing in my nerve endings. 'He's not going to skulk off somewhere. There's a perfectly rational explanation.' I shake my head, the scene replaying in my mind. 'You changed something. People saw what you did. Ordinary people. In the street!' Also, there's no way Daniel didn't see me. And if he did, then he must think I'm crazy. Have I just ruined everything?

'Don't worry, Evie,' says Jay. 'He didn't see us. I saw the look on his face. He looked right through us. And he was in his car by the time I got Harding back here. You're good.'

I grimace. Yes, Daniel has always seemed slightly more dense when it comes to fiction. But still. Something is desperately wrong.

Maybe I am crazy.

I pull my eyes from Jay's in the rearview mirror and take a long breath. And another. I block them both out of my head. This has got to stop. Breathe.

Clear, focus, breathe.

When I risk a glance in the mirror again, both Jay and Carolyn have disappeared.

I sag forward with relief. *Oh, thank you.*

11

11

When I get home I rush into my writing room and lock the door.

I need my cave. I need safety, and quiet.

I throw myself into the chair at my desk and tuck my legs up, hugging them. The picture of my dad and I stares at me from the wall. I'm so happy in that picture, and so is he. But I remember the turmoil of the night he died, that same feeling of being thoroughly out of control. I don't want to feel that again. I need to write.

Earplugs. Phone. Allsorts. Smock.

Once my things are in place, I start by deleting the last paragraph I wrote. Then I put my fingers on the keyboard. And wait.

Nothing. Just arid emptiness.

I was writing nonsense with Carolyn coming on to Jay, but now there's not even that. Just a gasping dryness, like the last breath of a dying man dehydrated in the desert (*interesting way to go*). And a bunch of other clichéd desert metaphors. If inspiration is something that flows then this is a cracked riverbed in a thousand-year drought.

I cast around for help and my eyes land on my new cults and sects book. I leap up to grab it from the bookshelf and accidentally jog my writing table. The bump sends my pile of handwritten notes cascading to the floor in a dry wave.

Curses. I like keeping my paper notes and hard copies of things, but I'm not great at filing. What a mess. I flip open the book. There's something in here, I can feel it, and it's more than large black and white photographs of crazy-eyed cult leaders.

But it's heavy reading. A lot of unpalatable personality disorders and good people who didn't survive the inevitable outcomes. And then, some time later, I realise I've been dozing. I rub my eyes and become aware that I'm not alone in the room.

I turn to see the Blade, too close to me.

He's wearing one of those scary gasmasks from the Second World War, the ones that make someone look like a *creature*, with wide, dead eyes and gaping mouth. My breath dries dead in my throat, stopping a shriek. He pulls the mask off, chuckling at me as if it's a joke between close friends. I can't speak. He lifts a cigarette to his mouth to take a pull and I notice his hand is shaking slightly. His eyes are very bright.

'Hi there,' he says, the exhalation of smoke mingling with his soft greeting. The scent of nicotine pricks my nose and the warm curves of his Southern accent smack me like ice. He's looking at me fondly, like I'm the love of his life, and this scares me. It's a personal look, somehow. This is no faceless shadow, but someone who knows me. Someone who has been thinking about me a *lot*.

'So this is where it all happens.' He gives a shallow smile and puts his arms out as if he's touring a palace instead of standing in my cramped writing room. 'Nice to finally see the place.' He tugs the blind so that it snaps open, revealing that the afternoon has turned to dusk. There's a pause, as if he's waiting for me to answer.

I can't. The edge of menace in the room is too tangible.

'But I'm here now,' he adds, though his tone is less jovial. 'Maybe I should go on ahead and make myself at home.' He steps back and kicks off his shoes, two scuffed brown loafers, and sprawls into my leather reading chair. His midsize frame lengthens as he stretches, and puts his hands behind his head, causing my eyes to be drawn to his pale face. The Blade doesn't have a single defining feature, except one: a slightly thickened nose from when he was hit in the face by his father as a young boy. He's average height and average weight, with mouse brown hair that can neither be described as dark nor light. His chin is halfway between round and square, his eyes halfway between brown and green, his lips halfway between thick and thin. He's forgettable. But I feel his gaze like a blade drawn sideways across the skin, the scrape of it.

Suddenly he bounces up and steps forward, suffocating my personal space again and making my skin crawl. I cringe into myself and he chuckles, leans in closer, and puts something onto my desk. Kindly, like it's a gift for a small child. I stare at it. It's a Hello Kitty brooch. The glossy pink and white plastic is bright and harmless, the tiny whiskers etched in black. He takes his cigarette, one end all wet where it's been inside his mouth, and presses it into the wood of my desk, close to my hand. The smell of scorching varnish rises.

I wake suddenly with the imprint of the keyboard on my face.

Heavens. Another dream? I look around the room, creeping horror covering me like a shroud. But the room is empty, just my books and my crazy-wall and the usual macabre clutter. He's not here. It's okay. It was a dream. I don't have to go and check my kitchen knives.

The thing about the Blade is that he looks so mediocre and uninteresting, but to be near him is to know that normal rules do not apply. He's not bound by any of the good fabric between human beings that keeps them safe in an ordinary world. Somehow he carries with him the scalding sense that he can tear that fabric at any time.

My hands are shaking. I can't believe I fell asleep. I twist my neck back into some kind of reasonable shape and realise that my phone is vibrating in its little shredded safehaven. I check the computer screen but the cursor is still blinking in empty space.

'Hello?'

'Hi Evie, it's Elise.'

'Elise, hi.' I rub a hand over my face. Elise is a friend from my writers' group. She's about forty-seven, single, kind of pudgy.

'Are you okay?'

'I'm fine!' I say. *Totally fine.* My ears prick at something. Was that a noise from the kitchen? *Don't be ridiculous.* I'm just freaked out by the dream. Still. Wouldn't hurt to investigate. I uncramp my body and unlock the door.

'Um, I was just wondering if you were going to the meeting tonight?'

The meeting. I'd forgotten about it. As I walk down the hall the sound I heard—is that *sizzling?*—gets louder. I open the door to the kitchen and stop dead in shock. Jay is standing at my stove, flipping stir-fry-style vegetables in a pan. As I watch he cracks an egg into the mix one-handed and pops a cherry tomato into his mouth. I gasp.

And watch in death-like stillness as he chews and swallows.

'I was wondering if you would be able to pick me up...?' Elise is still talking, but I have stopped paying attention. I put my hand over the receiver as Jay looks up and spots me. He smiles.

'Dinner.' He looks so content that for a moment I can't say anything. He's eating. Eating *food*. He seems to have forgotten that characters cannot interact with the real world. They can't change anything, because they aren't entirely here. And they definitely, definitely, definitely can't eat anything. Food and drink is a part of the real world, so it can never be a part of *them*.

I take my hand off the phone and blurt into it, 'I'll be there in ten,' and hang up. 'You're eating,' I say to Jay, holding—just—onto my calm.

'Yeah.' He's stirring the frying pan. 'You should eat something too.'

'Where did you get all this food?'

He uses his eyes to point out the new cardboard box of delivered groceries sitting on my kitchen table, opened and despoiled. A freshly bathed Carolyn walks into the room, her hair still damp, and smelling like my shower gel. She's wearing her trademark short skirt and heels, and her cheeks are pink and pretty from the hot water.

'Great. That looks amazing. I'm starving!' She grabs a neatly cut carrot stick and crunches into it, before catching sight of my look. 'What?'

'You're eating,' I say again. This has to stop. I close my eyes and breathe. Clear my head. Focus. But when I open my eyes, they're both still there, and now they're staring at me. Carolyn has her carrot stick midway to her mouth, like I just broke into a rap song about how my name is Bruce Willis. I need serious help. Like, stat.

'Ah, you know what?' I say. 'I've got to go. *We've* got to go. There's a writers' group meeting tonight.'

Carolyn turns sulky and annoyed. 'Now?'

'Right now.'

She plonks a hand on an out-thrust hip, all attitude.

'Well, can we stop and get takeout on the way?'

12

Elise slides into the passenger seat of my car. Jay and Carolyn are in the back. Carolyn looks like a grumpy teenager. Jay looks stern.

'Hi Evie.' Elise is awkward on the best of days. She's wearing baggy woollen pants with a shapeless turtleneck and cardigan. They're all shades of faded mud.

'Hi Elise.'

'Hi,' she says, to Jay and Carolyn in the back.

'You can see them?' My voice sounds like I spent the afternoon sipping strychnine (*interesting way to go*).

'Yeah,' she says uncertainly. 'Should I? Oh, are they your...?'

'My characters, yes!' I nod my head really hard, as if driving fictional people around in a car is something I often do. 'I decided to, um...'

But Elise is distracted by Carolyn's clothing. 'Don't you have a shirt just like that, Evie?'

'So!' I say, with way too much volume. 'How is your story going, Elise?'

'Oh, I've started a new one.' She fishes around in her pocket, and I hear the crackle of a wrapper.

'Wow,' I say. 'That's great!' Elise pulls out a chocolate bar.

'Would you like some chocolate?'

Carolyn responds, 'Yeah,' at the same time as I bellow, '*No!* I'm not hungry. *And neither is anyone else.*'

'Oh.' Elise is chastened by this, and I feel bad. She's always trying to lose weight.

'I just...' I suck in some air, trying not to hyperventilate, 'I already ate.'

I feel Jay's sternness intensifying in the back seat. I think the last thing I ate was that wretched Chinese stuff. 'But you go ahead, Elise. Tell me about your new story?' Elise takes a bite of her chocolate.

'Well,' she begins, 'it's about a writer whose characters actually come alive! I mean, really alive. In the real world.'

'Hahahaha!' My panicked laughter stops when I realise how rude it is. I clear my throat. 'Oh. Dear. That sounds...' I scrabble for an adjective. Carolyn, rebelliously addressing the window, interjects.

'La-ame.'

'Well, of course it's not an original story.' Elise is oblivious. 'But I have a good feeling about it.' She pauses and looks out the window. 'I hope they have cake tonight.'

'Me too,' Carolyn says.

'Well, we're here!' I yell, pulling into the car park like a race car driver crossing the finish line. We've arrived in record time. 'Let's all go inside, shall we? Don't want to be late! Quickly. Quickly, now!'

My writers' group is not exactly a hub of social networking. It's held in the library of a private college in New Rochelle, so it feels like it should be academic and stately, but there are only about fifteen of us, and our meetings tend to be such a mishmash of shyness and ineptitude that it's more like a gathering of Dorks Anonymous. I actually like this. It makes me feel good about myself. And it gets me out of the house once a week.

Mrs Andrews is the only sane one among us. If anyone can steer a lost literary ship into safe harbour, it's her.

I rush us through the main library with its calming taupe tones, rows of polished wooden stacks and long reading tables, and into one of the large private meeting rooms. Mrs Andrews is standing at the front as we enter, about to bring things to order, but as I charge through groups of milling people toward her I realise Carolyn has veered away from behind me. I swing around and see her at the refreshments table at the back of the room, already stuffing her mouth with cake. Holy. I make a beeline back and manage to bat the rest of the piece from her hand, much like a mother with a toddler who's been sucking on an electrical plug.

'Hey!'

'Carolyn, I—'

Mrs Andrews claps her hands. 'Well, shall we all sit down and get started?'

Oh dear. I'm too late for a private chat. I push Carolyn toward the door. 'Wait outside,' I say, as the chummy, chatting groups around us obediently separate and move toward a loose circle of wooden chairs.

I see Jay leaning against the wall and give him a *Pleeeease-can-you-go-outside* signal. Bringing them was such a bad idea, but I couldn't exactly *leave* them.

'Welcome, dear hearts.' Mrs Andrews smiles as everyone sits, clutching their coffees and laptops. 'Now, shall we get started? Who would like to share with the rest of us about how their story is going this week?'

I hurtle over to grab a seat next to Elise and stick my hand in the air, along with a few others. But I am way too keyed up to wait my turn.

'Uh, I have a question,' I say. 'It's not exactly sharing.'

'Yes, Evie?' Mrs Andrews' soft blue eyes focus on me.

'Yes. Well...uh, I was wondering if we could clarify what we know about our characters. We all know they don't have free will...'

Bob Geary, author of three books about Ancient Egypt, pipes up, 'But they sure have minds of their own!'

Everyone chuckles. I'm not surprised. One of Bob's characters is Cleopatra. Mrs Andrews is still looking at me, but her voice is gentle.

'Aye. They may be a wee bit hard to control sometimes but with effort we can always get them to do what we need them to do.'

'Right.' I pause. 'So, what happens if they, um, eat something?'

Yet another chuckle from the group, as if I have said something stupid, which of course I have, because everyone knows that characters can't eat. Now Mrs Andrews looks shrewd.

'That's not possible.'

'Maybe you need to write in some dinner scenes!' Bob folds his arms to hold in a belly laugh.

'But say,' I persist, 'hypothetically, it did happen. How could it?'

They're all staring at me as if I've gone mad. 'Elise is writing a story about this sort of thing,' I finish lamely. Beside me, Elise nods enthusiastically.

'Well,' Mrs Andrews purses her lips, 'as we all know, our characters are not part of us. The inspiration for them comes from outside us. No one knows where, but we all have our theories. We canna take credit for creating them, but we, as authors, *can* take credit for welcoming them into our stories. We meet them fully formed, in a sense, and it's our job as writers to discover more about their personalities and how they behave. But they're not a part of this world, the real world. They only exist in the story.'

'Yes, but if they start behaving in unexpected ways?'

'Well Evie...hmm. Let's take ye as an example. Ye've been writing about the same people for a long time. Nearly ten years, is it not, with some of your characters? That's a very long time to know someone when you're seeing them every day. It's natural that they should become more real to ye over time. Probably ye've become very close to them. The closer we are, the harder it is to lead them into things they won't like. But if they're not behaving, well, it's quite simple. They get cut from the story, and we find someone new, someone who will do the job that needs to be done. The story is the most important thing. After all, we always have to...' she does a little pause here to give everyone room to join in, which they do, '*just keep writing!*'

13

I leave during the break. I can feel Mrs Andrews' incisive gaze on me, but I can't stay. Something is decidedly, desperately wrong, and I can't sit there and listen to Melanie Baxter gush about her moody teenage vampire love triangle.

When I make it outside Jay is there alone. He's sitting on the stone balustrade of the entrance staircase, hands in pockets, shoulders hunched against the crisp night air, looking at the ground, thinking. He's basically just a silhouette in this light, and a very nice silhouette it is.

'Where's Carolyn?' I ask as I reach the bottom step. He looks up.

'She left.'

A heavy feeling comes crushing in. Carolyn can't just leave. Leaving is something she shouldn't even have the option of deciding to do.

'What do you mean, she left? You didn't stop her?'

Jay is quiet. 'I didn't see her go.'

I gulp, and look right and left. The campus is dark, and the only sound is a night breeze whispering in the trees.

'We have to find her.' Characters do not have free will. It's their defining characteristic and *Rule Numero Uno*. It's why they complain about going 'back inside', because they don't get to choose what they do in there. I work within the bounds of their personalities, yes, when I write them, but I'm the one who decides which parts of their personality to use at which time to move the story forward. I'm the one who knows where the book is headed, and I'm the one who decides how to get there.

They don't get to decide anything, really.

'Yeah.' His tone is stony, and now I register his attitude. He hasn't moved from his sitting position, hasn't taken his hands out of his pockets.

'What's going on, Jay?'

He lets out a terse sigh. 'Let's go.' He stands. 'I can make a pretty good guess where she went.'

I'm so grateful for this I don't say anything else until we're in the car and on our way. Jay is silent too after giving me a brief set of directions, which puts us heading south towards the city. We make it out of New Rochelle and cross into the Bronx, where the road winds past a golf course for a couple of kilometres. It's crumbly, narrow, and overhung with trees in new leaf, and I'm trying to concentrate on driving it safely when he says, 'So, I listened in at the meeting.'

I freeze. He continues. 'The fact that I could do that, and the fact that Carolyn had left by the time I got outside...'

'How much did you hear?' I ask.

'You mean what Mrs Andrews said? All of it.' His voice is hard.

My heart is beating way too fast and I have to pull over. Most of this road is bordered by a rusty metal guard rail overhung by thick groundcover but within the beam of my headlights I see that this gives way to a short gravelled shoulder and I yank the steering wheel and skid the car to a stop. I pull the parking brake, breathing heavily.

'You really shouldn't have done that,' I sputter. He shouldn't have been *able* to do that. Jay makes a noise of controlled exasperation.

'Listen. You...write me. But I'm here. Mrs Andrews said we can't exist in the real world, but clearly we exist in the real world. I mean, we changed stuff today.'

'Yes.' Heavens yes.

'She said you meet your characters fully formed. Was it the same for me?'

I gulp. 'Yes.'

'And? Explain it to me.'

I shift in my seat. 'And what? I don't know how to explain it.'

'You don't know? How about you try. I mean, geez Evie, you're the writer. You *must* know.'

I'm shocked at the emotion in his voice. Jay doesn't do anger or raised arguments. He's one-quarter Italian, which means he got all the looks and none of the passion. He's also four-quarters cop, which means he learned self-control the hard way. 'But I *don't* know!' I say. 'Yes, I write stuff down. I invent scenarios and plot twists, but generally things just come to me.'

'Come to you?'

'Yes. I didn't *make* you, if that's what you're asking. I *met* you, is more accurate.'

'Is it the same for all writers?'

'I can't be sure. I think so. All the ones I've met, anyway.'

'Has this ever happened before?'

'I don't know. But Elise is right. It's not a new idea. There are a lot of stories out there about characters coming to life. Or being alive, or whatever. Maybe it's happened to a writer before. Or maybe I'm having hallucinations.' I laugh nervously. 'I mean, you do hear about writers losing touch with...you know? They become hermits and they spend so much time with people who aren't real that they...that they...'

Wait. *I'm* a hermit.

I clear my throat. 'Oh dear,' I say. Then I have an idea. 'Wait. Tell me something. Something I don't know but you do because you're you.'

If Jay has free will, if he suddenly has existence and therefore knowledge I don't have, like a real person would, well, that means I'm not crazy, right? I cling to this twisted logic like a lifeline. Jay stares at me for so long I begin to wonder if I might have torn the very fibre of the universe by asking him this. Then his eyes drop to my lips and he looks away, and I get a surprise. What was he thinking about?

'I have a dog.'

This takes a second to register.

'What?' I splutter a bit. 'You do not have a dog. You're a workaholic, how do you have time for a dog?'

He purses his lips. 'I've got nice neighbours. They take him out and keep him company sometimes.'

I'm struggling with disbelief. 'What's his name?'

'Ben.'

'Huh. I guess I never spent much time in your apartment.' I hadn't taken the story there because there was no need—Jay was barely ever there himself.

'You never spent *any* time in my apartment.' He glances back at me.

'That's true. I haven't written a single word about it.' Jay's personal life isn't something that comes into the books much. Like a lot of cops, he *is* the job. I've never written big cosy scenes with him and Carolyn hanging out at his place, because they simply don't happen. He doesn't date, at least not the same girl more than twice, and his idea of free time well spent is weights at the gym or target practice at the range.

'So what you're saying is, that I just walked into the precinct one day and you decided to keep me?' Jay's tone is brittle.

'No!' I search for the right answer to this. 'Sort of. It's complicated. Carolyn was struggling. Those first couple of books she did fine, but she works better with someone to bounce off. I needed someone new, a new element. And there you were, suddenly. You were tough and smart—only a rookie detective but you'd come out of the Four-Two with a bunch of brilliant collars, and with the time you spent in Anti-Crime you had plenty of experience. You were more than a match for her. It was no wonder Manhattan South Homicide recruited you to the squad. You were supposed to be a minor character. But, well, you're you.' I'm looking at the side of his face in the dark. 'I don't know any more than that. I'm only human.'

'But if you had to explain this?'

'Then I would say...' I struggle for words. 'I don't know where the inspiration comes from. Nobody does. All I know is that yes, somehow you exist outside of me. Of all this. Of the books, the universe, somehow. But I don't think that's so different for me, or for anyone, you know? I mean, there's more to me than just what's physical. I'm more than just a body and a brain, right? I exist beyond my own story. It's the same with you.'

An unsteady pause. Jay breathes out.

'So we're the same.'

I swallow. 'I guess so.'

He drops his head into one hand to massage the skin beneath his eyes in a gesture that is so typical and familiar it's almost painful.

'So now what?' he says. 'Harding clearly has free will.'

I push myself back against the seat, my stomach clenching to hear him say it out loud. 'I don't know what to do,' I say, 'except to find her. Who knows what she's capable of right now.'

'Yeah, well.' He nods. 'It's a worthy goal.'

14

We reach Manhattan via the Triborough Bridge, and by the time we're taking the South Street exit off FDR Drive, I'm cringing. Trust Carolyn to choose the Lower East Side.

Jay points to a narrow parking space behind a lime green Honda, and I pull in right next to an overflowing trash can and a shady-looking group of guys who peer at my shiny car. Jay climbs straight out, and probably gives them his cop stare. If they can see him. I can't be sure, because my eyes are closed. This is one of those parts of the city that has yet to glimpse the persistent gentrification flowering elsewhere. It's dark, it's Saturday night, and out there it's all unsavoury smells, stains and cigarette butts. And danger.

Jay puts his head back in and gives me his cop stare too.

'You gonna sit here all night?'

He leads me down a cramped street of shabby shopfronts with graffitied roll-down gates and the metal skeletons of fire escapes spidering over the apartments above. I follow behind, feeling out of my depth. He's moving like he knows where he's going, but I can't tell what he's thinking. I've never felt this disconnected before. Jay pauses to cross the road, and I examine him as I stop beside him.

'Do you feel any different?'

He glances down at me and shrugs. 'It feels weird,' he says. There's a white neon bar sign above us, lighting the planes of his face. His eyes are in shadow. He looks like a statue, distant, cast in metal.

'Weird how?' I say.

'Like I just woke up. Like I'm at the start of something. Having the power to change things...' He shakes his head.

I've had the power to change things every day of my life and it hasn't made me feel the wonder and gratitude I hear in Jay's voice. He's thirty-four years old. That's thirty-four years of not getting to choose. I have an urge to lift my hand and run the back of my finger over the line of his jaw. Would it be rough? Does hair grow here if he has free will? He looks at me for a beat and then scrubs a hand over his cheek, like my eyes have told him this whole thought process. He says, 'We should go.'

'You know where she is?'

'Let's just say I got a clear sense of the general direction.'

About a block later we arrive at a dive bar advertising Guinness on tap in scrawled chalk. Jay doesn't hesitate when he chooses the place. We squeeze through a mash of people and the rough assault of electric guitars. Jay has to push people out of his way, which is a nice change. Women turn and stare at him, wide-eyed. Theoretically I knew this was the effect he had on people, but it's something completely different seeing it happen in front of my eyes.

'They can see you,' I say. Understatement.

'Yeah.' His tone tells me that he may have noticed, but he could care less. I feel quite cheerful, suddenly.

We find Carolyn drunk and dancing. And visible to everyone around her.

'Heeeeeey!' She throws her hands up, sloshing a drink over the semi-attractive boy-man she's grinding with.

'I can't believe she called *me* a cliché,' I mutter.

'Woo hoo, you guys made it! Drinks on me! Tequila shots!' Carolyn adds helpfully. 'Tastes waaaay better here!' She downs the rest of her drink and slides expertly through the crowd toward the bar. Boy-man follows, his leather pants gleaming in the neon lights, and I watch as he buys himself a drink along with five new shots. Jay and I share looks of disbelief, like Carolyn is an escaped chimp that needs wrangling. I'm struggling to believe this is actually happening. How did she get here? Does she have access to rideshare apps on her fictional smartphone?

I elbow my way up to the bar beside her.

'You're old enough to be his mother!' I yell. Carolyn doesn't heed this in the slightest, and it isn't true in any case. She only has five years on me, though Carolyn has a way of flattening out her feelings and pressing unflinchingly forward in her life that makes her seem older than her years. It's partly a result of keeping afloat while wading through the horror, blood and misery that is being a cop, along with the inevitable cynicism and loss of faith in humanity that comes with it.

It occurs to me that this lifelong hardening of heart might be contributing to the geyser of self-destruction I'm witnessing. Either that or her ex-husband Gareth. I try again.

'It's time to go home!' She downs a shot.

'Nope!' She actually pokes her tongue out. 'Don't want to go back. Whoops!' She stumbles a little.

Jay steps in and hoists her up onto his shoulder, then groans.

'Geez, Harding. You brought your weapon?'

Carolyn giggles. She keeps her gun holstered on her thigh, which is usually quite convenient since she wears her skirts so short. I took some artistic licence with her clothes. She would never get away with flaunting legs that long in a real-world detective squad.

Boy-man tries to step in as Jay hauls Carolyn toward the door, but Jay opens his jacket and flashes his shield. I watch this happening, then I catch sight of the remaining four tequila shots. *Yes.* The first goes down like a draught of battery acid. The next two taste like sunshine in Mexico. The last one I don't taste at all. Mmm. Good choice, me.

Jay is waiting for me at the corner, with Carolyn now passed out over his shoulder. At the car he dumps her in the back. I open the driver's side door and try to get in behind the wheel, but Jay takes my elbow and pulls me back out again. This shocks me.

'Hey!' I say.

'Don't even think about it,' he says, as he reaches for the keys in my hand. 'No way you're driving home.'

'Are you crazy? As if I'm letting you drive!' I evade him. He pushes me lightly against the trunk of the car and reaches again. His face is set.

'Don't think I didn't see you in there. And I know you haven't eaten anything again today.' Dammit. He really does see everything. 'In about forty-five seconds you're going to pass out.'

'No way,' I say. My motive is strong: do not let a person of questionable existence drive the car. 'You could disappear doing sixty miles an hour!' I add. Or at least I try to, but my tongue is a little unresponsive, and my arm as I swing the keys away from him does a wild arc behind me. Wow. Tequila really does work that fast.

Jay's response is to step right into me so he can reach my flailing hand, and the movement puts his other hand on my waist and brings the tip of my cold nose into contact with his neck. My waving has rucked my shirt up so his fingers are on my bare skin, and then his other hand connects with mine and we both freeze.

His whole body is against mine and I get a heady breath of his cologne, along with a shattering thud of chemicals crashing into my bloodstream. I can feel every millimetre where our skin touches. Holy. I've never touched him before. Not in fifteen books. And definitely not skin to skin, like two real people, with pheromones and chemistry and the slight prickle of a five o'clock shadow. He's so solid and utterly *there*.

My breath comes out in a rush. Jay steps back as if he just got burned by something, and we stare at each other for a second, breathing. It's too dark to see his eyes and I'm having trouble focusing anyway, but possibly he's as freaked out as I am. I swallow dryly, feeling unsteady. The reverberations of that chemical shock are still pounding in my veins. Then I realise he has my keys.

'Give!' I take a determined step toward him but he backs up and puts a 'stop' hand up, like I'm a dangerous animal that needs to be kept at a safe distance.

'Seriously, Evie, get in the back. You can hardly stand up.' His voice is a little hoarse.

'I can stand up.' But that's pretty much all I can do. I give in with a sigh and obey. Carolyn is slumped and inert on the seat beside me.

Dangerous animals, I muse as I close the door. *Interesting way to go*. A malfunction at the zoo followed by a good, old-fashioned tiger-mauling. Or maybe a nice elephant-trampling.

I close my eyes and try to clear my mind, which is quite easy, I find, with a head full of calming tequila-clouds. But as I open my eyes, hopeful, Carolyn, still very real, sticks her head out the window and throws up. Noisily. Jay, steely-faced in the front seat, hits the electric window as Carolyn gets her head back inside, and pulls out into the traffic, while my tequila-clouds turn into an unpleasant spinning. My phone rings. It's mounted on the dash, so Jay just presses the button for speakerphone and keeps driving.

'Honey?' Daniel's voice is rich with concern. It's Daniel! Oh, how nice. I experience a warm rush of feeling for him and then the dull sting of mortification. Hmm? I struggle to remember why this would be.

'Daniel?' Ooh, do I sound drunk? *Am* I drunk?

'Honey, are you okay?'

'Yes!' I clip this too short in the effort to sound sober, and suddenly come wide awake. 'Of course!'

'Hey hon.' He seems relieved.

Beside me Carolyn comes alive and yells, 'Danieeeeeeel!'

I grab the emergency fire blanket I keep on the back seat and push it squarely into Carolyn's face.

'Who's that?' Daniel asks.

I ignore this question. No need to have that can of worms opened on him right now.

'I've been trying to call you,' I say, making an effort not to sound accusing. Carolyn's voice, muffled by the blanket, carries across the car-noise.

'And the Asshole Of The Year Award goes to...!'

Thankfully Daniel appears not to hear.

'I'm sorry, Jane, I had to reschedule my flight to receive some clients this morning. The meeting was postponed, so I got to be errand boy for my father. It was an unpleasant day. How are you?'

Carolyn starts to struggle under my hand, apparently not enjoying being suffocated. She gets her mouth free and yells, 'Liar! You suck!'

'I'm fine,' I say, at ten times normal volume, trying to drown her out. 'I just...I'm glad to hear your voice.' I feel relieved, so relieved. There is an explanation. A logical and everyday explanation. I knew there would be.

'I can't hear you that great, honey,' Daniel says. 'Listen, I'm taking the jet tonight so I have to go but I'll give you a call tomorrow, okay? Talk soon.'

'Oh, okay. Bye then.'

'Bye hon.' He hangs up, and the glow fades off the phone. Carolyn rips the blanket off her face.

'What the hell was that? You're just going to let him walk all over you?'

'He hasn't done anything wrong!' I say. She glares at me for a few seconds more, during which time I realise I need to throw up.

And then I do.

15

What is this accursed light?

I squint at the ceiling. Early May morning sunshine is streaming through the window of the room, making joyful yellow patterns on the walls. Ugh. *How cheerful.* Where am I? Oh, in bed. My own bed. Jay must have carried me upstairs last night, because I definitely don't remember walking up myself.

I hear the drone of noisy snoring coming from the spare room. Ah. Carolyn. Facts drift back while I cover my face with the pillow. Carolyn escaping. Tequila.

The snoring reaches a peak, which isn't exactly conducive to falling back asleep, so I get out of bed and shuffle in that direction. Carolyn is in there, fully dressed, spread-eagled and unconscious, in an atomic detonation of tangled sheets. Well, at least she won't be going anywhere for a while.

I head to the bathroom, peel off last night's clothes and douse myself under the shower. I put on something that doesn't smell like a bar and head downstairs, the bump of each step bringing back a new memory fragment and making me feel proportionally more ill.

There's one coherent thought in my head, however: Daniel isn't cheating on me. I don't recall how I know this, but the residual sense of vindication from whatever I learned last night is undeniable. It's not over. I'm not alone. Daniel is a stable, trustworthy person. He was one of those jaded playboy heirs in the past, yes, and even the most basic internet search engine turns up a plethora of compromising paparazzi snaps as evidence of this. But twelve months ago he got his act together, started working for his father, and stopped having flings with models and superficial gold-diggers. He basically grew up and turned into someone any ordinary girl like me would be glad to have as a husband.

As I pass the living room I see Jay is asleep on the sofa, one arm thrown over his face, and shirtless. Hmm. Maybe I should recalibrate my definition of 'ordinary girl like me'.

Either Jay went searching through my cupboards or he knew where I keep the spare blankets. Either of those options makes me feel sicker. I tiptoe past, not wanting to wake him but he stirs, probably some kind of law enforcement instinct. I creep into the kitchen, and discover a half-empty bottle of vodka with the lid off sitting on my beige kitchen bench. Is this why I feel so terrible? I screw the lid back on then rummage through my new grocery box, which is sitting beside it. I pull out a fresh pack of PG Tips, sniff the life-affirming tea-ness, put the kettle on, take two painkillers, and hold my head.

Jay walks in, scratching. He has stubble and bed-hair and he's so human and real that I get a sudden pop of memory from last night, like being shot with a gun. I remember standing so close to him I couldn't breathe, and that if I'd lifted my chin just a fraction, my lips would have grazed the warm pulse in his neck.

Here's the part where I admit to myself that I have imagined what it would be like to kiss Jay. More than once.

But it's okay, I tell myself. It isn't terribly unusual for writers to be a little in love with their characters. It helps propel the story a lot of the time. And thank goodness, I've never told Jay this. Because I'm guessing not too many writers get the opportunity to have their lips bare millimetres from the warm, beating pulse in a character's neck and be a hair's-breadth from launching themselves at it.

'Hey,' he says.

Don't look at his abs, I reprimand myself. At least he pulled jeans on. I don't need the sight of his boxers burned into my imagination. My eyes move obediently, but where they land is no better. *Or shoulders.*

'Hey.' My voice sounds rusty, like I have a hangover, which I do, and he raises his eyebrows in an amused and knowing look. He comes closer to flick on the coffee machine, and then I say, 'Hey!' and grab his right arm and lift it. 'You have a tattoo!' I pull his elbow up so that the small script on his ribcage is revealed, dragging him into me. 'I can't believe you have a tattoo.' I never wrote a tattoo. I somehow feel like he has defaced himself without my permission. 'When did you get this?'

'About a year ago.'

'A *year* ago?' I put a finger near the dark blue lettering, careful not to touch him. He's ticklish.

It's the same colour as his eyes, and it looks good. The font is clean-cut and serious. *Fidelis ad mortem.* Latin. Official motto of the NYPD: Faithful unto death. He really *is* the job. How typical Jay.

I look up at him, feeling rather proud. And then I stop feeling proud and start feeling something quite different as I meet his eyes, and realise how close he is. All those same chemicals from last night are clouding off his bare skin. I see him swallow and I drop his arm like a hot poker and step back. 'I like it,' I say stiffly.

'You do?' He doesn't sound entirely convinced.

'It's perfect.' I take another step back. I can't help it. He's standing there looking like a blast of sunshine in my bland beige kitchen, all brown and healthy and strong. He's not long come back from a visit to his parent's house, hence the tan, which is something only days spent working shirtless in the sun could give. 'What did your mother think?'

I see the edge of a grin as he turns and grabs two mugs from my cupboard like he's lived here all his life.

'She thought it was perfect too.'

'Ha!' As if. Jay's mother is smart as a tack, and has a pretty sharp tongue too. I doubt she minced words when she saw it. She worries too much about him being a cop in the city as it is. His parents own a horse farm in South Carolina, which they bought when Jay was ten. Before then he'd grown up in Brooklyn, a city kid getting into trouble, but John and Cara Ryan had decided one day that fresh air and horses were what made healthy kids, and they'd acted accordingly. I don't think they ever regretted their decision. All Jay's sisters are happily married, and his older brother owns a hardware store in Charleston. Only Jay moved back to the city.

He pours just enough milk, and then hot water into my tea.

'How'd you sleep?' he asks, handing it to me.

I run a shaky hand through my damp hair. 'Like a freight train. Thank goodness.'

He grins again. 'So Harding's snoring up there?'

'Loudly. How did you know?'

'Please. You think I could forget Book Eleven, when she passed out in that dumpster after the fiasco with Claymore Reynolds? She could've woken the dead.'

I burst out laughing. 'I remember.'

Poor Jay had been the one who had to climb in and haul her out, after she'd been dosed with a potent concoction of benzodiaz-epines by a disgruntled pharmacologist.

'It took me three days to get rid of the smell.'

I laugh harder. 'I remember that too.'

'Yeah, well,' his grin meets mine, 'thanks for nothing.' We smile at each other for a moment more.

The doorbell sounds, and I start in surprise. Jay checks his watch. 'Almost noon.'

I dither a little. 'What if I pretend I'm not home?'

Jay rolls his eyes. 'Geez, Evie.'

Fine. I answer the door, and gasp. Jenna is on the front doorstep.

'You're alive,' she accuses.

'Barely,' I say, as she takes in my appearance. She looks amazing, as always, like a 1920s It Girl, petite and slim with her shiny bob and raunchy, super-chic fashion. Today she's wearing striking red heels that match her lipstick, and put her eyeline level with mine so I catch the full burn of her brown eyes. Jenna is pretty and vivacious, and she has a worldly air that goes beyond fashion and confidence and makes her irresistible to people—men especially. She's a few years older than me, and she loves the nightlife in the city and doesn't exactly do organic living, but somehow she manages to look eternally youthful, which makes the sweep of her inspection feel particularly incisive. I know I don't look my best right now.

'What happened to your car?' She points to where it's sitting in my driveway, and then scrunches her face as she steps past me.

'Come in,' I murmur, and peek out at it. 'Oooh.' Looks like Jay hosed it down last night but got distracted halfway through. Possibly by some semi-conscious companions. He might be the reason why the vodka bottle in my kitchen is only half empty and not fully empty this morning.

'If you give me coffee, I won't kill you.' Jenna is already halfway down the hallway, and I slam the door shut and hasten after her. 'Seven messages, Evie. It's a new record for you.'

I make it into the kitchen just in time to see her go up in a slow fireball at the sight of Jay.

'Well *hell-o.*'

Jay is leaning against my counter pouring coffee, and Jenna's predatory appraisal doesn't seem to faze him in the least. 'You want some coffee?' he asks.

'Yes,' she says. She's giving him the same inspection she gave me a few seconds ago, except this time it's bordering on pervy. 'And you are?'

'Jay.' Jay's tone has a careful reticence in it, and his eyes flick to me, a question in them. I open my mouth to give voice to a plausible explanation for Jay's identity, but my brain is not functioning nearly fast enough.

'Jay...?' Jenna's tone is sultry.

'Ryan,' Jay says, cool as anything. Jenna's mouth drops open. He hands her a cup in place of shaking her hand and leaves the room, hopefully to put a shirt on.

'Please tell me what's going on?' Jenna turns to me, her expression thrilled. Jenna loves drama. Especially other people's.

'Um...' How to explain, exactly?

'He has the same name as your character.' Jenna's tone is accusing again.

'Yes.'

'Like, really? Or, you know, pretend? Is he your Muse? Are you sleeping with him?'

'No!'

'You know,' she murmurs, 'he looks exactly how I imagined Jay Ryan would look.'

'Funny that,' I mumble. What I know is, I cannot tell Jenna who Jay really is. In fact, she's first on a long list of people I cannot tell, unless I want to get taken away and locked up forever. Jenna is eminently pragmatic. She may read fiction for a living but her success with it is based on an unfailing instinct for what sells and what doesn't, what strikes a chord and what doesn't. She doesn't do flights of fancy. She does realism. She might know that I 'spend time with my characters', but that's quite different to having one of them serve her a cup of coffee. Better she think Jay is some hot nobody than try to explain the truth.

'What about Daniel?'

'Jenna, nothing's going on.'

'Of course it isn't.' She winks. 'But does Daniel know?'

'Jenna, please. It's nothing like that. It's...' *It's that my fictional characters have exploded into living, breathing life. Nothing to worry about.*

'Listen Evie, I am definitely in favour of you doing whatever it takes to finish this book, and I've never been Daniel's biggest fan. He's been a disaster for your writing. But is this really a good idea?'

'I...wait, what do you mean Daniel has been a disaster for my writing? What do you mean you're not his biggest fan?'

'Well, obviously.' She flicks her hair. 'He's a walking cliché. And boring. You love him, good for you. But ever since you started dating you've barely been able to string a sentence together. And it's not like he encourages you. Haven't you noticed?' She takes a drink of her coffee like this isn't the most offensive conversation in history.

I frown. 'I...'

The doorbell rings again.

When I open it, it's Magdeline. The Bradley limo is idling at the curb behind her, and she looks glorious, like Paris Fashion Week is her next stop today.

'Evie!' A pause. 'You're not dressed!'

'Oh.' I look down at what I'm wearing. Apparently jeans don't count. Magdeline is wearing a tight white pantsuit that makes her legs look miles long and lights the golden brown of her eyes. Her blonde ponytail is straight as ever.

'Didn't you get my message about rescheduling?'

Possibly part of the message I deleted yesterday. But, 'Magdeline, it's a Sunday.'

'Yes, Evie.' Her tone is brisk but professional. 'Cintia is opening the salon for you especially.'

I wonder what kind of monetary incentive set this in motion.

'Hello, Magdeline,' Jenna pipes up from behind my shoulder. Jenna dislikes Magdeline, and in the same cold, unapologetic way that she dislikes child slavery and animal testing.

'Hello, Jenna. How nice to see you.' Magdeline is a model of restraint: nothing to hint that Jenna is possibly one of the most difficult bridesmaids in history. She motions behind her to the limousine. 'Evie, we really need to go. I managed to make this appointment for you, but obviously it'll be the last one available with Cintia for some time.'

Then her mouth drops open. She peers over my other shoulder and when I turn to follow her gaze I see that Jay has appeared on the stairs, holding a towel. Apparently he knows where my towels are too.

'Who's that?' Magdeline's tone is full of disbelief.

'Uh...!' My mind is blank.

'Do you mind if I grab a shower, Evie?' Jay is all politeness.

'Go ahead!' I say, my voice strangled. I don't look at him.

Magdeline's golden tiger-eyes are like lasers. 'A friend of yours?'

'He's a detective from downtown,' I gasp. 'He's helping me with my latest book. I've been having a little trouble with it.'

Jenna nods in agreement beside me. 'A *lot* of trouble,' she adds. 'Very helpful. You know,' she muses, and her expression tells me she is enjoying herself immensely, 'I think you should head off for that appointment, Evie. Don't want to be late. In fact, perhaps we should all go?'

16

The dress that Cintia Lareu has designed for me is exquisite. It's all flowy silk and antique lace. It highlights my curves and makes me look tall and slender at the same time, and the creamy shade brings out my eyes and makes me look startled and Bambi-esque. In reality, I am startled, and have been on a permanent basis since yesterday. And Bambi is a pretty apt metaphor for someone who lost a parent to an act of violence.

Behind the curtain, Cintia fusses with me in her pretty accent.

'See, I bring it down here, because it show off your bust, yes?' Excellent. Thank goodness Magdeline marched me back inside to retrieve my wedding-day underwear. I refused the limo, though.

Leaving had been such an awkward business. Carolyn was still comatose, but I wasn't willing to leave Jay unattended for an extended period, and so I asked him to come with us. Actually asked him, something I've never done. Clouds of steam brushed past me as he cracked the bathroom door, his hair all wet, his eyes gleaming, and I realised he had the power to say no. And I could tell by the look on his face he realised this too. But he didn't. And then Jenna gleefully drove everyone here in her brand new red Audi.

'So does Daniel know about him?' I discover Magdeline has insinuated herself behind the curtain with us. Outside, Jenna is touching up her makeup on the plush viewing couch, and not so subtly coming on to Jay, who sits beside her with his elbows on his knees and his head down.

The car ride was awful. Magdeline repetitively grilled me on everything to do with the wedding—'I need you to remember that it's only two weeks away, Evie'—while Jay sat in the front with Jenna like a disapproving stone. Magdeline asked him a couple of polite questions about himself, like which precinct he works, which department, what year he graduated from the academy. All things that would fail the most basic identity check if she chose to look into him. Then she pointedly left him alone, and I'm fully aware that she probably thinks I'm having some kind of torrid affair with him.

'Of course he knows about him,' I say. This isn't a lie because I've talked to Daniel about Jay, the way I've talked to him about all my characters.

'So he's met him?' Magdeline sounds justifiably suspicious.

'Not exactly. But Daniel's read a couple of my books so it's kind of the same thing. At least, I think he's read some of my books.' I ignore Magdeline's confused look.

'*Ya!*' Cintia tucks in a final pin. 'You must not get more *flaquita* before the wedding. Or we must take it in again. Already you are too thin.' I remember I only had tea for breakfast, thanks to Jenna. 'Go to show your friends.'

'Oh, no, I...'

'*Vaya!*' She pushes me through the curtain and I lurch into the main salon, where Jenna stands and plants shrewd hands on her hips.

'It's okay?' I ask, and in response Jenna gives a hard nod. This, from her, is tantamount to a long emotional speech. I hear a sniff behind me. I turn. Is Magdeline *crying?*

'Are you crying?' Jenna makes this sound like the seventh sin.

'I...' Magdeline brushes the tear away, almost angry. We all stare at her. 'It's an emotional moment, seeing the dress.' Magdeline runs for the curtain, where Cintia has a tissue waiting.

Jenna widens her eyes at me. 'Geez. Maybe she's getting over a break-up or something?'

I grimace. It's possible Magdeline is shedding tears of agony because she thinks I'm cheating on Daniel, but I'm not about to announce this to the room.

'Or maybe she's upset because she thinks you're an adulteress,' Jenna adds.

Thanks Jenna.

The door to the salon opens and Morgan the assistant appears carrying a huge bottle of Dom Perignon, followed by Eileen Bradley and Juliana.

'Hello, darling!' Eileen comes straight over and hugs me. I'm briefly held in a safe haven of finely woven fabrics and subtle, expensive scent. Eileen is wearing soft pink and feminine heels and has her dark hair swept back into an elegant chignon. 'You look so beautiful!'

Juliana hugs me too. It's like being embraced by a winter branch.

'Hello.' I smile, thrilled to see them. 'I'm so glad you're here.'

'Well you know, sweetheart, I didn't want to be the overbearing mother-in-law during this process, but I just couldn't bear to stay away from the second-to-last fitting. And I see you've done me justice.' Eileen's smile is real, her lovely brown eyes a little misty, and she hugs me again. I hear Morgan pop the champagne open and suddenly I have a glass in my hand. It's official: I have an amazing mother-in-law.

'Lace,' says Juliana, in a slightly bored tone. 'Mm.' On the other hand, Juliana is the kind of person who clicks her fingers in the face of desk clerks when they aren't processing her Presidential Suite reservation fast enough, or who only drinks coffee made from the overpriced beans pooed out by those special Indonesian monkeys. Or civets, or whatever. How Eileen managed to have a daughter so careless of other people is something I cannot understand.

'Now, who is this?' Eileen has caught sight of Jenna and Jay.

Oh no. I take a slug of my champagne.

'Ah, you know Jenna, of course, my agent, and dear friend, and soon my bridesmaid. Obviously I couldn't have this fitting without her.' I clear my throat. 'And this is Jay.' There could be no weirder place for an intense unknown male to be than sitting on a velvet couch watching me try on my wedding dress. The moment is more than awkward, but thankfully Jenna chooses this key second to place a proprietorial hand on Jay's knee. Jay's mouth quirks and then he blinks, and about fifty points of IQ drop out of his eyes, making him look exactly like Jenna's latest man-toy, and I collapse inwardly with relief.

'Ah, yes, hello Jenna.' Whatever Eileen's discomfort, it is well covered by experienced social graciousness. I'm hoping that since she and James Bradley have heard me talk in full about Jenna's personality, the oddness of her bringing a date to my dress fitting will not be out of context.

'She does have lovely bone structure,' Juliana muses to her mother, having been observing me, which makes me feel somewhat like a new artistic piece the Bradleys have acquired, perhaps *Girl in Vanilla Milkshake*, which they are deciding where to display to best effect. 'You'll wear your hair up, of course.'

'I'm not sure,' I say. I think I have an appointment with the hairdresser in the next couple of days, but frankly I've been trusting Magdeline to keep me up with those things. The wedding has been far from my mind. Two weeks. I get a fantastic jolt of reality. In two weeks I'll be married to Daniel.

'The skirt isn't a little long?' Juliana asks.

I take another slug of my champagne. Juliana hasn't touched her champagne, so it has helped keep her powers of criticism sharp, it seems. She's looking at the gorgeous creamy trail of my skirt, which is dragging on the floor. I lift it sheepishly, revealing plain red Doc Martens, scuffed with use. I bought them in England five years ago when I last went home to see my mother. It was the last time I saw her. Her funeral was three years ago.

'I forgot my shoes.' Kind of. The wedding shoes Magdeline convinced me to buy are painfully uncomfortable. And these boots are...I just needed these boots today.

'Oh.' This one word conveys Juliana's whole opinion about my choices in life.

'Where is Cintia?' Eileen makes a graceful turn, looking for her. 'I must congratulate her on her beautiful work.'

'She took Magdeline out the back,' Jenna says.

'I'll go and pay my regards. Juliana?' Juliana follows her and they disappear.

'Yeesh.' Jenna drains the last of her champagne. I catch sight of Jay.

'So,' I say. There's a pause where I try to read the expression in his eyes and not feel light-headed from the alcohol. I want to ask him what he thinks, but I feel too awkward for some reason. 'Too much lace?' I shuffle.

'You look good, Evie,' he says in a low voice. 'I think your dad would've been proud.' I drop my gaze to the ground, unable to speak for a second.

'Come on. Can't even shed a tear?' Jenna nudges him, oblivious. 'It cracked Magdeline.'

'Cops don't cry,' I say. I give a wobbly smile, trying to make light.

'Not in your books.' Jay quirks an eyebrow.

This is true. I have a tendency to paint all cops as heroes. Tough guys who never need help. Probably some kind of psychological complex left over from my father, who was a real hero. I suddenly miss him a whole lot. I wish he could see me in this dress. I feel pretty, beautiful even, and I don't want to get married without him there.

'You're right,' I say, quelling my feelings with another weak smile. 'In fact, I think Tillman is the only one who ever cried. And that was only because...' I gurgle to a stop, as a shuddering possibility hits me. 'Tillman.'

Jay's gaze sharpens. 'Do you think...?'

I clutch my throat. 'Oh dear. Do you think he's here? In the city?'

'I think we should find out.' Jay is already standing. I turn to Jenna, who's been watching this conversation with a breathless delight I have no time to analyse.

'Jenna, there are some things I have to explain to you. But I can't right now. There's no time. Will you please...?' What on earth could she do that will help this situation? In answer she lifts up her right hand and opens it so that her car keys are on display.

'Go with God, my child,' she says, and drops them into my palm. I gasp a thank-you and run for the door.

'Dress!' Jay says.

'Right!' I skid back toward the dressing room.

A wedding dress will definitely slow me down.

17

Jay drives fast.

'I can't believe we left,' I say, squirming with delayed guilt. 'I can't believe we just abandoned Eileen. What will she think? What will Magdeline say?'

Whatever Jay's feelings are on the disintegration of my life, he keeps them to himself. It's Sunday traffic, so we make good time, but I know he wishes we had a strobe for the roof. Then he swerves the car to the curb and stops.

What? We shouldn't be stopping. We need to find Tillman. If he's here. Is he here? His name is like a threatening drumbeat in the back of my mind. *Tillman, Tillman, Tillman.*

I watch Jay pull his wallet out of his back pocket and check there's cash in it. He pulls out a handful of notes.

'You think this'll be good here?' He flashes me a grin, then jumps out and strides into a Shake Shack. Er...? Is he planning to buy something with fictional money? Six minutes later he comes out again with two bags, gets in the car and says, 'Eat,' dumping one bag on my lap and throwing the other into the back seat. He accelerates us back out into traffic, and I open the bag and see a cheeseburger with everything, including—sweet heaven—smoked bacon. Suddenly I'm ravenous. Ooh, he got fries too.

'How many days since you ate a proper meal?' It's possible he's freaked out by my grizzly bear-style attack on the fries.

'Too many,' I say. 'Clearly. I can't believe you bought me food.' It's good. So good.

'So where's Tillman?' Jay is concentrating on the road, swinging between lanes. I swallow my mouthful and resist the urge to put two more fries in my mouth before I answer.

'I don't know. You and Carolyn have been staking out that house but I don't know if it's actually his. This is the first time I haven't had a story come together neatly in my mind. I have pieces but it just feels like—'

'Like everyone's doing whatever the hell they want. So he could be anywhere.'

'Yes. Oh no.' I clutch at my fries. 'I'm responsible for unleashing a psychopath on the city. I'm like one of those people who create diseases and then releases them into the population.'

'Biological terrorist?'

'Yes!'

'Hardly.' Jay slants a penetrating glance at me. 'Is he responsible for Orson Bidgood?'

I pause. Orson Bidgood was the dead guy who opened Book Sixteen. It was his *pieces* that were in the bag on Edgar Polton's fire escape in SoHo.

Tillman had been the obvious suspect from the beginning, since Jay and Carolyn's frequent contact with him throughout the series meant a thorough knowledge of his different quirks, most notably an obsessive-compulsive tendency toward collecting the city's free papers—like *The Village Voice*—which he kept stacked in precarious towers wherever he lived.

And that was why Carolyn and Jay had been staking Tillman out in Chapter Three. Because although it was out of the question that poor, wilted Edgar Polton might have precipitated such a heinous crime, it was just the sort of thing Tillman would be involved in, and *The Voice* was a dead giveaway. Either way, it was almost certain he knew something.

But now Jay is asking me flat out for plot reveals. This feels like very dangerous ground.

'He might have been,' I say carefully. Tillman is the ideal henchman. His placid lack of moral compass combined with his childlike enjoyment of being helpful has made him the go-to man for a number of crooked masterminds in the series.

But Tillman isn't known for ground balls, and there's something Jay and Carolyn aren't aware of yet: that Bidgood was a PI, and he was also the investigator Edgar Polton's business partner had hired to keep tabs on him. Which makes Polton look less than squeaky clean, despite his solid alibi.

'Either way,' I say, 'I get the feeling Tillman is in trouble. He's gotten involved in something that turned out to be bigger than he thought.'

The thing is, so far Book Sixteen has been standard detective work. But somehow I also know that Edgar Polton is the tip of the iceberg. I just don't know what that iceberg is. There's something brewing in the background, I can feel it. Book Sixteen is bigger than any of my other books have been.

'And Tillman could be here right now,' Jay mutters.

'He could be anywhere,' I say. I look out the window like I might catch sight of him. 'We need to find him.'

'What we need is Harding. She has a killer instinct when it comes to Tillman.'

When we arrive home I take the stairs two at a time and charge into my spare bedroom. Carolyn is curled beneath the sheets. I rip them off.

'Noooooooo!' Carolyn's newly-wakened eyes are tiny, her voice all cracked and papery. Her blonde hair has the look of a roughly gathered pile of garden clippings, and she burrows back into the sheets like a worm dug up with a spade. I catch Jay's eye, who has followed me in. He shrugs. What now? I have a brainwave. I head back downstairs and three minutes later I lean over Carolyn and hold the Chinese medicine mixture under her nose. She springs into a sitting position. 'I'm up! I'm up!'

Fifteen minutes later she's hunched on the leather chair in my writing room, dishevelled and clutching coffee, and wrapped in Jay's blanket, which she dragged off the sofa as she went by. The second cheeseburger is half eaten on the bookshelf beside her. Jay is pacing the room, avoiding the tumbled pile of my notes on the floor, and I'm sitting at my desk, my knees tucked up on the chair.

'Tillman wouldn't go far,' Carolyn says. 'He's a prime EDP but he's a little weasel and he has all those tics. Public transport gives him a rash, and he hates taxis. And I doubt his skinny little legs could run that far.' Her eyes are still tiny, but no longer from sleep. The idea of Tillman loose in the city has enraged her into immediate and incisive sobriety.

EDP is her cop-talk for an emotionally disturbed person. But Tillman is more than that. Much more. He's a killer. Jay stops pacing and folds his arms. He's wearing a blue t-shirt and the movement stretches the fabric and draws my attention to his Glock and leather shoulder holster, which he hasn't bothered shrugging out of, probably because he believes Carolyn is minutes away from cracking Tillman's location.

'You think he's staying with someone?'

'Yeah.' Carolyn picks up the burger. 'I think if he found himself here with free will the first thing he'd do is go burrow into a friendly hole somewhere.' Jay nods. Carolyn chomps into her burger and I watch them, rapt. They have that crime-solving electricity zapping between them. I've never seen the zing of it for real before. Jay starts pacing again.

'What about that guy he used to hack into the State Health

Department records database that time?'

'Bleechman. No.' Carolyn shakes her head at him. 'I get the feeling Tillman never trusted him. What about his friend from school, they worked on that import scam together?'

'I know the one.' Jay walks over to my bookshelf. 'That scrawny, stuttering guy from Book Eight.' He runs his finger along the black spines of the most recent edition of the series and chooses Book Eight, pulling it out and fanning it open. He spends a moment flipping pages and then says, 'Darren Hinds.' I blink. How did he know how to find that so fast? He and Carolyn never read their own books, obviously. That would be weird.

'Right,' says Carolyn. 'He was Swiss or something.'

'Swedish,' Jay and I say at the same time.

Jay turns his attention to me. 'Are they still good friends?'

I think about this and say slowly, 'They are.'

'Didn't he live near here?'

'Yes.' I clutch my throat. I wrote him into a Bronx neighbourhood only about fifteen minutes away. 'You think he'd be there?'

'We could check.' Jay snaps the book closed.

'No,' I say, 'what I mean is, he's not a character from a current story. If every murderer and maniac I've ever written about is living and thriving here right now, in the *real world...*'

'Relax,' Jay says. 'If that's the case then the rest of the guys you wrote about will be in jail right now. Harding caught them, remember?'

I try not to whimper. Jay drops Book Eight onto my desk where my pile of notes used to be and addresses us both.

'Okay. I'm gonna pay Hinds a visit. I'm taking Jenna's car. You,' he says to me, 'write. Write where Tillman is. You,' to Carolyn, 'help her.'

18

'WHAT is Tillman doing in there?'

The curser blinks. Carolyn lolls on the leather chair behind me with a large vodka tonic in her hand. She's showered, but she came down wearing my brand-new save-for-when-I'm-married underwear again, and not much else. She's really taking the whole free will thing to a new level. This kind of liberation could badly upset my neighbours.

'That stuff smells disgusting.' She screws up her nose and takes another sip of her vodka, ice clinking.

I have a fresh pot of the Chinese herb stuff beside me at the computer. I haven't been able to bring myself to drink any of it, but having it there at least makes me feel like I'm doing something, since I haven't written a word in the last two hours.

'Aargh, can't you get rid of it? It makes me want to throw up. *Why do I feel so gross?* I've *literally* never been this hung over before.'

I refrain from pointing out that this is thanks to me, that I haven't let her get into a situation where she would be this hungover before.

'Maybe you should stop drinking,' I suggest.

'It's the best cure.'

'Do you really trust your source for that concept?' The whole 'hair of the dog' idea is something she got from Gareth, who was Irish, and thought that a solid pint of Guinness for breakfast the morning after a bender was the quickest way to cure it. Carolyn glares at me in a way that would set me on fire if I were made of wood. Referring to Gareth, even obliquely, is not for the faint-hearted when Carolyn is in the room.

'Well, this is a cure too,' I say, giving my mixture another sniff and pretending I don't want to gag. 'It's supposed to make me more creative.'

'Blegh. Please, how hard can it be?'

'You're meant to be helping me,' I say.

'Geez, what do you want, a foot massage?' She takes another large sip of her glass and then gets up to examine my crazy-wall. 'In case it hadn't occurred to you, I'm not exactly dying to go back inside. Just put some words on paper. So to speak.'

'Carolyn,' I massage my temples, 'please go away.'

Just then the doorbell rings, and Carolyn flounces out before I react.

'That's for me!'

For *her*? I rise to follow her, but as I do I notice something hidden by the edge of my keyboard. A little incongruous bit of white plastic set against the dark wood of my desk. What...? I move my keyboard to the side, and my heart constricts.

It's a Hello Kitty brooch.

I move the keyboard a few centimetres more and there in the wood is the small blackened circle of a cigarette burn. No. My breath goes all gaspy as bolts of hot and cold rush down my arms. But it was a dream. Wasn't it?

I remember something that has been pushing at the edges of my memory all day. Sally Carston. She was to be the Blade's next victim. He'd been stalking her for months, had planned her death down to the last detail. And she's real. She's here, in a morgue somewhere, and the papers are reporting it.

He's here.

That worst-case-scenario horror I felt when I saw her name in the paper yesterday is actually reality. I cough, now really gagging, sick to my stomach, as disbelief sucks at me. He has killed someone. Not a fictional someone. A person.

Because of me.

I hear voices at the front door and I rush out there, my chest tight and frightened, but it's just a pizza boy, standing there gob-smacked at the sight of Carolyn's outfit. Her silky kimono (*my silky kimono*) is tied too loosely and her long, perfect legs are on full display as she plucks a little knot of cash from under the strap of her lacy camisole. The pizza boy looks like he might faint, but he manages to hand her a pizza box. Just when I think this can't get any worse, Carolyn turns and reveals even more of herself as she waves to someone outside the door.

'Hellooo!' Joyfully, like she's a Christmas elf come to bring good gifts to the world. The pizza boy is stumbling backward down my front path, and I see him pass my neighbour Leslie, who's frozen in place in my front yard.

'Leslie, hi!' I elbow Carolyn out of the doorway and try to think of a way to explain this situation but can't, so I slam the door closed, cutting off the sight of Leslie's shocked face. Carolyn takes all of two seconds to open the pizza box and start a slice.

'Well that was rude,' she rebukes me, her mouth full. I slump against the door. 'You know,' she adds, 'your yard is really messy. Your grass is longer than everyone else's.' That was probably what Leslie was coming over to complain about, but right now Leslie is the least of my worries. That Hello Kitty brooch is every worst nightmare I have come to life. I need help.

'We have to go,' I say.

Carolyn sighs gustily. 'Again? Can I bring my pizza?'

'Bring whatever you want. But *please* put some clothes on.'

19

The most qualified person I can think of for this situation is Mrs Andrews, and her house actually isn't that far from mine, only about a four minute drive. It's quaint and tiny, a stone cottage like something straight out of Grimms', with wild roses framing the front steps. When we arrive a muted sunset is staining the sky, kindling the slate peaks on the roof and the blowsy tangles of the garden.

This is one of those storybook streets in the Village of Pelham, with a willow trailing softly on the corner and a surprising sense of old-world sweetness. My own house is part of a more pamphlet-ready, American-dream style neighbourhood, my home one of many similar townhouses in a sculpted, upmarket community. It's very orderly and secure.

Mrs Andrews opens the door just as I manage to tear Carolyn's pizza box away from her and frisbee it out of sight.

'Hello, dear!' She's wearing a dainty apron and her white hair is pinned into a little knot on top of her head with combs in either side to soften it, making her look wonderfully kind and wise.

'Hello, Mrs Andrews,' I say.

She turns to Carolyn and clasps her hands. 'And this is Detective Harding! Och, I'd know her with my eyes closed.'

I shuffle. 'Do you mind if we come in?'

'Of course not, dearie! Come, come in! I was just putting on a pot of tea, so ye've arrived at the right time.'

She settles us into her cosy living room, where the soft green walls are decorated with floral paintings. Potted plants trail leaves on the mantle, and the old-fashioned chairs are upholstered in thickets of rosebuds, making me feel like I'm in a greenhouse. If a greenhouse had an abundance of doilies and knick-knacks, that is.

Mrs Andrews fusses in the kitchen for a little, before appearing with a tea tray. On it are two china cups and a plate of homemade shortbread. 'Well this is a nice surprise, dearie.' She sets a strainer into one cup and proceeds to pour. 'Milk?'

'Yes please,' I say, grateful. Obviously she doesn't offer any to Carolyn who, thank goodness, I was able to force into jeans before we left. Instead Mrs Andrews pours my milk, puts my cup nearer to me, and then proceeds to pour her own. I say, 'It's actually not a social call, Mrs Andrews.'

'No?'

At this point Carolyn reaches over, takes my teacup, plops three cubes of sugar into it, stirs, and then slurps heartily. With her other hand she plucks a shortbread off the plate and stuffs it into her mouth. Mrs Andrews watches all of this in shocked silence and then says, 'Ah.'

I swallow. 'Yes.'

'So those weren't hypothetical questions ye were asking in the meeting last night.'

'No,' I gurgle. We both watch Carolyn chew and then swallow like she is a newly arrived, interstellar being. 'Mrs Andrews, you said this wasn't possible.'

'I did.' She slides her eyes away with an oddly crafty look I've never seen before. I receive a small shock.

'You lied?'

'A little fiction.'

'Fiction?'

'Weel, fiction is all lies, is it not?'

'I...you...no. You always said fiction is all about telling the truth. Only, through other people.'

'Ah.' She looks pleased. 'And so I did. I'm glad ye remember.'

'Mrs Andrews. Could you please tell me what's happening? Am I losing my mind? Am I having some kind of supernatural experience?'

She twinkles at me and passes me the second cup of tea. 'Most of what we do in life is supernatural, dear.'

'I...Why is this happening?'

'My dear, I did tell ye most of the truth. Ye've been writing the same series for eight, nearly nine years, is it? It's true your characters become more real to ye over time.'

'But clearly you didn't tell me everything.'

'No dear, of course not. I told ye what was best for ye to hear. It's dangerous for authors when they don't focus on the plot. They get lost. Things happen.'

Things.

She continues, 'Ye know what my old English teacher used to tell us? Of course it was a long time ago now, but he used to say, "Forget plot, trust your characters."'

I shake my head. 'You've never said that to us. You always told us killing off our characters was better than letting the plot go.'

'Aye. Because trust is a powerful thing. When ye start to trust your characters, dearie, it means ye respect and appreciate them. And of course that's important. Respect and appreciation helps us write them. But it is possible to...well, to cross a line. To feel more. And our deepest, truest instinct toward those we truly care about, ye know, it's to give them room to grow, space to be themselves. To give them good things. And what is the best, greatest good thing? Well, that's choices, dear. Freedom. The ability to truly be who we are. The ability to choose. The space to live and breathe and be. Free will.'

'Mrs Andrews,' I say, 'what do you mean, cross a line?'

'I'm talking about love, dear.' She pauses here, as I look at the soft, kindly lines of her face, and the alert, gentle blue of her eyes. 'Real love. Somewhere, in your heart of hearts, ye began to truly love them. The selfless kind of true love that sacrifices for the good of the one it loves. And so somewhere deep inside, ye started to give them the space to choose their own path. And when that happens to a writer,' she looks at Carolyn, who has moved to the other side of the room, and is peering into Mrs Andrews' china cabinet, eating her third shortbread, 'things happen.'

I think about this. There is no doubt I've got used to having Jay and Carolyn around. I prefer them as company to pretty much anyone else on the planet. Even people whose company I should prefer. I like watching them. I like seeing what they do and how they react. I love watching them make decisions, the way it reveals their hearts.

Oh dear.

'Has this ever happened to you before?' My voice is strangled.

She regards me. 'I have had a wee bit of trouble with my characters in the past, yes,' she says. 'But it's quite easy to solve. Ye simply decide that ye don't want them to have free will, and then ye write them back into the story. A couple of sentences will do, usually. A paragraph, in extreme cases. Just write them back where they belong. Writing their story is the same as exerting your will over theirs.'

I grimace.

She eyes me. 'Ah.'

'I've been trying,' I say. 'Nothing comes.'

'Ah,' she says again. 'Ye know, in my experience dear, when ye don't know what to write next, it's usually because ye *do* know what to write next, ye just don't *want* to write it.'

'What's that?' Carolyn says. She's been prowling around the room with her tea, lifting Mrs Andrews' knick-knacks and peering under them as though Mrs Andrews is a potential murder suspect. Now she's pointing to a frame on the wall. It isn't a flower painting, but rather a single white page with some faded typewritten text on it.

Mrs Andrews has a funny little smile on her face. 'That there is a last page. An important last page.'

'A last page?' Carolyn turns around and puts a hand on her hip. 'There's no *The End*. It ends in the middle of a sentence. "*And then he...*" She reads the ellipsis out too, with extra scorn: '"*Dot, dot, dot.*" Mrs Andrews, no offence, but we need someone who can help Evie finish a story, not leave it hanging. Tillman is a smart guy. If he's figured out that people can see him, and that he can change things here, then he probably doesn't want to go back to work.'

'Oh dear. Tillman is here?' Mrs Andrews turns worried eyes on me. She knows my books. She knows what that means. But oh, if only it were just Tillman.

'We're not sure,' I say. 'If what you've told me is what has happened, I don't understand how he could be here. I certainly don't feel, er, you know, love toward him.'

'Weel, it's possible that your feelings toward one or more of your characters are strong enough that they've opened the door for everyone. It may be that Tillman is...overflow.'

I frown. This does not compute. I don't have strong feelings. I have people in my life and I have a job to do. I don't get intense about people, because when they die, it hurts too much. It's common sense.

'I don't think that I, er, er...' I stutter. 'I mean, I don't—'

'Och, anyone can see that ye care about them, Evie. I see it in the way ye are with them. I saw it in the way ye looked at Detective Ryan the other day when I met ye in town, dear.'

'You did?'

'And I think it's quite clear, as well, that their story has become so important to ye, that ye've neglected the writing of your own. Would that be right?'

'My own?' I say.

'Aye. Ye've begun living through theirs, instead of living your own. That's a dangerous way to be for a writer.' I stare at her with my mouth open. 'Ye must keep writing your own story, dear,' she says.

My eyebrows are *way* up.

'Look, Mrs Andrews,' Carolyn says, 'all this talk about feelings is getting us nowhere.' She has gone all businesslike, and I find it improbably comforting. 'Evie's got problems,' she motions critically toward me, 'we get that. The point is that if Tillman *is* here, then he might see Evie as a threat, the only one who can put him back in the story.'

A chill lances through me. I hadn't considered myself as a specific target. 'I mean, why go back where you don't get to choose, when you could stay here and...' She leaves the sentence hanging, which is worse than the hundred or so suggestions that pop into my mind. Who knows the havoc Tillman could be capable of if left to his own devices. And then there's the Blade.

'Aye,' Mrs Andrews agrees.

'So she needs to write.' Carolyn's voice is flat. Mrs Andrews regards her for a moment, and then she goes all businesslike too.

'I've always liked you, Detective Harding. No wonder Evie wanted to write about you. The two of you are like different sides of the same coin.'

'Ha!' Carolyn barks.

Okay, Carolyn doesn't need to sound so offended.

'Oh yes.' Mrs Andrews smiles. 'Ye remind her of herself, ye

know, except that ye do all the brave things she's too afraid to do herself.'

'Ha!' Carolyn and I say this together, and then don't look at each other.

A door slams. Two seconds later a sprightly, jolly man in full Tudor regalia enters. He's in the doublet and lace ruff and everything. His long legs are clad in red hose, and he has one of those wide, soft hats on his head, tipped rakishly to one side. I get a strange feeling, like I've seen him before. His hair and beard are pure white and he looks about seventy-five. He's athletic and strapping, and there's no doubt he was very handsome in his day. Even now he's exceptional, hose and all. Mrs Andrews' eyes light up. Carolyn chokes on her tea.

'Ah, hello everyone!' he says cheerfully. Then he turns a warm, special smile on Mrs Andrews. 'Hello, my darling. Oh, marvellous. Tea.'

'Hello, dear.' Mrs Andrews accepts his kiss on the cheek. 'Evie, I don't believe ye've met my husband?'

The outlandish man comes forward and shakes my hand, causing the feather on his hat to billow. I squint at him. I haven't met him. Which is strange, I guess, since I've known Mrs Andrews such a long time. But she never talks about her husband. And yet he seems so familiar.

'Please, call me Edward,' he says, twinkling. This strikes a chord too. Edward. Edward was the name of Mrs Andrews' most famous character. Sir Edward Winterbourne, third Baron of Harrowdown. I've read a number of Mrs Andrews' books, and they were a fun read, mostly because of Edward Winterbourne, who was a rather roguish noble in the Tudor era...My mouth drops open.

Who looked exactly like Mr Andrews.

No, he can't be.

'You're...!' I turn to Mrs Andrews, and then back to the man claiming to be Mr Andrews. 'Are you?' I gasp.

He seems pleased. 'Ah, she recognises me!'

I look to Mrs Andrews, aghast. 'Is he...?'

'Is he who?' Carolyn is impassive.

Mrs Andrews twinkles. 'All my readers did love him so much. And so did I.'

Gah. It can't be. To Carolyn I squeeze out, 'Mrs Andrews used to write a very popular series about a baron in the sixteenth century who...' But I see the penny has already dropped for her.

She looks his costume up and down, and says, 'And you still wear that?'

Mr Andrews gives a warm laugh. Mrs Andrews laughs too, in her melodic way.

'Oh, no dear, he's been down rehearsing with the local amateur theatre society.'

Mr Andrews grins. 'I always did have a flair for drama. Even at court.' He winks, and he and his wife share a flirty moment.

Carolyn eyes them both. 'Eew.'

20

'That was disturbing.' Carolyn grimaces.

We're sitting in my car in front of the Andrews' house. The street is dark, and we both stare through the windshield like the night-time ordinariness of suburbia might bring back reason.

Mrs Andrews married a character. That is either amazingly romantic or amazingly freakish. Right now I'm opting for freakish.

I'm not so much disturbed by the Andrews' evident love for each other, even forty-five years after she stopped writing her last story about him. I'm disturbed by what else is evident: that when this happens, when characters get so real that they take control of the plot, as in, *the* plot, the real world, Planet Earth Plot, it's possible for them to remain outside the story forever.

Which means that unless something is done, the Blade could be here until he dies peacefully of old age, having set new records for atrocities in his gleefully long life. He's already started killing here. And it seems the only way to stop him is to write him back into the story. So the only way for me to save the world from the Blade is to write.

Ha. Save the world. Me.

I have that same scary feeling about Carolyn, too. Like she's a force I can't control.

I say, 'Something's been bothering me about the story.'

'No kidding.' Her words are rebellious, but she's lost that adolescent body language.

'What's the thing that stands out most to you about the Blade?'

She purses her lips. 'He's here.'

'You knew?'

'It was logical.'

'But you didn't say anything.'

'I didn't want to freak you out. You don't exactly cope with hard stuff, Evie.'

I find this harsh but I ignore it for the moment.

'So tell me what stands out to you about him.'

She snorts. 'Aside from being a serial killer you mean? Aside from taking the lives of seven innocent women in six years?' She shakes her head a little, and the movement reveals something deeper than the bare sarcasm in her tone. I pause. It's guilt, I realise. Personal guilt. *Seven women in six years.* Though never articulated on the page, Carolyn has carried the responsibility for the deaths of those women like a weight. That first strangled girl six years ago had a similar backstory to Carolyn's own, and she was also the same age and build, found not too far from where Carolyn lived at the time. The case was one of the first Carolyn ever worked as a rookie detective, and the only major one she's never cracked. Every time a new girl was found dead, the twisting of regret and failure grew.

'Profiling suggests a narcissistic personality disorder,' she says, her dry tone revealing nothing.

'And?'

'And,' in a voice like she's humouring me, 'clinical psychopathy. Obviously. Antisocial behaviour, inability to make loving relationships, lack of guilt. Reason is intact but used wholly for selfish ends.' Trust Carolyn to know the definition verbatim. 'Typically impulsive, but also dedicated to planning long-term to inflict pain or revenge.'

It's kind of frightening to have her lay it out in this bare way. Suddenly we're talking about a real person. Someone who's not limited by moral qualms or remorse about harming others. Harming me, for example.

'What else?' I say faintly.

'Rampant misogyny. He kills women.'

'And?'

'And,' she shrugs, the casual movement hinting at that deeper layer again, 'he likes to play with them. I think it goes further than a lack of regret or remorse. Not only does he not feel bad about what he does, he enjoys it. He gets a kick out of their terror. I think he thinks they deserve it. I think he feels like he's doing a good thing when he kills. Something praiseworthy.'

'But why does he kill?' I prod. 'As in, the specific women he kills?'

She breathes out. 'I think it's because they're women who somehow made the mistake of hurting his feelings, or making him angry. That's how he deals with pain. Erase the source.'

I pause. She's exactly right, of course, and it's because I've left her enough clues through the series to get this far.

'The source,' I repeat. The word sounds a note inside me. A big, creepy bass note. There are things about the Blade I've always avoided looking at. But he's here now, and he has the power to do damage—if that cigarette burn and Sally Carston are anything to go by. And he's definitely planning to do damage. I can feel it.

'Evie, what's this about?'

I need to write. Because as clear as Carolyn's definitions and analyses are, I realise I don't understand what the Blade's true motivation is. I haven't spent any time with him, because I've been afraid to, and now I have no idea what's truly going on inside him.

'Do you know where he is?' Carolyn's tone has turned steely.

I don't answer. I remember that when I looked down at the Blade's shoes yesterday, there was a splash of paint on one. The Blade is not that careless. Everything is planned, every detail is orchestrated, always. And I remember how Tillman had a really strange smell on him when I saw him in the train. Like chemicals.

'Evie. If you know something, you should tell me.'

I look at her, at the clinical ice blue of her eyes. She's using her detective voice, the one for recalcitrant witnesses. Cold, and intended to make you feel like she doesn't care if you live or die. It's disconcerting hearing it in person. But I don't think I should tell her anything. I think the last thing I should be doing is revealing stuff to her that Detective Carolyn Harding doesn't know—*shouldn't know*—inside the book. I need to get her, and everyone else, back in that book.

'Do you know why you've never caught him?' I ask.

Her eyes have narrowed. Carolyn has wanted to stop the Blade for a long time. She's given so much of herself to do it, and she hasn't succeeded. She is driven and determined, and she hates anything that obstructs justice. Especially recalcitrant witnesses.

'He's careful,' she says. 'He has a bunch of aliases. He never gets seen, never does anything suspicious. He's smarter than Ryan and I put together. Evie, have you seen him?'

Carolyn hates the Blade. Hates what he has done, and what he will continue to do, if he's not stopped.

She leans down and pulls something out from underneath her seat, and though it's dark I see that it's her gun. She must have stashed it there earlier. It's a Smith & Wesson, and like all service pistols it's a solid piece, not the kind of gun that fits in a purse. Carolyn prefers the heavier stainless steel construction to the Glock or SIG options at the NYPD.

'What are you doing?' I blurt.

She holds it lightly in her palm for a moment, looking at it. I swallow.

'Let me ask you again, Evie. Do you know where he is?' Her voice is low and flat. She reaches into the pocket of her jeans, pulls out a narrow steel oblong and inserts it into the grip with a practiced smack. That's the magazine, and I know there are fifteen 9mm jacketed hollow points in there. She releases the slide with a snap, and puts both hands on the grip. I see her nudge the safety with her forefinger.

I don't know where the Blade is, but I have a hunch. It's less than a knowing, though more than a feeling. But I definitely do not want to go and find out if he's there. Not if someone paid me a million dollars. Not if it could solve this whole whacky fiction/non-fiction drama in one go.

'Carolyn...'

Without looking I feel her raise the cold metal barrel in my direction. Oh. I have underestimated her feelings. Her frustration. My mind flips through the stats on what happens to a human body when it meets with a JHP at close range. Of course, I've thought about this kind of situation before, but in a theoretical way. Right now the blood squeezing through my constricted capillaries is not theoretical, and Carolyn is an excellent shot. The single-minded elements of her personality manifest themselves in a physical talent for precision and accuracy. She could nick my right ventricle at fifty paces if she chose to.

'Don't be ridiculous,' I say. 'What are you doing? You would never kill me.'

'Don't think I haven't thought about it in the last twenty-four hours.' I stare past the barrel at her stony expression.

'Is that true?' It's more shock than an actual question.

She shrugs. 'I'm not perfect.'

'You don't know what would happen if you did that.'

'No, I don't.'

'If I died you might get stuck here,' I stutter, 'without a job, without an identity, and on the run for murder. You might die, yourself. Or disappear into nothing. At the very least you'd have to start wearing pantsuits and sensible shoes like the rest of the women in the NYPD.' My pathetic joke is flat.

'Or maybe I'd be free. Worth taking a chance on, maybe.'

'I don't believe you,' I say.

But her face tells me the truth of it.

'There's nothing wrong with wanting freedom,' she says levelly.

'You wouldn't kill me,' I repeat, but with less certainty. She's silent for a long time.

'No,' she admits finally. 'But I'm not against giving you a good scare if it will snap you into reality. It's time you started dealing with hard stuff, Evie. You need to tell me where the Blade is. And I will shoot you in the leg unless you drive me there. Now.'

I watch as her movements go into slow motion. She flips the barrel toward the back window, and pumps the trigger. The sound deafens me, and the rear windshield shatters with a crack. Safety glass splatters the back seat in thousands of gemmy lumps.

'Now,' she repeats.

21

The old paint factory is run-down and dark, a huge cinderblock monstrosity that must have been abandoned decades ago. There are a few recently repaired windows on the second floor, and the peeling paint of a faded logo on the front.

I don't want to get out of the car, but Carolyn does that terse pointy thing with her gun that criminals do when they want their hostage to move. I'm still half-deaf and shaky from having a semi-automatic weapon fired near me at close range, but I get out and hasten obediently over to the grim metal gate.

'The lock's new.' Carolyn has taken the flashlight from my glove compartment and is peering at the shiny gold padlock holding two loops of old chain together.

Squinting through the small square opening in the main gate reveals not a single security light, either inside or outside the building. This seems ominous rather than reassuring.

Carolyn has her face pressed to the opening. 'Can we get inside?'

As if I want to get inside. Suddenly Carolyn grabs me and pushes me roughly back against the wall and into the shadows as an armed security guard passes through a semi-distant pool of light in the factory across the road. 'Why this paint factory?' she hisses. 'Why not the other one ten blocks from here? It's more isolated.'

'Too close to the water,' I say. 'He needs somewhere dry.' I'm not sure how I know this.

She narrows her eyes at me. 'I want to see inside.'

No. No, no, no.

'Carolyn, we are not trespassing.'

'Actually, that's exactly what we're doing. Why? Because the little fiction author has a hunch. I agree that you don't belong here in the big dark factory. You belong in your little crime cave surrounded by all your crazy crime stuff. But you're the best lead I've had in six years, Evie. And frankly, it's nice to tell *you* what to do for a change. Now, come.'

She shoves her gun into the back of her jeans, grabs my elbow and yanks me forward, and this time I don't resist. We start moving toward the side of the property where the factory is bordered by the tussocky wasteland of an empty lot, and the fence is made of twisted wire and doesn't meet the uneven ground in some places. In the starlight these dusty dips are filled with shadow, and before I know it I'm on my knees and sliding into one so I can crawl under the fence on my belly. I rip a hole in the back of my shirt as I do this, and feel the sting of a scratch. We pause for a moment, listening, and then Carolyn runs over and tries the side door. This is metal. It's locked.

'You thought it would be open?' I hiss.

'Never hurts to try,' she hisses back. 'Remember Book Seven?'

I do. I'm surprised she remembers, actually. That was in the middle of her whirlwind romance with Gareth. She could barely string a coherent thought together for the whole book. She cups a hand to a grimy window and peers in. 'It's too dark to see.'

'Well that's it then,' I whisper, 'time to go home.'

Carolyn steps back and scans the side of the building.

'There. That window is open. Give me your foot.'

It's high, higher than I think it's going to be possible for me to reach, but I put my foot into her palm and she hefts me vertically with her strong, toned arms. I grasp the window ledge but there's no way I have the strength to pull myself up. My feet scrabble at the wall until the toe of my boot finds a tiny crevice between two bricks. It's enough to help me get my elbows over at least, and then I'm able to pull my torso in.

It's one of those windows that opens from the bottom and pushes out. I have a queasy feeing as I squirm through—it's not the kind of window you forget to shut. It's the kind of window you deliberately leave open to entice unknowing fools into a trap.

I turn and reach a hand to Carolyn, and I'm able to pull her as far as the ledge. From there she hoists herself inside. She's agile and quieter than I was, but I don't hear anything to suggest we're not completely alone. It's pitch dark.

Carolyn pulls out my flashlight and sweeps the beam over our surroundings. We're in an old office, the kind they build into the top of tall warehouses. There's the smell of stale carpet, and also a chemical undertone in the air, although perhaps that's to be expected in an old paint factory. The desk is covered in papers. The torchlight is dim, but a layer of dust is visible on top of the filing cabinet and the ancient computer keyboard. I glance over the papers on the desk. There doesn't seem to be as much dust on them, but there are no names or words that jump out at me.

'Here,' Carolyn passes me the flashlight so I can hold it steady while she photographs a bunch of documents with her phone.

'Crap.' The screen blacks out as her battery dies. She shoves it into her back pocket. 'Come on.' She strides out, and I'm forced to follow her beam of light as it rakes from side to side. We move through two more offices, more or less derelict, and then down some concrete stairs. At the bottom there's a corridor, all white walls and pristine linoleum. Brand new.

There are three locked doors on either side and at the end there's a final door, and this door is nothing like what we've seen so far. It's metal but hugely thick, with a heavy glass window and apparently airtight, bordered with a black rubber seal. Carolyn tries the massive lever, and it opens with a sucking noise like a monster opening its lips and breathing in. We find a narrow chamber with showerheads along the ceiling, and metal grates in the floor.

We enter, and I have a claustrophobic moment in the dark, as one door closes and Carolyn goes to open the other. This is exactly the way the Blade would like to kill two women in his ideal world. Put them in a tiny metal chamber and rain down something poisonous on them. He's that sick.

My throat constricts and I clutch at my sides. Yet another of the ways I'm afraid of dying. I'm forced to admit to myself, as I stand there in the dark waiting for the sound of that second door opening, that all my detached musings on Interesting Ways To Go is basically me trying to deal with the fact that I'm terrified of all those things. I'm terrified of being burned in a fire or trapped in a tiny space, of being suffocated or gassed or crushed. The idea brings back the darkest childhood fears for me. It's something that catches at my deepest self, and the only way I can deal with it is to think in terms of fiction, of it happening to someone else. Not me. Just an interesting way to go, for someone.

Carolyn hoists the large handle and there's a metallic gasp as the second lock unseals. My heart rate slows down and I gasp a few breaths of air. I hear Carolyn curse in a low voice, and I look up to see the beam of the flashlight sweep over some kind of specialised laboratory. It's large, and against three walls there are complicated networks of metal pipes, all suspended in place and connected to one another like a grotesque, futuristic spider's web, along with cylindrical metal canisters of differing sizes, pressure gauges, valves, and several machines I can't begin to imagine a use for. Or maybe I can.

'I don't think he was making paint here,' Carolyn says. She walks around, examining things.

'No,' I say.

'It's clean.'

She's right. There's the sense here of a job completed, of a location closed down as no longer necessary.

I say, 'I think he's already finished.'

Carolyn shines the flashlight in my face, making me squint.

'Finished what?'

Before I can answer, the beam of the flashlight picks up something over my shoulder that snags her attention and she strides past me.

It's a computer system set into the wall. I have a sudden terror of a booby trap that blows the whole place when the computer is restarted, but Carolyn doesn't go for the switch. She zeroes in on the keyboard, where there's something stuck between the keys. I follow and look over her shoulder.

She turns to me with it in her hand, almost accusing.

'What is this?'

She's holding a stamp. It's not an ordinary stamp. It's English, and old, the tiny straight-cut edges showing up bright white in the light. It's for me, like the Hello Kitty brooch. Somehow I know this.

'It's a penny black,' I say.

'What the hell is a penny black?'

'It's a stamp.' I know this because of research I did for Book Four, the first book the Blade showed up in. Penny blacks were the first postage stamps manufactured in Britain, sold for a penny, with Queen Victoria's profile etched against the black background. The stamps are not particularly rare, but they're definitely not something that float around or turn up by accident in the States.

'Yeah, I can see that. Why is it all stained?' Carolyn is peering at it.

'It's been cancelled.' When penny blacks were cancelled, they were stamped over in red, marking the stamp as already used. These days, cancelled stamps are worthless, but this one, quite clearly, has wavy red lines snaking over the womanly profile of the queen, like an execution order or an insidious gas cloud. This stamp didn't cost much, but it didn't get here by accident. My hand reaches into my pocket where I have the Hello Kitty brooch stored, and I hold it, feeling the hard plastic against my palm.

'Evie?' Carolyn repeats. 'Is this him?'

I say nothing. I get a sensory prickle down my spine, like someone is watching me. I turn and stare into the far corner, but it's lost in the darkness. Carolyn, seeing me spin round, shines the flashlight that way, but all it picks up is the network of metal pipes and pressure tubes. We both breathe out.

Slowly, she lifts the beam. There, almost completely hidden in the very top corner of the room, is a shiny black globe. A camera. Goosebumps scatter down my arms.

Behind us, in a sudden strobe of blue, the computer system flares to life. The screen lights up the whole room, and on it, dead centre, is a timer.

$$[\ 1\!:\!00\!:\!00 \ ]$$

We stare at it.

'One minute or one hour?' Carolyn mutters.

It starts to count backward. A hundred milliseconds are already gone before I react. My head starts screaming and I push Carolyn toward the only exit—the door we came in through.

'Run!'

22

Carolyn yanks open the heavy door and we scramble through it and the next, along the corridor, up the stairs. I don't know what the Blade has planned for when that timer goes off, but I spy another black globe at the top of the staircase and I know he's watching us. My legs feel like they're made of lead, like I can never get there, never move fast enough to get away.

We fly through the abandoned offices. I fall over a chair, and Carolyn gets ahead. She's already hanging from the windowsill when I catch up to her. She jumps to the ground, and I start to get myself through the window, agonisingly awkward, not flexible or swift enough. I feel sure a minute has gone by. My jeans snag on the catch and I tear the pocket pushing myself out and away. I ignore the ringing jar that goes through my body as my feet hit the ground and I do a running dive under the fence. Carolyn drags me the rest of the way, and we sprint, arms pumping, through the darkness and scratchy vegetation of the abandoned lot. There's no cover here, and the far side is bordered by the high brick fence of another factory, so we veer towards the road. But before we reach the sidewalk the world lights up around us and I'm thrown face-down on the ground. A wave of intense heat blasts us.

'Evie!' Carolyn is pulling me around the corner of the next building by my shirt, getting me out of the line of the explosion, and all the pieces of hot corrugated iron and cinderblock that are flying past and down around us. I scramble after her and cover my head with my arms, pressing myself against the brick.

'He blew it up!' I say breathlessly. 'He actually blew it up.' I can't believe it. The Blade never uses fire. Never. Not after his parents. It's special for him, something he reserved just for them. They had to be wiped out completely. Somewhere in my mind, I didn't think that little timer would result in an explosion, because the Blade has never hated anyone like he hated them.

I can hear the fire roaring, gaining strength on whatever debris was left after the explosion.

'I can't believe all that evidence is gone. Dammit!' Carolyn thumps the wall we're leaning against with a fist. She has no idea what this means. She doesn't know about the Blade's parents. Or about the first three girls he killed. 'What the hell was that?'

'About six pounds of Semtex,' I say. 'If I had to guess.'

'What makes you think so?'

I rub a shaky hand across my face.

'I mean, it's simple elimination. Nitro-based explosives and ANFO are too unstable. Military-grade C-4 would be an obvious choice, since it's about 91 per cent RDX.'

'So?'

'RDX was used extensively in the Second World War, and the Blade has this thing about that war. It's one of several obsessions.' The others are Ancient Egypt, venomous spiders, and stamps. 'But there are too many good clamps on C-4 here.' I thunk my head against the bricks. 'Semtex, on the other hand, also uses RDX, and it's stable and brissant, and became freely available on the black market in 1994. The Czechs manufacture and export it to any number of undesirable countries. Or let it "disappear" from their warehouses. It can be bought for the right price, and it's odourless and therefore theoretically easier to smuggle.'

I can feel Carolyn's knife-like stare, though I don't open my eyes. It's the look she gets when her sharp mind is working overtime.

'That wasn't a minute, you know,' she says.

'What?' I open my eyes.

'It was more than a minute.' Her blue gaze is like cut glass. 'More like a minute twenty. That timer was phony. He was watching to make sure we made it out before he blew it. He had his hand on the trigger the whole time. He was playing with us.'

We stay still, bits of ash floating past us, until a siren starts up in the distance. I have my breath back, but my face and arms feel raw, and I'm aware of every scratch and bruise, like they're all pulsing alarm signals into my body at once. Carolyn sighs.

'What an asshole,' she mutters.

I stutter a shaky laugh. Only Carolyn would treat an explosion that destroys a whole industrial block like a frustrating act of delinquency by a less-than-worthy foe. 'Come on,' she says, 'let's get out of here. Now I'm glad we parked so far away.'

We stagger there, and I don't question her when she takes my keys and climbs in behind the wheel. My car is covered in a thin film of ash. It has a strange oily texture, and as I slump into my seat I realise it's covering the inside of the car as well, since Carolyn shot the back window to bits. So now I've probably stained the butt of my jeans as well as torn the pocket. The small injustice overwhelms me for a moment. I really liked these jeans.

Then I remember there's a fictional serial killer who wants to make me into charcoal. So, perspective.

Carolyn starts the car and cold air rushes through the back window as we start moving. The explosion begins playing itself out on repeat in my mind.

And other memories.

The thing is, my father was killed in a hit when I was fifteen. So this isn't my first real brush with violence. Back then, the event was more than shocking, too Hollywood for our sleepy village of Auldbourne. It was in all the county papers for weeks.

And it wasn't as simple as a drive-by shooting. My father was abducted and tortured, his body found later, washed up in our local river.

A year later my mother sent me to the States for a holiday with my aunt and uncle. She hadn't coped well with my father's death, and had diminished rapidly from the feisty woman I had known, becoming fearful and reclusive. When it came time for me to go home to England, she called Aunt Jo asking them to keep me for longer, and that longer gradually became always, as my mother slowly disappeared from my life.

But Aunt Jo was a loving substitute; sweet and open, and so like my father in a lot of ways that over time, my life transformed from that of a traumatised, displaced girl to someone, if not quite American, then at least firmly settled here. Jo and Uncle Allan hadn't been able to have children of their own, and my uncle was a natural father-figure and mentor. He was a cop too, working the Seven-One at the time, and happy to answer all my questions and foster a growing fascination for 'the Job,' as cops call it.

I guess it was a way for me of working out all my issues. My father's killer, though suspected, was never charged. Rodney Boyle. He was exactly the kind of powerful underworld figure I found appearing again and again in my books, a man without any sense of the heinous nature of his actions.

He was serving a long sentence when my father was killed. He'd chosen to reach out through his extensive network and put a stop to a fairly simple investigation my father was conducting into the protection racket Boyle had established in a nearby town, which was snaking its way into Auldbourne, and crippling the businesses of people my father had been friends with for years.

My mother shifted counties when she sent me to New York, trying to escape what had happened, I think. But a decade later she passed away in a government mental facility.

Her death impacted me deeply. I had been full of anger towards her, and when she died, something snapped inside me. I stopped doing interviews. It became easier not to go out. Somehow, the world seemed too evil a place to engage with.

I could deal with fictional evil, and I did, and it gave me some control over my feelings. But who knows where I would have ended up if the Bradleys hadn't appeared in my life.

23

We're silent on the way home. I hold the stamp in one hand, and the brooch in the other, and think about Rodney Boyle and the Blade. They're not at all alike, except for the menace they form in my life, and the fear that uncoils in the pit of my stomach whenever I think about them.

But I must think about them. Or at least, about the Blade.

I focus on the stamp. His father was an avid collector. But why this stamp?

Queen Victoria. England. That's me. Queen Victoria was a strong woman who was leader of a country and mother to a bunch of children. Okay, so not exactly me. But the English thing and the woman thing, yes.

The brooch. Hello Kitty is a fluffy icon made for pre-adolescent Japanese girls.

These two things have absolutely nothing in common.

Carolyn is thinking at a million miles an hour too; I can tell this by the way her hands are clenched on the wheel. She would very much like to throttle the meaning of the stamp out of me, but I don't know the meaning. Yet.

She pulls into my driveway with abrupt precision, where my pretty, ordinary house is a picture of comfort and safety. The simple farm-house style has gabled windows and dove grey paint, and the lights I left on downstairs make it homey and welcoming. I open the car door, relieved to be back, when a gleaming black Jeep screeches to a stop on the road behind us like some kind of sexy armoured tank. It's weirdly familiar. A new Jeep Wrangler Rubicon four-door, with a hard top and telltale off-road mud sprays around the rear wheel rims. From a road trip or a farm visit, for example.

That's Jay's car. Down to the numberplate.

Jay's car exists.

As I open my mouth to articulate this, Jay leaps out of it and throws the door closed behind him.

'Where have you been?' he demands, as he comes striding toward me. I blink. He's furious. 'I've been trying to call you!' I pull my phone out of the back pocket of my jeans as he reaches me but the screen is cracked and in any case it's been dead for hours. He turns a glare on Carolyn.

'Don't look at me,' she shrugs, standing beside my car with her arms folded. 'I didn't exactly pack my charger when I landed here.'

Jay grabs my elbow and pulls, hauling me toward the house.

'Get your computer. We need to get out of here right now.'

'Stop it!' I shake my arm out of his grip as we make it to my door. I'm very tired of being bullied by people who shouldn't exist. I fumble my key as I try to insert it, and he takes it off me and drills it into the keyhole.

'We need to go, Evie. You can't stay here.' I can hear an anxious undercurrent in his tone that sends me toward my writing room once we're inside, but then I pause, stalled beside the wide entrance to the living room. Jay stops not far from me with his arms loose at his sides. He looks like a blackbelt expecting a fight.

Then his posture changes, as if he's just seen me properly. 'What happened to you?' He takes a step toward me and stops. I imagine that in addition to the ripped clothing and scratches, my ashy smudges have me looking a little charred.

I shake my head. 'Jay, tell me what's going on.'

He takes a breath. 'Get your computer, and whatever else you need to write. I'll tell you in the car.'

Carolyn has followed us inside and is standing behind Jay. I can see her brain is still working overtime.

'No.' I hold my ground. 'Tell me now.'

He folds his arms, tucking his fingers in but leaving the thumb of each hand on the outside. This is a unique tell of his that means he's holding on to the end of his patience. His physical strength means that he could easily be a bully, and he was once or twice, with his brother when he was younger. It's something he didn't like about himself. But he had a good father, who taught him how to respect other people, and now he consciously practices patience when stressed. Since I feel like he has already bullied me tonight, I know something big must be going on for him to behave this way.

'Hinds is dead. And Tillman,' he says.

'What?' This information punches the air from my lungs and I totter over to collapse on the sofa. 'How do you know?'

'They were both at Hinds' apartment. Looks like there was a struggle, but it was execution-style. Their hands were tied. Single entry wound. Close range.'

'I can't believe it,' I say. 'Not Tillman. Why? Why would someone kill him?'

Carolyn makes a noise. 'Besides the obvious?'

Jay ignores her. 'The scene looked exactly how I would expect if someone wanted information,' he says. 'We have to assume he wasn't just killed, he was killed after he stopped being useful.'

My focus narrows on him. 'What are you saying?'

'Evie. Do you understand? Tillman has been here multiple times. Here, to your house. He knew exactly where you live.'

I remember that phone call from Uncle Allan when he mentioned how the people from *The New Yorker* were pressing him to know where I lived, and how weird that had seemed at the time. Had someone been trying to find me?

'You think he was killed because of me?'

Jay shifts on his feet. 'I think he was killed because he knew something about something. Probably too much about something. Maybe it's got nothing to do with you. But we can't take any chances.'

'Jay,' I say, 'can we be candid here? Are you talking about the Blade?'

He glances toward the window. 'This isn't a safe place for you to be.'

He won't say it, because he thinks, like Carolyn, that I can't handle hard stuff, and by all that's holy, he's right.

'I'll get my computer,' I mumble, getting up and walking toward my writing room. I can feel Jay's eyes burning into my neck.

When I get there I close the door on him and lock it. Not my proudest moment. But I've never pretended to be brave. Writers are known for not being brave, in fact. We hide away in our rooms and we live our lives through other people. Through our characters. And that's fine by me.

I hear Jay curse and then his striding footsteps on the other side of the door and I back away. Hiding in this room comes naturally. I feel better, knowing I'm safe in here. I take an uneven breath.

'Dammit, Evie! Open this door.'

Not a chance. Everything in me craves the darkness and quiet of this sheltered sanctum, and I'm pretty sure this whole terrifying, deathly mess will go away if I just stay in here long enough and keep breathing. And write a sentence or two.

Easy.

I drop to my knees and start to gather up my notes from the

floor. Everything is there—every storyline, every idea, detailed bios on every character. All neatly colour-coded and stored in a way that I can find whatever I need.

Jay starts pounding on the door, furious, and I almost smile, my cave is so completely secure and impenetrable, when suddenly the window next to my desk smashes inward.

Something flies through it and explodes against my bookcase. I fling myself back against the underside of the desk, covering my face as shards of hot glass spray me, and when I look again half my books are on fire. The smell of gasoline fills the air. My mouth drops open as orange flames chase upwards to my ceiling. A molotov cocktail?

The hammering on my door has stopped and there are louder thumps. Jay is throwing his weight against the lock, trying to smash it open.

Bullets spray through the room. My brain registers the dulcet tones of an LMG and that gets me moving. I squirm further under the desk. The big hardcover cults book thumps to the floor along with two mugs as my weight rocks everything, and I grab the book and hold it against me like a breastplate. Out there in the dark, some lunatic is firing automatic rounds over my nice tall fence and into my house. An Ares Shrike 5.56 or a Stoner, I think. Both of them under ten pounds. Perfect for dragging up onto Leslie's roof.

Mown down by light machine gun. *Interesting way to go.*

My paralysed senses detect a pause from the hall. Then the door crashes open, but there's no one there. I see Jay swing an arm around the doorframe and fire four times through the shattered window. The spray of machine-gun fire stops.

'Evie!'

I'm pressed there in the dark, under my desk. Jay crawls forward, grabs me by the arm and barks into my face, 'If you want to live you need to leave this room. Do you want to live?'

I stare at him.

'Do. You. Want. To. Live?'

Do I? I don't want to die. Reality is a scary place, but I definitely want to be here.

I do want to live.

I scramble out from under the desk and through the door, assisted by his big warm hand clamped around my arm. He pulls me down the hall where I stumble, still clutching the cults book in the crook of my arm.

I see Carolyn heading through the kitchen door ahead of us with the bottle of vodka in one hand and gun in the other, when Jay suddenly throws both arms around me and drags me to the floor. We crash heavily, and I get a nasty jolt through my shoulder, though it must have been infinitely more painful for him with my full weight on top of him. I watch a line of bullet holes tear open the section of beige wall where I was standing. Whoever the shooter is, it seems the volley Jay sent that way wasn't discouraging enough to stop them pressing down on eight hundred rounds-per-minute through my spare bathroom window. I scramble off him and get out of the line of sight.

'Back door,' he says, rolling onto his hands and knees. He sounds winded but I can tell he's keeping his voice low and calm for my benefit. 'Stay down.' The hall is filling with smoke. I crawl toward the kitchen, but as I reach the door I remember.

'Wait!' I say, trying to push past him and go back the way we came. 'My computer! My notes!'

'Leave them.' Resolute, he pulls me toward the kitchen.

'Jay, you don't understand. I need that stuff, I can't leave it here.'

'You have to leave it. Keep going.'

Carolyn has flipped off the kitchen light, which means it's dark but we can see easily into the obscurity of my backyard through my kitchen windows and the pane of my back door. Jay keeps low and propels me toward the door with a hand on my back, saving me from bashing my shoulder on the counter as we go. My back door leads out onto a wooden deck and then down three steps onto the lawn. Behind us Carolyn drags a chair from my kitchen table over to prop the door to the hall shut and then we all three peer out into my yard. My eyes have adjusted and there doesn't seem to be any movement out there, other than the fitful ripples of deeper shadow beneath my one big oak tree. Jay eases the back door open. I hear a crash from the front of the house and realise it was the sound of my living room windows smashing.

I am so getting voted out of this neighbourhood by the Neat Street Committee.

Carolyn says, 'Time to go.'

Jay reaches inside his jacket and pulls out his Glock. 'Okay Evie, when I say *go* you're going to run straight across your yard and climb the back fence. Use the rails to jump over and keep running. Cover us, Harding. Evie, go.'

My mind is blank but he flings the door wider for me and I take off, dragging the cults book up with me, and sprinting the deck. I leap over all three stairs with only a momentary wobble and run as fast as I can into the darkness. The lawn is thick and tangled and for a second I really wish I'd listened to Leslie and had it mowed sooner. I hear Jay behind me, and nothing else: not gunfire from Leslie's roof, not the zing of flying bullets. Is the shooter gone?

When I hit the back fence I put a foot straight onto the lowest railing. But climbing over isn't going to be as simple as Jay made it sound. The fence is taller than me and made of fitted wooden pickets, and I'm stiff from being rugby-tackled to the floor a minute ago. I heft the heavy book over the top like a discus and into my neighbour's yard, then fit the toe of my boot onto the narrow railing and propel myself up to grab the top of the palings. These are pointed and splintery. I pull, and get my second foot onto the middle railing. Then Jay is behind me with his hands on my butt, helping me get higher, except that he's giving me too much momentum. I slap him away but he ignores me, which means that although I manage to get high enough to manoeuvre myself on the narrow awkwardness of the top rail, my inexperienced jump into the darkness on the other side includes a crash landing.

Ouch. It's possible I've pulled something. Or a couple of things, like my pride. This yard is pitch black too. I feel around for the cults book. My fingers discover its smooth solidness right beside me, and I heft it up and scramble to my feet. I can hear Jay and Carolyn climbing the fence and I start moving to get out of the way, but a few strides in, my right foot hits nothing but fresh air. I tip forward. Lots of fresh air. How could I have forgotten my privacy-obsessed back neighbours are digging a swimming pool? Freaking wealthy neighbourhood.

I fall in with a squawk and land hard at the bottom, having flung the cults book in the process and put my other arm out to break my fall. There's a grinding snap and then a lancing pain so sharp I hear it as a sound.

I gasp, and then groan. Oh no. Above me, I hear Jay curse. What a moment to be so clumsy and brittle. I hear a thump beside me. Jay, landing on his feet like a cat.

'Evie, are you okay?'

'I'm fine,' I lie.

He calls to Carolyn to warn her and pulls me to my feet by the elbow.

'You gotta keep going.'

'Argh,' I grind out, as I envision the bone in my arm having broken the skin. My senses have split open at every end. I press my back teeth together, use my left hand to hold my right wrist against my chest, and let Jay help me out of this hideous hole in the earth, which luckily is only about chest-deep. I use my elbows to claw my way out onto the grass while he lifts me from behind.

I think I'm going to faint, but I don't. I run. Carolyn is with us, assassin-silent. There's a children's playground in the next yard but none of my senses are receiving information properly. I break out in a cold sweat, my mind narrowing down to the pinpoint goal of keeping as close as I can to Jay's broad back as he runs us along houses, across streets and through side gates.

At one point he has me crouch down in the shelter of a hedge and I nearly lose it, feeling like I can't go any further. I sense Carolyn's presence beside me and then it's possible I zone right out for a while because when I come back to myself they are arguing in hissed whispers. Carolyn wants to go back and get Jay's car. Jay wants to call the station and get backup. Then it gets fuzzy again.

I hear Jay say through gritted teeth, 'Yeah, we can. *Everything exists.* We gotta call it in. Ten-thirteen *forthwith.*'

And then Carolyn arguing, 'Let me go back there. Come on, if he wanted her he would have taken her and we wouldn't even have realised she was gone. Or that shooter could have picked her off in the backyard. But he's had two chances tonight. And both times he let her live. On purpose.'

'Two?'

'I'll explain later.'

'What makes you so sure this is all about her?' Jay says. 'He must want you dead, too. All three of us.'

'He wants his freedom. But he also wants to make her suffer. To him, she's the one who's kept him prisoner all these years.' There's silence, before she says, 'Trust me, Ryan. I know you know exactly what I'm talking about.' Another pause.

'You're not going back there alone.' Jay's tone is staunch. There's a reason cops work in pairs. They keep each other safe.

'Those guys'll be gone by now,' Carolyn says, sounding very

certain. 'Whatever he wanted tonight, it wasn't her, dead. This time. Probably it would have been a bonus, but it wasn't the focus. And look at her. She's white as a sheet.' A slight huff. 'Looks like she found out that real bullets are a little different to written ones.'

'We can't move her again.'

'I'll get the car. You stay here with her. I'm serious, I'll be fine.' Carolyn pauses again as if she's waiting for Jay's nod. Then she says, 'One five.' It's their code. 'One five' means fifteen, which is how many minutes to wait before the other takes action. A jingle of keys being passed and she's gone.

'You okay, Evie?' Jay's voice is close but not gentle. It's hard and practical. He's probably angry at me, and I can't blame him. I put all our lives in danger. It was immature, and cowardly. I should have done what he asked me to.

'I'm sorry,' I say. I have my eyes closed and my teeth gritted and I'm pretty sure my face is as white as they say since I can feel all my blood thudding near my heart. My fingers and toes feel cold. 'I shouldn't have...'

'Ah, geez. Lie down a little, will you?' His voice has softened up a tiny bit. I feel a warm blankety thing come over me and realise he's covered me in his jacket. 'I doubt it would've made any difference,' he adds. 'You probably just saved us meeting those guys on the street.'

'Nice of you,' I mumble.

'This'll be over soon,' Jay soothes. 'It's gonna be okay.'

What a lovely voice Jay has, I think. It's a deep, reassuring voice, though he sounds so far away. It's like I'm sinking underwater and his words are getting duller and more distant. But it's still a very nice voice. If I needed a police officer for some reason, he's the one I would want.

Oh, wait. I do need a police officer. Someone just set my house on fire.

'Don't fall asleep, Evie. I need you awake. Stay with me.'

Yes, Officer. But nice police detectives like this one might have better luck doing their jobs if they didn't try to do them underwater. 'Evie? I'm serious. Stay awake. Talk to me.'

'Jay,' I say.

'Yeah?' he sounds relieved.

'My computer...'

'It's okay.' He's still being soothing. This is his voice for victims of crime, specifically for females. 'You don't need it. You can write by hand. You've done it before.' This wakes me up. I take a breath. I feel all gaspy and I can't seem to unclench my teeth.

'How do you know?' I open my eyes and look up at him. I must have my head in his lap.

He looks at me and doesn't answer, and then his eyes do a sweep of the empty backyard we're in. How on earth could he know that I've written stuff by hand?

'It might be a problem,' I say. His eyes zero back in on me. 'I'm pretty sure I've broken my wrist.'

24

My gaze wanders the ceiling as I breathe in again and hum a little tune to myself. Night-time Emergency Department noises float through the door, the controlled turbulence of beeps and groans and raised voices.

This is a nice room. Small but state of the art. Much nicer than I can afford. I don't remember which hospital we're in—Lenox Hill? NYP?—but my boots have made muddy scuffmarks on the sheet of the bed I'm lying on and I feel bad about that. Everything is so shiny and new in here. I have a crackly memory of a chaotic arrival, and the discovery that the insurance upgrade James Bradley's assistant talked me into a month ago entitles me to some kind of special treatment. I smile lovingly at the ceiling. Mmm. Daniel.

Jay and Carolyn are talking together a couple of metres away, hunched in with their crime-solving chemistry zapping. Jay's jacket and jeans are scuffed and dirty, and Carolyn's hair has a twig in it. I giggle. Honestly, those two are *adorable*. Just look at them, their heads all close together the way they get when they're trying to hide something from the person they're talking about. I wonder who they're talking about.

Maybe me!

This realisation causes a fit of laughter. I look around a little more and see the IV in my left arm and the X-rays of my wrist on the lightbox on the wall. Yikes. Like a horror movie, bones everywhere. I wheeze in another breath through my oxygen mask, needing more air for giggling. They do say that laughter is the best medicine.

My right arm is stretched out beside me on a little bench and covered in a cloth. The bone had broken the skin, as I thought, which strikes me as funny. The doctor covered it up after he was done examining it. He was so handsome, and now I lament not telling him so. People need to be told these things. Dr Richards. He went to get the stuff to make the splint. Apparently I can't have a full cast for a couple more days, until the swelling goes down. I feel disappointed about this. I had my hopes set on coloured plaster.

Plaster cast. I chuckle to myself. Rhymey.

'So you're telling me...' a fierce pause from Carolyn, 'that you called the station house from Hinds' apartment, and when the squad showed up it was Eddie and the rest of the boys.'

Jay says nothing, but she reads the answer in his face.

'And they recognised you? They knew who you were?' I can hear the disbelief in her voice.

'Eddie offered me a ride back down to the precinct but I took Jenna's car.'

'And the precinct?' Carolyn raps out the question with the relentless bite in her tone that scares everyone she knows, except Jay.

'Exactly how she wrote it. Evans was working the front, and in the same foul mood as always. My desk is there. With my name. With the exact same paperwork piled on it that I didn't finish before we left for that godforsaken stakeout.'

'And did you see the Cap?'

I feel a prickle of emotion. The Captain.

Jay shakes his head. 'I found my car and left. Eddie called me two minutes out to tell me the Cap was looking for me, because

Hinds and Tillman weren't the only DOAs they found tonight. Frankie Rimmer is dead, and the Manouli twins.'

Carolyn curses, her tone surprised. 'And he thinks it was the Blade?'

Jay's eyes answer this.

She curses again. 'So what's his objective?'

'This feels like a clean-up. Till now, he's been killing women. That we know of. And being careful about it. Tracks covered, those marks he puts on them like a tally on a scoreboard. And only one or two a year. So we've had enough to follow the lead but he wasn't out of control, and I think it's because Evie would only let him do that much. Now, he's acting like someone who just got out of jail.'

'Or like someone who just got handed free will. And who doesn't want to give it up again. You think he killed these guys because he's looking for her?'

'Either that, or he used them for something he doesn't need them for anymore, and they knew too much about what he's been doing.' Jay glances my way and lowers his voice. 'Evie said she felt like Tillman had got involved in something that was way over his head. All these guys were low-grade perps. The kind he could have paid to set something up that's finished now.'

'When we were in that factory, Evie told me he was already finished,' Carolyn says. 'Whatever he's doing, he's got it ready.'

'What did you find?'

'Some kind of laboratory. Brand new. And not an ordinary fit-out. I want to know where he got the money for something like that. And he knew she would show up there. He was counting on it. I think he's leaving clues on purpose. For her. Because she's the only one who knows him well enough to put them together.' She pauses. 'And he likes the game.'

'This feels bad. We've always run behind him, trying to save the next girl on his list. This time he's not acting in character.'

'Or is he?' Carolyn glances over at me. 'At least we know who the next girl on his list is.'

Jay curses softly.

'Think about it, Ryan. It's the first time we've known that in advance.'

'You said he deliberately let her live.'

'Yeah. The timer in that factory was a hoax. And he didn't need to mess around with goons and machine guns at her house. I mean, molotov cocktails. What is this, the Belgian mafia in the seventies? There wasn't a single shot fired when we ran her yard. I bet they had instructions to scare her and get her out of the house, nothing more. He's toying with her. That *is* in character. He's probably feeding off her terror right now, wherever he is. But there's no doubt he'll want her dead, eventually. Whatever this big thing he's doing on the side is, I think he's going to use it to draw her in and kill her. We could work that to our advantage.'

'No. She needs to go as far into hiding as we can get her. If he really wants her dead, she'll be dead.'

A pause.

'You gotta let this go, Ryan.'

Dr Richards arrives. Behind him is a female nurse carrying a large plastic basin with bandages and goodness knows what else. I push down my mask with my left hand.

'Hello Dr Richards!'

'Hello again, Evie. We've come to put your splint on. How are you feeling?'

'Fine!' I say. How could I not be fine when Carolyn and Jay are being so cute? 'You're very handsome,' I tell him. He's about thirty-five, I think, and he's tall and professional-looking. Jenna would go crazy. He looks at Jay.

'Did she eat anything today?'

'For once.' This is Carolyn, who is standing beside him, her arms folded.

I giggle and tell the doctor, 'They're the food police.' Although I really appreciated that burger today. 'And they're very good at it,' I add kindly. Jay's eyes are like volcanic stones. 'You're very handsome too,' I tell him. I frown. 'A bit too handsome. Hm. It's unrealistic. I never thought about that before. It's dis. Um, dis.' *Disconcerting?* 'Dis-trac-ting,' I say. 'It's distracting.' I beam at him. Carolyn rolls her eyes. The doctor puts my mask back on.

'As you know, it's a severe compound fracture. Thankfully it doesn't need any pins, so no operation today, but we've given her morphine, as well as the nitrous oxide.' I push my mask down.

'Happy gas!'

The doctor pushes my mask back up. 'I need to straighten the bone, so I'm going to give her a light sedative. She won't remember any of it.' He pushes a syringe into the IV intake beside me, and then sits down and takes the little blankie off my arm to start cleaning the area with alcohol. This is uncomfortable but somehow hilarious. My poor snapped radius is sticking whitely out of the skin on my arm, with quite a lot of accompanying blood. I push my mask down.

'I'm so glad you guys are here!'

Jay turns to the doctor. 'How long until this wears off?'

'The gas won't last long once we take her off it. The rest will make her pretty woozy for a while.'

Carolyn puts her face near mine. 'Evie, you need to tell us what you know about the Blade.'

I blink. 'Oooh!' I feel overwhelmed by affection all of a sudden. 'You guys make such a great team! You know I've always thought that. I'm glad you have free will.' Jay gets a surprised look. I love his surprised look! 'I like you so much.' I sigh happily. 'You're my favourite people, did you know that? I love to watch you be yourselves.'

'Evie.' Jay comes closer to my bed so I'm looking right up into his face. His brown hair is scruffy, and his chin is shadowed with stubble. Turns out hair does grow here when you have free will. 'Do you think your uncle Allan would be open to you staying for a few days?'

'I don't think it's a good idea to get her family involved,' Carolyn says.

'Allan's a retired cop,' Jay argues. 'He would want us to take her there.'

But I'm shaking my head. If *The New Yorker* knew their phone number, then the Blade definitely knows where they live.

'Nope,' I say. 'We need to call them and get them to go away. Bobby knows where they are. And anyway, that's probably the first place he would look.' This catches their attention. Suddenly they are both one hundred per cent focused on me. C.U.T.E!

'Bobby?' Carolyn says.

I nod. 'Bobby Laidley.'

'Bobby Laidley?' Jay repeats. The doctor is moving my arm now, pressing and stretching, getting the bones back into place, I guess, and I'm distracted by it. I can feel my face going white again, though the pain is a distant, manageable thing.

'Mmm.'

Carolyn looks into Jay's face and says meaningfully, 'B. LAID-ley.'

I really have their attention now.

Jay says, 'Evie. Have you ever seen Bobby Laidley?'

'Of course.'

'You could pick him out of a line-up?'

'Yup.'

'When did you see him? Recently?'

'Uh-huh. I dreamed him. Twice. Although I don't think that second time was a dream. I think he was really there. It's how

I knew about the paint factory. He gave me a present.' My voice goes a little breathless. Both doctor and nurse are leaning over my arm. It's been sheathed in gauze, and they're laying a long rectangle of damp plaster over the uppermost side and moulding it to my arm. My fingers are free but the plaster extends all the way to my elbow, and I can see from the rest of the implements in that basin that there are crepe bandages in my future.

An exaggerated sigh wells up. I'm so uncool.

'A present?' Jay persists.

'A brooch,' I mumble.

'Did it mean anything to you?'

'I'm not sure. Umm. I need to think about it some more.'

'Do you know what he's doing? What he's planning?'

'Mm.' I sigh. 'Something big.'

Jay and Carolyn have a silent conversation with their eyes as the doctor finishes up and the nurse takes the tub of unused bandages away.

'Well, that's it for now,' the doctor tells me in a gentle voice. 'Just stay there for a few minutes until it dries properly, and then I'll be back in to check it before we discharge you.' He's so nice. And so handsome.

'You're very handsome,' I tell him again.

'Don't worry, she'll be back to normal in a few hours,' he says to Jay and Carolyn. He leaves, his white coat swishing. Mm. I wonder what time it is? It must be the early hours of the morning by now. It will be so nice to go home and have a little sleep.

'I want to go home,' I say.

Jay and Carolyn look at each other.

'Maybe later,' Jay says.

'Okay,' I say.

'So what now?' he asks Carolyn.

She looks at me like someone might look at a pet after it peed on the carpet.

'I'll call the Cap. Get a unit to her aunt and uncle's place and get them out of there. And I'll update him about the paint factory and the rest of the situation while I'm at it. Can I borrow your phone?'

Jay hands it over and she leaves. He pulls up a chair beside my bed.

'How's the arm?'

I look at it in surprise. Oh, right, my arm. It's lying there all stiff and crepey. I try to lift it and find it's heavier than I thought. I must be tired.

'Crepe bandages are so ninth grade.' I sigh. 'I wish it was blue. I like blue.'

His eyes have the tiniest smile in them. 'Me too.'

Behind him a male nurse comes in and sets a small tray down on the little bench beside my bed.

'Like your eyes,' I say. I examine them. 'I like your eyes.'

The edge of his mouth curves up ever so slightly and I get a little shivery feeling in my upper chest. Behind him the nurse lifts a syringe and flicks it, and then moves toward my IV. I watch, fascinated, and my attention makes Jay turn and look too.

'I thought the doctor said she wouldn't be needing any more,' he says.

'This is just a little something extra because she—'

Jay stands up abruptly, so much so that he knocks his heavy plastic chair over. He has put a restraining hand on the nurse's chest and must be applying pressure, since the nurse takes a step backward, looking both surprised and offended.

'Because she's what?' Jay says in a blank distracted voice, and then yanks off the nurse's ID badge and glares at it.

'Excuse me!' the nurse says. He has short dark hair and the thin, pallid features of someone who spends all their time caring for other people. What is Jay doing? Upstanding hospital employees who give out more medicine should be *welcomed*.

I am equal parts wondering whether I should mention this to Jay or drift off into a nap, when the nurse, looking like he has re-evaluated how his day might turn out, quickly lifts the hand holding the syringe, as if to raise it in surrender. Jay drops the ID badge to the floor and steps forward, pushing the nurse so hard that he falls over backwards, the needle flying.

'Not a good enough resemblance,' Jay mutters, and unholsters his Glock in a fluid movement that is as visually pleasing as it is practiced. Hm? I suppose as off-duty law enforcement the hospital let him bring his weapon inside. But he couldn't possibly need it. He's overreacting. The poor nurse has scrambled to his feet, looking very wary now, and no wonder. There's a pause as the two face each other.

And then something odd happens. Jay lowers his right hand from its position on the Glock and pumps his fist twice, like he has a cramp or something. At the same time he takes a small side-step and shakes his head slightly, as if he's having trouble keeping his balance. I watch the nurse reach into the pocket of his navy scrubs with his left hand, and then drop that same hand down again, holding it next to his leg. With his right he gently raises a pacifying palm and says, 'Sir, are you okay?'

He has an accent. I blink concern at Jay. Is he okay? He must be very tired, he's having trouble holding his gun in position, as if it's too heavy. There's something not quite right about this but I can't figure out what it is. My brain is moving with the calm lethargy of a day at the beach.

The nurse moves forward, stepping around Jay's fallen chair, still with a pacifying arm outstretched, as if he's going to try to exit the room. But the movement somehow lacks the peaceful intention it implies, and brings him closer to Jay's personal space. There's a flash of movement. I blink. The nurse has surged into

Jay, beneath the wavering barrel of his weapon, and now the two men are wrestling, whirling like a rugby scrum, heads down. Jay's left hand with the gun hangs useless over the nurse's right shoulder as they struggle, and I wonder why Jay doesn't push himself away so he can use it. Then I realise that Jay's focus is taken up in trying to stop the nurse from stabbing him in the right side with something silver. A wicked, sharp little blade. Ah, I remember what it's called! A scalpel. Jay has the nurse's knife-hand pinned hard to his own hip, and the nurse is trying to get it free. They are locked together, both needing to stay close to stop the other using their weapon. They crash into the foot of my bed, shoving it sideways, and then into the lightbox on the wall, causing my X-rays to crash to the floor along with whatever flimsy materials lighboxes are apparently made of.

Ooh, now I get it. This is a fight scene! I've written these, but I've never seen Jay's ability in person like this. It's rather glorious. I have a vague feeling I should be concerned for my safety, but I also feel very pleasant, cocooned in my own wellbeing. I hear a scraping sound and look that way. I have to concentrate to focus, and I see that somehow Jay's Glock is on the floor on the other side of my bed. It must have slid underneath across the linoleum and ended up there. Huh.

I look back to the other side of the room to see that Jay and the nurse have separated, but the nurse hasn't dropped the scalpel. They're over a metre apart, and Jay is in a ready stance. He's standing like a barricade between the nurse and the gun, his back to me, but he makes no move to turn and retrieve it. The nurse attacks. He leaps forward, rushing the scalpel upwards at Jay's abdomen. Jay doesn't have much space to move since he has his back to the bed, so he parries hard to the left. The scalpel grazes the mattress as the nurse's momentum carries him forward, and Jay steps into the space it creates, whipping around and elbowing him hard in the face. Really hard. The nurse crumples backward and down. Jay spins again, drops a knee and punches him a second time while he's on the ground for good measure, right in the diaphragm. He grabs the scalpel and tosses it into the corner, then steps back and rests his hands on his knees and catches his breath a little. He opens and closes his right fist again, like he's getting back the feeling in it. The nurse is both dazed and wheezing. Jay leans down and carefully drags him into the recovery position.

The ruckus has brought a group of frightened people to the door. Carolyn pushes past everyone.

'Geez, Ryan, I leave you alone for five minutes.'

'Stolen ID badge.' Jay points to the end of the room where the nurse's syringe had flown. 'Trying to give her something.

'What was it?'

'I don't know. But he scratched my hand with the syringe and it was enough to half-paralyse me on the right side.' As he says this he flips up the back of his jacket and pulls a set of handcuffs out of his jeans pocket. The nurse groans from the floor. 'I'm guessing it would have killed Evie.' Jay leans down and I hear the click of cuffs.

Carolyn's eyes flick to me. 'He knows where we are.'

'This is fun for him,' I tell them, and then wonder if my cheerful tone might be a tad inappropriate.

Jay says nothing but moves around the bed, stoops to pick up his weapon from the floor, checks it, flicks the safety and re-holsters it.

Carolyn watches this, and nods. 'She's right. So what now?'

Jay moves back to the nurse and pulls him to his feet by one arm. 'Let's get her out of here.'

'I thought you'd never ask.' Carolyn comes over to my bed. I smile up at her cool blue eyes, and then I feel something cold go around my good wrist. She snaps a handcuff in place.

'Evie Howland. You're under arrest.'

25

The interior of Jay's car is just as big, black and sexy as the outside. Unfortunately it's also cold, since two of the side windows have been gunned in and there are bullet holes along one side. But at least I'm not sharing the backseat with a killer nurse. Jay called for a squad car to take that particular criminal to the precinct, while *this* particular criminal gets chilly personalised service in a roughed-up Jeep. Poor Jay. He loves this car. Finding it neatly parked near the precinct last night must have felt like winning the lottery.

'You have the right to remain silent. Anything you say or do can and will be used against you in a court of law. You have the right to an attorney...'

Carolyn's voice is strident. She's in the zone. She's snapped back into the predator mindset she gets, with the bloodthirsty attitude of a large cat chasing down a frightened mammal. I'm pretty sure I'm not the mammal, the Blade is, though after she perp-walked me out of the hospital I can't be certain.

My cheek moves on the leather seat as Jay takes a corner. My left arm is cuffed to the grab handle above the door, which means that if I don't mind getting pins and needles in it, I can be lying down almost flat. I'm so tired, and kind of fading back and forth. Now Carolyn and Jay are arguing in low, tight voices in the front.

'And I'm telling you,' I hear Carolyn growl, 'that taking her to the station is both the safest place for her and the best course of action. The sooner we get hold of Bobby Laidley, the sooner she'll be safe for good. And the best way to do that is for her to tell us everything she knows.'

Jay answers, but too low for me to hear. Carolyn huffs.

'How about obstruction? Being an accessory after the fact, and possibly before the fact? Withholding information? She's a material witness, Ryan. So to speak. The fact remains that she has vital information and she's not going to give it to us unless we scare it out of her. Good news is she basically wets her pants at the first sign of danger.'

I frown, but can find no argument for this in my woolly brain. I wish I could join in the conversation. I feel annoyed at them, but in a distant, sleepy way. I wonder what time it is. It must be around eight o'clock in the morning, as the sun was well over the horizon when Carolyn bundled me into the car.

I have the right to an attorney. I wonder if I should call one. Maybe Mr and Mrs Bradley know someone? And then I realise a whole day has gone by since I spoke to Daniel. All of a sudden I have a deep yearning to hear his voice, and be comforted by his efficient care of me.

'Do I get a phone call?' I ask loudly. I don't care if it's a cliché. People get a phone call. I sit up, or at least try to. In the front seat they both stop talking. I see Carolyn fold her arms and look out the window. This means that she feels some tiny uncertainty, at least, about whether arresting me is the best course of action.

Jay adjusts the rearview mirror so he can meet my eyes. 'I want my phone call,' I say, as forcefully as I'm able, which isn't very. My voice is spindly and abstracted. Jay takes a hand off the wheel and gives his phone to Carolyn, who passes it back to me without looking at me. Jay's phone is black and shiny, like his car, a detail I have never thought about before. I dial Daniel's number one-handed. It rings a few times, and then his voice comes on, rough with sleep.

'Hello?'

'Daniel, it's me.' I sag back down into a lying position, clutching the phone.

'Honey, are you okay? It's like...ten o'clock at night.' So he's still in Hong Kong.

'And you're asleep?'

'Long day.' There's a huff as I hear him roll over and rub his face with his other hand, waking himself up. I imagine him there in his hotel room, blankets untucked the way he likes it. I experience a flush of feeling for him. Daniel could choose to spend the rest of his life doing nothing more taxing than improving his tan. He could be wasting his days in one of the Bradleys' grand houses in Costa Rica or Florida, buying boats and being idle, but he doesn't. He's been diligently manning the container shipping side of Amiton, working under his father as head of the subsidiary that James Bradley regards as his personal baby. Daniel chooses to work this hard.

'I love you,' I say.

'Mmm,' he says sleepily, 'you miss me.'

'I do,' I murmur, feeling emotional.

'What's wrong? Is everything okay?' For a fleeting few moments I consider telling him everything: that I was nearly exploded into little bits last night before a group of armed thugs barged into my house, and now I'm under arrest with a broken arm. But none of that sounds even remotely real. It sounds like...like a *book*.

And anyway, if Daniel came rushing back to the US to spring me from jail, my being there would make it into the papers. Do I really want the Bradleys knowing I've been arrested? Also, and most importantly, if I could just write a single paragraph there's every chance this whole situation might disappear like it never happened.

'It's okay,' I say. 'I'm okay. I just needed to hear your voice.'

'Well, I'll be home soon. Tomorrow morning, your time, so maybe we can do something, go get some breakfast together.'

I sigh. 'That would be nice.' I hear a noise in the background, like a door opening. 'What's that?'

'I just flicked the TV on. You planning to write today, Jane?'

I eye Carolyn and Jay for a moment. 'Yes. Definitely. You have another meeting tomorrow?'

'Meetings, plural.'

'Have you been able to go out and see the city at all?'

There's a rustly noise, which I kind of imagine is him rolling his eyes. He's been to Hong Kong a hundred times, like he's been most everywhere a hundred times.

'I had dinner last night,' he says, and I can hear the smile in his voice. 'Sushi.'

'Oh yes? A nice place?'

'Very nice.'

'Ah. You ordered room service.' The Bradleys own a glamorous hotel in Victoria City, one of a fancy chain that forms part of Amiton Corp's holdings, and the second most expensive in Hong Kong, which is really saying something. The sushi was probably made with seven different kinds of rare seaweed, hand-harvested by Japanese virgins dressed in organic cotton, from the backs of wild dolphins.

'Yeah.' I can hear the smile in his voice.

'Shame on you.'

He huffs a laugh. 'Please. Like you have any credibility. You'd be the first one ordering room service if you were here.' This is true.

'I wish I *was* there.'

'I'll be home soon. Hey listen honey, I should go.'

'Alright.'

'See you tomorrow.'

I hang up, and press Jay's phone against my lips.

'How's Hong Kong?' Carolyn asks, the sarcasm evident.

I don't answer.

Carolyn is this cynical about Daniel for a reason. 'I guess he's just been worried *sick* since he hasn't been able to get in touch with you for the last twenty-four hours.'

'He's busy,' I say, and I hear her snort. This is exactly what she used to tell herself when she didn't hear from Gareth, and I cringe.

'He's not Gareth,' I add, and then regret it. Carolyn doesn't answer, but I can feel her become radioactive in the front seat. Because of Gareth, pretty much nothing will convince Carolyn that Daniel isn't having an affair.

The Gareth issue is painful for me. He sprang into the story without any warning, and Carolyn fell for him right away. He was an academic—an associate professor of anthropology, over from Cambridge—and much smarter than her, which was an obvious turn-on, as hardly anyone is. He'd grown up in one of the rougher suburbs on the north side of Dublin and he was tall and handsome, and slightly dangerous, not nerdy at all. He wasn't intimidated by her in the slightest, and he fell for her too. Hard.

She met him at NYU, where he was a guest lecturer, and she was investigating the suspected homicide of a student. It was love at first sight, or if not love then something hotter and brighter than Carolyn had experienced before. The whole thing felt like a train-wreck the second he stepped onto the page, the kind where the emergency brakes have failed and the train is barrelling out of control. I felt powerless to stop it, but that didn't mean I couldn't have.

I could have chosen to stop writing. I could have gone back and deleted that paragraph where he walked out of a lecture hall and into Carolyn's life. I could have transformed her day into something ordinary, where she chased a clue and caught a killer. Because I knew from the first moment that Gareth was trouble.

But I didn't. And I still struggle with this. Did I do the right thing?

I wanted her to have the choice, I realise. To insert myself at any point in that relationship would have been to compromise her choices. I wanted her to choose what was best for her willingly, consciously. I didn't want to make her do it. I loved her too much, respected her too much to mangle her freedom like that. And free will isn't free will *unless there is a choice*.

Carolyn had plateaued. She was successful in her work, but she was so focused on it that she was on a one-way ticket to a lonely old age. She needed to snap out of the dead-straight path she was walking and open her eyes to other possibilities. People. Love. Growth. Change. I didn't want to force her to do that, and it hadn't needed to be Gareth. She could have chosen it at any point, listened to a million other tiny telltale moments or signs in her life. But she didn't. And I let her choose him.

Hazarding her heart in a relationship and then marriage had been huge for her. And I know the pain she's been feeling for the last three books is intense. But I also hope she's going to come out of the experience a better person—freer, more whole. Happier. Once she gets through this tender healing stage.

She just needs to see Gareth for what he was.

A gift. From me.

26

'Harding.' Jay's voice is low as he pulls up in front of the precinct. 'Try to remember she's a friend.'

But Carolyn's forceful hand on my left arm doesn't feel terribly friendly, as she marches me into the building while Jay parks the car. Her grip tightens as we enter, and I feel her wonder and her nervousness. She can't believe everything is exactly the way I wrote it.

And neither can I.

Ironically, I wrote MSH—Manhattan South Homicide, Jay and Carolyn's squad—into the real-life Ninth Precinct station house because the building looks fictional. The orderliness of the historic stone facade is perfect, friendly green lights glowing beside solid brass doors, the lunettes above classically rounded and symmetrical. Why bother inventing something when reality fit so neatly?

Every New York City precinct has its own detective squad, but I created MSH—an elite, eight-man specialist squad that reports directly to the Commanding Officer, Captain Bill Stubbings—so that Carolyn, and later Jay, could more or less have the run of Manhattan without concern for precinct borders or Police Service Areas, a necessity once the Blade arrived on the scene.

I look around, overwhelmed and shaky. Everything is here, down to the last detail. *Have I created an alternate universe?* My brain

is too blurry to process this. The last ugly paint job is in place, as
well as the chipped edges of the grey formica front desk, and the
faint scent of disinfectant. Even that drooping pot plant, a peace
lily, which Evans' grumpy wife gave him. Exactly as I'd seen it in
my mind's eye.

Holy.

Carolyn scribbles down my pedigree information and empties
my pockets while the desk officer grumbles at us, and I wonder
why I couldn't have written a more cheerful DO behind the front.
I sign the voucher and she takes me past Evans to the elevators.

'Karen!' she yells, as we emerge onto the third floor and into an
open bullpen. I guess the '8 to 4' shift is slowly revving up for the
day—there's a level of subdued activity here and the smell of fresh
coffee. I see several neatly dressed men and women with their
heads already buried in paperwork. The space is quite large: the
eight desks used by the Manhattan South squad aren't separated
from those of the Ninth's regular detectives, and the bullpen takes
up most of this floor, aside from the CO's office, a couple of interview rooms, and a temporary holding cell.

I'm relieved: I guess I won't be going through the ordeal of
getting fingerprinted or taken straight to the precinct cell. Carolyn
has that much compassion, at least. I see a thin girl, aged about
twenty-five, hurry over. Carolyn is facing the other way. 'Where
the hell is Karen?'

'Here, Ms Harding.'

Carolyn looks her up and down. 'Oh, good, you exist.'

Karen blinks. She seems smart and efficient, but timid, just as
I envisioned her. A police administrative aide in a green cardigan,
possibly knitted by her grandmother. And that's all. Huh. A stick
figure.

Carolyn sighs. 'I was so hoping you'd have more backbone, here.
Where's Jones?'

'I believe he's currently booking the suspect you arrested, Ms Harding,' Karen says.

'And Davits?'

'He's scouring the RTCC with the information you gave him.'

I blink. The Real Time Crime Centre exists too. I wonder if, of the millions of criminal records in the database, half of them are fictional now. Or were fictional, but are now non-fictional? My head is too fuzzy for this.

'Anything?' Carolyn snaps.

Karen clasps her hands together. 'Not yet.'

'Did the retrieval team find what I asked for?'

'I heard Eddie say that Garcia is bringing it now.'

'Where's the Captain?'

'He's in his office.'

I start. I have that same tingle of emotion as before, when Carolyn mentioned the Captain, and feel myself go rigid. He's here, right now, in the building. With me.

'Good,' Carolyn says. 'I'm going to deal with Miss Howland, and then I'm going to talk to him. I want you to speak with Davits and then get me a copy of everything he comes up with. Do you understand?'

'Yes, Miss Harding.'

'And I want it five hours ago.'

'Yes, Ms Harding.'

'And Karen, I think you can find a better cardigan than that, don't you?'

Karen looks like she might burst into tears and I want to apologise to her but Carolyn drags me away to our next stop, which is one of the precinct's shabby questioning rooms. She removes my cuffs and tells me to 'sit'. I sit. I'm grateful she doesn't cuff me to the table, but the wait is long.

An hour? Two? I can't tell. My temples are throbbing, but my arm throbs more. I put my forehead down on the cool table, where I watch the little mist my outward breath makes on the metal. It's possible I sleep, but then I hear the door open, and something slides onto the table near me.

'I got you tea.' Jay's voice.

My head snaps up.

His eyes are hooded. He's holding a doubled paper cup with a teabag tag hanging from it. English Breakfast. Not PG Tips, but he must have sent someone out for it, and I feel a pulse of gratitude. I realise that what he slid onto the table is my cults book. I put my bandaged right hand on it. 'You found it.'

'There's a retrieval team at your house.'

'Did they get my computer? My notes?'

His eyes tell me a story I don't necessarily want to know. There's compassion in them. I'm guessing my computer is long gone, along with everything else I owned. I imagine my scruffy lawn, now a kind of smouldering black wasteland. I reach out my left hand, and he puts the tea into it. His fingers brush mine. I try not to notice.

'There's candy in the vending machine if you want,' he says. 'But not liquorice.'

I shake my head. I feel queasy and exhausted. 'I think it's time I gave it up.'

'I see. But not tea.' There's the ghost of a smile in his eyes.

I clutch my cup tighter. 'No. Not tea.'

He sits down opposite me. The one-way mirror on the wall reflects his profile and the greenish tinge of the fluorescent lights. The walls are grey and scuffed. I wish I'd written better decor in here.

'Just so you know,' he says, 'your aunt and uncle are okay. They're being held in a safe location. They're worried about you, but the Blade isn't going to find them anytime soon.'

This warms me and I nod thanks as the door opens and Carolyn comes in. She dumps a laptop on the desk, closes the door and leans against the wall, facing me. Jay doesn't look at her. I can tell they've been arguing.

Generally Carolyn does all the talking in interviews. She's great at it, shrewd and skillful. She has a natural gift for making lateral connections and it comes out with beautiful clarity when she's asking subtle questions and articulating detail. Jay, on the other hand, is the one who does all the watching. His gift is observation and reading people. He catches every nuance.

'There's a sketch artist on the way,' he says to me. 'Harding thought you might be willing to look at some mug shots while you wait.' He pushes the laptop in my direction. I frown. I don't need to look at mug shots to know that the Blade is in the system, or what petty crime he was charged with, or under what alias. They can forget it if they think I'm playing this game with them.

'How about a pen and paper instead?' I say. *So I can take away the Blade's free will. And yours.*

'And what good has that done you so far?' Carolyn fires at me. 'It's time you admit that you can't control this story, Evie.'

I lean back in my metal chair and stare at them. Jay's eyes are still hooded, but I take a good look in them and what I see there surprises me. He agrees with her, at least on some level. Jay doesn't want to go back in the story either. He wants this to be solved another way. He wants me to help them.

No, no, no. For some reason this information causes me a kind of pain under my ribcage. I put my head on the table again and try to block out their desires and feelings. I have plenty of desires and feelings of my own.

'I want to see the Captain,' I announce to the table.

Silence. I look up. Carolyn just stares at me with her snapping, summer-blue eyes.

Jay says, 'Why don't you tell me about the brooch, Evie? And the stamp.' He's talking in the singular, ignoring Carolyn, separating himself from her, letting me know I can trust him. If we were doing clichés this would be *good cop*. His presence and integrity are a natural fit for it.

'Don't do your cop thing with me, Jay,' I say. 'I must have written a hundred scenes like this for you and Carolyn. I want to see the Captain.'

'You think that's a good idea?' he asks.

'I told you we should be treating her as hostile,' Carolyn mutters from behind him.

'Stop, Harding,' Jay says, his voice quiet. I watch them. They're like well-choreographed dance partners. The kind who rehearsed together for years, and know each other's every move. If I were any ordinary mope, it would work on me.

'I'm not telling you anything,' I say. 'Not until I see the Captain.' I press my lips together, and clamp down on my fluttering heart. 'I want to see him,' I repeat. Jay's eyes gaze into mine, seeing all the emotions I'm pretending not to have right now.

'Why don't you answer a couple questions first?' he says. 'And then we'll see what we can do. There's no reason not to talk to us.'

Ha! There are a million reasons. The longer these two are out, doing their thing, and the more I tell them, the harder it's going to be for me to write them back in.

'Let's send her to the Tombs,' Carolyn says, sounding bored. 'See how she feels about talking to us after that.' The Tombs are the pens in the basement of the Criminal Courts building on Centre Street, where people sometimes wait for days in crowded, smelly obscurity for an arraignment.

I scowl. Since they haven't booked me yet, I don't think Carolyn has any intention of wasting time by sending me to see a maybe-fictional judge. But I wouldn't put it past her to let me stew overnight in the precinct holding cell.

Jay ignores her. 'Just tell me a little about Bobby, Evie. Something simple. Tell me about his childhood. Then I promise you, I'll get the Cap for you.'

I clench my good hand against the cold table. 'Listen. I don't want to talk about Bobby. Or his childhood.'

'Why not?'

'Because it was ugly,' I say. 'It deformed him.'

'Okay, then,' Jay says, his tone reasonable, 'tell me where.'

'Alabama.' I see the tiny flicker this sends across both of them: brand-new information. I kick myself.

'Why was it ugly?' Jay asks.

'Does it matter?' I snap.

'Evie. Hasn't it occurred to you that maybe we can help? Maybe we can do this together. You just have to trust us.'

Which is exactly what got me into this mess, according to Mrs Andrews.

Carolyn bursts off the wall. 'Why don't you want to talk about it, Evie? Huh? Because in general you just sit back and watch while terrible things happen to people and you don't lift a finger to stop it? Do you even care? Or worse, you write it on purpose?'

I blink at her. Oh. This isn't a clichéd *bad cop* moment. She's really angry. I shouldn't have mentioned Gareth earlier. This is about him.

'Harding.' Jay is repressive.

'*Do you care?*' she spits. Her blue eyes are like diamond-cutters, and they don't move from mine.

'Harding!'

'Is it painful to think about all the terrible things you've allowed to happen?' she continues, as I quail inside. 'Does it make you uncomfortable? And he's here now. *Bobby's* here. You can't choose what he knows or what he decides. You have no control whatsoever. That's no fun, is it? No fun at all.'

'You think I don't know what it feels like to have no control when bad things happen?' I snap back, surprising myself. I blink. The old hurt is there, on the surface, choking me. How could she think I don't know that? 'I'm sorry about Gareth. I knew he was wrong for you. I knew he would cheat.'

'What?' Carolyn deflates instantly, shocked.

'I knew from the beginning.'

'You...what?'

'I knew. I knew exactly what he would do. Okay?'

'You knew.'

'I'm sorry.'

She starts breathing little pregnant breaths, and pacing the room. 'You're sorry? What's that supposed to mean?' She folds her arms across her body.

I shake my head. I can't tell her that her freedom was important to me, more important than controlling the story. That's the last thing she needs to know.

'I'm sorry for the pain it's caused you,' I say, in a lower tone. 'It wasn't easy for me, either.'

'Easy for you?' She laughs, sounding hollow. 'That's funny.'

'It's true,' I say. What else can I say?

'Why? Why the hell would you let me make that kind of mistake?'

I steel myself. 'What you learned with him...it will help you, Carolyn. For your future. I hoped you might see that. One day.' I swallow.

'What I learned?' Her voice rises. 'How to be humiliated and heartbroken?'

I feel tears prick my eyes. She hates me, and I can't explain it to her. She can't see things from outside. The thing is, I have this certainty that Carolyn's perfect match is somewhere near. About to come into the story, waiting in the wings so to speak. And though Gareth was a setback, it doesn't mean that what she learned can't be used for a better outcome next time. On some level she's more ready for the real thing. After all, being real and being a little broken go hand in hand. There needs to be at least a tiny glimpse of the true, vulnerable Carolyn visible beneath the hard shell she wears, before any star-crossing *Romeo and Juliet* thing I might try will work.

But I can't tell her this.

'Would you have listened,' I ask, 'if I'd warned you?'

There's a long moment of silence.

'Well guess what, Evie?' Her voice is brittle. 'You don't get to choose anymore.'

She turns and exits the room, slamming the door behind her.

27

Jay regards me. I put my head back on the table and squeeze my eyes shut.

'Evie.' Jay sounds pained. 'Please don't cry.'

'I'm not crying,' I say. But I clearly am. 'It's the drugs,' I tell the table, sniffing. 'I'm okay.'

'Evie, can't you give me something? Please.'

I lift my head to look at him. He has removed his weapon and holster, so he looks a fraction less intense, and what I see is the face of someone who's my friend. There's strain around his eyes, and he has his jaw clenched. I remember that he hasn't slept in twenty-four hours, either. His eyes flick to the one-way glass.

'Is he in there?' I breathe, my heart constricting at the thought. Jay drops his eyes to the table.

'You need to give me something, Evie.'

Oh. Carolyn is right, I realise. I'm not in control of this story. I've been arrested, and I have to cooperate to get what I need. Jay is a cop, and he has a boss. He needs me to cooperate, too.

I take a breath. 'The Blade killed his parents.' Jay's blue eyes rivet in on mine. I force the words out. 'A long time ago, when he was fifteen, nearly sixteen. He's forty-one now. His parents were... strange. In fact, they were two very screwed-up people. They had strong opinions on raising children, and a lot of it involved locking Bobby in a dank basement alone for days or weeks at a time.' I pause, pierced unexpectedly with a flash of real grief for that little boy. The days he spent crying and asking to be let out, just wanting to be wanted, to be loved. I swallow. I never thought about that before. I never really looked at the heartbreak Bobby lived when he was vulnerable and alone. I only thought about how it changed him, how it maimed his ability for reason and compassion.

Jay pulls a notepad out of his pocket and starts scribbling. 'Names?'

'Jed and Barbara Laidley.' They were so twisted, so weird.

Jay's straight brows knit together. 'But he's always killed girls.'

'Yes. But not that time. Only since then. The first girl he killed was Nancy Last. She was a distant cousin he met once. She'd said something that hurt him. But he didn't do it till years later. He planned it.'

'You said he killed his parents when he was sixteen. Was he questioned? Did he go into foster care?'

'No. The police assumed he'd died with them. But he'd robbed their nearest neighbour, Ronald Harvey, who was a recluse and a hoarder, and ran. Ronald had been receiving an army pension he hadn't cashed for years, living in mounds of trash and suspicious of banks and governments. Bobby moved to Iowa and set himself up as Ronald's twenty-one year-old son. He lived off Ronald's pension for two years.'

'Where?'

'Jackson.'

'Tell me about the other girls.'

I tell him. Chelsea Grey. She lived in the same trailer park in Jackson, and used to walk past his trailer in pink trainers with her dog. Carrie Marsden, who had the misfortune to cross Bobby's path when he was in the middle of a delicate bank fraud. I have trouble pinpointing the moment of the birth of his hatred of women, but the outworking of it I know in all its gory detail. It's all there, and too vivid.

He strangles them. He likes to feel the domination as the life leeches out of them. It's a visceral enjoyment he takes in the last few minutes. Usually he uses his hands, or a cord. A scarf for Sally Carston because she wore it the day she offended his sense of personal greatness. He has no empathy for them, so he absorbs their desperation as a kind of excessive proof of his brilliance, and his strength, and the rightness of his actions.

'These girls aren't counted in the tally,' Jay says. 'Which means we didn't know about them, but also that Bobby doesn't include them either.'

'I know,' I say. To be honest, it's starting to feel like a relief to get it off my chest.

'You've known about them all this time.'

'Bobby didn't include them because he didn't want interest from the Feds,' I say. 'He's always been careful not to link himself to crimes in other states. It was the smarter move to limit who noticed him, and you know how good he is at staying hidden. In any case, those first girls were...well, he was figuring out how to... what he...liked. What he wanted.' I pause, swallowing nausea. 'And he developed a particular appreciation for you and Carolyn. He knows about you. He liked it being just between you and him. He likes the chase.' I falter. 'I can't do this, Jay.'

'Okay,' he says. 'It's okay. Tell me some more about Bobby as a child. Did he have any friends?'

'No. They lived miles from anywhere on this horrible, swampy farm. The nearest thing was the Redstone Army base. When he wasn't locked in the basement, Bobby would go walking in the swamps for hours and hours. He became fascinated by the...' My voice cracks to a stop.

Bam, bam, bam, bam.

I snap my head to the side and stare at my right arm with its conspicuous bandage. It's still clamped atop the cults book. Knowledge hits me with physical force, like a beating, a whole handful of discrete packages of realisation, shocking and almost painful. I gasp a breath of air then pull the huge book toward me and start flipping through it with my left hand, searching.

'What?' Jay says. 'What is it?'

Holy. How could I have been so blind? The Blade was fascinated by Redstone. He used to sneak in and traipse for hours around the site. Not because of the army installation there, but because of the history. Redstone is well known for the stockpiles of chemical weapons that were buried there after the Second World War, ugly substances stacked in long trenches that go for miles. The government has been in the process of finding and destroying the stuff for years, but the task is enormous. And when Bobby was young, that task had barely begun. There was a toxic stew of lethal substances buried beneath the surface: containers of chlorine, white phosphorus, tear gas, smoke bombs, and incendiary bombs. Blister agents, choking agents, vomiting agents, nerve agents.

On one of his day-long rambles, escaping from his volatile, abnormal parents, Bobby Laidley had stumbled across discoloured drums sunk halfway in water. It was like a confirmation, and a promise. It lit something inside him. A fascination. A kind of passion.

There. I find the page I've been looking for. It's about Aum Shinrikyo, a super creepy Japanese cult that killed a bunch of people and injured about five thousand more in a 1995 attack on Tokyo's subway system. The cult members had used bags of liquid sarin, one of the deadliest nerve agents there is. They'd punctured the bags and left them on five trains heading for central Tokyo. The sarin had vaporised and killed those it came into contact with instantly.

'Do you have them?' I put out my left hand, palm up. A beat, and Jay puts a plastic security envelope into it. It contains the stamp and the brooch. They were taken off me when Carolyn tossed me on arrival, but somehow I knew Jay would have them. I lay them on the table.

Hello Kitty. Japanese. And the stamp. The etching of the queen being enveloped in wavy red lines. England. Wait...no. Great Britain? Something tugs at my memory, and all the millions of little factoids I've acquired over the years about how to kill people. Great Britain.

The military designation for sarin is GB.

I rock back into the metal chair. Do I have this right?

'What is it, Evie? What have you figured out?'

I have a mental picture of the Blade, laughing and enjoying himself as he watched Carolyn and I scramble for our lives out of that paint factory. My terror had been a bonus. He'd wanted me to find that place, had delighted in leaving me that clue. He'd been making sarin there.

I thunk my head on the desk. For starters, it's a freaking cliché. Sarin. Like every wannabe terrorist and his dog. And it doesn't fit with what I know about Bobby. Chemical weapons isn't his style. Too impersonal. Too many risk factors, too many moving parts. It's out of character.

But how would I know that, really? When have I ever looked at Bobby closely enough to know? I've never looked at him, treated him, like he's a real human being.

But he is a real human being. And I think, against all probability, that he's using sarin.

Sarin is a toxic nerve agent. A single drop is enough to kill an adult human within seconds. It is a colourless, tasteless and odourless liquid at room temperature, and like all nerve agents, exposure means overstimulation of muscles, salivation, tears and rapid death through asphyxiation or heart failure. It's so deadly that people who receive a non-lethal dose suffer permanent neurological damage.

What have I done?

'Evie. Tell me.'

I tell him. He frowns.

'Chemical weapons?'

'I don't know how he plans to do it,' I say. 'I don't think he has munitions, and sarin isn't easy to weaponise. It degrades easily and vaporises slowly. But he'll have thought of a way. At the very least you can trace the chemicals used in its manufacture. They had to be making their way into that paint factory somehow.'

'Are they hard to come by?'

I grimace. 'Not very. There's only four, and two can be bought on the shelves. The others can probably be ordered online through any regular chemical supplier. But he would need larger than domestic quantities. The logistics of making nerve agents are phenomenal. The process is very difficult.'

'And he's already finished. You're telling me that right now, the Blade has large quantities of one of the most deadly chemicals known to man, and he has free will.'

I swallow. 'It seems so. That's why he needed that specialised installation. Do you have someone chasing the money?'

Jay stands and begins pacing the room.

'Davits traced it as far as a shell corporation in the Bahamas. Does Bobby have access to that kind of money, or are we talking a backer here?'

A backer? I know about shell corporations because of research I did for Book Five. The Blade has made contacts over the years, but I can't see him working closely with anyone. Yet there's no way he could have accumulated those sorts of funds on his own. At least, I don't think so. Certainly, I never wrote it.

'I can imagine him exploiting someone wealthy,' I say. 'Like all narcissists, he finds it easy to be naturally charming and believable. But not having a partner.' I point at the Aum Shinrikyo page. 'These guys had everything going for them: a whole bunch of rich, brainwashed cult members, and a three-storey facility, staffed by workers with chemistry and chemical engineering expertise who designed and built proper process controls. And it cost them $30 million. That was back in the nineties. We're talking a lot of people and a lot of money.'

'So, someone powerful.' Jay is still pacing. 'Someone who can buy countries. And possibly wants to destroy ours. And a bunch of chemists who are well paid to keep quiet or who are now dead and real quiet. You don't have any idea how he could get access to that kind of money?'

I shake my head. Why don't I know?

'Do you know where Bobby is?'

'No,' I say, and it's the truth. It was nothing but a trap last time, in any case. He has anticipated me too well at each turn. He *knows* me.

'A bomb?' Jay says. 'Is he going to set off a bomb?'

I gulp back a little crest of panic and shake my head. 'I don't think so. A bomb would be the most effective way to disperse the sarin—it would both heat it and spread it over a large area at the same time. But he wouldn't use fire. That's how he killed his parents. It's special for him.'

'He used it on you.'

I look at him, not willing to verbalise what this means about the Blade's feelings toward me. Jay scrubs a hand through his hair, cursing, then slams both hands on the table. 'You need to write.'

I stare at him. 'But I thought...?'

'We don't have time to solve this. Not before he's killed everyone he wants to kill. And that includes you. You need to write,' he repeats, heading for the door. 'We need to get you out of here to somewhere you can concentrate.' He yanks it open.

'Jay, wait!' I jump up. 'Please...' I beg him with my eyes. 'Please let me see him.'

28

I freeze in place when I hear the door open.

Is it him? I wonder if Jay is behind the one-way glass, watching. What argument did he use to get the Captain in here? I don't know where Carolyn is. They both know what this means to me. They've seen the photo.

The man who enters has grey hair. Greyer than I remember.

I gulp for air.

Here's where I admit there's one other way to bring characters into a story. It's if they are people the writer already knows—or knew.

It's possible to write real people into a story. Not the actual person, obviously, but someone exactly like them. Since you already know their traits and mannerisms—or better, their deeper self—it's one of the easiest routes to meeting new characters. And the most difficult. Because this man—this man is my father.

He has an easy efficiency about him as he closes the door and sits opposite me at the table. He's a great CO. My dad never had a chance at being a leader back in England, but the Captain is exactly the kind of boss everyone most appreciates: an active, courageous cop, although his is technically a supervisory position; intelligent; good with people. Not deadened by the wreckage of humankind that has been his daily bread for decades, but calm and fair. Good at seeing people for who they really are. Good at talking to them.

'Detective Ryan said you wanted to speak to me.'

I nod. He has a different accent, but it's my father's voice, and it pulls the string of the deepest feelings I have. My hands are clasped together in a tense prayer position and the Captain is staring at me, not unkindly. He has green eyes, like mine. They're the deep colour of the English Channel, though my own are lighter.

He's here. He's real.

'Was there something you needed to tell me?' he asks. His tone is so polite.

I fight the urge to burst into tears. He's waiting patiently, wondering why I'm staring at him. He doesn't recognise me. In the books, he has lived a different life, has a different daughter. I'm an unknown girl to him, and worse, one that is scraped in dirt and ash, with dried blood on her shirt and a crazy look in her eye. Why was I so desperate to see him? Why did I feel like I was dying of the need just to be near him? Because sitting across a table from someone I love so much, and have wept over and wanted for years, and not to be able to hug him or pour out all the words of yearning and need and love, is a far worse feeling. This is torture.

'I just wanted to meet you,' I croak.

His eyes are shrewd, assessing. 'Detective Ryan said you're aiding them with their investigation.'

'I'm trying to.'

'Good girl.' This validation, however flippant for him, means an embarrassingly deep amount to me. 'I've given him the okay to get you to a safe place,' he says. 'You'll be released without charge.'

'Thank you,' I say.

'I've decided to bring in Jack Archer from the Financial Crimes Bureau to help Ryan and Harding chase down the benefitting owner of the shell corporation in the Bahamas.' This information gives me a little tingle. Something tells me Jack Archer and Carolyn are going to get on really well. Eventually. 'Do you know Jack?'

I shake my head. *Not yet.*

'We're doing everything in our power to find Bobby Laidley,' the Captain continues. 'It was brave of you to tell us what you know.'

'I'm not brave,' I say.

He observes me. 'That's what you think.' He muses for a moment. 'You remind me so much of my daughter.' I swallow a sudden lump in my throat. His eyes glance at the one-way glass. 'Ryan tells me you're a writer,' he adds. 'In fact, he tells me you're The Writer.'

My mouth drops open. So that's the argument Jay used. It says a lot about the respect and trust he has for his boss.

'Yes,' I say hesitantly.

'Probably best you don't tell anyone else here.'

Of course no one in the precinct knows that I'm the writer, because I've never thought much about anyone here. As Jay complained so recently about Karen, they're just stick figures. I haven't bothered to bring them into my life or have them over to hang out near me in their downtime while I pondered their personalities. I wasn't interested in developing them as characters. And thus they don't recognise me as the one who, until recently, made the decisions in their lives. And my own father, or at least the man sitting across from me, was too painful to think about much. I throw a furtive glance at the door.

'Do they all know...have they all noticed that they suddenly have free will?'

'Of course,' he says.

'But they're all still here. Working. Complaining. Doing everything they normally do!'

'Of course.' He sits back. 'Does that really surprise you? Human beings are creatures of habit and comfort. And free will has its own boundaries. The boundaries of respect and safety and love. The desire to provide for their families, to do the right thing, to earn a decent day's wage. These are all good things, and not worth throwing away just for the sake of suddenly doing what they *think* they want.'

The door opens. It's Jay. The Captain stands up. 'You're free to go, Miss Howland. Evie.' He looks me in the eye. 'I'm sure you'll make the right decisions.' He pauses. 'I'm proud of you.'

He leaves, and Jay stands there holding the door open. His eyes are unreadable.

'Time to go,' he says.

I breathe in and out a few times, and then get up and move toward the door.

But as I near Jay I can't seem to help moving into him. My arms go around his waist and my nose goes into his neck, and I settle naturally into him. His arms come right around me and we stand that way for a while. I like the sound of his steady, beating heart. I feel safe.

'You asked him to tell me he was proud of me, didn't you?' I mumble.

'Is that okay?'

'Yes.' I blink moisture into his shirt. 'Thank you.'

29

It's late when we pull up to Daniel's apartment. The musky scent of dry cleaning and dog pee is in the air, and the streetlights are glowing that artificial gold that makes me crave starlight.

Reynaldo gets a cautious look when he sees Jay, but I don't bother explaining. What I want is a familiar, safe place and a really long shower. And Daniel's apartment is the plushest, safest place I know. Jay seemed sold on the idea when I told him Daniel would be back tomorrow and we could ask him about possible rich suspects for the Blade's backer.

As the elevator doors are closing, a quick, feminine hand with short nails stops them. It's Carolyn.

'I should have known you'd be this stupid.' She steps inside and glares at us as the elevator rises. I don't have the strength to keep fighting with her. Jay has two days' growth of stubble and a reckless look about him, and I'm surprised Carolyn has the nerve to pick a fight with him. 'Evie was in the social pages with him only last week, Ryan. The Blade has to know they're together.'

'If it helps her write, I think we can risk it.' Jay's face is impassive. It has remained pretty blank ever since I told him I wanted to go to Daniel's apartment.

I leave them outside the elevator doors in a kind of stand-off and head for Daniel's apartment with my key, but I can hear them talking.

'I can't *believe* you, Ryan. You are literally incapable of thinking clearly. You would let her do whatever she wants. It's not about what she *wants*. It's about what's *best* for her.'

Oh, the irony. I stick the key in.

'Wait.'

I feel Jay charge up behind me and then gently push me out of the way. He turns the key slowly, unholsters his Glock, and cracks the door like he expects a bomb to go off. The apartment is in darkness. I reach past him and flick the light switch, and follow him inside. The first room is a narrow vestibule with a high ceiling, painted to look like something from one of the sixteenth-century palazzos on the Grand Canal in Venice. The floor is black and white chequered marble, and Jay moves across it with the silence of practiced stealth.

'Seriously.' Carolyn says at full volume, standing in the open door with her arms folded. Jay continues down the hall, gun drawn. 'Really?' Carolyn is looking up at the ceiling and the frescoes there. Okay, so Daniel's apartment is a little over the top. Actually, it's a lot over the top. It says more about how much money he has than how much he understands the concept of home. She rolls her eyes. 'Ugh. At least Mommy and Daddy paid for state-of-the-art security.'

'Leave them out of it,' I say, but without ire. I turn to press my fingerprint to the glowing control panel, but the security system isn't armed. I frown.

'Why, because you're way more in love with them than you are with him? What did he say when you called?'

'He didn't answer,' I say, gritting my teeth. I move forward down the hall, both wanting to catch up to Jay and escape Carolyn.

Carolyn scoffs. 'Wait...is that an ice sculpture?'

I close my eyes. 'No Carolyn, it's...oh.'

It *is* an ice sculpture. I blink. We've reached Daniel's spacious chef-style kitchen, gleaming with hanging copper pans and an oversized range, and there's a dripping sculpture propped on the marble benchtop of the centre island. 'It's the same as the one Magdeline wanted for the wedding,' I murmur. Two dewy doves form the shape of a heart with their spread wings. Kind of tacky, I thought, when Magdeline suggested it, but then I wasn't in the habit of arguing with Magdeline. Maybe she brought over a trial version, so Daniel could approve it?

Just then Jay walks back into the kitchen, his expression unreadable, his Glock re-holstered. I open my mouth to ask if everything is okay when I notice something else I'm not used to seeing when Daniel isn't home. In the spreading puddle from the melting sculpture sit two empty wineglasses, smudged in crimson from recent use. I stare at them for a moment, and then start walking toward the bedroom. Jay, who was busy making eye contact with Carolyn, is about two beats behind me.

'Evie, wait.'

I speed up. Daniel's apartment has the square footage of a Las Vegas casino but it doesn't take me that long to sprint to the master bedroom. Jay catches up to me as I throw the door open and flick the light.

I step back, straight into him. Someone is asleep in there, tangled up in the sheets of Daniel's bed. It's Daniel. And someone else. My eyes rake the room, snagging facts. Daniel's gaudy interior design wears an additional air of refined debauchery, if not wild sex. High heels and women's underwear.

I breathe out.

'Evie?' Daniel lifts himself from the pillow and turns over, blinking in the light, naked and impossibly attractive.

'Huh.' Carolyn has come up behind Jay and is peering over his shoulder. 'My money was on Magdeline,' she chirps, and I stiffen.

But her chirp is brittle. She's lived this exact scene herself. She knows what it feels like. She drops the chirp altogether and adds, 'Who's this?'

'It's Jenna.' Jay's voice is gravelly and threatening.

'Really? I would have picked his secretary, or his PA. There's no cliché here. Oh, wait. Isn't she your best friend?'

Questions clog my throat but they are unnecessary. This whole scene is so out of context that I can't process it. Or is it? I try to say something, but all I manage is, 'Neh.'

'Evie? What are you doing here? What's going on?' Daniel has pulled the covers over them both.

'Righteous indignation?' Carolyn answers, her disgust turned on full.

'Neh,' I say again.

Jenna is waking up. She swipes a hank of her cute haircut out of her eyes, and her sleepiness bottoms out into horrified recognition.

'Evie,' she says, the single word hinting at yet-to-be-plumbed regret. I wonder if she's going to say, *this isn't what it looks like.* The Jenna I thought I knew would probably try to justify this, or to explain it, at least. I always found it reassuring, how strong and confident she was.

In any case, it's exactly what it looks like. Also, ugh.

I turn around and push past Jay and Carolyn, who shepherd me back down the hall.

'Let's go,' Carolyn says. 'This was never the ideal place, anyway. I can't believe it was Jenna. I thought I was a better detective than this. I'm disappointed in myself.'

'She's my friend,' I mumble, and realise how small and forlorn I sound. I turn and run back toward the bedroom. I'm not sure what I intend to do, possibly point a threatening finger at Jenna, or beg Daniel not to be such a selfish jerk. Because he's ruined it. I can't marry him. I can't be one of the family. Part of them.

But I don't get to do any of this, because Jay catches me and hefts me up so that my running feet are lifted high off the ground.

'Don't do something you'll regret,' he says as I struggle, dragging me back down the hall. He plants me on my feet next to the sink, careful to avoid the puddle of water on the floor from the sculpture. But Daniel isn't far behind us anyway, tying on a robe and squinting with still-sleepy eyes. His hair is flat on one side from the pillow and he looks ridiculous, caught off guard like this. I want to leave, to get away from the reality of it, but another part of me, with the steely presence of Jay and Carolyn at my back, has to understand.

'You lied about Hong Kong,' I choke. Oh no. There are tears coming.

'Evie, what are you doing here?' Daniel still has that tone, as if this is all my fault for showing up unannounced. 'Why are you so filthy? Is that dried blood?' He points. 'And who is this?'

The effect this tone has on me is catastrophic, perhaps even more so than the effect of the visually identifiable facts. This tone says Daniel isn't upset about hurting me, that he doesn't care. He doesn't love me.

Jay, who is standing close to me, steps forward. As Daniel gets his robe straightened and looks up, Jay punches him hard in the face. Daniel's head snaps back and he goes down.

'Because she nearly died twice in the last twenty-four hours,' Jay says in a monotone.

Daniel climbs back up, straightening his undignified outfit, as Jenna runs to his side.

'Danny!'

Danny? Double ugh. But I feel my face crumple. The tears are here. I try to keep them silent by gulping down that twisting, tight feeling in my throat, but I'm not fully successful.

'Who the hell do you think you are?' Daniel yells at Jay. I think he's pretty brave, yelling, with the expression on Jay's face right now. 'Do you know who I am?'

'Jenna,' I squeeze out, 'why?'

'Aaaand the bubble bursts.' Carolyn is watching all this from the other side of the kitchen. I turn wide eyes to her. She couldn't possibly be smug about this. Her gaze shies away from mine, as if she got poked by her conscience. She narrows a glacial glare at Daniel.

'We're going to call your parents, you know. We're going to tell them all about this.' She waves a vague hand at the general sordidness. 'And you're going to regret it. You're going to regret it with every atom in your tiny brain. I'll make sure of it.'

I blink at her. I know for sure she isn't talking to Daniel right now. This is the speech she wished she had given to Gareth. I wonder how Daniel is taking this weirdly personal threat from someone he's never met before, but to my surprise he looks taken aback. And perhaps a little afraid.

'Let's go,' Jay says, holding his right fist in his left.

'Evie, who are these people?' Daniel has raised his voice again, but there's anxiety in his tone. 'How dare you bring them into my apartment!'

'I'm sorry,' I say, the apology automatic.

'You're apologising?' Carolyn drips disbelief.

'My father doesn't need to know about this,' Daniel adds.

'Evie, it just happened.' Jenna's chic bob is all messed and frumpy and I realise that at some point she must have started crying. Her face is wet, her cheeks pink. She's pulled on a gown too. My gown.

'This is the first time,' she continues. 'And only time. I never thought...' She pauses and wipes her eyes on the satiny sleeve, then looks at Jay. 'It's the guy you brought to the fitting!' On cue

Daniel spins to land an accusing gaze on Jay. Jenna looks back to me. 'Magdeline told me…You brought him to Daniel's apartment?'

'No, I…we…you don't understand.' I shuffle, hampered by rising sobs and wondering if a plausible explanation exists. 'He's…I…'

'Evie!' Carolyn's voice cuts through my own. 'Stop explaining yourself to him.' She points at Daniel. 'You. Listen up, rich kid. We don't have to explain anything to you. You are an asshole.' She grabs my arm and drags me toward the front door.

'And we are definitely calling your parents!'

30

We're standing outside a door. Huh. It's very grey and ordinary.

Whose door? I have a vague memory of spending a car journey staring at nothing in particular. It's possible there's severe turmoil going on inside me, but if there is, I can't discern it. It's like being in a coma, but with moderate use of my faculties.

Jay opens the door, and a big black Labrador noses his way out and sticks his muzzle into my hand. A thin memory makes it to the surface of my brain. Jay has a dog. Named Ben.

'Ben,' I say.

'He's an excellent guard dog.' Jay rolls his eyes.

Ben rushes to his master and goes through the doggy motions of being thrilled to see him. Jay fends him off affectionately. 'Come in,' he says to us.

I don't know what I imagined when Jay started talking about his apartment two days ago, but I'm pretty sure it wasn't this. It's nice. Homey. The kitchen, dining and living areas are all one space and it feels quite large, for the city. There are lots of dark masculine colours but it feels light somehow, and it's clean. Jay trained with the Navy SEALs for over a year before a tiny heart murmur disqualified him for service, and there are signs around the room of a military-grade attitude to organisation. There are books everywhere, and they're coordinated by exact size and lined upright on every shelf like soldiers. I walk through, gazing. Only one folded sweater and a dirty coffee cup mar the neat picture of order and self-discipline.

'Australia?' I hold up a dog-eared travel guide with my left hand. He shrugs.

'Um, bedroom through there,' pointing, 'shower down the hall.' I nod, and run my fingers over a stack of more travel books for other countries. Uruguay, Norway, Ethiopia. He did a year of backpacking straight out of high school. I hadn't considered that he might want to travel more.

'How long do you think we've got here?' Carolyn asks. She's been checking rooms. Ben offered her a lick, but quickly saw they were not kindred spirits. He's currently receiving a head massage from Jay, who's using his other hand to check the fridge.

'With two cars outside, someone on the door...' Jay's face gives nothing away. 'Less than twelve hours.'

I wander into the bedroom. The bed is made up military-style with a dark grey duvet tucked into precise hospital corners, and there are books here too: a bookshelf beside the closet and a neat stack of weighty paperbacks on the bedside table. Beside them is a framed picture of Jay with his father. I pick it up and examine it. Jay looks about seventeen and they're both filthy but laughing, as if they've had a day of sheep shearing or mucking out horse stalls. I blink back something in my eye, as I hear Jay come in behind me. He has a plastic bag and tape.

'I thought this might help in the shower.'

'Thank you.'

I reach to take it but he says, 'Let me.' I watch him as he fits the plastic bag over my splinted arm. My eyes go back to the photo.

'I like your dad,' I say.

He gives a half-smile. 'So do I.' He pulls off a piece of tape with his teeth, and gently sticks the bag to my arm, making it waterproof. I tear my mind away from the sensation of his skin touching mine. 'He reminds me of yours sometimes.'

I sigh. 'The Captain...isn't my dad. Not quite. It's complicated. But I like to think our dads would get on well, if they ever met. I always loved it that your mother and father decided to leave the city so you and your brother and sisters could grow up in the outdoors.'

'Yeah. Sometimes I miss the smell of horses so much I don't mind when my mom calls for a chat.' His smile is white and beautiful, but too fleeting.

'I was sixteen when my dad...'

He glances at me. 'Yeah, I know.'

'How do you know?'

'I've known you for a long time.' Our eyes meet. 'And I'm a good detective.'

'Uncle Allan's been so great all these years,' I say, 'helping me with the books...' I glance out the window. We're in Brooklyn, I recall, on the fourth floor of a red-brick walk-up. 'When I'm writing it, the good guys can go home to their families. The bad guys get convicted. Carolyn doesn't rest until there's justice, and justice gets done. But when my mother died three years ago...' I can't finish the sentence.

'It's normal to want family, Evie,' Jay says softly. He finishes the last piece of tape, but his fingers linger on my arm. 'What do you need?'

I pause. There are a lot of answers to that question.

'To write,' he clarifies. 'What do you need to write?' He moves over to his closet, pulling out a baggy grey hoodie. He holds it up. 'Close enough?' It bears such a resemblance to my writer's smock that I feel overcome with gratitude.

'It's perfect,' I say, with a wobbly smile. He comes near and hands it to me, with a pair of his sweatpants, and his eyes catch mine. I see they're about three shades darker than normal, the exact colour of the night sky seen from an open field. I imagine looking up at the stars with a night breeze full of the scent of grass and horses, two warm hands linked gently around my waist from behind. I gulp. I'm staring into his eyes, and he's staring back. Has time slowed down? He's giving me the sweater and I'm taking it, but neither us are doing either of those things. We're not moving at all. 'Thank you,' I say, my voice tangled and unsteady.

'Shouldn't she be writing?' Carolyn is leaning on the doorframe, her expression like a bucket of ice water.

'Let her shower first,' Jay says. Then to me, 'Towels are in the bathroom cupboard.' I nod and move toward the bathroom, head down. When I glance back, I see Jay stalk across the hall to the kitchen, and Carolyn follow him like a terrier.

'She should be writing,' she hisses.

Jay throws her a warning look but says, 'Let her get comfortable first. You know she likes to have her stuff in place.' Then he gives her another look, the kind that would flatten a grown man. 'You're gonna rush her into it, Harding? Because I know you're just dying to go back in, huh?'

I go into the bathroom and close the door, but not all the way. Carolyn sighs gustily.

'Obviously not. But if it has to happen I just want it over with.' A pause. 'Listen I...' A longer pause. I find myself surprised at her tone. She knows she has annoyed Jay. 'I know I haven't been...I know I'm not exactly selfless, these days. I know it, okay?' I don't see the glance they must exchange here, but I know what it would look like. Despite Carolyn's rough tone she's being humble, which is difficult for her. Jay would appreciate that. 'But you don't need to worry about my motives, okay? I know what's the right thing to do.'

'I know you do,' Jay says. 'I trust you.' There's another pause, and I hear a sound that might be dog biscuits getting poured into a bowl. I move over to the faucet and turn it on so that I'm making some bathroom noises in here, and sneak back to the door.

Carolyn says, 'So what about yours?'

'My what?'

'Your motives. Because you're not exactly rushing her either. You could be less obvious, Ryan. She's The Writer. It's like a pet monkey falling in love with its owner. There's a name for this, you know. It's called Stockholm syndrome.'

'That's enough, Harding. You want me to trust your motives, that goes both ways.'

'Come on.' Though their words are confrontational, I'm warmed by their gentle tone. They only talk like this when they're alone. They have room for each other's faults, because they care about each other. Carolyn continues, chiding, 'She's like a scared little mouse. What's to like?'

Jay answers, 'And sometimes, you're like a boot to the face, Harding. But I like you. I know you're here because you care about her. Don't tell me you've come this far just because you have a job to do.' They're speaking very softly now, and I feel like an intruder.

'You gotta think this through,' Jay continues. 'There isn't a single thing she's done for you where she didn't have your best interests at heart. She's never once tried to deliberately hurt you. She loves you. You see that? Because if you don't start looking at things differently you're gonna end up the lonely, bitter old lady she's trying to save you from being. And you and I both know, that either here, or inside, she's the truest friend you've got.'

'What about you? You're not my friend?' Carolyn's voice has gone very small.

'Yeah. And I'm your partner. That's why I'm giving it to you straight.'

There's a pause, like they're having a moment, or they're wondering why the shower isn't running. I dash over and blast it on, turn off the faucet, lean on the vanity and stare at my face in the mirror. It's not exactly my best look. There's a hint of crystallised shock in the coastal tints of my eyes, and my cheeks are mottled with a mixture of dirt, ash and tears. But I'm cheered by how honest Jay and Carolyn are being. I appreciate more than ever how deliberate they've been in keeping their relationship solid. Especially now they have free will.

I close myself into the shower and use Jay's soap and his shampoo, which is for sure going to make my hair look like the end of a broom. I find a razor and shave my legs, and when I get out and wipe steam off the mirror there I am, at least partly human again.

Ben greets me when I make it out of the bathroom. I can hear Jay and Carolyn talking in low voices in the living room, but exhaustion is pulling at me. I should write, but I also think it might be nice to take this clean, warm cloud I'm in and have a nap.

The decision is made before I finish asking myself the question. I fall into Jay's bed, tug the rigid covers loose, and burrow down like a mole that's been kept in the sun for too long.

A really, really sleepy mole.

31

I wake quickly, shivering with a strange dread. It's dark. I turn my head and find myself face to face with the mournful brown gaze of a doe-eyed Ben. I blink at his huge black form stretched out beside me on the bed like a hairy bodyguard.

Well. No wonder Jay doesn't have a girlfriend.

I turn my head the other way and am confronted by the photo of Jay with his father, thinly visible in the darkness. The dread is still there, and that photo seems to have extra meaning. A pain similar to the one I feel when I look at the photo of my own father.

I stare into the darkness, analysing. I remember something Mrs Andrews said. She said a lot of things, and frankly not much made sense at the time. But one thing...*in my experience dear, when ye don't know what to write next, it's usually because ye do know what to write next, ye just don't want to write it.*

Is there something I don't want to write?

I sit up and see that Jay is lying on the floor beside the bed, freshly washed and shaven, and deeply asleep. Seriously, the floor?

I'm not sure what time it is. I creep out of bed, and peer through Jay's blinds to see early rays of light streaking across the sky. I pad out to the living room to investigate, and find Carolyn there, awake, and with an eye to the blinds, also. Her gun is on the coffee table. She turns when she hears me.

'Sleep okay?' She sounds wary. I rub my eyes.

'Yes, thank you. Did you sleep?'

'Yeah. Ryan took the first shift.'

'How long has he been asleep?'

'About an hour. I got you some clothes.' She points her chin at a pile on the arm of the sofa. I can see a blue knit top, and a pair of dark jeans.

'Those are your clothes.'

There's a second's pause. 'Yeah. I figured it was time I returned the favour.' She meets my eyes to give weight to this. We look at each other for a moment.

'Thank you,' I say.

She purses her lips. 'Yeah. Thank *you*.' She puts her hands on her hips, looking uncomfortable. She takes her hands off again, but they clearly feel weird at her sides, so she folds them in front of her. 'So I've been thinking. That I never gave you credit for...for how you wrote me. And I've been thinking that the decisions you made, weren't to deliberately hurt me. And that maybe they were good decisions. I just didn't see it. So far.'

This is so unexpected that I stare at her for a moment. I feel a huge wash of gratitude to Jay.

'I never wanted you to be hurt,' I say, wishing I could hug her. Carolyn doesn't do public displays of affection.

'No, I don't think you did.' Her blue eyes are piercing. 'And I am grateful for...what I learned. Or at least, I expect I'll be grateful. Eventually.'

I say, 'I care about you.'

She drops her eyes. 'Yeah well, Mrs Andrews pretty much outed you on that one. I didn't believe it, you know. I didn't want to believe it.'

This makes me uncomfortable. I don't really want to acknowledge what Mrs Andrews said. Her *real love* terminology was way too intense. *I don't get intense about people because when they die it hurts too much. It's common sense.*

But, of course I care.

'You and Jay are my favourite people in the world,' I say. As if I have a lump in my throat. As if I'm on the verge of tears.

Carolyn drops her head and blinks a couple of times. 'Ditto for me,' she tells the floor. She looks up and I see her lashes are damp. We share a tentative smile. 'You want to go back to bed? There's still a couple of hours before sunrise and we'll have to move you sometime early today. You could get some more rest.'

'No,' I say. 'I'd rather stay here and keep you company.'

She nods slowly before she answers, as if this really means something to her. 'Thanks.'

An hour later, Carolyn and I are hunched over Jay's kitchen table, clutching Jay's coffee cups, as the rising sun touches Jay's windows.

'So what about the evil nurse? Didn't he have anything to say?'

'The guy from the hospital?' Carolyn shakes her head. 'He started speaking a small-village dialect from one of the Slavic nations, and refused to understand English. I don't think they've managed to track down the right interpreter for him.'

'Eastern Europe?' I huff. 'Really?'

'I know. Cliché.'

'And there's no word on the chemists the Blade used?'

'Some.' Carolyn toys with her empty cup. 'A number of chemical engineers entered the country in the last six months on H-1B visas for the business the Blade set up through Soman Corporation, the shell company. Ostensibly a new paint factory, looking for the perfect shade. Or whatever. But they're all missing now, presumed dead.'

'Six months ago,' I say. *This started six months ago?* That was when

I began dating Daniel. How is that possible? 'Where were they from?' I ask.

'All over. Mostly members of the EU. No word yet on the contacts within those countries, who put them in touch with the Blade to begin with, or the associates here he was working with. And his name appears nowhere, since the business is managed by Soman, and Soman is bogus and anonymously owned.'

'So no leads there either?' I'm trying not to feel defeated.

'I mean, yeah,' Carolyn says. 'Just not in our time frame. Turns out Soman is the subsidiary of another shell entity in the Caribbean, one of many, probably, which means there's already about a hundred layers between us and the benefitting owner. The registered agent that set it up was White Incorporating Services in Nevada, basically just another questionable corporate service provider creating shell companies for frauds and terrorists. Soman is legally registered to an address that about two hundred thousand companies are registered to. Thanks to Nevada's conveniently lax rules on business incorporations, White are under no obligation to disclose anything about ownership unless compelled by a court or by law enforcement, which we're working on. It's in the hands of the Financial Crimes Bureau now.'

'You've been in touch with Jack Archer?'

'Yeah. I talked to him late last night. He's a jackass. But it seems he knows his stuff.'

I keep a smug look off my face. I was so right about them.

Then I have an existential moment. Wait. Is Jack Archer a character or a person? I can see him in my mind's eye, and I'd had that feeling about him and Carolyn as soon as his name was mentioned. And yet I've never written about him. Is he someone from the book who I just haven't met yet, who has landed here along with everyone else? Or is he someone from the real world who's getting caught up in the expanding ripples of something that still is, essentially, fiction?

'Jack Archer is blond, is he?' I'm trying for nonchalance.

Carolyn eyes me. Possibly I have *Existential Crisis* written all over my face.

'Yeah.' So she's read his profile.

'Brown eyes?'

'Yeah. Six-two. Two-ten. Type A. You okay?'

'Fine!' There's no doubt in my mind that Carolyn and Jay are real, right now. Any doubts I might have had about that were shaken off the moment Jay's skin touched mine two and a half days ago on the Lower East Side. But are they as real as everyone else? Or more pertinently, are 'real' people just as capable of being part of a story? Carolyn is giving me her knife-sharp stare.

'Evie. The Blade is smart, yeah, but this is a huge operation. As far as we know, he hasn't run anything like this before. He's bound to have made a mistake somewhere. We've got plenty of leads. What we don't have is *time*.'

'Carolyn? What was the retrieval team supposed to be bringing you?'

'When?'

'When we arrived at the precinct yesterday. Karen said the retrieval team was bringing something. But if my computer and notes were destroyed...'

'No,' Carolyn shakes her head, 'that wasn't what I was looking for. Your computer and notes were all missing, in any case. Not destroyed. We can only assume he's got them, and that's the reason he stormed your house. No, what I wanted was copies of your books.'

'The books?'

'Yeah.' She barks a laugh. 'The retrieval team was at the bookstore. I figured they were as good a source of information on the Blade as any, since you probably included information in the narrative that you didn't allow Ryan and I to discover.'

I shake my head. 'I never hid stuff from you. The only place where there's information you don't have is in my notes. Everything is there.'

She grimaces. 'I know that now. After a team of five people speed-read three books each in four hours.' We share a smile. It's not funny, and technically it's time wasted, but I think we might be giggly with exhaustion, and frankly, I'm enjoying sharing this feeling with Carolyn.

'Why did he steal those notes?' she asks. 'Is there a clue there? Something he wanted to get hold of? Or something he wanted to hide?'

I shrug. 'Maybe. I made a lot of notes. Everything from the beginning of the series until now...every idea, every plot point, every motive.'

Carolyn eyes me. 'Well whatever it is, he has it now, and the only other place it exists is in your head.' She stares at me like she wishes forcible extraction were an option. 'It could be the clue to unravel all this, the one thing that can shut him down for good.'

I shrug again. If Carolyn thinks I can pin down one random fact from the millions of scribbly dot points I've made in the last ten years then I need a lot more sleep and gallons of tea before I try.

'What I don't get,' she muses, 'is how Edgar Polton fits into all this. There's more to that story.'

Edgar Polton, the softly spoken orthodontist. There was something I needed to tell them about Polton. Something to do with Bidgood. What was it?

'Could a dentist be a good front for bringing chemicals into the state?' she asks.

I shake my head. 'Not these kinds of chemicals. Well, the sodium fluoride, maybe. But it's easily accessible by anyone, not just dentists. Another, methylphospho-something, is a Schedule 1 substance under the Chemical Weapons Convention. It's both reactive and corrosive, and it has basically zero uses other than making chemical weapons. An orthodontist would be just as suspicious as anyone else, trying to get his hands on large quantities of it.'

Carolyn eyes me. 'Geez. Your brain. What other knowledge have you got in there?' She frowns. 'What I don't get is how you can be so smart but miss the whole Jenna thing. There had to be clues.'

The lack of segue takes me by surprise. But landing back at Jenna and Daniel isn't as painful as I would have thought. Logically I can see, now, that Jenna going after Daniel fit perfectly. She's the kind of person who feels she's worth more than what she already has, and she goes through men accordingly. Daniel must have looked like the ultimate trifecta to her—a handsome, smart, point-one-percenter, someone who met the kind of inner celebrity standard she'd made for herself.

I'd always known she was driven and slightly shallow, but we've known each other a long time, and I loved her. She was the one to take that first clumsy story written by my nineteen-year-old self and help me turn it into not just a successful, ongoing series, but a long career. She has faithfully cheered and championed me all the way.

In short: no, I didn't see the clues.

'Am I emotionally blocked, do you think?' I ask.

'Definitely,' she says. 'Or maybe just emotionally dense. Like a spongy kind of undercooked emotional cake.'

'Er, rude.'

Carolyn grins, and there's enough self-awareness in it to make me grin too. She knows her own emotional cake isn't perfectly cooked, either.

'At least it's tasty,' I say.

'That remains to be seen,' she says. 'Maybe you're too soft to be tasty.'

'Soft. You mean nice. I'll take that as a compliment.'

'I didn't really mean it as one.' We exchange smiles.

'You're much better at being facetious than I thought,' I say.

'Yeah well,' Carolyn's eyes meet mine, 'I've got a good friend who's English. It rubs off, I guess.'

I get a warm glow in my chest. *A good friend.* We exchange another smile. Then I ask, 'Carolyn? What makes you think Edgar Polton is involved?'

'I don't know,' she muses. 'He was too nice.'

'Cynic.' We hear a noise from the direction of the bedroom, probably Jay's alarm, waking him up.

'Carolyn?' Her blue gaze flicks back to mine. 'You think the Blade will come here?'

She sits back. 'I think that if what you told us about his childhood is true, then he probably blames you for it. I think it's safe to say that he hates you more than any other woman he's ever met. And he really hates women.'

'Great,' I murmur. *But it's not hate.* Hate implies some kind of reckless feeling. Bobby Laidley believes he's doing the world a service by getting rid of women. But why?

'Evie, it's okay. There are at least six cops in plainclothes outside and the Captain has a team of people from all over working on this. It's different now that there are chemical weapons. That makes the Blade a terrorist. The FBI and the CT Division are involved. And no one does counterterrorism better than the New York City Police Department. If you still haven't written anything in the next couple of hours, you'll be moved to a safe house out of state. And nothing he does will be able to stop you writing there. But you should write.'

Her eyes meet mine, and I register both the resignation and

the determination in them. We both turn as Jay emerges from the hall, looking rumpled and adorable. His eyes are clear dark blue, thanks to some much-needed sleep, and he takes us both in.

'Carolyn's helping me work out some story elements,' I say.

'Good.' He yawns. 'You guys want some breakfast?'

32

32

The kitchen is warm and bright.

Jay scrapes fresh coriander into the Spanish omelette he's just mixed, and the green-fresh scent hits me and makes me think of sunshine and Saturday mornings.

'Mmm,' I say, sniffing, 'I love coriander.'

'It's called cilantro. And, I know.' He gives me a brief look that tells me he had it brought especially but regards it as an obnoxious genetic mutation. 'You're the only person I know who does.'

'I *know*,' I reply. My equally dry look meets with a grin.

'Remember Book Six,' pipes up Carolyn, 'that guy who thought the world was going to end unless he did that crazy ritual?'

This has grown into a cosy *Remember When* time, stories from the series drawn out by the sounds of cooking and the smell of comfort food. Danger feels very far away.

Since Carolyn's ability in the kitchen extends only as far as buttering toast, Jay lobbed some bread in her direction, and I managed to cut a few tomatoes one-handed and lay the table. Jay moves around the rest of the ingredients with the ease of a swimmer in seawater. We've never shared a meal together. It makes this whole scene seem unnecessarily significant.

Jay picks up the frying pan and flips the omelette in a fancy move without the help of a spatula, but half misses and only saves it from disaster by a slim margin. He looks at me and grins, like he knows I won't take him seriously. Heavens. Cool and serious Jay I can almost handle. Goofy, homey Jay is something I need protection from.

I smile back, glad for the distraction from the muscles in his forearms. He's wearing a knit sweater and has pushed up his sleeves. His knuckles are split from where he punched Daniel, and I imagine the beat of his pulse under the golden skin of his wrist.

I shake myself, hard. This is not me. Feelings like this—no, not *feelings*, thoughts like this—put me in the same category as all those tragic women who are secretly in love with Mr Darcy. And if anyone had first dibs on him it was Jane Austen.

She managed self-restraint. I can too.

I sit at the table and focus on my plate.

'Lenny Blythe.' Jay pushes the omelette toward me and sits down with Carolyn and I. Carolyn cracks up, remembering.

'Oh, yeah, Lenny.'

I laugh too. Book Six was a fun write. 'He had such a weird relationship with his mother.'

Carolyn shudders. 'Blegh. She was nuts. She kept talking about Oedipus, with that sleepy smile of hers. It was creepy.'

'Remember when we were in that abandoned church in Queens and Lenny slipped over on the way to get his bow and arrow?' Jay says, pouring coffee.

'I remember,' I say. The food is so good. I can't stop eating.

'I thought we were never going to get out of there.' Jay shakes his head. 'And then he trips over his own feet and knocks himself out cold.'

'And Carolyn goes, "Whoops,"' I add, as Carolyn beams. I laugh again.

'I told his mother he'd been arrested for stupidity,' Carolyn says, as she scoops more tomatoes onto her plate.

'Even as I wrote it down, I couldn't believe you did it.' It's been quite a ride. I really do love these two. I'm stopped by a sudden realisation. I don't want to write them back in. Especially not…I look at Jay.

'Harding, geez.' He's watching Carolyn feed Ben a piece of toast under the table. 'It gets stuck in his teeth.'

'He looks like he's starving,' she says, turning an accusing glare on the dog.

'It's an act.' This seems to be true, since Ben is hardly rake-thin. He devours his toast and turns big sad eyes back on Carolyn and I.

'Well,' Carolyn brushes crumbs off her hands, 'your dog is a con artist. I can't believe I fell for it. I'm gonna go shower.' She stands up, effectively ending the warm pocket of comfortable camaraderie I was enjoying, and puts her plate by the sink. I haven't finished my food, and Jay and I eat in silence for about thirty seconds before I abandon the last of my omelette and stand up too. I start clearing the table, because sitting there with him feeling all domestic is not good for my heart. Besides, I need my head back in a place where I can write. Enough of this tranquil downtime.

But Jay stands up too, and then we're clearing the plates together, which is even worse. I rush into the kitchen to dump them and escape.

'Don't worry about the dishes, Evie.' He comes too close and eases them out of my good hand. He smiles at me but doesn't move away. Rather he rests a hip against the counter and folds his arms.

'Thanks.' I smile back but avoid his eyes. I'm finding his proximity intoxicating.

'So. You okay?' He asks this so seriously that I know he's at least partly talking about Daniel. Possibly his sharp eyes have seen the glassy, unprocessed state my feelings are in.

'I think so,' I say, aiming for offhand cheerfulness, but it comes out a little forced. I risk looking up. Jay says nothing, and so I add,

'I was marrying him for his money anyway.'

Jay doesn't smile at my joke. He studies me for a moment, and I feel the slice of his intelligent gaze reading my face like a crime scene. The moment feels awkward. My heart starts to beat uncomfortably. He clears his throat.

'Uh, I guess you want to work in the study? You can use my laptop if you want.'

'Um...' I swallow. My fake bravado is gone. This is it. This is where I put him back inside. 'Yes. Thank you.'

It's serious to him, too. I see the deliberate indifference in his body language that's designed to hide how much he doesn't want me to do this.

He stares at me for a couple of seconds. 'Great.' He pushes off the counter.

I steel myself. 'Jay?' And then I don't know what to say, because I didn't really have anything to say. I just wanted to delay the moment a little longer, because my instincts are all pushing me to hold on to this time with him for as long as I can. 'What's it like, not being able to choose?' I want to kick myself.

Jay cocks his head a couple of millimetres to one side. This is another tell of his. It means I've caught his curiosity, and his intuition is amping up. Damn.

His gaze narrows and his lips twitch briefly in the shadow of a cynical smile. 'Well, I like being able to choose better.'

I nod, unable to reply.

'I like it but it feels dangerous.' His voice is low. 'There's stuff I've wanted to do for a while, but it's fragile, here. Things get broken easily. One careless word or action...There's no delete key if you make a mistake. Just because I can do something, doesn't mean I should do it. Turns out not having free will isn't the only thing that can stop a person doing what they want.' His eyes brush over my lips, and I'm reminded of that moment in my car three days ago when he surprised me by doing that exact same thing.

He abruptly steps back and says, 'I'm gonna get the laptop. You need anything else? Earplugs?' He could be joking, but his tone is too lifeless to be funny. 'I can send Owen for some if you do. He's right outside.'

I shake my head, feeling sick with a kind of unnamed grief. I'm grateful to him for trying to lighten the moment, but how can he joke about this? If I write them back inside, then I'll be alone. I don't want to lose them. I don't want them to lose their freedom. I want them to be able to make their own decisions. Carolyn and Jay are like my family. And Jay is...Jay is...

I say, 'If I write the Blade back into this story, that means you'll go back in too.'

'Yeah.' His voice is steady.

I blink at the dirty dishes. 'You know...maybe you would be free forever—'

'Don't.' I see the last ray of a bleak smile. Something inside me twists painfully. 'Don't do that.'

'Right,' I say in a brittle voice, crossing my arms to hide their shakiness. Something is pulling at me from the inside, little hooks all over my heart that are more dangerous than the Blade could ever be. Jay scrubs a hand through his hair.

'It doesn't matter. It doesn't matter what I want. Or what Carolyn wants,' he says, his voice still low. 'There are innocent lives at risk. Including yours. And I can't protect you—*we* can't protect you from him.'

'I understand,' I say, in an unconvincing monotone.

Jay nods. 'Listen Evie, we're not unhappy in there. When you write, you take care of us. It's a good feeling, knowing there's someone behind everything, someone kind. Someone who...cares about us.' Something flickers in his gaze. 'It's gonna be okay.'

But this sets off a tremor in me. *Someone who cares.* Mrs Andrews' words float back to me again. *Something I don't want to write.* What? I grasp vainly for it.

Jay watches me. He moves closer, like giving verbal comfort makes the impulse for giving physical comfort automatic. But he stops before actually touching me.

And I'm relieved. Jay respects the rules, he honours the lines, he does the right thing. I remember the first day he walked into the story, that Monday morning when the Captain introduced him to Carolyn, and he quipped back her little displeased jibe so fast and firmly he had her respect from that day on. Seven years ago.

The best seven years of my life.

And then it hits me. The ending.

I'm crushed by a blast of intangible truth. I feel it like a mushroom cloud in slow motion.

I see the end. Not the whole plot, not the way there, but the end. New understanding drowns me. It's like being born under a waterfall.

'No,' I breathe.

'What?' Jay's eyes rake over me. 'What is it?'

Book Sixteen is the last book. And Jay dies. The series ends with his death.

'No,' I say again.

'What is it, Evie? Tell me.' He steps forward and puts his hands on my arms, and it's close to unbearable. I clasp my hand over my mouth like it will keep the truth in. 'Tell me,' he repeats.

'It's the ending,' I whisper, through my fingers.

'You see it? You can write it?'

I shake my head again. Tears start pooling, and I start to babble.

'No, I can't. She was right. Mrs Andrews said something to me, that there's something that's stopping me from writing. I've just been so...*blocked.* She thought...she said...it was because there was something I didn't want to write.' I try to stop there, to stop talking, and find I can't. 'And then I...it just came. I saw it. I do know what has to be written. I know what the bigger picture is. I know how it ends. I've known all along.' I stare at him, blown bare by nameless horror. 'This is the last book. It always was.'

His look of disappointment would be devastating enough, but he says, 'And?' Jay is too smart to think that's all there is.

The words won't stay in.

'And you...die a hero.'

His hands fall from my arms. I don't think he takes a step back, but it feels like he does. *I can't write it.*

He looks away from me, into a distance that's further than the wall or the window, his eyes pure blue.

'I see.' His voice has flattened out.

'Jay, I—'

'You gotta finish it,' he says. 'It's the only way. You'll be safe.'

No rage. No questions. He doesn't ask me how I think I have the right to take away his life. He doesn't tell me I have to change the ending, or even ask me if I can.

Can I change the ending?

'I stand by what I said,' he says. 'This isn't about what I want. And I trust you.'

'Jay.' It comes out on a sob. The sight of his face is blurry with tears. It's not normal, that kind of...that level of...what? Courage? Selflessness? Resolve?

Not normal, but not a surprise either. Part of me is desperately grateful for this predictable nobility of character. It's like a refuge, a place of safety and stillness. But another part of me wants to say, *No, fight! Fight back. Fight*—what? Me? I gulp like a pitiful child and say, 'How did you know I'd written pages by hand?'

He stares at me for so long I think he isn't going to answer.

'It felt different.' He reaches out slowly and grazes one of my fingers with one of his, causing a frission of sensation. Our two hands hang in mid-air a moment, as if magnetised, his brown, mine pale, before he pulls away.

'Write the damn story, Evie.' He turns and walks toward the study.

33

33

I hold my stomach, feeling sick.

This isn't right. How can this be? Why this ending? I have that certainty in the pit of my stomach, like always, that this is how things are.

Jay dies in the line of duty. The series ends. But what, or who, gave me that certainty?

Where do the stories come from?

Like all the writers I know, I've always felt like I was tapping into something bigger. Cosmic, even. The characters show up and the story starts flowing and I have that hot flushing, hands shaking, unearthly feeling of inspiration blasting through me. Of loosing something other.

But where is it all coming from if it isn't from me? Who's really telling this story?

Jay trusts me. And yes, this is what writers do. They use their characters to achieve their ends. Does that mean I have the right to kill somebody?

I pick up the pile of Carolyn's clothes and bolt to the bedroom. It's slightly cooler in here. I take a breath. Ben is lying on the bed in some kind of post-breakfast coma, and I sit down beside him.

Innocent people are at risk.

Innocent girls, I realise.

Another of those shattering grenades of information bursts inside my chest. That's the deeper meaning of the Hello Kitty brooch. It's made for young girls. It's why I had that feeling about *the source*. Bobby Laidley wants to destroy a whole generation of women, not just one or two. Whatever he's planning, it's going to involve killing children. Little girls.

I change into Carolyn's clothes. Both jeans and top are skin-tight. Carolyn doesn't see the point of buying clothes that don't show off her assets, so although my skin is covered my body feels very visible. Not exactly a writer's smock. And no liquorice.

No matter. I can do this. I can ignore this storm inside me, and write. I've had plenty of practice—almost nine years of avoiding any kind of reality—channelling all feelings into words on a page and managing, masterfully, not to experience any of them. Ever since my father died it's been so easy to keep my heart clamped down and forge all my emotions into books.

So here we go. Words. The next part of the story. Any part of the story. I close my eyes and will away the dryness.

I hear the bedroom door open, and look up to see Jay come in.

'I'm coming,' I say, glad for the reliable, granite edge in my tone. I don't have feelings. I have people in my life and I have a job to do. Jay closes the door and walks toward me. I frown. 'What...?'

He picks me up by the waist and walks me backwards until I'm pressed against the bedroom wall. Then he puts me back down and looks at me.

It's a look that silences my question, and takes my breath away. He leans in, and kisses me.

Holy.

Turns out I was wrong about Jay having no passion. This kiss is like being caught in an avalanche. But not snow. Heat.

His mouth is hot and unyielding, and he pins me to the wall with his body. This isn't the patient, controlled man I've written about for seven years. This is someone else. And this person's mouth and body, which feel so good against mine, are pushing at all the carefully compartmentalised parts of my consciousness, making me feel...

I start to struggle. Jagged fear is fluttering around behind all the closed doors in my heart. I wanted them closed. I prefer them closed. I push against his chest. I'm not choosing this. I had decided not to feel this.

He pulls back, and we both gasp for breath like two people in hand-to-hand combat. His eyes are the colour of the sea in a midnight storm.

'Why are you fighting me?' He sounds both wild and confused.

Great question. I feel like I'm fighting myself more than I'm fighting him. But I can't articulate this as sudden tears press behind my eyes, tears I don't fully understand. And so rather than let them fall I grab for anger.

I open my mouth to tell him—anything. Anything that will make him leave. There's a quick change in his expression—he sees things too clearly not to register my intention—but he drops his eyes away from mine and looks down. When I follow his gaze, I see what has drawn his attention. It's my own traitorous left hand, clutched in his sweater. I stare at it. It's as if some unconscious part of me is trying to hold him close even as I'm desperate to push him away. I make a huge effort and tell my fingers to unclench themselves, and they do.

'I see,' he says. His voice is flat and dry. I can't see his expression. 'Did you wanna tell me something, Evie? You wanna tell me you don't want me to kiss you? You wanna tell me I'm not real?' He looks up and I realise I was wrong about him not being angry. And I'm pretty sure he has more reason to be than me.

I squeeze my eyes shut as hard as they will go, like a terrible coward. Maybe it will work this time. Maybe he'll be gone when I open them and I won't love him. But I can't bring myself to truly try. I don't want to wipe him away. I want him here, and when I open my eyes again, still breathing hard, he's right there. His look is hurt and resigned, and tender. It's a tenderness I don't deserve.

I stare into this, locked into the truth of his feelings, as he says, 'No.' He brings his face closer to mine. 'It's my turn to choose. You're not going to get away with this. You're not going to avoid this for one second more.'

I stare at him. 'This?'

'Me.'

He dips his head, and I'm aware of a visceral surge of hope, thinking he's going to kiss me again, but he doesn't. He just hovers, too close. His lips are only a breath from mine, like an offering, or an invitation, and he waits, as still and steady as only Jay can be. There's a hungry tempest in my bones that's starting to shatter me. Is he going to stand there all day, implacable, like a wall? The beat of each millisecond feels like an hour, until I can't help myself any longer. I lean in and press my mouth to his.

He ignites beneath my hands. It's that same avalanche of earth and heat and reality, the kiss burning between us. His mouth is so insistent and full of unsaid things that I start to lose my grip on whatever it was that I was keeping back from him. He presses against me and kisses me harder, with lips and tongue and teeth. My feelings are finding the surface, and they're blazing out of control. It's like trying to defend a small stick-built village from a battery of heavy tanks.

Why was I keeping them from him? I don't remember. I'm lost in the sensation of him. He hooks a finger in the neck of Carolyn's sweater and pulls it down over one shoulder, drops his head and brushes his lips there. Holy. My breath leaves me, and my hands slide into his hair.

This is better than writing. Who would write when they could experience it with their own skin, feel the beat of someone's heart under their hand? I've never felt so present before, or enjoyed being alive, and real.

He senses the change and lifts his head to look at me, and that's the moment. The truth is in my eyes, and I can't hide it.

'I love you,' I whisper. We're both breathing hard. I cannot write him back in.

He sighs deeply and puts his arms around me. My lips are against his neck, just like I wanted. His pulse isn't exactly even, and I can feel the strong thump of his heart in his chest. I care so much about that heart.

'I love you too,' he whispers. He leans back to brush a gentle finger over my cheek. 'I've watched you for seven years,' he says. 'I've loved you for seven years.' He swallows. 'If I had free will, things would be different. That's all.'

He kisses me again, only this time it's all softness and sweetness, and so tender I feel tears prick behind my eyelids. His hand is at the back of my neck, his other arm tucking me tightly into him. And I'm holding him tightly too, like I'm going to lose him. I'm kissing him back like it's my last chance to show him how I feel. I realise that this kiss, which has all the elements of desperation and endings, feels like a goodbye kiss.

Because it is.

I hear a voice from the doorway say, 'Hmm.'

We jump. Carolyn is standing there, disapproving. 'Guys. This isn't exactly a plot twist.'

Jay steps back like he's been caught stealing evidence. I'm reeling from the reminder I've just had, every cell in my body rebelling against it. *Goodbye.*

'Cap's on the phone for you, Ryan.'

'Yeah.' He leaves the room.

Carolyn keeps her eyes on me as he goes, then raises her

eyebrows further. 'You think that's smart?'

I don't know what I think. I put a hand to my mouth. Certainly Daniel never stirred up such crushing things in me, just nice fillips of pleasant anticipation or enjoyment.

Because I was in love with Jay.

Carolyn is closing the door when I say, 'Wait.'

She stops. 'What is it?'

'We have to keep Jay out of this.'

She regards me. 'Why?'

'He's in danger. I'm not sure how, but we have to do something. You have to help me keep him away.'

'You think that's possible? Ryan's his own person, Evie. Maybe you didn't fully realise that, writing him. But he makes his own decisions. And he knows how to make smart choices. Despite what just went down here.' She raises her eyebrows again. She thinks I'm just starry-eyed and in love, I realise. Or tanked on emotions and hormones, like she was with Gareth. She doesn't know what I know.

'This is important,' I say. But her face is impassive.

'He can take care of himself.' She pulls on the door. 'He knows what the stakes are.'

What are the stakes? I wonder, as the door clicks shut. If Jay dies, does that mean I can't write him alive again? I think about it. Tillman died. And I know, somehow, that he's dead for good. Dead here, means dead there. And dead there, means never coming back here again either.

I slump down on the bed. I poke Ben, wondering that he slept through that whole passion tsunami, and realise that he's really out of it. Like, unconscious. Or *actually* unconscious? Weird. I look closer and see a tiny silver needle, almost invisible in the fur around his jaw. What? I feel a sudden prick in my neck and go to scratch it, and my fingers come away with another silver barb.

Like a sewing needle but finer, and without the thread.

I look up. No wonder it's so fresh in this room. Jay's bedroom window is open. My ears are ringing, and I vaguely realise that my vision is clouding. Huh. And I can't move. Oh no. Distantly I feel my body slump to the floor.

Too quick-acting to be ketamine. Too little dosage to be sodium thiopental. Etorphine? I watch, paralysed, as two black-clad legs drop into the room from behind the blind, aware of how hard my heart is beating and of rising nausea, the sign of rapidly dropping blood pressure.

Two milliseconds of panic before my vision goes dark.

34

Full consciousness is slow in coming. I lie in a groggy half-state for ages, convinced I'm inside a hurricane. I have the sense of wind blowing around me but my limbs and skin are numb. What was in that dart? If it was Etorphine, it would have to be measured in nanograms. But maybe the guys he hired are that good. I mean, they had to be good to blow that dart straight into the vein. That's not easy. And they had to be good to vanish me from the room.

How does one find such people? Ninja-abductors.com?

I become aware of a cramp down my left arm, which seems to be caught behind my back, and my broken wrist is throbbing. My face is planted into something hard but smooth. I crack my eyes open. It's dark, but I can see it's piles of paper, and I recognise my own handwriting. My notes. The cyclonic sound I can hear is some of them blowing around the back of the vehicle I'm in, being driven at speed. I'm mashed among the metal footings of some brown vinyl seats, half in the well near a sliding side door. So some kind of bus or van. I cling to my hard-won awareness. The wind is coming through two open windows, one on each side. But attempting to look through these gets me nowhere, as my ankles are secured firmly to my arms, behind me. And I've been gagged.

This is it, I realise. Everything I've ever feared is in motion at this moment.

It's just the Blade's style to disappear me out the window. I bet all the plainclothes cops guarding the street are either dead or have little needles in their necks. What does he plan to do with me?

Well, there's no question, really. Kill me.

If I could write something, maybe I could save myself. I grope around behind me as gusts of wind blow more of my notes from their folders. But there's nothing but ancient brown carpet around me and it's too awkward in any case, with my hands secured the way they are.

We brake to a stop. My notepaper dies mid-flight and settles in ghostly drifts around me as my heart rate lurches into a painful gallop. I know there's no point trying to scream through the gag. He wouldn't bring me anywhere that my screams could be heard.

The van makes a slow, sharp turn with a bump, like we're pulling in somewhere. I hear the crunch of gravel and the sound of a second vehicle creeping along behind us. The van stops, and a second or two later the second vehicle stops too. I hear both cabin doors open at the front, and the creak of two occupants sliding out. The doors on the vehicle behind open and softly close. Crunching footsteps, and the low murmur of a voice, then another in brief answer. None of it sounds rushed or furtive to me, just careful—professional.

The side door flies open. This is it. I squeeze my eyes shut.

'Aww, come now. There's no need for that.' The Blade sounds gleeful.

He's here. *I'm going to die.*

I force myself to open my eyes. A weak interior light has come on with the open door, and there's the barest hint of daylight outside. Dawn maybe. It's enough to see him by. His ill-fitting suit is the same brown as always and too big. I'm struck afresh by how Bobby doesn't look anything like a maniacal killer. More like a weedy public servant with too much debt and no imagination. You would think, being a narcissist, that he would take more care with his appearance. But he's brutally, intelligently aware of the effect he has on people. This look holds all the boyish appeal and harmless innocence he could desire to achieve his aims. It set the girls at ease.

'Well, hi there,' he says, speaking at normal volume, and quite cheerful. 'Here we are finally. You and me, after so long.' I force myself to meet his gaze, and he smiles, also cheerfully, which sends a glacial slide down my spine. I want to squirm further away from the door but I'm wedged. I try to look past him to see what kind of place we're in, but he's taking up the whole narrow opening of the doorway. Can I hear the ocean? He sees me looking.

'What are you looking at, little girl? Penny for your thoughts?' He chuckles, apparently gladdened by this little cliché, and not bored in the least by his one-way conversation.

Penny?

'Ah,' he says, seeing my expression, 'you found my little clue, didn't you?'

The stamp. A penny black. I should have known he had another meaning layered in there. 'I thought it was real nice and fitting,' he continues. 'To give you a penny for all those little thoughts of yours. All these years, wondering what you were thinking, wondering what you were going to dream up next.' He makes me feel like the word *dream* is poison in his mouth.

He lifts his left hand slightly, as if to emphasise the point, and I see he's clutching a thin sheaf of papers, gripping them so hard he's crushed one end into deformity. As I focus on them I catch a written phrase. Oh, no. It's a section from my notes, the part I wrote about his childhood. The page or two where I jotted down every awful thing that happened to him, as it came to me. It must look like a list of torture to him.

I think I'm going to try screaming through this gag. Even if no one hears me, I can't just lie here and do nothing.

'Oh, dear,' Bobby says, sounding anything but concerned, and causing me an unpleasant, slithery sensation. 'Not enjoying having your hands tied? It's hard to see all the things you'd like to do, all the places you'd like to go, and have someone else decide for you. It's a hard lesson to learn, isn't it?' As he speaks he crumples the sheaf of notes in both hands, crushing it into a deliberate ball, staring at me the whole time. His breathing has changed, become laboured, as if he's imagining something that excites or angers him. He tosses the paper ball over his shoulder with a giggle.

My heart is thumping convulsively, and waves of terror-spiked adrenaline are leaving me weak and shaky. I would like very much to burst into tears but I'm too scared. Bobby opens his jacket with a little swagger, pulls an old-fashioned switchblade out of his pocket and opens it. I recognise it, and the tears begin regardless. He stole that knife from his father's toolshed the day he killed his parents. It's the one. The one he always uses to cut the girls.

I see the breathy thrill of excitement glitter in his eyes. He's going to slice the skin open on my neck, nine neat incisions. He always marks the girls. It's his tally.

'Hold still now,' he says sweetly, as he moves nearer.

No.

I want to struggle and thrash but I'm stuck in place. And I know it will only make it worse. This is his favourite part, the part that brings him the most satisfaction, even more than killing them. I hold myself still. Maybe I can get away—maybe I can change the outcome. But not until he's done this. He's going to be happier afterwards, pleased with me. I might be able to talk to him. Submitting is going to make me feel dirty, and weak, but it will be worth it.

It might be worth it.

I feel the first sting like a caress, and grit my teeth on the musty gag, trying not to whimper. Is this what it feels like not to have free will? This shaking horror and shame? As if my very essence, everything that makes me good, makes me valuable, is shrivelling and crumbling into nothing?

I squeeze my eyes closed. *He never cuts deep*, I tell myself, as I feel the next. They're just marks. Nothing more serious than paper cuts, enough to be noticeable when the body is found, that's all. This part is the least violent of his whole sick process, really. But I can hear his excited breathing, and I'm aware of the rush he's feeling as he gets to prove his power over me.

Eight, nine. Are the cuts bleeding? The answer is a little warm drip down my neck. I unclench my teeth and gasp in a ragged breath or two.

'There now. All done.' He steps back into the darkness. I hear his eager breathing for a few more seconds, as if he can't stop looking at his handiwork, and then two big guys step forward, their faces covered by black balaclavas. This gives me a shock. They're dressed in black too, and I would probably spend some time pondering where ninjas buy their uniforms if I wasn't feeling the burn of those nine marks in my body and my soul. I'm overwhelmed by their nearness as they grip hold of my arms and legs, and by the instinct to struggle as they pull me out of the van.

The reaction to forcing myself to lie still while he cut me expresses itself in a kind of wildcat resistance now. There's panic too. I mustn't let them take me to the place he plans to kill me. Once there, he'll be too hungry for the outcome to listen to me.

I struggle so much that whoever is holding my upper body loses their grip and I hit the ground with my shoulder. It hurts, but it wakes me fully out of my stupor. And beneath my shoulder the ground feels like pea gravel. What do they use pea gravel for? Driveways? Garden paths? I can definitely hear the ocean. Loudly.

But I can't see anything except an inky sky and some kind of formless, bushy landscape.

The ninjas take a better grip of me. I thrash, but I'm lifted and carried, and wherever we're going they seem keen that I get a scratch from every prickly bush we pass. Which there are a few of. As well as swaths of what might be overgrown lawn. Is this a garden? It's almost light enough to see, but not quite, not enough. How long was I out? Twenty-four hours? I guess Bobby made sure I stayed unconscious long enough to suit his timing. Seaside murders are undoubtedly best executed in the night-time. Pun intended.

There is a slightly off-key note that sounds like the whine of an iron gate opening, and then we burst out into the open air. Oh no. No. This must be it. I struggle afresh, but I'm held too securely.

There's a wild wind blowing, and the rush of waves is deafening. The ninjas drop me and I hit the ground hard for a second time. Onto concrete. I absorb the jolt, and peer around in the blur of the gloomy shadows. We are at the top of a cliff, I think. I can make out a wire safety fence beside me, the tracery of the metal in the darkness like a cage or a spider's web. A little further along there is a sign, probably advertising danger. In the opposite direction, the direction we came from, is a tall fence of sharpened iron palings, shrouded thickly behind by vegetation, possibly a hedge. There's no moon, and the dawn isn't advanced enough to add depth to what I'm looking at. But I think this might be somewhere I recognise. I've seen this place.

This is Rhode Island, one of the cliffs around Newport. I've been here before. There's a popular cliff walk here, miles of pavement skirting the edge for tourists. My aunt and uncle brought me to see it when I was sixteen years old and new to the States. It was a good day. It had been sunny and they were kind, and seeing the wild shoreline kind of eased the wildness inside me.

The ninjas must have carried me through the grounds of one of the many stately mansions that border the coastline. No wonder they weren't in a hurry, or worried about me screaming. Some of the properties in Newport are preposterously vast. Maybe they knew the owners were away. Maybe they killed the owners.

These cliffs are about twenty metres at their highest point. Maybe I could survive that. People have survived more. Maybe I could scream my lungs out when Bobby takes the gag off. Or maybe I could be an undignified discovery on the rocks for an unlucky walker later this morning, with my limbs all wrenched and twisted. Great.

That's how I'm going to die. A vertebral compression fracture. Or maybe by drowning. Wrists and ankles wound with electrical tape. Or maybe a fractured skull. Death by ninja.

Interesting way to go.

But no. He'll strangle me. He strangled all of them, at least the eight he counts.

The two guys who carried me have melted away into the darkness but another ninja tramps past me, his arms full of something. I watch, weirdly sickened, as he ducks through a ragged hole cut into the wire safety fence not a metre from my feet, and continues across pale, uneven stone to the verge. The horizon is a black, slick line before him and I imagine the breathtaking drop, the grisly waves making a mess of the stones below. I squint, and see the ninja lift the pile he carries to throw it over the edge. Sheets of paper go swooping on the wind, separating and flying out like dying seabirds. My notes. All that hard work gone. That's ten years of diligent thought and the regular repression of difficult emotions.

And this destruction communicates Bobby's intentions more clearly than anything else. The slithering fear in the pit of my stomach increases. My lungs are frozen, like lumps of ice in my chest. He wants to erase me. *Erase the source.*

My skin prickles and I realise he has knelt beside me.

'Any last words?'

Another ninja—which I think makes four—pads silently past and, with a small metallic chink as his clothing scrapes the wire, more of my notes explode. The Blade's eyes look black in the gloom, and although his voice is soft it's also flat and offhand. As much as I've tried to avoid knowing him in the last decade, I recognise what's going on inside him. It was the same for all the girls. I don't provoke any feelings in him other than a sense of his entitlement to do what he wants with me, an acknowledgment of his power over me, and a recognition of his superiority. His main desire is for me to comply with his expectations, because his sense of his own greatness is so strong.

I see the white of his smile in the dark. 'Surely *The* Miss Crime Writer must have some memorable words? You know I always let them have their final words.' He giggles. 'Because you wrote it.'

I try to writhe away from him but I don't succeed in getting anywhere. The safety fence is too close. I'm flopping on the ground like a worm, terrified, and I loathe myself.

'Now, now,' he says, and I can hear him smiling, enjoying it. He has loved this whole game. He's fed off it.

'Let's get rid of this old thing.' He bends down, slides the cold blade of his knife beneath the gag and saws it, scraping my cheek with the blunt edge until it gives way. I gulp air for a scream, but as he pulls the putrid cloth free he uses his left hand to place a vice-like grip on my neck. It isn't enough to totally cut off my air, but it's enough to stop me screaming. The feel of his skin touching mine is sickening, and his grip causes the cuts below my ear to pull and sting.

'Now, do you have any words for me or not?' He's speaking to me like a naughty child. His hand releases pressure just a fraction.

I scrabble together the incoherent terror beating about inside me and try to force it down.

'If you kill me, you disappear,' I breathe. My words are without substance, but he hears them. He twists his head, like a cobra coming in for a look at its prey. All the girls try to talk their way out. He gives them this moment, and all of them ask him, beg him. Every single one of the girls he killed. I feel his fingers clench around my neck.

I use all my will to speak. 'You disappear,' I repeat.

Of course, I don't know this for sure. But he can't *not* know it for sure. None of the other girls had a single speck of power. But I do. I try to put a triumphant look on my face.

'No,' he says. 'I've got a life of my own, now. You die,' he uses his right hand to hold up a finger, like a numbered list, 'the story goes unfinished, and I stay here.' He holds up two more fingers and smiles, gladdened by his own logic. 'That's the beauty of it, darlin'. We all have unfinished stories. Well, except yours. Yours'll be done.' He cracks up laughing, as if he's told a terrific joke. 'And then, in less than twenty-four hours, forty per cent of the girls aged between five and fifteen in this state will be dead from nerve agent poisoning. A little bonus. An ugly way to go, but quick. I'd say that's a good beginning, wouldn't you?'

So I was right.

'Why are you doing this?' I ask. I feel sickened but I want to keep him talking. 'Why women? Why girls?'

He *tsks*. 'How can you of all people ask me that? But maybe you never realised how I met Morton.'

Morton Tillman? I frown, not understanding. The Blade hates women. But I don't see what that has to do with Tillman. They met when the Blade was twenty-three. At the time Bobby was halfway through ten months in Rikers for petit larceny which he was caught and convicted for soon after moving to the state, though under his false alias as Ronald Harvey's son. That jail time was the only mistake he ever made, and one that yielded him a wealth of knowledge and contacts. That was right after he'd killed Nancy Last, his first girl. He'd enjoyed killing her, but he hadn't killed her because she was female. He killed her because she piqued his pride. His somewhat brittle self-opinion had been only slowly hardening into princely certainty back then. The next two women he took came soon after, trips back to Jackson to take revenge of past hurts, 'thrill rides'. They made him feel powerful.

'What does Tillman have to do with it?' My voice is a whisper.

'Oh, honey, you don't know? Tillman was the one who told me about you, Evie.' His use of my name makes my skin crawl. 'He told me all about you. He'd been to your house. The girl who thought she could control me. The girl who thought she had the right to decide what happened in my life. *The girl* who took away my freedom.' It's definitely getting lighter, because I can see spittle in the corners of his mouth, and all the cold hatred toward his parents in his eyes. 'I realised what a sick, conceited plague you really are. No one takes away my freedom.' He smiles.

He's done all this because of me? Disbelief crowds into me.

'Because you couldn't kill me?' I gasp.

'You deserved it. But so did they. You were the one who made me realise how much.'

'Did you kill Tillman?'

'He needed to be taught a lesson.'

'He betrayed you?' My voice is broken, but his fingers have slackened the tiniest amount. I feel a tiny sliver of hope.

'He went and made a fuss with that PI. Trying to draw attention to me. Almost ruined Polton for me.'

I frown. 'Edgar Polton?' I say. 'What does he have to do with it?'

'Oh dear. You haven't figured out very much, have you? Polton was my best effort so far.'

Agh. Comprehension comes in a sickly rush. Bobby *was* Edgar Polton. An assumed identity. Meaning the real Edgar Polton was an unfortunate casualty of the Blade needing to stay invisible. He could be anywhere. I'm assuming dead.

'What happened to him? Did you kill him?'

The Blade flicks a hand. 'He was in the way.'

And Orson Bidgood, the private investigator hired by the real Edgar Polton's business partner to investigate the real Edgar Polton, he was just a guy in the wrong place at the wrong time. He must have been sneaking around, and so Bobby sent Tillman after him. But Tillman made a fuss, put Bidgood on show, and included *The Voice* so Carolyn and Jay would come asking questions. He was trying to tell them to take notice of Polton. *And me.* Tillman was trying to make *me* take notice.

But I hadn't. I hadn't bothered taking the time to look closely at Polton. I didn't recognise him, so neither did Jay or Carolyn. Carolyn had dismissed him as a marshmallow. They had the Blade, and they never knew it.

Bobby's grin widens as he sees understanding dawn on my face.

'He was a funny little fellow. I enjoyed being him. The kind of man no one would ever suspect, *ja*?' He says this last in a perfect Afrikaans accent.

'I'll give you whatever you want,' I say, as desperation pushes up in me. Because this is it. He's finished his evil-guy monologue. He's bragged about his genius. All he has left is to get on with the task of killing me. I try to keep my voice level, not fall into pleading. 'Money, land, power. I can, you know. You could be the richest man on the planet. You could be king of your own country.' But it's a mistake. This angers him, and he roars, squeezing his cold hand around my throat, pushing his face into mine.

'I don't want a country. I want my freedom.' He lets go and slaps me, hard, with an animal snarl.

'No one has freedom,' I rasp, gasping for air. 'Not really. Not the way you see it. That kind of freedom doesn't exist. In the real world, everyone's freedom is dictated by consequences, and you wouldn't have me around to manage yours. You can't hurt people and get away with it. Either internally, or externally, you will suffer consequences. It's cause and effect.' But this logic only enrages him more. He lashes out to grasp my neck again, squeezing, but this time he takes a handful of my hair with his other hand, too, and uses both to spin me clockwise so my head is facing the hole in the safety fence.

'I'll take my chances,' he growls.

The hard ground is taking the skin off my hands and arms, still secured behind me. I see, very near, the sharp edges of the crudely cut gap in the wire. 'Help me,' he commands someone nearby, and there's a scrabble of movement out of my line of sight, and several black-gloved hands on me. I struggle as I'm half shoved and half lifted through the hole, then scraped another metre to come face to face with the crumble of the edge. There are no plants here, only dust and gravel. The crash of waves is impossibly loud. My instinct is to use what movement I have to thrash backwards, away from the drop, but Bobby grabs me by my hair again, at the temple, and turns my head so that I'm looking down at the grey rocks below. They look sharp. I have tears running down my cheeks again. I'm actually snivelling.

I don't want to die.

'You're nothing but a writer. You're as human as anyone else. I kill you, and all it means is...'

'If I die, you disappear,' I pant, empowered by some final throb of desperation. 'That's how it goes. It all disappears. All your plans. You can't take a risk like that.' I've given up trying to sound brave. I'm pleading, my voice high and frightened. Begging for my life from this psychopath, who loves every second of it. In theory I knew how his victims felt, but this terror is more consuming than I could have imagined. 'You don't know for sure that killing me won't change everything for you. None of your plans will happen. Everything you've worked for. I know it matters to you.'

He growls, furious. He's strong, and he shakes me. I think he's going to hurl me over, as the wind dries out my eyes and the foamy crash of waves goes all blurry in front of them. 'You don't know,' I say, like a chant. 'You don't know for sure. You can't risk it.' I close my eyes.

I feel myself dragged back by my collar. Relief rushes through me as I look up into his contorted expression. 'You can't risk it,' I murmur. I have no strength left to struggle. Has he changed his mind? I watch him draw back his foot like he's going to kick me in the face.

35

I stare hard at the bottle of water. I have a thumping headache, either from dehydration or being booted in the face by Bobby's cheap loafer, but I'm alive. And I'm so thirsty I could die.

But the seal has been broken, and I'm too scared to drink it, so I've been staring at it for the last hour. I know Bobby put it in here to torture me.

I'm in a small white-painted room with one tiny, high window, one door, and sawdust on the concrete floor like there's been a spill of some kind. I tried the door but it's locked, with two brand-new deadbolts.

I look up for the hundredth time, searching the corners of the ceiling for a CCTV camera, and again I don't see one. I can only assume that Bobby didn't expect to be keeping me alive in here, otherwise he would have arranged for there to be one. He wouldn't want to miss this.

I look back at the bottle of water. Is it laced with sarin? If it was I wouldn't know. Sarin is endlessly soluble in water. I'd be dead before I put it to my lips. But maybe drinking it is better than waiting around for whatever Bobby has planned for me.

No woman has ever survived the Blade. Not when he set his mind to killing her. Only the threat of losing his own life has been enough to stop him, and it has won me a little more time, at the very least. But he must be furious.

I massage my temples. I have the blurry memory of Mrs Andrews' voice floating around my mind. I can't remember what she said, but the echo of it is comforting. My wrists are unbound, though a sticky residue remains from the electrical tape, and one of my feet is bare. My boot is upturned across the room, like it came off during transport and one of the abductors just tossed it in here after me. I guess the ninja service doesn't extend to shoe replacement. I haven't bothered to put it back on. Instead I've spent an unknown portion of time staring at the water bottle and crying my eyes out like a great big baby.

The thing is, I've spent most of my life being afraid. And where did it get me? Dead, almost, and into this tiny prison cell. But I was in a kind of prison already, too scared to go outside, too scared of a real relationship, too scared to live. Yes, I lived some grief as a child. But did it have to affect the rest of my life?

I push myself up against the wall and ease into a standing position. I hobble over and put my shoe on, and then use it to kick the wall in frustration. My head is killing me. I can see the bottle of water out of the corner of my eye.

In a rush I lunge over, sweep up the bottle, throw off the cap and guzzle the whole thing. I stand there and blink as if I'm about to see that bright light everyone talks about. *Am I dying?* I take an internal catalogue. No sweating or saliva or tears. No agonised cramping of muscles, breathing difficulty, or heart overstimulation. I'm alive.

I did it! I experience a moment of heady euphoria. Ha ha!

But it's gone almost instantly. I'm still in here, trapped. If only I could do something. Anything! My gaze catches on the sawdust.

I regard it. The floor is concrete, and it looks like there was a leak in here at one point, and someone emptied a pile of sawdust onto it to soak up the liquid. Hopefully nothing toxic. I sink to my knees and brush the very tips of my fingers over it, feeling how loose and dusty it is.

I don't want to be afraid any more. I don't want to be the victim of my circumstances. I want to *do* something, as Carolyn said in my car the other day. I want to break something.

I feel something inside. A glossy kind of electrical newness. This is the same feeling I have when the story starts to bubble inside me. A zing of knowledge or understanding. Or power.

Does scrawling words in sawdust count?

Doesn't matter. I'm going to try anyway. My hand hovers over the shavings, one finger extended, my broken wrist blocky and immobile in its bandages. This is it. Book Sixteen. Chapter Three. Writing the story is the same as exerting my will over theirs, Mrs Andrews said. This is my chance to end this whole thing.

No words come forth, but that's not going to stop me. The Blade is going back inside, along with his whole Evil Incorporated conglomerate.

And Carolyn.

And Jay.

And...nothing. The well-known emptiness scours through me.

'Aaaaaaagh!' My cry of frustration sounds like wind in leaves, thanks to my damaged throat. I wrap my arms around my knees, rocking a little.

I still have Mrs Andrews' voice rolling softly around my mind, probably connected to some kind of concussion from when Bobby kicked me in the face. The memory of her advice comes into focus. Something about writing my own story.

Ye must keep writing your own, dear.

My own?

I'm pretty sure Mrs Andrews was being metaphorical. Of course she was. You know, be the lead character in your own life, *carpe diem*, that kind of thing. But it turns out I've got some skills with making real stuff happen, when I write.

An idea is coalescing. Maybe I could apply those skills...to myself.

Er...Okay? Worth a try. But what is my own story?

I hunch back onto my knees, and my finger hovers again. I press it into the sawdust, and mark the letters carefully.

Evie is

I pause. And gather myself. What am I? What can I be?

brave.

I poke a period in. Better make sure I've got proper punctuation happening. This is my story after all. Aim for excellence. I pause again, and close my eyes, searching inside for some kind of difference.

Nothing.

All my feelings, everything, are exactly the same. These three words have no power. Why?

There has to be more than this. Somehow, everything I've written in the last ten years has turned into a kind of alternate universe. That's not a normal thing.

I grit my teeth. But I don't make the stories. All I do is write them down. The inspiration either flows or it doesn't.

So if I'm not the one who creates the stories, then logically, whoever or whatever does probably knows my story too. All I have to do is let it flow.

I scrub out what I wrote, smoothing the sawdust back into place.

'Let's do this,' I mutter, wondering if I really am talking to some kind of cosmic force that's about to blow through me like the glorious fiery affliction I feel at the start of a new story.

Or, you know, to myself.

I let out my breath and let my mind open.

I start with 'I'.

I am fearless.

It's almost a shock, but it feels right, and the buzz I'm familiar with fizzes unexpectedly up. My hand starts to shake and my skin gets hot.

I keep going.

I am strong.

Wow. It's violent perfection. It's orchestrated chaos. It's like sliding star-bound on sheets of raw...something. I remember what Jay said the other day, that I know how to do a lot of things. I just never do any of them. Maybe there's no reason why I can't put what I know into practice. And learn some new stuff too? So I keep going.

Words cover the sawdust, and I have to write smaller. My lettering gets firmer as I go. Details come. This sense of flooding inspiration is how it used to feel, back when Jay and Carolyn were at their best. It's the part I enjoy the most: the flow. The visceral sense of power and ability.

As I'm nearing the other side of the room, I realise my head has cleared. Huh.

I stand and brush the sawdust off my hands by wiping them on my jeans.

Something has happened.

I'm not entirely sure what. But something is different.

Am *I* different? I bounce on my toes, feeling loose and agile. I do feel stronger. I take a look at the far wall.

I gather myself, push off my toes, and run straight at it, feeling strength inside. When I get there I use the momentum I have to step one, then the other foot onto the wall, and as I gain height I fling myself backwards into space, a quick twisting flight, efficient as an acrobat. I feel the full control I have over all my muscles, as if I'm aware of every single one. My knees bend as my feet connect with the ground. I take a deep breath. I want to laugh out loud.

Holy. I can backflip off a wall. I mean, it's one thing to write about physical strength, and it's another to...well. Do that. There's a slight pressure in my neck, so I tip my head to one side and it cracks with a satisfying click. I smile.

Time to do some damage. I check the door behind me, focus my senses and listen for the sound of someone coming. Nothing.

Could I...? Would it work if I...? I take two running steps and slide baseball-style to the floor at the end of my last sentence, thinking fast.

I have

Can I give myself something tangible as well as skills and courage?

Well. Here goes nothing. My handwriting gets messy as I scrawl. I think I prefer a Glock, given the choice. And I don't want a compact pistol. I want a Glock 17. If we're going full supernatural here, might as well be specific.

I finish the sentence and take a breath. I reach behind me, still holding my breath. I slip my hand to the back of my jeans.

I can't believe it. There it is. I pull it out of my waistband and hold it in my hand. I just *wrote* a semi-automatic handgun into existence. I check the magazine. Yep, seventeen rounds. I snap it back.

On second thoughts, no. This is way too real. And it's not like I could shoot anyone. I put the gun down and brush the words away with my hand.

When I look again, the gun is gone.

Heavens. I see. Words have power. But this is crazy.

That gives me an idea, though. About things I *don't* want. A few

seconds later my clunky splint is gone. I look at my bare right
wrist and flex my fingers. Maybe...

I try writing away the glass from the tiny window, but nothing happens. I'm unsure what that means. Maybe it's that I can't
change things around me, I can only change myself?

My story. Me.

So I won't be writing the door open, I guess. I brush those
useless words away and consider a rifle, just for show. But what
am I going to do, a big Butch Cassidy and charge out of here with
guns blazing? No. Who knows how many people there are in this
building. I glance up at the window again and decide.

I'm going out through there, through that little slice of possibility, and I'm going to get the police here as soon as I can. Not
to mention the whole freaking military. Ooh. How about now? I
write a little more and pull a phone out of my pocket. Ha! I love
this. But then I realise, who do I call? It's not like I know Carolyn's fictional number off by heart. I don't even know the number
for dispatch at the Ninth to get them to put me through. Never
mind. There's no time. I'll call 911 once I'm out of here. My prior-
ity is getting away.

I slide the phone back into my pocket and look at the tiny
window. Hmm. Pity I can't write a folding ladder into my back
pocket, too.

But when I leap for it, my fingers make the ledge, and when I
pull myself up, my body coordinates on its own and my arms work
with minimal effort. I *am* strong.

The ledge is wide enough to pull my knees onto it and balance
there. Now that I can see out, I realise this room is really high up.
The angle is awkward, but the vibe I get is of an abandoned industrial park that got built during a boom, and which has the air of
a post-apocalyptic city, streets and fences and offices, all self-con-
tained and separated from the rest of humanity by kilometres

of unwanted real estate. Probably this place was founded in the 1800s, remodelled in the 1950s, went out of business in the nineties, and has been accumulating black mould and property value since then. We could be in Red Hook, or anywhere in the nearest three states. Or maybe this whole place didn't exist until recently. Maybe it landed here right out of fiction.

I can see there's a blocky Holland-style building beside this one, like a red-brick six-storey factory, and probably the one I'm in is identical.

There's a padlock on the catch holding the window closed. No one can say Bobby isn't thorough. But I thought of this already, clever me. I slide a little slim-line set of picks out of my other pocket. I choose two of the smaller tension tools and push them into the padlock. I manipulate the pins, twist gently and...bingo.

I ease the window open and push my face outside to see if there's a way to climb down. There isn't. Red bricks sheet smoothly away in every direction. I assume there are windows on this side of the building, since I'm sticking half out of one, but from this angle I can't see them. They will be recessed like this one maybe, without any fancy brickwork jutting out to announce their existence or provide a handy foothold. In any case, they're probably spaced too far apart to use for climbing, even if I have become some kind of supernatural instant-gymnast.

About a metre to my right I see a drainpipe that runs the whole height of the building. Happily, it looks like every drainpipe in every action blockbuster ever made, and everyone knows what happens when the hero puts their weight on it—the rusty screws detach from the brickwork and the whole thing goes plummeting backwards.

I twist on the ledge and put one foot and then the other through the window, and lower myself down so I'm hanging from the outer sill. I'm not certain that what I'm attempting is a good idea, but I swing my left leg sideways and manage to get a foot dug into the other side of the pipe. This increases the pressure on my fingers, which are taking all my weight. About this time I realise that writing myself a nice sturdy zipline with a good solid stainless steel claw for an anchor on the sill would have been smarter. Or some of those sticky gloves from *Mission: Impossible*.

Note to self: be more creative.

The pipe is painted the same colour as the building, and I reach for it with my left hand and manage to touch it with the tips of my fingers. With my left foot I feel a bracket on the further side of the pipe, about in line with my shin, and slightly loose. I jam the solid toe of my boot between it and the bricks, just in case.

As I do this, my right hand begins to slip from the sill. My fingers slide toward the rough edge of the brick as my weight, pulled awkwardly by my foot on the pipe, drags me down and I grab hopelessly with the fingertips of my left hand on the metal surface of the drainpipe, trying for a hold. But my arm isn't long enough and all I achieve is to send a few desiccated flakes of old paint fluttering into the breeze before my right hand loses purchase and I do a breathtaking plummet into gravitational acceleration.

I clamp my feet together on either side of the pipe, but this isn't what saves me. My left foot, wedged into the bracket, gets stuck, and so my body has an anchor as it drops out and down. I also feel newly strong core muscles engage to slow this process, which means I don't end up plummeting to my death, but rather tip backwards until I thump into the pipe with my back.

Holy. I hang upside down, breathing. Probably I should have written *I am graceful*, because that move was major amateur hour, and now there's about six storeys of fresh air between me and the ground. The view is dizzying, and my left foot, jammed behind the bracket and taking all my weight, is killing me.

I blink. There must be a loading bay on another side of the

building, because I see a blue van pull around the corner and drive away. This gives me a bad feeling. Is this building bursting with criminals and chemical weapons? Then I see another van. And another. Oh, no. Am I watching nerve agent get shipped out to unsuspecting women and children? This galvanises me. The thought of the Blade actually succeeding in his hideous ambition because I'm stuck on a pipe is too much.

Why didn't I write *I am a ninja?*

I become aware that my butt is vibrating.

The phone. Lucky Carolyn's jeans are so tight on me or it wouldn't have stayed in there. I manage to slide it out and get it to my ear without dropping it.

'Hello?' The tone of my greeting is a little short and unfriendly. In my defence I'm quite busy.

'Evie?'

I frown. 'Who is this?'

'It's Jenna.'

Seriously? If I hadn't been upside down, I would have checked the screen.

'How did you get this number?' I ask.

'This is your regular number.'

'Oh.' Clearly I'm a genius. 'Listen Jenna, this really isn't a good time.' I eye the sheer drop stretching away below me. My face is heating with the blood pooling in my head and it isn't a great feeling.

'I thought you'd say that, but I had to talk to you.' She sounds like she's crying, and has been crying for a while. 'I've been trying to call you.'

'Okay, that's really nice Jenna, but—'

'I went to your house. It was all burned.'

Some encouraging news I didn't need to hear right now.

'Jenna—'

'Evie, I'm sorry,' she chokes. She's definitely crying and doesn't sound like herself at all. I've never heard Jenna so...broken. She's always chic and together, like a shiny hard plastic shell and not a real person at all, I realise. A stick figure. 'I can't believe I did that to you. When he came on to me like that, I just lost my mind. I don't know. Not that it matters. There's no excuse. I'm sorry. I know what I did is horrible. Horrible. I'm so sorry.' She's babbling, and deep inside me I'm a little touched.

'Jenna! Okay, yes, that's all fine. I appreciate the call. Lovely. I forgive you.'

'I think it's just that when I realised you were sleeping with that guy, the hot detective guy, it made me think...I...I don't know what came over me.' There's a pause, while I gape. 'Are you still with him?'

'Jenna, I wasn't...' I sigh. And then I say, in a rush of personal growth, 'Yes, I'm with him. I love him. I love him with all my heart.' Wow. Despite the fact that I'm suspended above certain doom, that felt really good to say.

She hiccups. 'I knew it. I'd never seen you look like that.'

'Like what?'

'That morning, at your house. You looked so...alive, or something. Happy. You never looked like that with Daniel. And so I thought...'

'Right.' I roll my eyes, which isn't all that comfortable when they feel like they're bulging. 'Good work, Jenna, conscience clean. I'm sure you and Daniel will be very happy together.'

'No!' There's a series of huffs, as if she's sobbing. I wonder how I ever thought I knew her. 'He broke it off with me.'

'Oh.' That's not a huge surprise, I suppose. 'Well. Probably for the best,' I say. 'He was a giant asshole after all, and as you said, a colossal, stupefying cliché. So I forgive you, and we can move on from this. I need to ask you a favour. I need your help.'

'What do you need?' She hasn't returned to her old self but she does sound like she wants to be helpful.

'I need you to call Detective Carolyn Harding at the NYPD and tell her to ping my phone. This phone. Tell her that Edgar Polton is the Blade. Tell her she needs to put every girls' school, girls' club, women's group and female *anything* in the state on high alert. And tell her that they need to get some choppers in the air looking for a bunch of blue courier vans. Bright blue, with painted back windows.'

There's a pause.

'Are you making fun of me, Evie?' Her voice is quivery and disbelieving.

'No!'

'Detective Carolyn Harding?' she chokes. 'The Blade? Really? You are making fun of me.'

'No I'm not. And believe me Jenna, by the time you've finished helping me you'll wish I was. We need to SAVE NEW YORK.'

36

Okay, so maybe that last bit was a little forceful and dramatic.

In any case, Jenna hangs up on me. And when I go to handle the phone, it slips out of my fingers and I watch it spin majestically down to the ground to smash into a million pieces.

'*Crap*,' I announce with feeling.

It's time to go. I'm starting to get nervous about being found up here. If Bobby's in the building then no doubt he will want to look in at me soon, just to enjoy a tickle of pleasure at knowing I'm trapped in his web. And I left that window wide open.

So, enough with this clumsy stuff. The good news is that I don't feel afraid. All I feel is a thousand points of data flashing through my mind at once. So writing 'fearless' worked. But how do I get down? If I grip the pipe with my hands, below my head, I could release my feet and my body might fall into an upright position? Except that my head will be in the way as my body swings downward with gravity. But maybe if I could do it in such a way that it happens sideways? Like doing a cartwheel more than a somersault.

Either way, I don't see what my other options are.

I put my hands behind my head and grab onto the pipe. Whatever happens, I must not let go with my hands. I must focus all my energy there. I wiggle my butt to the side of the pipe where my foot is wedged but keep my head locked on the other side, so that my hands are slightly uneven. My feet are going to fall outward as well as down, but I might be able to control this. I try to wiggle my left foot out so that it releases my weight.

Everything happens very quickly as my foot comes loose. I feel my abs engage, and as I fall, I'm able to curve my body and use the distance between the pipe and the wall as a space for my head, which means I don't break my neck as my body flips over, but I also don't create too much outwards velocity and lose grip with my hands. In fact I grip so hard that as the front of my body thumps into the pipe, I stay stuck there, clinging like a mollusc.

I'm not dead.

In fact, I'm right way up and ready to go all Spiderman and shimmy down this thing. Or at least, to perform a weird upright crab method, where I alternate gripping with my knees, feet and hands in stages, part sliding, part squirming, while muttering encouragement to myself. The struts hold—thank you, unintentional starvation diet—and when I get a foot on the ground I take a moment to kick my phone innards into a weedy crevice and run. Like an Olympic sprinter. I want to get away from here as fast as I can, and I want to find out what's in those vans.

This is an old industrial park, I was right about that, the kind photography students gush about in their nerdy blogs. The buildings are crumbly and historical, and empty, I think. They are useless to me, other than blocking the sight of me from Bobby Laidley.

I head in the same general direction I saw the vans go, and find an overgrown grassy area and beyond that a high wire fence. There are reels of razor wire twined over it, glinting bright silver. New. So I won't be getting over there fast enough to stay unseen.

There's also a gate in the distance. I crawl through the scratchy undergrowth for a while, to get closer, and get a good dose of burrs and grassy hay dust in my lungs for my trouble.

Aha. As I suspected, someone is doing guard duty. There's a little booth to keep the guard nice and comfy in the late spring sunshine. As I watch, another blue van heads out, and I squint to make out the writing on the side.

KCI Courier Service. The lettering is white, the font fresh and elegant. *KCI?* I frown as this reverberates in an odd way, like it's familiar. As the van gets to the gate it stops, and I watch a stocky figure amble out of the guard shack and chat briefly with the driver. As he turns, and his single earring glints in the sun, I recognise who it is.

Johnny Diamond. Small-time petty thief and all-round scumbag through Books Two and Three. I smile. Because if Johnny's here then so is his fabulous bike. I risk sticking my head out of the grass and spot it, slouched in the shade nearby. A black Ultra Limited, buffed to perfection. That's 103 cubic inches of glorious gut-wrenching Harley-Davidson, and my ticket out of here.

I wait until the van is through the gate and then snake my way over, counting on the fact that Johnny is almost certainly the worst guard in history, because any time he sits still he immerses himself in game-hunter blogs. A tiny peek through the window affords the view of a sweaty slice of butt crack as Johnny leans forward, scrolling his phone. Two silent seconds later I'm at the bike.

In theory I know how to hot-wire one of these, but damn, it's a big bike. It's black, and sticking half out of one of the panniers is the polished walnut stock of a gun. Excellent. It's the Winchester, an 1897 shotgun Johnny stole off a wealthy collector a decade ago. Thank goodness he doesn't have it with him, or I would be risking a spray of shot as I rode past his door. Or worse. Maybe he has slugs in there.

Looks like I get to Butch Cassidy this after all. I pull the gun out and slip it into the leather strap meant for a pillion, praying it will stay put during transit. I swing my leg over, which is like climbing onto a leather sofa, and brush my fingers over the massive polished petrol cap set in the centre of the body, and the two little glowing gems artistically pinioned into it. If I'd had any doubt about whose bike this is, those diamonds are a dead give-away. And they give me an idea.

These bikes start with a keychain fob or, in the absence of this, a numbered code, and a lot of riders don't bother changing the factory setting of four zeroes. But Johnny loves this bike too much to be that careless. And I know what else he loves, almost as much.

I kick the stand, click the ignition over, and start alternating indicator buttons to input the numbers one, two, zero, seven, his mother's birthday. Johnny Diamond loves his mother, more than the Winchester, and more than anything except this bike. He's going to be so mad. His darkened Oakleys are there so I put them on, because I'll need eye protection from the wind, and I clunk his smelly helmet onto my head too. I push the starter button and get enveloped in a giant honeyed roar. The feel of the engine rips through me as I hear a yell and I see Johnny's face appear in grimy window. But he isn't going to be fast enough to stop me. I squeeze the clutch and click my left toe down into first, rev the guts out of it, let my left foot brush the ground for balance as I make a tight circle around the shack to line myself up with the gate, and burn out of there in a spray of dust and stones.

37

I squeeze the throttle and fly after that last blue van. Because by the time the authorities find a KCI vehicle and haul it over, the rest of them may already be at their destinations. I need the facts on the Blade's plan. And I think I know the driver.

Johnny Diamond wouldn't look up from his reading material and leave that guard shack for just anyone. He would wave the drivers through, barely lifting his eyes. So the driver of this particular van must be an associate of his. A friend. And Johnny Diamond only has one friend.

I press into upper gears, the rasp of high-speed air currents snagging my cheeks. The emptiness of a failed industrial area peels off into a low socio-economic neighbourhood, complete with potholes and boarded shopfronts.

There isn't much traffic. The van is almost alone on the road. And whoever is driving is obeying the speed limit. I can picture some written instructions outlining this, obediently destroyed before leaving the depot. If the Blade is the one giving the orders, he wouldn't give them in person. He's not a leader. He's a controller. A manipulator.

But somehow, I don't think he's the one giving the orders. I bet whoever is writing his cheques is organising the people stuff. Bobby might have had the vision for this operation, and he might be loving the way it's turning out, but I'm unsure how much of the string-pulling in this show is actually him. Regardless, he has to be stopped.

I catch up fast, narrowing my eyes against the air snaking in around the Oakleys, and think of Rodney Boyle, the man who had my father killed. He was a controller too. He was a huge, muscled bald man, with fingers like tree roots and a bespoke set of knuckledusters, and he controlled people to such a degree that, even from prison, he could decide that a man must die, and that man would die. Rodney Boyle had decided he wanted my father dead, and my father is dead.

But my father didn't die for nothing. Because there's me, and I'm not going to stand around being a victim anymore, while people like Rodney Boyle or Bobby Laidley have their way.

The van stops at a set of lights. It doesn't run the yellow. It is conspicuously not drawing attention to itself.

I have visions of pulling in close and slamming my fist against the driver's side window to get his attention. But in reality one Ultra is more than enough bike for two hands, especially for someone my size. It's made for big hairy men with beer guts that work like leather-vested ballast. I'm too lightweight for fancy moves. So I punch down through the gears until I come up slow behind it. I put a finger inside the helmet near my ear and loosen it, and then follow the van sedately like any ordinary rider. And as I do, I wonder for the hundredth time what's inside it.

The blue paint job is clean and professional. Not a law-enforcement blue, but a catchy commercial colour that looks like a new business trying to draw clients with their speedy up-to-date services.

I keep a safe distance behind, my eyes on the rearview mirrors. The van has a high roof and a long wheelbase, and it's not hanging low at the axles, which means the load is light. Not a massive, aerosolising bomb then, to be parked, set and abandoned in a target-rich environment. Although it doesn't take that much sarin to hurt a lot of people. *Is* it a bomb? Could the driver touch a button and arm it from the cabin? I have to assume no. Bobby is more subtle than that. He likes elegant crimes, a beauty and fittingness that takes more than an average brute to execute.

About three blocks further on, the van slows to a smooth law-abiding stop for another red light. I pull the bike around it with a burst of throttle and slam to a stop right in front, blocking its forward path. I'm counting on the driver's surprise to buy me a couple of extra seconds, and it does. I kick the stand, plant my foot and swing my other leg over the seat in a wide arc behind me, and slip my helmet over my head so he can see me. My hair is loose and I shake it out, and beam a big winning smile into the windshield, like I'm some kind of swimwear supermodel on wheels.

Like I know him. Which I do.

I keep my eyes on him, drop the helmet to the ground from my right hand, and with my left pull the Winchester out of the pillion strap. I swing it up and around until the shaft hits my right hand and at the same time I step up onto the front bumper, which puts me at eye level with driver. I jam the stock into my shoulder, rack the slide, and fire a round into the empty passenger seat.

The windshield splinters as a hole the size of a golf ball crashes into existence. It's got slugs in it, like I thought. The glass holds, though. Front windshields are mostly glue. In my peripheral vision I see passers-by duck and scream and run for their lives, away from the crazy girl with a shotgun. And I also see, through the blasted, sticky hole, that the driver is exactly who I thought it would be.

Wade Best. A nice name for the short, wiry man scrabbling one-handed toward the place he usually keeps a weapon. But I'm counting on the fact that he doesn't have one. The Blade wouldn't want anything out of the ordinary to cast suspicion on his drivers. Plus he doesn't care about their welfare.

'Don't, Wade.'

His left hand stills, but I see his right itching toward the stick, thinking to buck me off with a short stomp on the gas.

'*Wade*,' I repeat in a motherly tone, and I *tsk*. Something in my expression seems to stop him. Maybe he recognises Johnny's gun.

Wade Best is a cook and a father of two. Sweet, in theory. In practice he has the hard red skin and deeply drawn lines of a man who has spent decades in the elements, roughing up and occasionally killing enemies, the hard mouth of a lifelong smoker and the hard eyes of a dedicated meth-cooker. His two sons, both about my age, run the business for him, pumping out hundreds of thousands of dollars' worth of innocuous-looking, life-damaging substances a year in clouds of phosphine gas.

He's pretty minor-league, but nonetheless Wade Best is all about money. And I bet he's thinking that if a little girl with a gun gets in the way of his payday then she has to expect the consequences. So I rack the slide again and aim the gun through the cracked glass so it's pointing straight at his hard-skinned nose.

'Hands up.' He points blunt fingers toward the roof and says nothing, evaluating. 'Get out of the van,' I say.

His dark eyes, like shiny little baubles in his leathery face, spark at this, and he opens the side door and slides out. I jump down to meet him.

Wade doesn't take his eyes off me. He's wearing a uniform, a new button-down shirt and pants, both blue, with KCI logos, and a cap.

'What's in the van?' I ask. I keep my eyes fixed on him, but his are all over the place, and I'm betting there are people behind me, peering round corners, finding safety in numbers and probably calling the police. Good.

I repeat the question.

'Take a look and find out.' It's the first words he's spoken, and they show off a full set of nicotine-stained teeth beneath his impressive moustache. Then he smiles.

'No,' I say, 'you're going to look.' I use the barrel to point, much like Carolyn did with me a couple of days ago. Wade regards me for an insolent amount of time and then turns and walks that way, following the length of the chassis, without any hint of fear, which at least reassures me that the back isn't wired with some kind of booby trap. I refrain from nudging him with the muzzle and ask, 'How many vans are there in total?' He glances over his shoulder at me.

'What, at the company?' he says.

'No need for games, Wade. I want to know how many vans Bobby Laidley sent out today.'

He blinks. 'Who?'

'How many?' I ask, in the same tone as before. He doesn't answer. 'Where are they going?' I had made that guess about girl's schools and clubs. There would have to be about a hundred and fifty all-girls schools in this state alone, and it would make a convenient way for the Blade to be specific about his chosen target range.

Wade reaches the back, then turns and smiles again, ignoring my question. 'It's locked.'

'Where are the keys?' I growl.

'In the ignition.' He grins again. He knew that, but he walked all the way down here anyway.

'Listen Wade,' I say patiently, 'I don't have to put lead in you to kill you. There's a lot of things I could do to you that will hurt a lot more.'

Wade doesn't blink. Behind me, far in the distance, I hear the sound of a police siren. 'I could threaten your sons,' I say, 'who, though you have never once verbalised the words *I love you* within a hundred kilometres of them, you would defend to the death. Maybe a car accident. Maybe cancer. I could burn your house down with your business inside it. Or we could go the other way. I could have you win a nice long cruise to Antigua. I could make you invisible to the police. I could make Mandy love you. Just tell me what I want to know.'

Wade still hasn't blinked. In his defence, he's not the kind of man to exhibit facial expression when he's coming to the conclusion that he's talking to a crazy person. The sound of the siren is getting closer, and for the first time it occurs to me that it might not look so good, holding a neatly uniformed courier at gunpoint in the middle of the street. I need that van open.

Wade shifts his weight.

'I don't know who you are, girlie. But you're in way over your head.'

I'm running out of time. I consider shooting Wade in the leg, but at this range the damage from a rifled slug would be catastrophic and he would bleed out before they could get an ambulance here.

'Okay then,' I murmur, 'it looks like I'll have to kill you. Or maybe I should just shoot the lock off.' I lift the sight toward the handle of the back door in demonstration.

Wade twitches like a marionette that just had its strings jerked. 'Don't do that.'

Ah. I'm pretty sure Wade knows the damage a 1oz slug at 1800 fps would do to the lock on that van. In fact, it would blow through the whole contents of the van like a torpedo, shattering whatever containers or mechanisms are in there, releasing their contents or exploding their triggers. Looks like Wade doesn't like the idea of asphyxiating on the street in a cloud of evaporating sarin.

'Talk to me, Wade.' He seems to evaluate, though staring at his face is like examining a brick wall.

'There's a key in my pocket.'

'Then get it out,' I say. 'Slowly,' as his hands start to drop.

He keeps his eyes on me as he reaches stubby fingers into the crisply ironed pocket of his new shirt. He pulls out a key and turns toward the van, and I move around him so that I can still see his hands. He pulls the doors open, and I move again so that I can see what's inside. And frown.

Boxes.

Black heavy-duty plastic containers, stacked into a metal framework set into the cargo area so they act as drawers. The interior looks industrial and ordinary. Exactly the way I would expect a courier van to be laid out. It means the whole of this back area can be at capacity, while still retaining easy access to all the stowed packages. The shelving would also, I think, mean that whatever is stowed could be packed securely and safely in some serious insulation to prevent the pre-emptive release of dangerous substances. I keep the gun up high.

'Pull one out,' I say. 'Show me what's inside.'

Wade leans in and pulls out a drawer. He reaches inside and takes out a white cardboard box, big enough for a cake. I blink at it, and can't help following it with the gun for a second, instead of Wade's skinny ribcage. I can see there's a white, printed sticker on one side, with what looks like the name of a receiver and an address, though I'm too far away to be able to read it, and I'm not about to step up close.

'Open it.'

Wade does what he's told and tugs its folding lid loose, lifts it, and reveals the contents.

A gift set.

An elegant gift set: an expensive-looking box with a glass front containing scented hand sanitiser, soap and potpourri. The whole effect is sweet and feminine. The dried petals are in their own meshy little drawstring bag and have been dyed to make their colours prettier. There's a small earthenware bowl and a bottle of essential oils to augment the fragrance.

The world goes silent while I examine this, my mind racing. Where's the danger here? Did I get this wrong? And yet, I couldn't have.

I glance at Wade. The careful, conscious way he's holding the box tells me there's something very wrong here. And based on some hasty calculations, I'm guessing there are about a one hundred of these boxes in the van. Every last one of them filled with freaking potpourri.

Potpourri. Perfect for freshening a room. Perfect for aerosolising a scent. Or anything else for that matter.

'Where were you going with this, Wade?'

'I don't know anything.' Defensive. 'I'm just delivering packages.'

'Yeah, I know. You're innocent. But who were you delivering them to?'

'Run sheet's in the cab.' He smiles at me again and I resist the urge to throw the gun down and throttle him.

'Was it a school, Wade? A girl's school?'

He says nothing, and to the untrained eye there's no alteration in his expression. But mine is not the untrained eye. I see the microscopic flicker in his marble-hard look that's nothing less than a flash of surprise.

I glance back at the box. Those little glass canisters of 'essential oil' would be a perfect carrier for GB. And I'm betting the hand sanitiser bottle contains a healthy dose of GB too. Give this gift pack to a teacher and the first thing they will do is pump some onto their hands, for quick relief from grimy kids. Imagine what happens when instant collapse occurs and all the children in the class come running, only to touch or inhale the chemical as they bend over their fallen teacher.

It's both elegant and utterly fractured, and exactly like Bobby Laidley. I'm guessing the flowers of the potpourri have special meaning for him, something tortured and vengeful. Maybe it's an allusion to the flowers he could see through the tiny porthole window in the basement his parents kept him in most of the time, a private nod to the thin kid he was, climbing the bookshelves and trying to glimpse the outside world he was denied.

I need to call Jay and Carolyn. It's possible these boxes are being delivered to a school at this moment, wheeled in on a hand trolley and given out, like some kind of Care for Our Teachers program. One for every classroom.

It's then, as the ambient sounds from the street around me come back into focus and my brain blasts into overdrive with a *Disaster Aversion To Do* list, that I hear at least three cars screech to a stop behind me. I freeze. A bunch of doors snap open, and I register the sound of the first round jolting into the chamber of a Glock 19, multiple times over.

I see a kind of calculating resignation flicker in Wade's eyes. I lower the barrel of the rifle and look behind me. There are four police cars in a semicircle around us, and their flashing lights are strobing red across the shabby shopfronts on both sides of the street. Men and women in uniform with serious expressions are pointing their firearms at us from behind the shielding of car doors and trunks. These are white and emblazoned with the blue lines and bold lettering of the NYPD, so at least I know which state I'm in.

'Miss, put the gun down and put your hands up.' The loudspeaker is harsh and uncompromising in the emptiness of the deserted road.

Yes, time to put the gun down and get to business.

The breath congeals in my lungs.

38

I'm suffocating. I drop the Winchester and double over. Blindly, I'm aware of movement around me. I'm gasping for oxygen like an asthma sufferer, but it isn't because I can't get any. It's because parts of me are fizzing down to their elements and evaporating into the atmosphere. Like I'm losing myself.

Something has happened. But it isn't sarin.

It was the Blade. The Blade happened. I'm not sure how I know this, but my mind comprehends that about ten seconds ago he threw the door open to the room I was held in, and onto the words I'd scribbled in the sawdust. And he swept and kicked them into oblivion. He already knew I was gone, but his rage hit peak, and he vented it by scrubbing away what I wrote before making his escape from that factory.

All those words about myself, with their unexplained, cosmos-altering power, deleted. And me left a quivering heap in the street with nothing but shaky hands and a sodden clump of terror in the pit of my stomach.

Note to self: write my story on something more permanent next time.

I close my eyes. I can hear Wade talking as I'm pushed down onto the pavement and patted down for a second weapon. It isn't until I feel the cuffs go on that I react. Although technically I guess it's called *resisting*.

'No! Stop! This is a mistake!' My tongue is thick and my thoughts garbled and I struggle, but I'm no match for the blank-faced officer who heads me firmly and unstoppably toward the open door of the nearest squad car. 'Wait!' I yell. Wade cannot be allowed to continue on in that van. 'I'm a terrorist!'

Okay, not my best idea. But all I could think was that Wade would never admit to transporting sarin, and I'm not coherent enough to convince them of the whole story. I start to babble on about how the van is bursting at the seams with chemical weapons, and it produces the desired effect. Tension fires up around me, several police circle the vehicle, and now Wade is being questioned more carefully. I'm firmly escorted right back to where they had intended to put me in the first place, into the nearest squad car.

The door slams closed, muting the noise of the scene outside. I squirm a little, trying to get into a more comfortable position with my hands cuffed behind my back. Nobody told me I was being arrested so maybe I'm not. I'm just *detained*. I'm not sure how long being detained will take. I squeeze my eyes shut and spend some time trying to put myself back together. I know time passes because the cuts on my neck and the bruise on my left cheek where Bobby kicked me start to hurt again, and a faint beating pain in my wrist gets stronger. Is my wrist back in a cast? I try to wriggle it, and open my eyes to look at it.

Curses.

The car door opens, letting in a rush of fresh air and noise. I blink, as if the daylight flooding through is new and unexpected.

'Jay.' I'm half hoarse. The bruises where Bobby squeezed my throat are tender again.

Jay is staring down at me, an indescribable look on his face. He puts a hand inside my elbow and pulls me out of the squad car. I go awkwardly. I've lost all my energy and flexibility, and I'm stiff and sore. He helps me stand upright. I teeter for a second, and he folds me into him.

'Um.' I'm not capable of anything more eloquent, but I'm glad to see him. And it's not like I need to speak. His hand is behind my head, and I feel his lips on my hair. My own lips are pressed up against the little dip in his neck where his pulse beats and that's enough for me. He and Carolyn must have heard the call and come straight here.

'Evie.' The relief in his voice is evident. 'Are you okay?' He shifts me gently backward with two hands on my shoulders.

'I'm okay,' I say.

He leads me a little way from the squad car and I go willingly. Then he stops me, and turns me slightly so he can unlock my cuffs. My arms come apart with an internal scream of relief and I breathe out. Jay stares intently at my left cheek. Possibly it's red and swollen.

'You're hurt. I thought...' He tucks a hand under my chin and his eyes finish the sentence. 'You've been gone for days.'

'What day is it?'

'Thursday.'

Sheesh. Two whole days?

'I'm okay,' I say again, needing to reassure him and that look in his eyes. 'I escaped.'

'How?'

I point my chin toward the glowering Harley. Jay flicks a glance at it and I see the intelligent glint in his eyes sharpen. He knows there's more to that story, probably. He looks me over again and this time his hand comes up to brush back my hair and expose the side of my neck. Oh. The tally. Jay's mouth hardens, and I shrug. There seems to be a world of things in his expression, and there's certainly a world of things I could say about coming so close to being the ninth girl in that tally. But neither of us speaks. Then Jay says, 'Where is he?'

'Close.' I look around, remembering. 'An old factory building, about ten or fifteen minutes away. A big abandoned industrial park.'

'Which is it, ten or fifteen?'

I squeeze my eyes shut, thinking.

'Thirteen. South-west.'

Jay strides off to talk to someone. I sag against the car I'm standing beside. Whoever Jay spoke to barks orders to those near him. I squint. Not whoever. The Captain. He's here. And so are a lot of other people. The place has bloomed with police since I last took a good look around.

I feel a wave of wobbly tiredness. Jay makes a call, talks to the Captain again, and heads back toward me. He looks beat. He hasn't shaved and he has the slack yet tightened movements of someone who's been holding himself together far past the point of exhaustion.

'There's a team heading there now,' he says to me. 'Don't worry, Evie. They'll find him. Every girls' school in the state is on lockdown, and there are half a dozen choppers in the air running down those blue vans. We've already disabled one, in fact, and the rest won't be far behind. ESU is dealing with the contents. Can you tell me how you think he's planted the GB?'

'They're like little gift packs,' I say. 'I think it's in the sanitiser. And the oil bottle.'

He nods. 'Okay, good.' He runs his thumb over my cheek. 'Good. I'm gonna make sure you get to a hospital to get checked out.' He takes my shoulders again. 'You did it, Evie. You beat him.'

I blink at him. I did it. 'How did you know? About the vans and the schools?'

Jay smiles the slightest smile. 'Jenna called.'

Jenna. I sigh, grateful and relieved. Jenna came through.

'Where's Carolyn?' I ask.

'Where do you think? In a chopper with the aviation division.'

I nod. Of course. Like a wolf after prey. 'Is this it?' I murmur. 'Is this really it, Jay?' I gaze up at him, hopeful. 'It's finished?'

As I ask the question I feel the sedan behind me buck a little as someone gets into the driver's seat and closes the door. Someone else comes into my line of vision and stands just behind Jay's shoulder, like he's waiting. He's wearing a suit and tie, not an officer's uniform. I guess the Feds are here too. He's sandy-haired and looks nice. I smile at him. I feel like I want to be friends with the whole world.

'Almost,' Jay says.

'Almost?'

'Evie, is it true you told them you're a terrorist?'

I frown. Jay is holding my fingers in his, which is nice, but there's a handcuff dangling from his other hand.

'It was the only thing I could think of at the time,' I say.

'You know how serious that is.'

'Yes. I know it wasn't smart. I just couldn't let Wade get away with the van.'

'And you resisted arrest?'

'Resisted...ha!' I try to pull my hand out of his, but he tightens his hold. 'I mean, the exact definition of resisted has to be...Okay, yes, I resisted slightly. What else was I supposed to do under the circumstances? You can fix that, right? I mean, clearly I'm not the terrorist.'

'No, you're not a terrorist,' he says, but his tone isn't reassuring.

'Exactly,' I say. 'If anything, I'm a superhero.' I deliver this deadpan, and although I wasn't expecting him to smile, the fact that he doesn't gives me pause. 'Obviously, not the flying kind,' I add. 'I can't be arrested, Jay.'

Jay's eyes shift from mine, and realisation dawns. He takes my left wrist, snaps the cuff on it, and secures my hands in front of me.

I should have known Jay would do things by the book. How annoying that his integrity is the thing I admire most about him.

'Jay! You're not seriously going to arrest me a second time!'

His eyes flick back to me, sharp. 'They won't take you to Central Booking, Evie, they'll take you to Bellevue. You need medical attention.'

'And then?'

'This is Special Agent Henders,' he says, motioning to the sandy-haired suit behind him, who seems much less nice than before. This is a black FBI sedan I'm standing next to, I realise. 'You'll be in the custody of him and his partner, Special Agent Hewitt. Since you've been claiming you're a terrorist, it's their right to question you about that, regardless of the NYPD's stance that you're inno-cent. You understand how the situation works, Evie. He and his partner will take you downtown after you've been seen by a doctor. I know you don't like it, but this way you'll have a guard on you the whole time. You'll be safe.'

'So you're going after Bobby from here? Without me?' The answer is all over his face. 'No,' I say. 'No. I'm coming with you.'

'You're definitely not coming with me.'

'You can't send me away, Jay. You need me! And you don't know what might happen!'

All I can think about is the certainty in the pit of my stomach that Jay will die. Either inside or outside the book. That it's going to happen, and I'm powerless to stop it.

He's implacable. 'Exactly. And that's why I want you as far away from anything that might happen as I can get you.' He dips a hand in his jacket pocket and pulls out a folded piece of paper.

'That—' I open my mouth to tell him it's the dumbest thing I ever heard.

'Do you recognise this man?' he asks, ignoring me. He unfolds the paper and shows me a photo of a person of interest. An older caucasian man. Kind of grey, with dark circles under his eyes, like he works long hours. I squint at it. And something starts thudding in my chest. This is a man I recognise. The circles under his eyes make him look like a ferret.

I remember him. And, I remember Daniel with him. He was the older man I saw Daniel talking to at the Bradleys' social gathering a few days ago. I start to get a bad feeling.

I swallow and hold my voice in check. 'Maybe. Who is it?'

'A suspect for the Blade's backer. We got the documents Carolyn photographed in that warehouse off her phone, and Archer tracked him down. His name is Leonardo Vyper. Does it sound familiar to you?'

Vyper. He sounds like a bad guy straight off the fiction shelves. I stare at Jay for maybe a beat too long and shake my head. My conscience rebels at the lie, but the instinct to keep Jay out of this is too strong. I don't want him to go chasing down leads that get him killed.

Jay stares back as though something in my blank expression has caught his attention. 'There's no clear evidence linking him to the Blade.'

I shrug.

Jay narrows his eyes. 'Apparently he spent some time in Austria with Edgar Polton last month. Did you know anything about that?' I keep my expression blank and Jay continues. 'It was where Polton got his skiing injury. Seems he's got friends in high places. Polton did tell us his parents were well connected.'

My head spins. Jay is talking about Polton and the Blade as if they're two different people. Doesn't he know they're the same person? Did Jenna forget to pass on that priceless piece of information?

Leonardo Vyper is connected to Edgar Polton. Skiing together in Austria, supposedly, though Bobby could have easily faked Polton's broken leg. Which means Vyper is connected to the Blade. His backer? But most importantly, if Daniel is doing business with Vyper, then...what? Is Daniel caught up in this somehow? Has Bobby drawn him into the story?

A nasty uncertainty is creeping up my spine. I have to talk to Daniel.

'Jay—' I'm about to ask him to help me do this when I remember that my goal is to keep Jay as far from the heart of this debacle as possible. And then I remember he's about to arrest me. 'Don't do this.'

He steps closer and goes to put his hands on my arms. I shake him off, but he pulls me into him. He splays a hard hand in the small of my back, and I feel something slide into the back pocket of my jeans. He holds me close to him and speaks softly.

'You should write, if you can.' I pull away from him and do my best to laser him to a pulp with my eyes. 'I have to follow the rules, Evie.' He's nowhere close to pleading, but his voice is gentle. 'I have to work within the boundaries of the world.' He waits until I meet his eyes. 'But you don't have to.' We stare at each other. 'You can make things right.'

He takes two steps back. Henders opens the door of the sedan, takes me firmly by the arm, ducks my head with his other hand, and tucks me into the vehicle.

39

Hewitt starts the engine as soon as Henders slides into the passenger side. I spend the first sixty seconds of the journey rage-sulking, while the back windows cloud up with the righteous steam pouring from my ears.

How could he? How dare he! Thinks he knows what's best for me? The only one who knows what's best for me is me! But it doesn't take too long for the honest edge of irony to split that delusion wide open. The fact is, I don't like having someone else decide what's best for me. Which is exactly what I've done every day for nine years to Jay and Carolyn. To the Blade.

I can't say I even know what's best for me. I know what I want, but that's an entirely different thing. And I can hardly be indignant at being arrested. What I did was really stupid. Why should I get to skip out on the consequences of my own actions? I should have been smarter.

Still. I mean, Daniel would never have...

And it hits me. All Carolyn's quips about Daniel being Mr Perfect were too close to home. He *was* behaving perfectly. Daniel never did anything I didn't like.

On purpose.

And it wasn't kind of him, so much as a tiny bit...manipulative. More the act of someone being one-dimensional and insincere, than someone who loved me. He was always so careful to notice how I was feeling and make sure I was happy. Carolyn complained that he was a fairytale, and now it's embarrassingly clear he was playing at Prince Charming. Never 'I love you,' it was always 'I adore you' or 'you are beautiful,' or something equally head-turning and dreamy.

Yet his insincerity had been enough for me.

Because I had been insincere too? I was more interested in Daniel's warm, ready-made family to fill the void inside me, and content with a boyish billionaire as a happy bonus. And thus lacking a certain scope of honesty about my true feelings, it seems. Which had been enough for him, too, apparently.

But why would Daniel go to such trouble? It's not like I'm in his league. I'm English, but that hardly befits me for the kind of New York aristocracy he's a part of. Fame? He doesn't need that. Desire? Clearly not a selling point, since he leapt into bed with Jenna. It can't be money as I don't have any, comparably. Not the kind of white-water river of it that Daniel has, thanks to whatever English manufacturing company it was whose success meant that three generations ago his family boomed into supersonic wealth.

I frown. Actually, I remember the name of the company. I researched it a while ago, the way I research everything. It was Kent Chemical Industries, a British company founded in 1907 that used to be the largest chemical manufacturer in Britain. It competed with DuPont and IG Farben, producing paint, fertilisers, insecticides and explosives, among other things. I blink.

Paint.

Explosives.

But that isn't all. Now I remember, with the pinpoint clarity of dawning horror, that KCI was one of three chemical companies working on organophosphorus insecticides in the early 1950s that independently discovered their extraordinary toxicity. The first of them to be marketed by KCI, branded Amiton, was later withdrawn as being too toxic.

And then those same compounds became known as the V-series of nerve agents. Awfully similar in effect as the G-series, discovered by the Germans in the 1930s. Of which sarin is one.

I gulp.

KCI was broken up and sold off in 1989, having made millions for the family heirs along the way, some of whom are Bradleys. The fact that James Bradley used the name Amiton for the company he built with his share of the profits is a testament to how much he liked the idea of a substance that obliterated expectations. He'd always been a man who admired power. He expanded into container shipping, financial services and luxury hotels, and now Amiton Corp. is a holding company whose subsidiaries employ some ten thousand people and generates around $4.6 billion in annual revenue.

All founded on the discovery and commercialisation of deadly nerve agents.

How could I have missed this?

Kent Chemical Industries. KCI.

What is the Blade trying to say with this? There's no way his use of KCI is a coincidence. Nothing directed at me—he'd planned for me to be dead by now. This is a little piece of pretty symmetry for his amusement alone, surely. I have to talk to Daniel. Which means I have to get out of here.

I glance around me. I'm pretty sure that what Jay slid into my back pocket was his notepad. He's never without it, and he knows what having something to write with means to me. At least, he thinks he knows.

But it's difficult to get something out of a back pocket with front-cuffed hands while sitting in a car. It takes me several minutes, the whole time trying to be nonchalant and surreptitious, and watching the steadfast Henders and Hewitt in the front. My pick-pocketing skills come in handy. Learning to be nifty with my index and middle fingers means they have a little extra dexterity in sliding a leather-bound notepad out of Carolyn's tight jeans.

I keep it low beside me, and flip it open. Jay's scruffy shorthand is there: the notes he took when questioning Edgar Polton's neighbours. I push the pages forward until I find a clean sheet, and pull out the small pen from its leather holder. What to write?

I hesitate. The shock of having those other words wiped away is still with me and faintly horrific. And I'm not sure I like the person I became last time. I was a little...ruthless.

Was that supposed to happen?

It's possible that being entirely fearless isn't a good thing. A little of the right kind of fear might be healthy.

I breathe slowly out.

I am free.

Left-handed. It's messy, but my cuffs snap open of their own accord with an audible click. I whip my head to the side and glare out of the window like I'm still sulky, just in case Agent Henders wonders what the noise was and decides to turn around. He doesn't.

I slide the metal off my wrists and start scribbling.

I clean myself up—write away the splint, my black eye, and the soreness and dehydration for good measure. I take a chance and try writing a gun into my lap, and it works. So, laps and pockets, good to know. I stare down at it for a beat, then write a phone into my jeans.

Now it's time to get creative. Because the Blade is long gone from that factory. Of that I'm sure. There'll be plenty of evidence there, but the Blade will have disappeared. And Carolyn is on her way there in one of the NYPD's Bell 429s, which means she's heading in the wrong direction. Where is he?

I hover Jay's pen over the notepad. I need to know what's going on.

I glance up, seeking inspiration, and look straight into the shocked eyes of Agent Henders. He has turned around and is staring at me as I sit there fresh as a daisy with a shiny new handgun in my lap and cuffs abandoned on the seat beside me.

'Pull over!' he yells at Hewitt, and the car swerves.

I grit my teeth and shove the gun into the front of my jeans. If I can change everything else about me, surely I can change my geographical location?

Time to find out.

I scratch a hasty sentence, and hesitate at the last word, careening forward in the backseat as the car brakes.

'Henders,' I say forcefully, 'tell Detective Harding to call me.'

I've got to stop leaving messages with distracted people. Henders is slamming out of the car and drawing his weapon. I've run out of time.

I scrawl the last word, and nail the period in place like my pen is a sledgehammer.

40

The air leaves my body in a rush as the ground blasts up to meet me. I'm flung forward onto all fours in the lacquered light of a rooftop sunset, my head fizzing. It's windy, and I'm high up. I blink and look around. It's the Amiton helipad.

Okay, the next time I write an address, I'll be sure to specify the floor. I lurch to my feet, the unparalleled view of a glowing sun-gold Manhattan rushing at me from 360 degrees. Since downtown rooftop landings were banned after 9/11, the Bradleys schedule all their flights out of the heliport on Pier 6, like the rest of New York's busy executives, and so this circle of black tarmac sits abandoned.

I check myself over. The Glock and phone are still in place so apparently that's a thing, but the notebook, which was on my lap, is gone. I'm feeling a bit odd internally but otherwise healthy. I stumble down the tiny flight of steps from the helipad to the roof and sprint over to the door. It's locked, but I grab a small piece of concrete rubble from beside a nearby air vent and scratch a sentence into the faded paintwork. The skewed lettering looks like adolescent graffiti but it does the trick: when I stick my hand in my pocket there's a big silver security key in there. Ha. I *am* creative. I fit it to the lock, and it turns smoothly. I experience a tiny inner swell of rational discomfort, like the last mew of my logical brain fighting the impossibility of all this. But there's too much to do right now to indulge in wonder. I pound down the twelve sets of stairs to Daniel's office.

I burst onto his floor, panting. There's bustle here, the two receptionists at their solid oak desk beneath the twelve-foot brass Amiton logo, and a handful of well-dressed employees visible in the long glassy corridors to the left and right, giving the place a sense of refined efficiency. Amiton is one of those work environments where the staff don't like to be seen leaving for home, even late in the afternoon. James Bradley can be quite imposing, I guess. His business runs with the precision of a Swiss timepiece.

I greet the receptionists, who know me, wishing for a moment I had written a hair tie into my pocket along with that key. I'm sweating and scuffed, but I ignore the little glance they give each other, stick my head down and walk straight into the wide entryway set into the wall beside their desk. This doorway is recessed in such a way that it's invisible from most viewpoints in the reception area, and the passageway behind, named The Avenue by an uncommonly pretentious architect, is angled so that the destination can't be seen from the entry point. Once inside it widens out into panelled wood, brushed steel and a myriad of cosy downlights. But it's basically just a shortcut that leads directly to the most important offices on the floor, and I walk down it like I'm very rushed and important, which obviously, I am.

I make it to the tastefully designed open area at the end, which serves as a receiving space for prized clients as well as a waiting room for people visiting James or Daniel. One wall of this is all glass, giving sweeping views of the splashy sunset reflections of the surrounding buildings, and the other wall is exposed brick covered in the framed splotches of a Jackson Pollock. I sprint across the polished concrete floor, through the artfully arranged three-piece sofa in natural tones, narrowly avoiding a priceless bronze sculpture and almost tripping on the designer rug before arriving at the oversized mahogany doors that lead to Daniel's office. These were stolen from some ancient church in Italy, which Juliana's husband brought over when they married. They clash with the rest of the industrial, designer décor on this side of the building, but I guess James Bradley, whose office it used to be, didn't really care about fitting in. Or, you know, World Heritage listings.

Daniel's secretary is here at her own desk, pink shellac nails clicking on her keyboard. She's very pretty, her blonde hair shiny and sleekly styled. Her expression is dispassionate.

'Hello, Evie. What a surprise to see you here.'

'Hello Ellen, is he in?'

She nods. 'He is, yes, but he's just in the middle of a short meeting with James and Eileen—'

The sound of Daniel's raised voice makes it past the muffling of the huge doors. Ellen stiffens neutrally in her yellow Chanel power suit and gives me a manufactured smile. 'I'm sorry, Evie, but you'll need to wait. You understand.'

I hesitate. Ellen is one of those unrealistically toned women who keep a taser in their top drawer and does hours of kickboxing after work. I briefly wish I'd written the ninja thing again.

'The hell she will.'

I spin and get the shock of my life. Magdeline is stalking toward us, looking like a gold Amazonian goddess. She must have been standing by the wall in the waiting area, but now she's towering over Ellen and I in velvet skyscraper heels.

She folds her arms, and her tiger-eyes zero in on me. She nods. 'So you know he's sleeping with Jenna?'

I blink. I suppose I have that look about me. 'Yes,' I say. 'I found them in bed together.'

'What a cliché.'

'Yes.'

'You called the wedding off?'

'In a manner of speaking,' I say.

'Good for you.' She looks sincerely pleased for me, and I feel quite touched.

'How did you know?' I ask.

'Daniel came on to me once.'

'Oh.' I had meant, *How did you know it was cancelled*, but that works fine too.

'Actually twice,' Magdeline corrects herself. 'Once about three months ago. The second time about three days ago. The day right after my boyfriend broke up with me. Daniel wanted me to "check" that the ice sculpture was going to work for the wedding. Like that's a thing,' she scoffs. 'Why did you think I was so awkward about planning your wedding?'

'Oh, I, um,' I clear my throat. 'I thought, er...never mind.'

'He's also sleeping with Ellen.' Magdeline points and Ellen's mouth drops open.

'It that true?' I gasp. Ellen begins stuttering something but I find I'm not interested enough to wait for her to finish. His secretary. The wedding planner.

'He's an asshole,' Magdeline states matter-of-factly, and then she sighs. 'I'm so tired of assholes.'

'Do you know what they're arguing about in there?' I ask.

'You, I expect.'

Warm and fuzzies. My proxy-parents standing up for me, after discovering their son is a spineless baby-man. I hope they've been giving Daniel a good deep-frying.

'He asked me in for this meeting,' Magdeline says, 'as a "family friend". He wanted me to tell James and Eileen how "strangely you've been behaving".' She gives a tiny smile. 'I told them about Jenna instead.'

Wow. I re-evaluate my opinion of Daniel's intelligence and

also his troubling level of self-confidence. I also feel a poignant moment of regret at not giving Magdeline more credit all this time. She's sensational.

'Thank you,' I say sincerely.

I take a step toward the doors but Ellen bounces up like a rubber duckie Death Star and glides to a stance in front of them. I purse my lips, but Magdeline has my back. She looms toward Ellen like a warrior princess.

'I'll hold her,' Magdeline growls, and makes a move like she's going to immobilise Ellen's arms, maybe permanently.

'It's okay,' I say, and pull the Glock out of my jeans. 'Just step out of the way, Ellen.'

'Evie!' Ellen looks flabbergasted and sidles fearfully to the left. I heft myself into Daniel's office.

The huge doors make a big entrance impossible to avoid. Mr and Mrs Bradley turn to gape at me, there brandishing a gun like an out-of-control cowgirl, and I'm aware of a blanket of tense horror that strangles the room for a moment. It's the kind that's laced by fear because of the presence of the Glock, but also the awkward, superior kind, that hints I'm making a terrible faux pas in this place of security and luxury. I whip the gun out of sight and shove it back into my jeans.

'Evie!' Daniel shouts. Daniel's office is obscenely spacious and all windows, so he's backlit behind his tennis court-sized desk. Upsettingly, he's wearing my favourite suit of his, a grey Valentino, and has his hair neatly styled. He looks extremely handsome.

'Darling!' Mrs Bradley is wearing soft blue linen and moves tentatively toward me in a way that tells me she was very shocked by the gun. But her eyes are also full of regret and apology. 'Is everything alright?' She gives me a hug and I hug her back, grateful, feeling the press of her pearls against my collarbone and the softness of her cheek as it briefly brushes mine.

'What are you doing with a gun, Evie?' Daniel sounds shocked, but doesn't wait for my reply. 'Didn't I tell you, Mother? You said yourself she was odd at the fitting. She's behaving outrageously. Bringing strange people into my apartment, one of whom physically attacked me! Tell them, Evie!'

Well. He really did call his parents in here to make me look bad in front of them. He really didn't ever love me. I step awkwardly back from Eileen.

'Yes, I'm afraid that's more or less true,' I say.

'Darling,' Eileen speaks straight to me, in a kind tone. 'Daniel told us the whole story. We're perfectly capable of reading between the lines.' I look in her lovely dark eyes.

'You know about Jenna?' I murmur.

'Yes, of course. And Ellen. And all the other inappropriate women Daniel's been involved with in the last ten years. He is our son, but I'm sorry.'

'You can't dictate to me who I'm with, Mother,' Daniel interjects.

Eileen sighs. 'No, apparently not.'

'Daniel,' James Bradley's uncompromising tone comes from the other side of the room, where he's been observing us. 'Enough of this.' His suit is black and double-breasted, the kind businessmen wear to look serious for a distasteful task, like firing someone. He's radiating anger, and his presence seems to loom. 'You're going to marry this girl. You don't deserve her, or anything else we've given you, it would seem. But you're going to learn, once and for all, what it means to be loyal. Loyal to family, most of all. As I have explained to you, what we Bradleys do not do, is cheap flings and social scandal. We do not draw attention with frivolous, pointless actions. What we do, what we show the world, is decency and class. Our agenda is bigger. It's not small and selfish, like this.' He points a threatening finger right at Daniel. 'We keep our promises, and we sacrifice for the greater good. I don't think I need to remind you, *how important to the family this is.*'

I've never heard Mr Bradley speak in this tone of voice. This is what must strike fear into the hearts of his employees. Even Daniel seems to shrink. In the short silence that follows, I manage to raise a hand.

'Er...' I fade a little as Mr Bradley turns his stern eyes on me. I clear my throat. 'The thing is, I don't want to marry Daniel.'

'My dear.' Eileen pats me gently, like I've demonstrated a little mental incoherence.

'I don't want to marry him,' I repeat, more firmly this time.

James Bradley looks at his wife, as if handing the problem over to her and her womanly understanding.

'Then what are you doing here, dear?' she asks me.

'I need to ask Daniel how he's involved with Leonardo Vyper,' I say.

'Who the hell is Leonardo Vyper?' Daniel bursts out, surprising me.

I frown. 'You know him. I saw you with him.'

'I don't know who you're talking about.'

'Listen, Daniel,' I say, 'he's dangerous. If you're doing business with him then it's possible that you're being incriminated in a complicated plan to kill a lot of people.'

'*What?*' Mr Bradley shouts.

'What on earth are you talking about, Evie?' Daniel sounds legitimately exasperated. He addresses Eileen. 'Listen Mother, do you see? She's talking absolute nonsense. She seems unhinged to me. She's unsuitable. You can't hold me to this contract when she's turned out like this.'

I blink. Contract?

Eileen pats me again and says, 'What are you talking about, dear?'

'Leonardo Vyper is connected to a major criminal,' I say. I pause.

I was about to say *the Blade*. But I can't say that. James Bradley has read all my books. 'Er, Edgar Polton,' I finish.

'And what is that to Daniel?' Eileen is all patient encouragement.

'I saw you with Vyper,' I say to Daniel, whose expression is incredulous. 'I need to know what your involvement is. He's a criminal.'

'And how do you know this?' James Bradley regains control of the conversation, although technically I'm speaking to his son.

Er.

'Well, I...uh, through my research I, um...discovered a laboratory that had been used to make chemical weapons, and Car... um, a detective who was with me photographed some documents there.'

'And where is this laboratory?' James Bradley sounds both wary and intent. 'You actually went there?'

'Yes, well no, it was blown up.'

His eyes are fading to a kind of distant disappointment. Possibly re-evaluating everything he knew about me.

'You see?' Daniel snaps.

'It's true,' James murmurs.

'I told you she was too obsessed with her books,' Daniel continues. 'She's completely disconnected from reality. A bookish, distracted girl will be perfect, you said. Someone who's smart will do you good, you said. Respectable but shy and malleable, et cetera. But she has utterly lost touch with real life. The contract is void, Father.'

'Lost touch with real life,' James repeats. His eyes are still distant. Almost calculating.

I press dry lips together and mumble, 'Contract?'

'It did seem like a good idea at the time,' Eileen sighs, going over to her husband as if to console him. 'We weren't to know. She is nice, and ordinary and oblivious to money, James, as you said. But I think Daniel might be right, darling.'

'I am right,' Daniel says.

'Am I part of some kind of contract?' I ask.

'Not specifically, dear,' Eileen says, 'we just wanted Daniel to marry a nice girl before he became CEO, and stop all his...playing. He needed to settle down and prove to us he could behave like an adult.'

'It was a requirement of Father naming me his successor,' Daniel clarifies.

'You were forcing Daniel to marry me?' I don't feel ready to plumb the depths of how unflattering this is.

'They chose you,' Daniel says. 'Not me.'

'Now sweetheart, don't be petty,' Eileen rebukes him. 'You liked her too. Didn't you?'

'Well the contract is certainly void if you've been involved with criminals, Daniel,' says Mr Bradley. Daniel gapes. In response James Bradley gives him a hard stare, and there's silence for a moment.

'I don't know who she's talking about, Father!' Daniel says, his teeth gritted. 'This isn't fair.'

'Listen,' I say, looking from one to the other, 'this isn't imagined. Leonardo Vyper has potentially been financing a huge criminal operation, and making potpourri and manufacturing a toxic nerve agent so that all the teachers will...' I notice they're all looking at me with the kind of pitying, slightly distasteful expressions of people whose worst fears are being confirmed, and I falter. 'He...wait.'

I stride over to the desk, grab Daniel's engraved fountain pen and scribble *I have a photo of Leonardo Vyper in my pocket.* 'This is what he looks like,' I announce, and I stuff my hand into my jeans.

But there's nothing there. I try the other pocket. And the back two.

Nothing.

Daniel is looking askance at my fantastical sentence on his embossed *From the Desk of Daniel Bradley* memo pad. I drop limply into his chair, a horrid fear beginning to buzz beneath my thoughts.

I'm not crazy. I mean, it does sound like the non-credible tale of someone who's been slowly losing their mind. Because it's all out of a book I've been writing, isn't it? My own invented characters come to life. A wonderfully tired cliché.

The Bradleys haven't heard of Leonardo Vyper. Does he exist?

I grit my teeth. The surreal nightmare I've been living for the last week suddenly seems like it could be exactly that—a nightmare. I look down at my hands. They're perfect—no wounds, scratches or splints. Have I imagined this whole thing?

'Listen dear,' Eileen comes to put a gentle hand on my shoulder, 'you've been under a lot of stress recently.'

'Thanks to me, I suppose?' Daniel rolls his eyes. 'I've done everything you asked me to.'

'No,' Mr Bradley booms, and his voice carries such weight that I think the whole building must have stopped to listen with the same quaking I feel. 'What you have done, Daniel, is continue to live a reckless, immature and selfish life in secret, while outwardly you pretend to obey and respect us as your parents. You have disappointed me. There's nothing that can redeem that, now. Juliana will be CEO.'

'*What?*' Daniel begins to visibly vibrate.

'This is final. We will not wait for the wedding, since it's been cancelled, in any case. The paperwork will be drawn up immediately.'

'No! You cannot do this, Father.'

'Come, dear.' I look up and find that Eileen is talking down to me again. 'Let's leave them to argue. It might be good for you to go home and get some rest.'

'Oh. Yes,' I mumble. Her kind motherliness is very welcome at this moment. I feel shaky and fragile, and numbly uncertain as to whether I should go to a hospital and check myself in, or home for a long period of seclusion and recuperation.

Eileen helps me stand, and we are walking toward the door when I hear the sound of my ringtone. My phone. I pull it out and answer. As I do, something falls to the ground. A piece of folded paper.

'Talk to me.'

Carolyn's voice. I gasp and hang up, dropping the phone. A hallucination.

To hospital then, not home. I need a professional assessment of some kind.

From the floor the phone starts ringing again. I pick it up and answer it, scooping up the folded paper as I do so. I stare at it. It's a photo of Leonardo Vyper.

'Hello, Evie.' Hearing his tone is like being doused with a bucket of cold crawling ants.

My voice is a rasp. 'Hello, Bobby.'

41

I open and close my mouth a few times. 'How did you get this number?' I say.

'This is your regular number.'

Dammit.

'Where are you?' I know he won't tell me, but I can't help asking.

'On a little road trip,' he says, sounding more gleeful than he should, considering his big master plan is in the process of being dismantled. 'Go take look at the TV, would you darlin'?'

'I'm not near a television.'

'No, I suppose not. Well, look out Daniel's east-facing window.'

I move toward Daniel's windows like a person in a dream. There, too far below in the encroaching shadows of late afternoon to see the source, is a plume of smoke rising between the buildings on Broadway. I also see a lot of flashing lights heading that way, and I can hear the sound of a helicopter. A news crew maybe?

'What is it, dear?' Eileen has come up behind me.

'What is it?' I repeat her question into the phone.

'A van,' he says, as if it's the most obvious answer. 'A blue van.'

I turn to Eileen.

'You can see that?' I ask.

'The smoke? Of course, dear.' I hear the little panicky undertone in her voice. New Yorkers are jumpy about explosions.

'What did you do?' I ask the Blade.

'Oh, dear. You didn't look past all the little boxes, Evie,' he says in a gently reprimanding tone. 'Did you?'

'Past?'

'Yes, to where the little device was, with the Semtex and the little wires. The Plan B. There always has to be a Plan B.'

'You wired the vans with explosives?'

'Behind all the little boxes. All those little boxes just needed the right temperature. They just needed to be hot enough. Semtex is made of RDX, you know. It gets real hot. Real hot and firey.'

I swallow hard and put a hand against Daniel's clean glass, where it puffs out foggy marks. The cloud of smoke hangs between the buildings below, black against the last molten light of the afternoon sun. I wonder how many people have died and how many are going to, poisoned with the hot sarin particles in that deadly haze.

'Now what?' I ask. 'You park them all over the city and explode them?'

'Oh, no. They won't be parked. I have a remote signal. I can choose to make them hot and fiery whenever I like.'

'How did you know where I am?'

He chuckles. 'I didn't. You told me yourself. Anyway,' he says, 'if you saw my logo then I knew you'd figure it out. It was a nice touch, don't you think? And you are so predictable.'

Figure what out? I think. *Daniel?* That Daniel is connected some-how?

'Not so predictable,' I say, with the flat tone of an automatic drill press. I did, after all, learn how to pull off a plot twist or two. Suddenly I feel angry. He's silent, and I feel his anger too. Huh. I'm right. He didn't predict me escaping, and he didn't predict me foiling his misogynistic plans. And he's mad about it. Mad enough to explode those vans one by one. 'Have I upset you?' I ask sweetly.

There's an intense pause.

'You'll regret that soon, if you don't already,' he says in a tight voice. A shiver rushes up my spine. But then he says, more care-free, 'Now, I learned a long time ago not to get attached to things. Ideas are nice, plans are nice, but sometimes they don't work out, you know? And now I get to make different plans. And you're gonna spend the rest of your life looking over your shoulder, wondering what they are. Wondering if I'm behind you. And I will be. You won't last long, Evie. And neither will the Bradleys.'

'What do they have to do with it?' I ask, my voice a breath.

He cackles a laugh. 'Dear old Daniel. I have a little something special planned for him. Your fiancé.'

There's a rich vibration in his voice as he says this word. *He thinks Daniel is the love of my life.* And that hurting him will hurt me.

'You won't make it that far,' I say. 'The police know you were at that factory. The whole state is mobilised against you. There are roadblocks and helicopters. You've got nowhere to run.'

'Yeah, I know,' he says airily. 'That's why there's a Plan B.'

My heart sinks.

'Blowing up the vans?'

'That's gonna happen once every ten minutes unless I get my freedom, Evie. You're gonna let me walk away. Call off the hounds. I know you can.'

'I can't.'

'Well then, you'd better be prepared to have more lives on your conscience. Lots more lives.'

'Even if I could,' I say, 'I don't trust you. Once you're safely away you'll keep setting off the triggers.'

'Yeah. I suppose that's a risk you'll have to take, isn't it? Because unless that search shuts down, I definitely will. Do you know how many explosions that means?' He doesn't wait for me to reply. '*Lots of them.*'

'You have to give me something better than that.'

'Well, let's see. This phone I'm talking to you on is the same one I use to trip the triggers. Once the search is off, I'll destroy it.'

'That's not good enough. You could just switch it off and turn it back on later, and I wouldn't know the difference.'

'That's right.' He giggles. 'But you'll just have to trust me, won't you? Up to you.'

The line goes dead.

I stare at it in my hand for a moment. I start to redial the number Carolyn called me on, but then I realise she's the last person I should call. She'll never see reason when it comes to the Blade, not when she's this close. She'll refuse to call off that search, believing they can find him before the next bomb goes off. But I know they won't. He's too smart for that. Hunkered down somewhere so he can see when the coast is clear.

I'm distracted by some raised voices. It seems the Bradleys are getting impatient. Eileen has her coat on and she and James are moving toward the door. I dash in front of them, and pull out the Glock.

'Um, excuse me, I'm on the phone,' I say to them. 'Would you mind waiting?' All three move backward and away from me, into a polite huddle. Both men pull out their phones and dial. Calling security, I imagine.

I plant myself in front of the mahogany doors and spend a rushed and awkward minute with the search engine on my phone before I come up with the number for dispatch at the Ninth, and leave a message for Jay. Thirty seconds later my phone rings.

'Evie. Where are you?' The blast of worry in his voice comes with the equally loud blast of rotor-noise. He must be in a chopper somewhere.

'I'm fine,' I say, ignoring his question.

'Henders said you disappeared from the back seat of his car. He thinks he's going crazy. What's going on?'

I bite my lip. 'I can't explain right now. I need to know something. Are there roadblocks in place around that factory?'

'No. Harding doesn't think for a second he's still in the area. We got cameras on the bridges and tunnels, some with facial recognition, and we're in the process of setting up slowdowns on most of the interstates, which the city isn't gonna thank us for. We got a checkpoint at the exit of the Holland Tunnel, Jersey-side, because it would be the fastest way out of the state if that's what he wanted.' Jay pauses. 'Is that what he wants, Evie? Or is he heading upstate? Where's he going?'

I close my eyes. That's just the thing. I don't know where he's going. I have no sense at all about where he is or what he wants. There are thirty-two interstate highways in New York—nine main routes and twenty-three auxiliary routes. There's no way the police can sweep all of them in the next few minutes.

'Jay,' I use a careful tone, 'I need you to get them to stand down. Call in the roadblocks, and call off the hunt.'

Jay says nothing, and I continue, hurriedly. 'Bobby had a Plan B. We need to let him go free.'

'I can't do that, Evie.' Jay's tone doesn't give a speck of leeway.

'You have to try,' I say. 'His vans are also wired with explosives. He just detonated one near Wall Street. You know about that?'

Jay curses. 'I heard the call go out.'

'My guess is between twelve and twenty vans, and that makes one GB bomb exploding every ten minutes for approximately the next two to five hours unless we let him go. At which point there'll be so much chaos he'll probably slip through anyway. The next one is due to blow about five minutes from now.'

Jay says nothing and I listen to the aggressive burr of the rotor.

'Every ten minutes?' he asks finally.

'He's angry,' I say. Understatement. 'Where are you?'

'I'm with Harding. You know she'll never agree to this.'

'That's why I called you and not her.'

'I'm gonna talk to the Captain. Evie? Stay where you are.'

The line cuts and rather than wonder what he meant by that I hit redial on the Blade's call. I can still hear the rhythmic scream of a nearby chopper. There must be one inspecting the explosion. I frown and peer out the window as Bobby picks up.

'It's done,' I say.

'Good. Bye now, Evie. I'm sorry about Daniel.'

'What do you mean?'

'I have some people coming for y'all. His parents are there, aren't they?'

'Yes,' I say, feeling uneasy.

'I thought they might be. Ya'll are just one big happy family, aren't you? It seems a shame for it to end, since daddy's little boats have been so helpful. But you understand. I got eyes on the doors downstairs, so if I see them leave, I'll go ahead and bump the trigger on another van. That's fair, ain't it? It won't go outside our deal? Well, I don't suppose I care if it does.'

The line goes dead and I look blankly at the three Bradleys, huddled in the furthest corner. They don't look chastened, though. More like intolerant. Daniel tosses his head as if being forced to wait for someone else is beyond what he can bear in life.

'What's going on, Evie?' he demands, striding forward.

Something snaps.

'You,' I yell, lifting the Glock and advancing toward him. 'You. Are. A *jerkface*.' Daniel blanches. 'Sorry,' I amend, 'that was rude. *Nonetheless*,' I continue, regaining my momentum, 'perfectly accurate. You have been working with this man, haven't you?' I shake the photo of Leonardo Vyper at him as he back-pedals. His eyes go to the paper.

'Call security again, Father,' he says. 'She's definitely lost her mind. She's holding a photo of Raymond Drummond.'

'Who is Raymond Drummond?' I demand.

'Ray Drummond,' says James Bradley, as he comes toward me, 'is an old friend of the family.' He takes the photo from my hand and studies it. 'We went to business school together. He was invited to our wedding, for heaven's sake.'

'Have you been doing business with him?' I ask.

'Of course. We've been partners for years.'

'And does he import things on your ships from time to time?'

'Yes,' says James, in the voice of someone humouring a child.

'Are these things legal?'

'Ray is a man of integrity, Evie. I won't have you maligning a very close friend.'

But as James is speaking I see the expression on Daniel's face change.

'But he isn't, is he Daniel?' I ask him.

James' head whips around to look at his son. They stare at each other for a moment. Then Daniel looks at me, then back at his father. I have a weird feeling, as though they're having a silent conversation only they understand.

Then Daniel says, in an odd tone, 'He asked for a couple of special favours, Father. On a single crossing from Turkey in March. He paid double the price. I wanted to show improved figures for this quarter so you would...'

'So I would what?' James asks in a quiet voice.

'I did it for the company, Father,' Daniel says, but his tone has lost all strength and turned pleading. I stare. He's practically whimpering, and the big speech I would have liked to give at some point, about what a slithery, hateful slug Daniel is in my eyes, dries up from my mind as unnecessary. He is a slug at this moment, and he knows it. He only ever really cared what his father thought, and his father is universally disappointed. It's enough punishment for anyone.

'I think it's time we all went home,' Eileen says in a pacifying voice. 'Evie?' She comes nearer and makes a motion as though dropping my weapon would be appropriate now.

I do lower it, but I say, 'I can't let you do that, Eileen. I'm afraid you're in danger. I need to get you out of the building somehow without being seen, and take you somewhere safe.'

Exactly how I'm going to do that without going through the front door is beyond me, however. And even if I do manage it, we'll all have the Blade stalking us for the rest of our lives.

Lovely. Unless...

And there it is. Carolyn's words come back to me. When we were sitting at Jay's table, talking about my notes, and all the millions of facts stored there, or inside my head...*It could be the clue to unravel all this, the one thing that can shut him down for good.*

I know where he's going.

I raise my gun and say, 'I need you to move to the stairs please, Eileen.' She gapes at me. 'James, Daniel,' I add, using the Glock to point at the door. None of them moves.

'Where the hell is security?' Daniel barks, clearly worn out by his emotional day.

I quell an internal sigh. These people are Bradleys. The only thing they're used to doing is exactly what they want to do. Doing what they don't want to do doesn't enter into the equation. I point the gun at the ceiling and fire once. Plaster splatters as the report deafens all four of us. Eileen makes a dignified but terrified little shriek, and Daniel puts his hands in the air.

'If the three of you could make your way to the stairs, please,' I repeat.

With a sudden bang, the monstrous office doors burst open and Carolyn and Jay barge in. My mouth drops open. Jay has discarded his leather jacket in favour of a black Kevlar vest, Glock holstered on his waist. Carolyn is Kevlar too, with jeans, and she has exchanged her heels for motorcycle boots.

In less than two seconds, they register the scene before them, and I see them both resist the instinct to draw their own weapons.

'Evie,' Jay asks, 'why are you holding these people at gunpoint?'

'Good work,' Carolyn says, ignoring him. I'm too dismayed at seeing them to answer. I'd been counting on the fact they were far away and very much on the wrong track to be in any danger.

'What are you doing here?' I gasp.

Jay's eyes make a steady circuit to the Glock in my hands, then back to my face. 'By the time Special Agent Henders called Harding, she'd figured out that the factory was empty. She picked me up and we came straight here.'

'How did you know I was here?'

Jay's expression is dry. 'You left your forwarding address in Henders' car.'

I curse inwardly. His notepad.

'I'm trying to get the Bradleys to safety,' I say. 'Bobby's threatened them. As far as I can tell there's a truck full of his ninjas on their way here.' Or something equally terrifying. 'How did you get here so quickly?'

Carolyn points a finger upward.

Ah. They landed on the roof. Turns out using helipads is the prerogative of the NYPD.

Well, at least now we can get out of here.

'You got a plan?' Jay asks me.

'We can't take them through the front door,' I say. 'But if we can get them to the Hamptons, they can organise themselves and go into hiding. After you arrest Daniel,' I add, ignoring Eileen's dismayed reaction. 'We need to go now. Whoever Bobby's sent is on their way here.'

'Darling,' Eileen says to her husband, her voice high and thin,

'I think we should call the police.'

Carolyn claps her hands like a schoolteacher with an unruly class on excursion and unholsters her Smith & Wesson.

'Mrs Bradley, we *are* the police. Okay, everybody, let's move to the door. Time to go.'

She ushers them that way, while I do a swift turn and jog over to seat myself at Daniel's desk. The things I want right now are too big for my pockets. I wonder if writing them into my lap would work again?

I tuck the Glock back into my jeans, pick up Daniel's pen and write, and my lap gets heavy. I thunk a couple of Heckler & Koch MP5s onto the desk, and look up to see Jay's arms drop to his sides, the only sign of shock he displays. Our eyes connect, and I watch him assimilate this new information with me disappearing from the back of an FBI sedan. He glances at my neck and I remember that when he last saw me I had a tally there and a black eye, and now I look like I'm in the running for World's Healthiest Abductee. He says nothing.

Carolyn, who's having trouble moving the Bradleys out of the office without shooting them, turns and catches sight of the two machine guns as well as the large metal case I lift off my lap and sit beside my feet. I see the same series of conclusions ignite in her eyes, but I also see her thoughts brush past the existential maelstrom and zero in on the immediate benefits.

'I see you've started writing again, Evie,' she says, as she pushes past Jay and grabs the metal handle of the military-green case. 'I can take this one.' She heads for the door, while James Bradley begins loudly rebelling against being obliged to do something against his will. He's barking orders to his driver it seems, on his phone, but Carolyn grabs this off him and tosses it away. 'Go,' she says, and prods him through the door with her gun.

I tear the written-over page off Daniel's luxury memo pad, glad for how thick and weighty it feels, fold it tightly and shove it deep into my front pocket. These particular words are ones I'm keeping safe.

I push the fountain pen into my other pocket for good measure and jump up to follow Carolyn, passing one of the machine guns to Jay. I feel him close behind me as I reach the doors.

At which point all hell breaks loose.

42

I flatten myself against the protective mahogany as a stutter of automatic fire splinters the muted competence of the space outside. I guess the ninjas have arrived. I can hear, beyond the waiting area outside the doors, down the long glass-enclosed corridor where the rest of the offices are, the muffled sound of several voices rise into screams, and another voice, male, shouting commands.

'What do we do?' I whisper.

Jay is flat against the other door, the MP5 wedged in the crook of his elbow. It's a compact weapon, as far as machine guns go, and my eyes rake the stubby barrel with its narrow metal tip, and the curved edges of grip and magazine, before landing back on Jay. He's looking at me too, and the gun I'm holding. The metal casing is cool beneath my fingers. I gulp a breath of air. Should we be rushing out there to help Carolyn? The door is too heavy to crack open in a subtle way, so we can't see what's happening.

'Harding can handle herself.' Jay says, reading my expression, his voice low and calm. His eyes meet mine. 'Can you?'

I nod.

'Sounds like they're gathering all the employees together,' he adds.

That makes sense. That way they contain potential heroes and also pick the Bradleys off from within the group. Not that I think there are any heroes out there. It's just C-level executives and their underpaid administrative assistants.

'What's the best way to the stairs?' As Jay speaks, he locks the bolt back on the barrel of the MP5, checks the magazine, reinserts it and slaps the bolt with his palm so it snaps forward, ready. It makes him look like a badass but I almost roll my eyes. He watched me write *fully loaded* but he's too conscientious not to double-check.

'Through that open doorway on the far left,' I say. 'The half-hidden one.' Jay and Carolyn probably came the traditional way from the stairs, the roundabout one that shows off the full glory of the fancy offices. 'It takes you to the stairs by the elevators. If there's a second set of stairs in this building, I imagine they're at the far end. But I'm not sure.' Daniel gave me a tour of this floor once, but he wasn't exactly pointing out fire exits at the time.

'Any idea how many there are?' Jay angles the gun and uses his thumb to click the selector switch around to full auto. I take his lead and do the same. This time I know he isn't talking about stairs.

'Maybe four of them?' I say. 'I think there were four last time.' I remember that, from the horror of that night. Jay nods. My eyes snag on his Kevlar vest, and it gives me an idea.

I pull out my piece of paper and scribble the sentence, becoming instantly aware of the weight and tightness of the fabric, but still needing to glance down at myself to check that it actually happened.

'Magic,' Jay says, eyeing me, though his expression indicates misgiving rather than wonder. 'Stay here,' he adds, and yanks open the right-hand door, takes a quick look, and disappears through it.

Give me a heart attack, why doesn't he? I suck in my breath, fearing the worst. I hear another volley of machine-gun fire and I tense. Is it him? Or did it seem to come from further away? Then two quick ricochets. Carolyn maybe? One thing is certain, I'm not staying in here by myself. No sir. And I'm not writing *I am fearless*, either. I'm doing this myself.

I yank open the left-hand door and pitch myself through it on my hands and knees. I crawl behind Ellen's desk, dragging the MP5. Both Magdeline and Ellen are there. They make room for me, and I peer out and around the ugly ficus plant Ellen keeps next to her desk. Through the cloud of small green leaves I see no sign of Jay, but I do see the prone form of a black-clad man, and the telltale wires of Ellen's taser. Sensational.

I give her a thumbs-up. She gives me a terrified look in return.

'Which way did everyone go?' I whisper to Magdeline. She points toward the long corridor that leads to the far end of the building, where the lunchroom and executive boardrooms are. I nod and then point at Daniel's office.

'Safer there. I'll cover you,' I say, ignoring a surreal moment of ridiculousness. Magdeline nods and they start to crawl that way, her velvet heels dragging on the carpet, and I pop up with the gun to make sure the coast is clear. Then I have a brainwave. 'Magdeline!' I hiss, and she pauses her crawling. With a bit of twisting I yank the Glock out of the back of my jeans and toss it to her, and she palms it deftly out of midair. Wow. She's magnificent.

Once they're inside I creep out from behind the desk and start moving in the direction of The Avenue. I'm not sure this is a great idea but I figure maybe I can come at things from a different angle and surprise someone. I sidle toward it, keeping a sharp eye on the empty corridors, my right palm sweaty on the grip of the MP5. There's more shouting coming from the far end of the building, in the direction Magdeline pointed. I assume this is the ninjas. Whoever is yelling seems to be sporting clipped accents, and they sound angry, not scared.

I'm about to slip through the door to The Avenue when there's a burst of fire and a searing pain in my left arm. I throw myself to the floor, whip my gun up and squeeze the trigger. The stock slams into my shoulder with the pump of the recoil but I hold tight, loosing at least ten rounds before I manage to unclench my trigger finger.

I don't know if I hit anyone because my eyes are squeezed closed, but I do know I smashed a lot of things. I unsqueeze them with difficulty and look. No ninja. Just Ellen's empty desk and the priceless Anish Kapoor sculpture near the wall with a gash of bullet holes. I lurch up onto one knee—an awkward thing as my left shoulder is screaming and I have a sub-machine gun in my right—and as I do, I see someone in black, out of the corner of my eye. He's not lying wounded like his electrified comrade, but taking cover behind Ellen's ficus and possibly quite grumpy. Agh. I throw myself into The Avenue, and a pepper of fire hits the space where I was standing, thudding into the brushed metal near the entrance. But I'm sprinting, counting on the fact that the angle on this corridor means Ninja Two will have to run after me before he'll get another clean shot.

I'm right. I blast out into the main reception area at the other end. It's empty. I hesitate and then spin a sharp right and dive underneath the massive oak reception desk and crawl to the far end, pushing fancy designer wheely chairs out of the way as I go. I press my back up against the inner side so that I'm facing the way I came, and grit my teeth. Part of my view is a tiny sliver where I can see anyone coming through the doorway. I hold my breath, raise the sight on the MP5 and train it there. Is he coming? Did he follow?

Though I doubt a ninja would poke their head around a door. And this guy was obviously sent out to pick off strays like myself which means he knows what he's doing. My left shoulder is on fire and I steel myself to make a lightning fast inspection. Carolyn's blue sweater is torn and blackened, and I have a hot slice in my skin that's starting to bleed like mad. But the bullet only grazed me.

Just as I'm putting my focus back on the doorway I hear a tell-tale clunk, like something small but solid bumping on carpet. I drop the gun's sight to floor level, right in time to see the dark green baseball shape of a grenade go bumping past. Great.

It's not a stun grenade. It's the real thing. That means a kill radius of five metres and a casualty radius of fifteen. I hear a metallic thump as the grenade hits the elevator doors, which means it's about seven metres from me, plus the desk, which hopefully is enough to protect me from chunks of flying shrapnel. I make a spilt-second decision to drop the gun and protect my ears when—*crack!*

I feel the percussive wave and tighten into a ball as my body internalises the shock of it. Thank goodness for the desk. My ears begin stinging and I'm about to lift the gun again when I realise I'm too late. My little sliver of vision has a ninja standing in it, with an MP7 in his hands and an unfriendly expression in the holes of his balaclava. Heavens, an MP7. That's armour-piercing rounds. These guys aren't messing around.

I swallow. He jerks the barrel of the MP7 upwards a couple of times, which I interpret as ninja-speak for *If you wouldn't mind standing.* I push the MP5 away and get to my feet. As I rise he pulls something out of his pocket with one hand and holds it up. It's paper, and I'm guessing it's a photo, supplied by Bobby to make sure the job got done this time. Maybe the celebrity snapshot from the gossip feeds last week, or the dyspeptic author's photograph from my books. I seem to be correct because the ninja crunches it in his hand like he doesn't need it anymore and lets it fall to the floor. He raises his gun until it's at eye-level. It's the kind of action that doesn't have the air of someone about to usher me somewhere else, into a pack of hostages, for example. There's a finality to it. It looks like someone lining up the barrel for an execution.

Well. *This is it.* Death by ninja.

I barely have time to register the reality of this when there's a burst of gunfire. For one frozen moment I think it was the sound of my own fatal shooting, but when I realise I'm still alive and glance up to see how Ninja Two is responding, I see his masked chin drop as he crumples over. Dead? Heavens.

I grab up the MP5 and move on weak legs toward the elevators, which are pockmarked and torn from the grenade, looking around the reception area for the shooter. There's no one. The main corridors are empty too. Then who? I change position again and there's Jay, haloed in the warm lights of The Avenue, looking like a freaking superhero. I sag with relief. He steps over the body of Ninja Two and says, 'You're right, there were four.'

I nod. There's shock crowding toward me but I hold it back.

'You did good,' Jay adds.

'Yes,' I gasp, 'thank you. I distracted an assassin with my face. Where's Carolyn?' My breath is slightly short.

'She got the Bradleys upstairs already.'

'Well then,' I say, 'let's go.'

The NYPD's blue and white Bell 412 is obscured by semi-darkness by the time we make it to the roof, the blades a hot blur, the noise at full decibels. We run up the last metal stairs to the helipad as Carolyn shoves the cabin door of the chopper back. We climb in quickly, careful not to stay in the open too long. Though the wind was blowing the remains of the explosion away from Amiton toward the East River, there's no point taking chances with stray sarin.

I see that this is an ESU unit, with four plain black seats, one in each corner, of which the Bradleys are occupying three. There is barely room for Jay and I amid the ropes, rigging, spinal board and other emergency rescue equipment that takes up the rest of the space. Carolyn has a headset on and is arguing with the pilot and tactical flight officer in front as she wrenches the door closed. I guess they're not happy about the extra payload. The six of us would have more than maxed out one of the four-seated patrol choppers, but that doesn't mean they want to take off with two unsecured passengers.

I'm about to collapse onto the hard cabin floor but Jay yells something to Daniel who is sitting in one of the back-facing seats, and points at the floor between his parents in the front-facing seats. Daniel unbuckles himself and goes to sit where Jay pointed, while Jay takes me by the elbow and manoeuvres me into the vacated seat. Daniel is wedged onto the floor between his parents like a naughty child, which is kind of poetic, but I'm incapable of feeling smug about it. All three of them look blank, and kind of traumatised. Eileen's mascara has run, she's plucking at the edge of her blouse, and when she looks over and makes eye contact with me I feel terrible.

I look away and fumble through buckling myself into the seat as Carolyn plonks into the one next to me and does the same. Jay settles himself onto the floor beside me and reaches up to examine my bleeding shoulder as the chopper lurches and we begin gaining altitude. I grab one of the black headsets off the hook near me and stretch the cord to hand it to Jay, and then grab another for myself.

'You saved my life,' I say. Jay says nothing, since there are three other people listening to our conversation, but his eyes are communicative. He reaches into the space under my seat to unclip a metal box there, rifles through it and pulls out a plastic bottle and a packet of gauze, which he tears open with his teeth.

'It's fine,' I say. 'You don't need to—*aaaaaagh*,' I growl, as he squirts liquid from the bottle onto my shoulder, which must be alcohol since it burns worse than the wound. He presses the gauze to it.

'Hold this,' he says, and I replace his fingers on the gauze with my own. He throws the bottle and gauze wrapper back in the box as the chopper begins a turn that puts G-force on my left-hand side, pushing me nearer him. He hooks a finger on the bare metal leg of my chair and grips it for support. Against my leg on the other side is the large case I wrote into existence in Daniel's office, and I see him glance at it. He says, 'So. You want to tell me what's going on?'

'I'm not sure,' I say, which is the truth.

His eyes take in my bulletproof vest, and then he nods at the case again. 'How long have you been able to do that?'

'Not long,' I say. I rub my right wrist, still free of its bandages, and put my hands back on the MP5 sitting in my lap.

'You started writing a new story?' he asks, and his tone holds the meticulous patience he uses when he's gathering all the facts, yet another of my favourite attributes of his. I give a deliberate nod.

'Yes,' I say. 'My own.'

'Where are we going, Evie?' This is Carolyn now, barking in my ear.

I give the address. 'We can get James to call ahead and have his staff light the helipad,' I add. 'Also, don't forget to arrest Daniel.'

'Don't worry,' she says, 'I won't. I assume it has to do with some convenient shipping anomalies?'

'Yes,' I say. 'It seems so.'

'Like maybe bringing plastic explosives over from the Czech Republic and a lot of undesirable chemicals from the Balkans?' she adds cheerfully.

'Possibly. Through Vyper.'

'Ah, so easy to do when you're the chief executive's son. Shipping containers are easily messed with when you have plenty of money and permission from upstairs. Who's Vyper, anyway?'

'A man with aliases,' I say. 'The Bradleys know him as Raymond Drummond.'

'And he's the Blade's backer?'

'You'll have to ask Daniel.'

'Oh, I will.' She grins. 'We'll be there in twenty minutes. I'm looking forward to this.'

Jay's voice breaks into the conversation. 'Alderman? Any reports of another explosion in the city?' I assume Alderman is the tactical flight officer.

'That's a negative,' the answer comes from the front. I can see what Jay is thinking. *The Blade kept his word.*

But it's more likely the Blade was too busy making his getaway to set off a second explosion. There's no way he will keep his word if he can help it.

'Do you know where he is, Evie?' I feel Jay's eyes on me.

'No,' I say.

The truth. Just.

43

The helipad of the Bradley's Southampton home sits in the middle of a neatly manicured lawn behind the glass-enclosed swimming pool. It's haloed in floodlights, and as we land and I see that the reinforcements Carolyn called in have arrived. Some local cops from the Southampton Police Department are waiting in a grim and official capacity to 'accompany' the Bradleys, and particularly Daniel. I have to acknowledge the briefest smudge of satisfaction when Daniel is handcuffed and read his rights, over the slowing thud of the rotor blades against the night air. I hang back in the shadows of the cabin as this cheerless ceremony takes place, and the whole justice team marches toward the mansion.

I can see Carolyn's glee, and sense the heady breath of nearing victory she's inhaling at the idea that Daniel holds all the clues she hungers for. But I don't go with them. I sit tight. Technically I'm wanted by the FBI, and don't want to draw attention to myself. There's no need for me to be there, anyway. And more importantly, there's no need for anyone to be *here*, with me.

Both men in the cockpit are staying in their seats as the pilot runs the engine at about two-thirds capacity to cool it down. I assume they're awaiting instructions from NYPD Air Command before heading back out to join the manhunt for Bobby and his drivers. They're having a discussion about how much fuel they have, and deciding they have enough to make it back to base. This would be Floyd Bennett Field in Brooklyn, about eighty nautical miles away. This confirms what I see when I glance at the gauge over their shoulders—that the tank is basically empty. I look over at the big fixed cylinder the Bradleys have next to the indoor pool, which is kept diligently full of Jet A and which they use to top up the EC145.

I pull out the piece of paper I have in my pocket, which is getting a bit crumpled, and write myself a couple of sentences. And then a couple more. In theory, I learned how to fly a helicopter. I had a bunch of lessons and spent time in a simulator during Book Twelve. But it isn't until I dot the period on the last sentence that I start to feel I'm capable of a bit more than reciting flight procedures from a manual. Like last time in Bobby's warehouse, knowledge and experience and muscle memory trickle into my mind and limbs. In all honesty, it isn't an entirely good feeling. There's the thready sensation that I'm breaking some natural laws, or something. But on the other hand, it does feel good. It feels very good.

I wait until the pilot reduces the engine to idle and disengages the clutch, then I shove my paper back into its place, and from my other pocket pull out a couple of tiny stickers, like nicotine patches. This was one of my other sentences. I considered a taser, but really, since when is it a good idea to tase the person in charge of a helicopter? Regardless of whether or not the controls are engaged.

I pull the little plastic covering off both patches, careful not to touch the sticky underside. Then I angle myself so I'm facing the cockpit, and my arms are free. I set a patch to the neck of the pilot, and as he lifts his hand to inspect what it is, I lean further and stick the other to the neck of the tactical officer. And then I interfere with their attempts to get their fingers on the patches for the three seconds it takes for them to slump into unconsciousness. I let my breath out. Okay. That was easy. Not elegant, unless you count slapping at the hands of two grown men elegant, but it achieved what I wanted. Now I just have to get them out of here.

I reach forward and turn off the autopilots, the generators and the fuel valves, and complete the shutdown process to make these next couple of steps a little safer. I climb down out of the cabin, open the cockpit door, step up and unclamp the three-way buckle from the limp form of the pilot. I tamp down my nervousness. It's okay. Jay and Carolyn have only been inside about two minutes. They won't be looking for me yet.

For a brief moment I wish I could use the Bradleys' Eurocopter for what I'm planning to do, but since it's probably waiting on Pier 6 for James's usual ride home from work, it will have to be the Bell. Which means getting two large sleeping men out of the cockpit.

The embroidered badge on the pilot's navy flight jacket says Green. I pull his arms through the straps, which get snagged a couple of times, and mutter an apology as I take fistfuls of the material and attempt to roll him toward me. He does, thanks to gravity, and I almost take us both for a swan dive, face first into the concrete. He's so heavy. I get him onto the ground, where his helmet saves him from a concussion. He's going to have some bruises tomorrow. Oops.

Once I've finally dragged him, puffing, into the darkness a safe distance away, I lay him so his airways are clear, apologise again and yank off my vest, as it's a suffocating fashion option when trying to manhandle someone three times my size. I get my breath back and write myself yet more sentences. I need a better way of doing this.

I am strong worked really well last time, and it does again. I bounce up on steady legs, feeling the flexion and ability of every muscle. I get Alderman onto the ground and out of the way with more ease.

I dash to the Bradleys' cylindrical white fuel tank and unhook the hose, prime the pump, and head for the back of the chopper. As close as I can figure, Southampton to Wirt County, West Virginia, is over three hundred and fifty nautical miles, which is borderline for what the Bell 412 can do on a full tank of fuel.

And that's without taking a possible headwind into consideration or the fact that I'll be keeping below 500ft to avoid the radar horizon. And assuming I can find the Blade immediately. So to be safe, I should make it with a single stop. Making it *in time* is something else entirely. If I'm right, it's about eight hours of driving, so the Blade will be arriving at his destination somewhere between two and three in the morning. That's if he sticks to the freeway. And he pushes through without a break. *If* I'm right.

To fly the same distance...I calculate, as I tap my foot impatiently. Jet fuel fumes snake into the air and I sprint the hose back to the tank when I'm done. The Bell has a maximum cruise speed of about 120 knots, which means it's going to take maybe three hours to fly there, plus a fuel stop. So, a trip out of the way to Philly or Baltimore. So four hours total, maybe, if nothing goes wrong. The Blade has a long head start on me but it should be okay.

Because I want to be there before he arrives. I want to be waiting for him.

I lick my lips and head for the cockpit. The Bell 412 is a solid, high-powered twin-engine chopper. It has lots of modern flight tech and a digital automatic flight control system so start-up requires some precise steps, but theoretically all I need is a quick couple of minutes for a safety check and Carolyn and Jay will never be the wiser. I step up and lift myself toward the pilot's seat.

'Going somewhere?'

Dammit. Since the blades aren't running, Jay's dry tone is clearly audible. If I ignore him and get in, he will only follow me. I turn, just in time to see Carolyn step out of the shadows to stand beside him at the edge of the helipad. I should have known her killer instinct was far too sensitive to be sidetracked by Daniel. She's known all along that I'm the key to getting what she really wants: Bobby Laidley, impaled by justice.

She and Jay are glaring at me, arms folded. The floodlight over the helipad is austerely bright.

'Yes,' I say. 'I am.'

'Please don't tell me that body over there is Alderman?' Jay's voice is level.

'He was very tired,' I say.

'What exactly are you doing, Evie?' There's a hint of confusion in Carolyn's tone, something that never happens.

'She's going to fly it,' Jay says.

'Fly what?'

Jay's eyes don't leave mine.

'Just let me go,' I say.

'Fly the chopper?' Carolyn is still behind us, which makes me feel like I scored a coup of some kind, but then she catches up like a hunting panther and says, '*You know where he is.*' There's jackhammer-heavy accusation in her tone.

'No.'

'If she knew that,' Jay says, 'she would have written herself there already. But she probably has a pretty good idea.'

He's right. I did try writing myself there. Crouched over Green, realising what a task I'd set myself, I tried writing myself to a different location again. This time—both when I tried writing myself to where I imagine Bobby *might* be, in a car somewhere, or writing myself to where I think he might be *going*, a remote farmhouse with a big barn—nothing happened. For some reason, the words were empty and useless. Sure, I didn't have an exact address, like I'd had for Daniel's office, and now I wish I'd done more than vaguely research Wirt County five years ago when Bobby stole that AgustaWestland and stashed it there. But also, those written words felt powerless in a more cosmic way: I'm not in control. Their story, Bobby's and Carolyn's and Jay's, really isn't mine anymore. Somehow it isn't such a scary thought as it was a few days ago, though. I can't seem to write their story, and I can't write myself into it. I can't touch it, and I can't change it. But I can change my own.

I'm going to fly the helicopter.

Carolyn says, 'And stealing police property. I'd be impressed, if you hadn't planned on leaving without us.'

'You're still impressed,' I say.

A tiny grin flickers at the corner of her mouth, and I see her acknowledge how determined I am. What she doesn't know is that when I couldn't get myself to Bobby, I wrote myself another Glock into the back of my jeans, and a couple of clever sentences inspired by the shootout with the ninjas. So I'm more than just determined right now. I'm *ready*.

'Either way,' I say. 'I'm going to finish this.'

'We're coming with you.' Jay drops his hands so they're loose at his sides.

'No,' I say. The sticky irony is that I would prefer if they came. I don't want to do this alone. I want them with me.

'And what are you going to do, alone?' Jay's tone is moving toward angry. 'What's your plan here, huh?'

I say nothing, because I don't know. All I know is that I have to do this. This is personal. Bobby is here because of me. He's done all this damage because of me. It was my fault he smarmed his way under Carolyn's radar as Edgar Polton. I'm the writer. He's been my responsibility from the beginning. I'm not going to let him make a clean getaway, the way my father's killer did.

'We're coming with you,' Jay repeats.

'You'll have to shoot us to stop us.' Carolyn shrugs. 'We should arrest you right now, in fact.'

'I think you tried that already,' I say.

Carolyn shrugs again. 'You know you aren't a match for both of us, Evie.'

'Fine then,' I say, pulling out the Glock and pointing it at them with two hands squeezing the grip.

'Come on.' Carolyn rolls her eyes. Jay says nothing.

'I'm telling you to stay here,' I say. 'It's for your own protection.'

'No, it's for his, because you're going to kill him.' Carolyn motions to Jay, who is still as stone.

My lips part. He told her. They really have no secrets, the two of them. I feel like a murderer, even though I'm trying to prevent that murder with a high-powered handgun and all my heart and soul.

'So I don't see why *I* can't come,' she continues, nonchalant.

Actually, I don't see why she can't, either.

'Harding!' Jay puts a quiet roar of both shock and fury into that one word.

'Fine,' I say, ignoring him. 'Jump in.' She almost skips to her task, leaping blithely into the cabin, while I take two steps backward to the cockpit. 'I'm sorry, Jay. It's for your own good.'

But my plans to climb in and power up unhindered are derailed when Jay strides toward me like he plans to wrest the Glock from my grip. I raise it and it barges into his chest as he comes too close.

'Don't point your gun at me unless you mean to pull the trigger, Evie.'

'Don't!' I grit my teeth and grip the gun harder. He knows the safety's still on. His eyes are glinting in the starlight. 'Don't, Jay.'

'What, so you'll kill me now? Here? Is this how it ends? Stealing a helicopter? I thought you said I was gonna die a hero.'

'Just stay here, Jay! Can't you see I'm trying to keep you safe?'

'That's not your decision, Evie!'

Oh.

The strength goes out of my arms and the Glock wavers and ends up pointing at the ground near my feet. Jay's midnight gaze is like staring into eternity. He steps into the space made by my lowered arms. 'You want family? Well this is it. This is what it looks like. *We* are it.' He pauses, and I find myself hyper-aware of how close he's standing, the way he's inside my personal space, and I'm inside his. Because for seven years, being in Jay's space was impossible. I could never be close, and a part of me preferred it that way. And now, after all this, I'm still trying to keep him at arm's length.

Jay says, 'You gotta let me choose for myself.'

I see what I've been doing. I've been trying to write him.

He has free will. But in the way that human beings use words to build fences and push people away, I've been trying to hold Jay back. To keep my heart safe. I don't want him to die, the way my father died, or the way my mother died. So I've been trying, on some level, to keep myself safe by not letting him be who he is.

'Jay.' My breath hitches. 'Don't you see? If I can prevent it...if there is the smallest thing I could do to change things...'

'Could you change things?'

I stare at him.

His voice changes. 'Is there a chance?'

I swallow. 'I have to try.' *Because I love you.*

He looks at me for a few moments, as if reading everything in my eyes. Then he sighs. It's a deep, unexpectedly glad sound. Above us stars are shining like pinpricks in the fabric of the universe. Like another world shining through. A bigger world.

How inconvenient it is when the people you love have free will. And how glorious.

'It's time to let go, Evie,' he says. 'Let me make my own decisions. I know what I'm doing. You can trust me.'

Right on cue Carolyn pops her head out of the cabin door.

'Us. You can trust *us*.'

Jay waits until I meet his eyes. 'Do you?'

44

I study the instrument panel. Fuel valve on, battery on, oil pressure good, TOT less than 150, N1 good...

Okay. I'm nervous.

Jay pulls himself into the cockpit seat to my left as I check the controls for full range of movement and press the starter button with my right thumb. So many checks, all of them crucial. I push past idle and back again with my left hand before releasing the throttle. Okay. All the switches are in the proper position—transfer valve, balance pump—and now the blades are drifting off and I'm actually doing this.

Jay pulls his headset on.

'Where are we going?' His voice crackles into my ear, warm and reassuring.

'Baltimore.' I open the throttle slowly. 'There's a public heliport there that should let us do an after-hours refuel. If you get the Cap to vouch for us.'

'How long till we get there?'

'A couple of hours.'

I ramp the RPMs until the rotor screams, then take a breath and inch the collective up, adjusting torque with the left tail rotor pedal. I damp down the little trickle of doubt that says this is madness, and we lurch upward into the clear night air with only a tiny plummet of my heart and stomach.

I glance around, keeping eyes on the environment, and see the house and grounds pull away below us. The tennis court is in darkness, and the pool, as well as the woodsy area Eileen likes to take walks in, but the house is lit up. I glance toward the horizon. I'm glad it's a clear night.

'What is it?' Jay says.

'What?' I say, but Jay is talking to Carolyn, who is craned forward and peering through the cockpit at the house.

'Nothing,' her voice says in my ear. But she's squinting, concentrated, her body taut and twitchy at my shoulder. I put a little pressure on the cyclic and we start to move forward with a shudder, and the sprawling mansion with all its big windows and gables begins to creep out of sight below us. Carolyn slumps back into her seat.

'Nothing?' Jay repeats.

'Just a feeling.'

I keep us climbing with more tiny adjustments to the collective, and then, as we hit about three hundred feet, something explodes behind us.

Boom.

My instinct is to duck but I don't get the chance as a harsh blast of hot air buffets the chopper, and I react in a cold kind of panic while we jerk in the air and the torque gauge pushes dangerously into the yellow. I make iron-hard millisecond judgments with the controls, trying to keep us airborne without toasting the engine in the process, and simultaneously lift us away from any bits of flying debris that might have been part of the explosion.

When I have control again I hold us in a hover, breathing like a sprinter, and rotate us so we can all look back at the Bradley mansion. It seems to be intact. But across the lawn next to the pool there's an inferno.

'What was it?' I gasp, my voice lacerated and half-strength.

'The fuel tank.' Carolyn is peering through the window. I picture the fuel tank as I saw it last, a big white tablet on the lawn, hidden from the house by the glass enclosure for the pool. But that glass enclosure seems to be destroyed, and the poolhouse is on fire. The fuel tank is nothing but a burning crater.

'We should take a look,' Jay says.

I'm already pushing on the cyclic to take us back for a flyover. I skirt the opaque plume of smoke rising from the Bradleys' over-sized poolhouse. The glass enclosure beside it is nothing but a moonlit skeleton of metal framework over a mess of rubble and dark water. We peer down as I struggle to handle the controls, thanks to leftover thermals.

'That's a person,' Jay says. I look at where he's pointing. He's switched the high-def long-range camera attached to the chop-per to infrared, so even though it's dark in the cockpit, the video display shows the white glow of a human sheltering behind a tree in Eileen's woodsy area.

'Who is it, Evie?' Carolyn barks at me.

'Is it Alderman?' Jay asks. Oh no. Green and Alderman. They were so close to the explosion. Are they dead?

'I don't think it could be,' I say. 'They were both unconscious.'

I nudge the cyclic, dip the bird to my side, and glance through the window. I can't see Green or Alderman, and I can't see the unknown person in the trees, but I can see someone else. He's sprawled on the grass between the helipad and the woods, like a crumpled Ken doll, and it looks for all the world like he has a gun in his hand. A big gun. Like he just shot the gas tank to bits. On purpose.

'We have to go down there,' I say. 'That looks like it might be...'

I'm about to adjust the RPMs for a landing when the sound of automatic fire shears the air. My heart clenches and I pull up, listening in horror as I hear the fuselage take some hits.

'Get us out of here!' Carolyn shouts, and I do. I crank the collective in an effort to get us out of range and manoeuvre us back over the house.

'What do you see?' I say.

'Nothing.' Carolyn is peering through the window. 'It's too dark.'

'That guy is still in the trees,' Jay says, adjusting the camera. 'And he's got company.'

'Is that who fired those shots?' My mind is rushing through possible explanations.

'It doesn't matter,' Carolyn growls. 'There's not much we can do without reinforcements, and we've got more important places to be.'

I keep us gaining distance, my eyes raking the instrument panel. The gauges seem okay. It's possible the damage from the shots we took was only superficial.

Out of the corner of my eye I see Jay punch the radio to call it in. I look at him and he looks at me, and he nods. Like he read my mind. We keep going. Much as I hate to admit it, Carolyn is right. We don't have time to waste. And whatever is happening down there is secondary. Every instinct I have is screaming after Bobby.

I take a breath, ease the cyclic forward, and feel us gain speed. This is it.

45

Baltimore's Pier 9 doesn't operate twenty-four hours, but Jay calls ahead, pulls some strings, and arranges an after-hours landing for extra charge. We could have chosen to fly into Martin State Airport, but the Baltimore police choppers are based there. It's weird landing a police chopper at a commercial heliport, but it would be weirder still to make use of the facilities of the Baltimore PD without a flight plan and a formal collaboration. Maybe if *NYPD* wasn't emblazoned across the body of this thing, or we were prepared for a lot of questions I don't have answers for, it might have been feasible.

The Baltimore Heliport, on the other hand, is smack in the industrial part of town, which is almost deserted at this time of night, and an easy landing for me and my reflexes, which are getting blunt with fatigue. I bring us down heavily, and then power down while Jay jumps out to speak with the night manager. I take a breath, slide out of the cockpit, and give myself a talking to. I can do this.

But my thoughts are fragile and edgy, and the Bell's tanks seem to take too long to fill. I just want to get moving. I want this to be over. I keep thinking about the Bradleys. Are they okay? The situation back at the house looked messy. Who shot the fuel tank and why?

While I wait, I watch Carolyn. She took a call after we landed, and now she's at the door to the shed-like pilot lounge, still on the phone. The heliport is basically one long concrete landing pushing into the Patapsco River, and I brought the Bell down on the largest yellow circle, at the very end. Carolyn is too far away to make out her expression, but she has that taut set of her shoulders she gets when she's hearing something she doesn't like.

The night manager—a stocky, taciturn guy in a boiler suit—finally unhooks the hose, replaces the fuel cap and looks at us. There's a short but fantastical interlude where I realise that the price of Jet A is about the same as liquid gold, Jay realises he doesn't have enough fictional cash to cover it, and I'm forced to lie about getting some more from the cabin when what I'm really doing is hiding there while I write a few hundred dollars into my pocket. None of which helps my state of mind.

Once that's over, Jay pulls a flashlight out of the cabin and we investigate the fuselage for damage. There's only a benign burst of bullet holes across the doors and some near-miss nicks close to the transmission. Lucky.

'Lucky,' says Jay, verbalising my thoughts. He clicks off the flashlight, and we stand together in the semi-darkness for a moment, watching Carolyn. There's fear breathing at me from every angle, like the icy cross-breeze on this pier. What's going to happen when we get there? Will we find him? Will I have to kill him to stop him? The darkness of the old fear inside me might be enough to help me pull a trigger. Or it might not. Could I really kill another person, in real life? I grit my teeth, screwing up my courage. The truth is, I don't know.

'We need to go,' I say, shivering, and I move to climb back into the cockpit. But in the darkness, Jay puts his hand into mine. I still.

'We have time,' he says. His voice is quiet. He's as still as stone, as if this is an eternal moment, one that will hold true through endless days and nights till the end of time.

I take a shivery breath, and my heart breaks.

Everyone dies, eventually. The people in my life, especially. And moments are all we have. If you knew you were going to die, wouldn't you take hold of the moment while you could? Jay's hand in mine tells me that's what he's doing. I can hardly bear it. It makes me want to scream. I've been drowning in the idea that it was a mistake to let him come, that he was sitting right beside me but already lost to me forever, and now we're standing here holding hands.

'We have to go,' I say again.

'You can do this, Evie. I trust you.' I hear him breathe out. His hand is warm, and it's enough to melt at least some of the hard dread inside me. I let him pull me closer to him, like a tiny magnet to metal. I've always been drawn to him, this strength and purity he has that's irresistible.

'How do you know?' I mumble.

'Because I know you,' he says. 'I know you.' He pauses. 'I know you love cold weather, and your comfort food is shepherd's pie. When you're feeling stuck or lonely, you listen to that piano guy.'

'Chopin.'

'Yeah, because you say his music is complicated and calming at the same time, and it helps somehow. You wish you'd paid more attention when your aunt Jo tried to teach you to cook. You don't like trimming the hedges in your yard because they're rosemary and the scent reminds you of your mom. You can't dance. You're a bad liar. You eat liquorice because your dad liked it. And you love people. Whether you admit it to yourself or not. I hear your voice change when you talk to your aunt and uncle on the phone, and I know you paid for their new house. The top drawer of your desk is full of letters you wrote to your dad after he died, and I think the reason you suck at answering your phone is probably because even after all the years since then, you're still afraid it's bad news. It hasn't been easy for you, but you're getting there.' He puts a gentle finger under my chin and tips it up. 'Your courage is beautiful.'

'Jay, please shut up,' I say hoarsely. 'Stop talking like this. As if...as if...'

'Evie,' his tone changes, 'I need to say something to you, and it's not gonna sound great. I need to apologise. For kissing you.'

'What?' I can't see the expression in his eyes, which are mostly hidden in darkness, something I've been grateful for since there are tears streaming down my cheeks.

'It was selfish,' he says, and I'm caught by a vibration in his tone. 'I should've let you write. Maybe we wouldn't be here right now if I'd just left you alone. But I wanted to. I've wanted to for so long.'

In that moment I discover something about Jay. Kissing me was scary for him, too. It means the first thing he did with his free will was to be vulnerable. That strikes me as wonderfully brave. Yet he maybe feels as naked as I do about this. About me. He let me see his feelings, and it was a risk for him. Cops really don't cry. Feelings are a luxury they can't afford, to be able to do their job well. To put others first.

He doesn't want to lose me either. But he put his heart in my hands.

'You don't regret it, do you?' I don't want him to say yes.

A pause.

'I should.' But his voice tells me he doesn't, and I feel the brush of his fingers on my cheek.

He pulls me in nearer, so near that I can bury my face in his shirt. It's creased and he's smelled better. It's wonderful. He pulled his vest off on the ride here so the only thing between us is our clothes and I relax into him, feeling as though his warm solidity is all I could ever need.

I lift my head and say, 'You don't need to.'

He grazes a hand up my side to rub a gentle thumb over my cheek again, which makes me want to kiss him, but with effort I keep my focus and say, 'I'm glad you kissed me, and it wouldn't have made a difference if you hadn't, anyway. I needed to learn how to write my own story, and if anything, you helped me do that. You made me realise how much I'd been hiding. You helped me.' I take a breath. 'I have to finish this, Jay. I have to change things.'

'So how does it turn out? Your own story?' I hear that vibration again. 'Do you know?'

I bite my lip and look at the river. 'No. But I know it means I can't let being scared stop me anymore. I want a happily ever after, like anyone does.'

I feel him smile. 'You want the cliché.'

The ride-off-into-the-sunset cliché. I might as well face it.

'Yes. That's what I want.'

'Sunshine. Birds and stuff.'

'Yes. And rainbows. And a unicorn, preferably. If at all possible.'

'After what I've seen you do today, I'd believe anything's possible.' Something catches his attention over my shoulder, and I see Carolyn stalking back across the tarmac toward us. 'Time to move.' His hand drops back to my side.

'Jay,' I resist the space he puts between us as a cold slice of air sneaks in, 'what do *you* want?'

'Evie.' It's a sigh. 'I want a thousand ordinary things with you.' His hands on me tighten. 'I like the idea of a happily ever after. But I think maybe it's just peace of mind. What I believe in, is doing everything we can to make things right.'

'Everything.'

'Everything,' he says.

We stand together for a second more, my eyes lowered, my anger igniting at him again for being so damn noble, and then I turn toward the cockpit, my thoughts trampled and difficult. But Jay spins me back and pulls me into a hug. His lips brush mine before he lets go. I feel the reluctance and the determination in him, and it's awful.

Like a robot I climb into the cockpit and buckle up. I plug new latitude and longitude coordinates into the GPS, adjust my headset and start powering up. Carolyn slams the door to the cabin closed with extra fury.

Jay says, 'What is it?'

'That was the Captain,' she growls. 'He left the Hamptons about forty minutes ago.'

The engine is gaining volume. They both reach for their headsets, and Carolyn's voice continues in my ear. 'It was a freaking mess. All the Southampton cops shot dead. That was Daniel unconscious by the helipad. Bleeding out from gunshot wounds. Looks like he's the one who caused the explosion.'

There's a pause while I stuff down my emotions and request clearance for departure. I press on into the complicated balancing act between power, lift and torque that judders us into the air.

Then I say, 'It was Daniel?' Daniel was the crumpled Ken doll lying in the grass.

'He's okay,' she says. 'He's been stabilised and taken to hospital. But the rest...something isn't right. The whole house was abnormally scrubbed and sterile, and two very expensive cars missing from the Bradleys' garage.'

'Abnormally?' I say. 'I mean, the Bradleys have cleaning staff. A scrubbed house wouldn't be unusual.'

'Do they use sodium hydroxide on all the surfaces?' Sodium hydroxide destroys DNA.

A few seconds pass before I have us moving forward on a sensible incline. *The ninjas. Was there another team sent to the house? Did we leave the Bradleys there to walk into a trap?*

'Before he lost consciousness, Daniel claimed it was Raymond Drummond who shot him.'

This rocks me. 'Vyper? How? Why?'

'The Captain has no idea. He thought we should ask you. Also, James and Eileen are missing.'

I feel something heavy bloom in my chest. No.

I look out into the darkness. Flying at night means the horizon and most visible landmarks are gone as reference points, and so it more or less feels like manoeuvring through a distant cosmos or a dream. There are constellations of lights below us, the night-lights of Baltimore city, but I know these will peter out as we hit the Appalachians, and stay sparse as we head further into West Virginia, the lonely farmhouses and smaller towns only making faint blips in the sea of darkness below us.

'You think they were taken as hostages?' Jay is all business.

'It doesn't matter now,' I say. 'All that matters is finding Bobby.'

46

The GPS pings.

'Now what?' Carolyn's voice in my ear is tense.

I set my mouth.

Wirt County. A nondescript splotch in the north-west quadrant of the state. The county doesn't look that big on a map, but it's about 600 square kilometres, and the least populated in West Virginia. I realise that it's one thing to make it here, and another thing entirely to find a solitary farmhouse of generic characteristics, the only defining feature of which is that I will hopefully *just know* it's the right one.

There's nothing but rolling darkness below. I wriggle in my seat, feeling strangled by the harness. I want to know where he is—and I don't. And the turmoil of not knowing is sickening. What a mess I've made. He could be anywhere.

Jay and Carolyn stay silent while I set us heading due west, drop us a hundred feet, and slow to about half the maximum cruise speed. I plan to fly east–west vectors over the whole county at about two-kilometre intervals, and then complete the grid doing north–south laps of the same distance. That way, at least, we'll cover most of the ground, and have the most chance of finding the right place. Trouble is, it's going to take us all night.

Jay ramps the Nightsun, a white-hot spotlight attached to the outside of the cabin, and sweeps it around using a grey control console he unhooks from the instrument panel. The bleaching beam picks out densely wooded hills, fields and the occasional building or outhouse. But there's nothing to suggest we've reached our destination, and behind me I can sense Carolyn's impatience unfolding like a sail. She wants to fire questions at me, and wring out every bit of information she can. But she keeps silent. Instead, she begins to deliberately gather the tension inside herself, like a coil, like a cat ready to spring. The Blade will not get away this time, if she can help it. All her energy is fixed on that one outcome.

The sky starts to lighten around four in the morning and as it does, my frustration peaks. Jay switches off the Nightsun and the grey shades of the early morning sky seem to blur the view of the trees below us. *He's already there*, I think. *We've missed him.*

And then, when dawn seems too close but is probably still twenty minutes away, I catch sight of a distant pinprick—a red tail-light— and something inside me jumps. It isn't the first one I've seen, but this one is different. There's a car following the winding, wooded road that leads over the next hill. I take us that way, and drop us down another hundred feet.

I lose sight of the tail-light for a moment, as whatever vehicle it's attached to has turned, taking it deeper into a line of shrouding trees. It's a driveway, the kind of narrow dirt-packed track that leads into the heart of a large property. And it's not a car, it's a van. Not blue, though. The grainy light reveals that it's off-white and ordinary, like the van that drove me out to the cliffs in Newport. I pull up and put some speed on to get us ahead of it, and there, over the crest of a small hill, I see a ramshackle wooden farmhouse and the sloping roof of a big barn.

Carolyn catches my jump in heart rate as if she was listening for it, and flies out of her seat, almost wedging herself half into the cockpit in her suspense.

'Easy, Harding,' Jay says, but rather than acknowledge him, from the corner of my eye I see her turn back to rummage in the gear we brought with us, including the machine guns.

'Read the instructions,' I caution. 'Carolyn? And for goodness sake, let me bring us down before you start firing.'

The van has slowed and stopped near the house. The barn is about sixty metres from it, close to a low hill, and from the air both buildings have the slack, moth-eaten look of long disuse. As we get closer I see there's a litter of abandoned cars in an overgrown field beside the two buildings, and I consider aiming for the clearest space in this. It's a better option, safety-wise, as it will give us some cover if Bobby has a weapon. It will make for a difficult landing, but it's better than blocking the space in front of the barn, which would put us directly in the way of what Bobby wants.

Is it him? Something in my constricted cells tells me it is. We're only about forty feet in the air and I can't see the van's driver, but I would be a fool to land us too close. I have to assume Bobby will use any means to secure his escape. And he is surely armed.

It's light enough to see now, but the sun has yet to edge its way over the hills, so I take us in the direction of the field. Landing there will put us about fifty metres from the house, but it will allow us a clear shot to both the van and the barn. There cannot be any other outcome but one to this scenario. The Blade cannot leave this property free.

I'm inching the collective down when the thump of automatic fire cracks across us. It's him. He's standing beside the van in his too-big brown suit, holding an AK-47, like the cliché he is.

I'm so fed up with being shot at. I land us hard, dangerously close to a burnt-out pickup truck with weeds twining its crumpled frame, and power down fast. Before I'm done, Carolyn has thrown the cabin door open and she's firing back at him with one of the MP5s. Jay is out of the cockpit, crouching behind the scorched pickup with his Glock, close to the nose of the chopper. Bobby has run forward and hunkered down, taking cover behind the shell of a rusted sedan. There's fifty metres' worth of corroded farm vehicles and a wavy sea of thigh-high grass between us and him. And I know that if he keeps firing at the chopper, he's going to hit the fuel tank and we're going to go up in a fireball.

I tear off my headset and fling open the cockpit door, jump down to where Carolyn has climbed from the cabin, yank her out of the way and say, 'Get clear of the chopper while I distract him. He won't kill me,' then I fling myself in front of her and run. Actually, I'm not sure he won't kill me. We're too close to sabotaging his freedom. I don't know what he might do.

'Evie, no!' I hear Jay exclaim, but I keep going.

I run forward, stumbling in the long grass, straight for the last place I saw Bobby, waving my arms like some kind of lunatic human shield. As I get closer, I can see his white face, like a pale smudge behind the sedan's corroded fender. I keep running, until I can make out his expression. He doesn't know what to make of me. He doesn't know whether or not to shoot at me. And then I see the exact moment when his eyes go hard and he decides.

He pops up, lifts the AK-47 and fires a bank of 7N10 rounds straight into my abdomen.

I feel them hit me, and I fall.

I blink, down there in the grass. It hurts. From my position I see the Blade jump up and run toward the barn. That's where he stashed the AgustaWestland. He's been holding on to it all this time, with this particular contingency in mind. It's his ticket out of here, and once he gets in that thing, his getaway is assured. He's undoubtedly got cash, weapons and a thoughtfully prepared go-bag ready to use. He'll disappear.

Carolyn isn't firing at him. I wonder why? I hear Jay yelling my name. My gaze swivels toward the Bell, and I see Carolyn standing beside the open cabin door and holding something big. Ah, good. It's the AT-4. It's an anti-armour rocket launcher. I knew when I wrote it into existence that Carolyn would be the one to use it. I hope she read the manual. The thing has three safeties she'll have to disengage.

Without a beat of hesitation she yanks the stop against her shoulder, braces herself and aims it toward the barn. I watch her fingers flip down the red tab of the final safety. The load explodes out of the barrel with an ear-ringing report. I squint the other way. That weapon is faster than Bobby.

Boom! The barn ignites in a fantastic fiery mess. A beat later there's a second detonation, which means the fuel tank on the AgustaWestland just exploded too. Bobby's running form is thrown down by the impact, and heat washes over me. I smile.

I move my head again and see Carolyn staggering a bit. Launching that rocket without earmuffs has undoubtedly left her shaken and deaf. I also realise that Jay is kneeling beside me. He's shifted me so he can look at my stomach. His hands press me and his face is haggard, but there's confusion there as well. I put a shaky hand on my abdomen and it comes away clean. The pain is fading.

'Told you I'm a superhero,' I say.

I put my hand into my jeans pocket and pull out the crumpled piece of paper, on which I wrote the words *I am bulletproof.*

I wasn't sure they would work. I'm awfully glad they did.

'Evie.' Jay shakes his head. He seems unsure whether to be traumatised or furious. This makes me smile again, and then I'm not smiling anymore. There's a gun pointing at the back of Jay's head. Bobby, recovered after the explosion, has found a convenient hostage.

Jay's eyes lock on mine, and he puts his hands carefully into the air.

'Stand up,' Bobby says, his voice raised over the sound of the barn on fire, and Jay obeys.

'No!' I gasp.

'Step back from her.' The Blade skips back a little to give Jay space.

No. No.

Time slows down. This is it. This is exactly what I feared. Jay is going to die. And it's my fault.

I can see the calculation in Jay's eyes. Bobby is clutching his assault rifle like someone with nothing left to lose, and Jay is too far in front of him to spin and disarm him. I roll onto my front and jump up. My instinct is to launch myself between them like a human shield again.

But as I tense myself to do this, Bobby grates, 'Don't think about it.' His eyes are hollow, and they glance at me, to where he knows he shot me—with my un-bloodied clothing and my excellent state of health—as if he understands everything. 'He'll be dead before you take a step, little writer. Now tear up that paper you've got in your hand. *Slowly.*'

The scribbled page crumples between my fingers as I clench my fist. How could he know? Or does he only suspect? I look back at Carolyn, but it seems she's still recovering and has just managed to dump the spent cylinder of the AT-4 and grab up the MP5 again. In any case, she's on the wrong angle. Jay is blocking her shot.

'I said *now*,' Bobby repeats. But I can't do that. If I do that the guns will disappear and I'll be left like ash on the ground, as if half of me has been granulated down and vaporised in a supernatural wind. And Bobby will kill Jay. I swallow hard and drop my fist with the crumpled paper to my side.

'No,' I say.

'No?' Bobby snarls.

'*No*,' I say, glaring into his vacant eyes. As I do I crunch the paper, one-handed, into a ball and drop it behind me into the windblown grass. 'This is the end for you!' I yell, but I'm shaking all over. All I want to do is distract him from destroying the words I wrote, but I think I might be making things worse. 'The *end*,' I repeat, but my tone rings hollow.

Bobby starts to cackle. His features are slack and insane, and there's a cold finality in his eyes.

'Oh, dear,' he says, still cackling. 'Y'all had some surprises for me, didn't you? Well I got surprises, too. Back up, Detective.'

I look at Jay, who's still facing me, swamped by a wave of regret. I've failed. Bobby registers my expression.

'Ah,' he says. His eyes swivel between the two of us. 'I guess it wasn't Daniel after all.' He smiles. 'Will it hurt if I kill him?'

I'm going to be sick. This is all his dreams come true. To truly hurt me, that's what he's wanted all along. I've lost. Bobby will never be stopped. He's fragile and fractured, but he's a genius, and he'll find another faceless financial guy to fund another ludicrous plan that will hurt more people. He will kill more girls, and I won't be able to stop it. Not alone.

It can't end this way. I can't let this happen.

They're a good distance from me now. Carolyn has her gun raised, and she's inching steadily forward through the grass, but she's being careful about it. The MP5 has superb accuracy, and with selective fire she could tap out a single round if she wished. Her focus is zeroed on Bobby, like a short-range missile on a hot target.

Bobby starts to laugh again.

'Oh, man, I don't believe it. The trouble I could have saved myself. I could have destroyed you! I didn't know. It would have been so easy to kill this one. Just one bullet. It's a damn shame. And you,' he calls to Carolyn, 'Miss Harding. A pleasure. It sure has been a long game, but those are the best kind. It's been fine, watching you dance for me.'

With this he steps up close behind Jay and jams the gun against his right side so that it's pointing at Carolyn. I watch, helpless, from my position several steps away, as Bobby uses his other hand to press the point of his old pocketknife hard against Jay's neck, effectively keeping him in place. One flick and Jay will bleed out in minutes. Carolyn is still about thirty metres away, and Bobby is entirely covered by Jay's bulk.

'I think I'll kill all of you,' he murmurs.

Jay's arms are in the air and he's looking at Carolyn. She's looking straight back at him, and I glance between them. Jay widens his hands slightly, as if presenting a bigger target. Carolyn presses her lips together, apparently receiving loud and clear whatever it is that Jay is communicating to her.

Oh. My mind blunders into understanding.

No.

Bobby is so close behind Jay that any bullet Carolyn fired would hit them both. She has the stock jammed into her shoulder, squinting through the rear sight, and those are 9mm FMJs she has in there. I chose them for the ninjas in case they wore body armour. A full metal jacket will pierce a human body—bone, organs and all—and damage downrange. And in fact, although Bobby is lankier than Jay, he's almost the same height, and their hearts are lined up perfectly, one behind the other.

If Carolyn shoots Jay, she could kill Bobby. Hit Jay in the right place, and she definitely will. And now I see their silent conversation for everything it is.

No.

My mouth moves to shout, twisting my head back to Jay, but I'm too slow. He nods at Carolyn, just the tiniest movement: *Do it.*

I hear the burst of fire as Carolyn taps the trigger.

Bang.

She's an excellent shot.

Life warps into slow motion. Jay looks at me as he falls, his eyes deep and blue, like a hug, like a goodbye. He crumples forward, while Bobby's eyes go surprised and then blank, and he falls backward.

No.

I run, ears ringing, and skid to my knees beside Jay. I scrape the AK-47 out of the way and try to push him onto his back. Try to do something, anything.

But Jay's eyes are empty, and there's blood leaking out of the wound in his back where the bullet left his body. My head is full of noise. I think I'm crying, and my hands are getting covered in his blood, when Carolyn comes up behind me and pulls me roughly back.

She hauls me to my feet and yells at me.

'Write him back in Evie!'

What? I stare uncomprehendingly at the urgent stab of her blue eyes.

'*There's still time.* Write him back in, *now.*'

Write him back in. My mind latches onto this and I shove a bloody hand into my pocket for that crumpled paper. But it isn't there. Of course it isn't. I threw it away. I look around, but there's nothing except tall green grass in every direction.

No.

What do I do? Jay's face is grey. Carolyn is kneeling beside him, pressing her hands onto the hole in him. '*Hurry up Evie!*' Her eyes are full of rage and desperation.

My thoughts are colliding together with panic but I spin and sprint toward the farmhouse. There has to be something to write with in there. There *has* to be.

I throw my full weight against the door, and it bursts open. The dereliction inside pierces me. There's a moldering sofa and a bit of carpet. I stumble down a hallway pocked with empty bedrooms and an ancient bathroom and find myself in the kitchen.

No. No. There's nothing here but a wooden table, and Jay is gone.

I collapse against the sink. Tears and sobs are pressing at my throat and I squeeze my eyes shut. But as I do, something burns into my vision—a rusty knife. There's an old knife in the sink.

I scoop it up and whirl toward the huge kitchen table abandoned in the centre of the room. I begin scratching into the wood with the feverish need of a drowning person clutching at a life preserver. The wood is soft enough. It will work. But what do I write?

Write him back in. Write the story.

What *is* the story?

That same emptiness is still there. I was blocked before—I didn't want to write Book Sixteen. Deep down I didn't want to finish it because I didn't want Jay to die. I get that. Now I will write anything to keep him alive. But *anything* has never worked for me. I need the inspiration.

Because I don't make the stories, I just write them down.

And I still don't know how this story ends.

How does this story end?

'Please,' I say. To whoever it is. 'Give me this story.'

Please.

And then something happens. Or someone.

Something blows through the farmhouse, but it isn't wind. It feels more like water, the way it washes and cools as it goes, but it isn't that either. There are words, and they aren't mine. I feel a gentle hand on my back, light as a butterfly. Someone says, *I'm so glad you decided to write yourself into your story, Evie.*

It's like being sung to by the stars.

And then it's over. I slump over the table, gasping.

When I peel myself back there are words there, a whole paragraph in my handwriting, jagged and almost illegible. The kitchen table is covered with it. I run shaking fingers over the scratched-in words.

Jay?

The kitchen is full of sunlight. The sunrise is over, and the day is in full swing. I can see it through the filthy windows. I drop the knife and stumble outside to find that the brightness is almost blinding. I shield my eyes with my hand, squinting toward the barn and the place where the Bell should be, over to my left.

The farmyard is empty. The barn is intact. The Bell is gone.

I run to the barn and throw open the doors.

It's empty. Dust motes whirl in the big slashes of morning light.

The unkempt grass hushes gently in the breeze. The place is deserted.

47

The lights are blinding. I can't see the audience, not that I want to. It's a sea of benign housewives enjoying the sight of a very minor celebrity about to fumble her way through a live television interview.

I blink and smile at Marcia as the applause dies down. She's very pretty, even prettier in person than on television. She has that brisk, lacquered way about her that people seem to get when they've been a popular talk show host for a while.

She just introduced me, though I barely heard it—*New York Times* best-selling author Evie Howland—and now she's saying a number of other positive things, which it is her job to do. Her teeth are an icy, glowing white, all the better to chew on sensationalist tidbits. Here comes one now: *high-profile split with wealthy playboy Daniel Bradley.*

I don't flinch. All her questions and comments were cleared beforehand with my new agent, Lily, so I was prepared for this. Mostly. I smile blandly.

'Well I am a fan, as you know,' Marcia takes a little excited breath, 'and I think I speak for a lot of people when I say that I can't believe the series is ending! Is it true?'

I swallow. The lights are so hot.

'It's true.' I smile again.

'So everyone out there, yes, this is your last chance to curl up with a cup of cocoa and enjoy the company of Harding and Ryan. If you've loved being a part of their world then you definitely shouldn't miss this final instalment. And this last book is special, isn't it?'

I clear my throat. 'Yes...the series, uh, well you could say it ends with a bang.'

'That's right! So,' her sales-pitch voice kicks in, making her seem even more delighted to be near me, 'it's Book Sixteen and it's coming out soon. And here it is, we have an early release to see there,' she angles a new hardcover copy to minimise glare for Camera One, 'and I believe it will be out in a couple of weeks?'

'December First.'

'So, hitting the shelves in time for Christmas, and I'm warning you ladies, be prepared for some surprises. If you were left on the edge of your seats at the end of Book Fifteen, then I can tell you there's quite a ride in store for you.'

I widen my smile. This isn't the first splashy promotional interview I've done since the finished manuscript went to print. The smile is almost natural. Talking about Book Sixteen and raking deliberately over *the dramatic end to the series* has almost become natural too.

'Obviously I'm not allowed to give away any spoilers,' Marcia continues, 'but I have a confession to make. I wrote to your publisher and asked for an advance copy.'

This is unexpected. My smile stays in place, just. My publisher had been almost offensively joyful about me getting into the limelight and creating some buzz, especially since the series was finished. But I don't know how prepared I am to discuss the finer details.

Marcia looks a like a cat with a saucer of cream. Possibly I'm the cream.

'I had to sign all sorts of things to safeguard the actual plot,' she says, 'but I can say one thing, this book is your best yet.'

'Thank you,' I murmur. I'm beginning to wonder if I've underestimated Marcia and her generic chat-show plasticky-ness.

'It was quite unlike your other books in some ways, or when I say *unlike*, it was more that there was, well, more. In some places the action was so real, it was like you had lived it yourself. Where did the inspiration come from?'

Ah. The segue. A little more lip-smacking scandal. Marcia's teeth shine in the key lights. Because she, like the rest of the world, knows that Daniel Bradley is in a coma in New York-Presbyterian Hospital due to injuries received at his parents' Southampton home. They know there was an explosion there, and some kind of gun battle. They also know that James and Eileen Bradley are missing, and that Juliana has taken over as acting CEO of Amiton Corp., making her not only the 54th richest woman in America but also one of the most powerful. Unfortunately, the company is under investigation for a number of crimes, due to some suspicion cast by the preceding events, so she's had a rocky start to her leadership role.

'Well, I suppose I've had a little experience with real-life drama this year,' I say cautiously. I try not to look as nervous as I am. The truth is I feel unequivocally terrible about the Bradleys, and especially Daniel. And confusion and remorse look ugly on television. It would be nice to survive this with some dignity intact.

Marcia latches onto this like a snake with a small bird.

'Yes, you were in the news a little, back in early May,' she says with a gentle false timidity, a tone of voice designed to make me feel safe. She knows she's casting Lily's demands to the wind on live TV. 'I think we probably all remember.' As if she had forgotten the CNN broadcasts from six months ago for even a second. 'It was a little shocking. Did you want to talk about that?'

Oh, if only I could.

The one comfort I have is that Marcia doesn't know about West Virginia. How I walked along country backroads in the morning sunshine with Jay's blood on my clothes until I found a tiny diner outside a town called Elizabeth and used the pay phone to call the only people I knew would believe me about how I got there. Mr and Mrs Andrews. And how I spent four hours waiting for them to call back, after they had checked out exactly how things stood— such as, whether I was wanted by the FBI. Whether Daniel was alive.

I spent the first two hours drinking terrible coffee, wishing for tea, and staring at nothing, and the next two scribbling on napkins with a borrowed pen.

They wired me money, and I found a motel, checked myself in, and cleaned myself up. I didn't sleep, though. And when they pulled up the next day in their old neatly waxed Lincoln, and Mrs Andrews saw the piles of napkins in the room, the first thing she said was, 'Looks like you're almost done, dearie.' I promptly burst into tears.

Mrs Andrews gave me a spiral notebook and another pen, and I wrote all the way home. They drove me back to my aunt and uncle's house, and then I went and faced the music with the police. The real police, that is.

I had to, because some things had remained after writing everyone back in. Some things—far too many to be comfortable—had somehow become a part of real life. The charred wreckage of my house, for one, along with the dead ninjas at Amiton Corp., the bullet holes and the traumatised executives. It was huge news. Uncle Allan made enquiries and told me that the NYPD's best estimate on the ninjas' identities was that they were a group of professional hit-men brought into the country through links with the Czech mafia. But since there were no identifying documents or markings on any of the bodies, these were just educated guesses. The investigation is in the hands of the FBI, who are interested, I imagine, in finding out what Amiton or the Bradleys did to incite a personal attack on their headquarters. Like I said, it's very uncomfortable.

Other things skittered out of reality altogether, as if they'd never been anything other than fiction. Sally Carston, twenty-six, Brooklyn schoolteacher, was one of these. The five brave members of the Southampton PD who I thought had died inside the Bradley mansion were also untraceable. No one from that precinct had been called out that night, and all were currently living full lives when I enquired. Tillman, Hinds, Johnny Diamond, Wade Best and Orson Bidgood were non-existent too. Even poor old Green and Alderman.

And all of Bobby's machinations, including the GB warehouse, the exploded van on Wall Street and all the damages thereof—human and otherwise—well, none of it happened, apparently. Not here, not ever. Deleted from reality. And my aunt and uncle, thank goodness, had no memory of being rushed out of their home and into police protection. It was like it never happened.

What remained of the debacle, for me, was a missing agent—Jenna resigned the same day she called me, got in a taxi and disappeared—an unconscious ex-fiancé, a hectic pile of napkins covered in my handwriting and a public entanglement in some bona fide mystery. I spent long hours fielding questions from the police. *Did I have any idea who would attack my home? Did I know anything about Daniel Bradley's business dealings? Where was I when Daniel Bradley was gunned down at his Southampton estate?*

Thankfully Mr and Mrs Andrews provided willing alibis for a couple of these trickier questions. Meanwhile the tabloids told delighted tales of Daniel's wild living and life-threatening coma, accompanied by pictures of me—looking pale, jumpy and dishevelled as I left the police station—and footage of my burnt-out home. I lived with my aunt and uncle for a few months while my house got cleaned up, and I wrote. Aunt Jo worried frequently and out loud about my lack of sleep, but Book Sixteen was finished in record time. And I didn't see a single character.

My publisher rushed the printing to make it in time for Christmas, and I found Lily. It was she who recommended this series of interviews to clear up 'my side of the story'. And after everything I'd been through, a little limelight didn't seem so scary anymore.

'Well,' I say to Marcia, 'part of the inspiration did come from real life, I admit. It did make an impact.'

'Yes,' she says, now visibly endeavouring to sound caring. 'I mean, your home was the subject of an arson attack, your fiancé's—sorry, *ex*-fiancé's—family is being investigated for possible involvement with organised crime...kidnapping, attempted murder. I mean, this seems a little Hollywood, but there are a lot of people in your life either missing or under suspicion at the moment. Do you have any explanation?'

'Um. I guess everyone makes mistakes. I got involved with the wrong guy. It happens.' I feel horrid, shafting Daniel when he's in a coma and can't defend himself. 'There's a lot I can't talk about, obviously, because of the ongoing police investigation.' I throw this out knowing that Marcia will love it, and she does.

'But what was it like, having your home burned down?' She can't let it go.

'Well, it didn't burn down completely.' I wink. 'We women, you know, we move on, we rebuild.'

'We write best-selling crime thrillers!' Marcia tosses her head as if she's just been awarded the prize for Wittiest Feminist.

'Maybe. And do television interviews,' I add, and she titters.

'Success is the best revenge!' Her eyes catch mine. She would love to paint me that way, I see.

'No,' I say. 'I don't want revenge. The truth is I'm very concerned about Daniel, and I want him to be well. But that chapter is closed for me. That's all. I'm glad to be writing a new one.'

'Yes! A new start. With someone new? Is there someone in your life at the moment?'

'No,' I say. 'Not right now.'

'Well. But writing...Are you working on something new? Can we expect a new series, or do you have any other projects coming up?'

'Well...ah, there's always stuff happening. I needed some time after I finished Book Sixteen and after...everything. I've been in talks with some people about different, um, opportunities, but I'm just kind of taking time to get back onto my feet again. I'll see what comes up next.'

The cameras cut for the break and Marcia thanks me. I step down off the dais into the semi-darkness and three women appear out of the shadows to greet me. Lily, Mrs Andrews and Magdeline.

Lily is apologetic.

'I am so sorry, Evie. I had a nasty feeling she would pull something like that but I never expected—'

'It's fine,' I say, waving down her concern.

'In any case you did great, really great. You handled her beautifully.'

'Thanks, Lily.' She's a sweet slip of a thing with a little elfish face and bright blonde hair in a girlish up-twist. I like her. 'Thank you for coming, all of you.'

'Weel, dearie,' Mrs Andrews sparkles, 'I wouldna missed it.' She meets my eyes, and we have a conversation with that glance. She knows how far I've come in the last six months. I've spent a lot of time in her cosy living room, drinking tea. 'You're doing very well, lassie. New chapter. Very nice.'

'Please. It was such a cheesy metaphor, Evie,' Magdeline says.

'Och, wash your mouth out, ye wee tramp,' Mrs Andrews exclaims with a smile, and I laugh out loud. 'When ye've finished your own book ye can make comments about Evie.'

I laugh again, loving the dynamic between them. Magdeline has spent quite a lot of time eating shortbread at Mrs Andrews' house too. After surviving the attack at Amiton—something she doesn't remember all that well and is seeing an expensive psychologist about—Magdeline decided to abandon wedding planning and instead pen a tell-all book about the rich and famous. So I introduced them.

I make a mental note to talk to Magdeline about libel.

'In any case,' says Lily, 'that's your last dodgy interview. Only signings and trustworthy media contacts from here on. At least until you write something new, or you start dating someone moderately famous.'

'That won't be happening,' I say.

48

I pull into my driveway, and see that my front door is wide open. I drive a plain black hatchback these days. It's inconspicuous, and it has a turbocharged engine with a nitrous oxide injector. And bulletproof glass. Just in case. I like the idea of being prepared.

Not that I've written anything into existence recently. The last thing I want to do is try messing with reality again, after everything. I just want normality. Not weird supernatural stuff, thank you very much. I have no desire to experience whatever happened in that farmhouse, or any of it, ever again. In any case, I still feel like I've learned to write my own story, in a different way. I'm still making things happen—advancing my own plot, so to speak—but with actions, not words on a page.

From the outside my house looks normal and pretty, and although my yard is patchy and only half regrown, its appearance is masked by a clean layer of early snow. The inside still needs a little work.

I walk through the front door, cautious.

'Hello?' There are plastic sheets on the floor, like preparation for a tidy assassination. They lead to the kitchen and I go that way, enjoying the passion-red feature wall in my living room and the sight of my remodelled writing room. It's a spare bedroom now, painted the same colour as new-morning sunshine and looking fresh and ready for my aunt and uncle who are coming to stay next weekend. I'm taking them up to Rhode Island to do the cliff walk around Newport. To relive old times. And lay some ghosts to rest.

'Through here.'

I push open the door to the kitchen and see Bernie there, putting the finishing touches on my new shelves.

'Oh, hello Bernie. It looks great.'

'Nearly done. Saw you on TV.'

'Oh, yes? What did you think?'

'Think you'll have a bestseller on your hands.' He winks, and I smile. Of course he would say that. Bernie's wife is a fan, and I gave him an advance copy of Book Sixteen to pass along as a gift.

'Thank you,' I say. 'Are you alright to let yourself out when you're done?'

'Yeah, no problem. I won't be much longer.'

I head upstairs and change out of my short black dress and sassy heels. Magdeline chose my outfit for today, and Lily approved it, in her sweet way. I had felt satisfied, liking how good my legs look since I took up running.

I think about going for a run now, stirred by the idea of pushing my body through the bracing cold and clearing out the memory of Marcia and her cat smile. But something inside me is fluttering around, kicking up the calm I've achieved in this last little while. There's a shiver of something new. I haven't felt this in a long time. In almost six months, in fact.

I pull on jeans and a comfortable sweater—something warm and pretty—and pad down the hall to what used to be the second bedroom. When my house was being rebuilt I decided to change some things. I put my writing room on the upper floor, where I would have a view of the street through the big picture window, and where I could start afresh with some brighter, sunnier decor. The room is inviting, with a bunch of flowers on the sill, and no notes strewn around. The picture of my father and I didn't survive the fire, but I have a photo of my aunt and uncle.

I was vague with Marcia when she asked about new projects, and there was a good reason for that. There is a new project, but it's kind of secret. I've been talking to certain people, and those certain people want secrecy.

I flip open my new computer and click a blank document, running my fingers over the keys, wondering what will happen once I start pressing them, shaping words into order and meaning. Words have power. I know that now.

There's the small sting of hope, too, and of pain. I've tried this before and nothing happened. These last months have been hard. I've been lonely, and I feel the fragility of this moment and all the emotions I've come through to this point. And where I've placed them inside me. I don't flatten my feelings down into fiction any more. I've done my best to admit and then manage them one by one. Maybe they aren't neat, or ordered, but I'm learning. Figuring out how to be a human in the real world. Ha.

I take a look out my window at the artsy curls of the leafless trees on my street, wintry and glistening, and I start typing. The words come. They're there, and so is the old feeling—the burning sense of something bigger.

A couple of hours pass, I think, when there's a pause, and I have the sense of an eddy in the flow, a moment to catch my breath. I look up from my computer and realise that pages have gone by, the story telling itself under my fingertips.

The doorbell sounds. I blink. The room comes into focus. And with it, hope.

My heart picks up, and I look back at what I've written. It's not a crime novel. It's a new story. Something fresh. And close to my heart.

The doorbell rings again.

My whole body snaps to attention, and I fly downstairs. I fling the door open.

My neighbour Leslie is there, looking kind and homey in a flowered apron. The disappointment is like being buried. Of course it isn't them.

'Hi, Leslie,' I say.

My cheerful neighbour falters a little.

'Hi, Evie! Is this a bad time?'

'No! No, of course not. Come in.' I wave her in.

'I just came by to borrow a cup of sugar and see how the renovations are going.'

'Oh, sure. You want a cup of coffee while you're here?' I know she hasn't really come by to borrow sugar. Leslie has been giving me some cooking lessons in the last few weeks, so I know her cupboards are permanently and perfectly stocked. She's coming by for a break.

'I'd love one!'

I lead her through the plastic sheeting to the kitchen, but she gets sidetracked marvelling over the colour I chose for the living room. 'Oh, I like it, Evie! It's so brave!' Her voice floats behind me.

I'm not sure that's a compliment but I laugh because, either way, it's appropriate. I push open the kitchen door to see that Bernie is long gone, only a fine layer of dust as evidence of the fact that my kitchen has received the finishing touches of being rebuilt from scratch. I find the sugar, lined up in a neat row beside the flour and the cornstarch in my pantry, and pour a cup, then put on some coffee.

Leslie is talking, but I can't really hear her from here. She probably wants to remind me about the neighbourhood street party next weekend, which she's hosting, and which she's hopeful I will go to. Since I say yes to everything these days, I will likely find myself there with a name badge and a plastic cup full of punch. Turns out I'm quite popular in the neighbourhood these days, since the local clutch of elitist housewives adored their fifteen seconds of fame caused by my Hollywood-esque housefire.

I could take cookies. Maybe I'll try the shortbread recipe Mrs Andrews gave me.

I grab the milk, expecting Leslie to appear in the kitchen any moment, but I can still hear her voice from the front. She's talking to someone. And that someone has a low, serious voice that is crushingly familiar.

I walk out of the kitchen and down the hall, still holding the milk, my breath short. I stop halfway, frozen. Leslie has the door open, and she's talking to a person on the front step. When she sees me, she smiles tentatively, steps back, and opens it all the way.

She's saying something about hearing a knock, and just taking the liberty of answering the door, I think, but I don't hear her.

And it's clear that Jay doesn't hear her either.

He's looking at me. He steps inside, but stops, as if coming any closer is something he needs my permission for. His eyes are dark and serious. He looks like an electrical storm.

Leslie melts back, slightly awed.

There's movement behind him and Carolyn pushes through the door.

'It's *winter*,' she says accusingly. 'There's snow out there. Geez, how long since we were last here, Evie? Like six *months*?'

It's said in her old pointed tone, but when I glance her way, I see her sky-blue eyes are clear. 'Glad to see us?' A smile plays around her pretty mouth. Her new haircut suits her, but more than this, she looks lighter somehow, as if something has fallen away, some burden. Some bitterness maybe. It's an encouraging hint of her old self, and also of the fresh recruit she once was, back when she hadn't seen too much or been so hurt. A little shine of newness.

A happy Carolyn.

I nod, but I can't speak.

Leslie says, slightly tremulously, 'Are these some friends of yours, Evie?' I realise, belatedly, that she can see them. In fact, she's been able to see them since they got here. And I know for a fact that Leslie isn't a writer. She's just a regular person, the kind of person who shouldn't be able to see my fictional characters in the real world. Which means they aren't fictional. They're really here.

This information starts me moving toward Jay.

'Yeah, we are,' says Carolyn, watching me. 'Good friends.'

'Leslie needs a cup of sugar,' I say.

'Ah. Well, you usually have some of that. It's your second favourite food group after all. Follow me, Leslie.' Carolyn beams at her, then pushes past me, grabbing the milk from my hand as she goes. 'I'm starving. Shall I order takeout, Evie?' she calls this over her shoulder as the two of them disappear down the hall.

'Go ahead,' I say mechanically. I look at Jay.

'Harding's happy,' he says, his eyes following her.

'Yes, I...' I catch sight of a tall blond man at the front door, '...I might have something to do with that. Come in, Jack.' Jack Archer steps hesitantly through the front door. 'Good to see you.'

He nods in answer, looking slightly bewildered.

'You know Detective Ryan, of course,' I add. I motion to Jay, and he and Archer exchange greetings. 'Carolyn's in the kitchen,' I tell him. 'Would you like to go through? She's just about to order takeout.'

'Is this your house?' he asks.

'Yes,' I answer.

'Does everyone come here?'

'No,' I say. 'Only, um, only important people.' I make an ushering motion toward the kitchen and Carolyn. Archer steps past us and I turn back to Jay, to see he has closed the distance between us.

'Hey,' he says.

'Hello.'

'I like what you've done with the place.' His eyes sweep over the plastic sheeting. Then me. 'You look good, Evie.' Of course he thinks that. I've gained at least a kilo since I saw him last.

'So do you.' I don't manage much more than a whisper. He gives a faint smile that fades quickly. His eyes are deep blue.

'I've got you to thank for that.'

My eyes go to the spot over his heart. 'Is there a scar?'

'Here.' His fingers brush the place on his chest and my hand follows his. His skin is warm beneath his shirt, and I can feel his heart beating under my palm. He's solid and real.

'You're here,' I say. 'You're real.' He looks down at me.

'I've always been real,' he says. 'You didn't make me. You said so yourself.'

'Yes,' I say, 'I know.'

'But you did save my life.'

'I'm so glad you're okay.' My voice chokes a little. 'I thought maybe I wouldn't be able to write you back here. I've tried so many times.'

Just then Carolyn sticks her head around the kitchen door and yells down the hallway.

'What about Chinese?'

'No!' Jay and I shout in unison. Carolyn disappears again. Jay's eyes come back to me, a smile in them.

'What are you writing now? If the series is finished?'

'Nothing,' I say.

'Nothing?'

'Nothing for a while.' I give a faint smile of my own. 'I'm writing a screenplay. At least, I started it, this afternoon. I've been meeting with some producers. They approached me about a month ago. They want to make a movie out of the series. It's all a bit Hollywood. They wanted to give the author the first crack at the script.'

'I see.'

'I have six months to finish it, and if I don't then someone else will write it.'

Jay's eyes spark with understanding. 'Six months is generous.'

'Mmm, I'm not sure it will be enough time,' I say, my tone defeated. 'I don't think I'm going to manage it. Very sad.'

'No?'

'No,' I say. 'In fact,' and I smile, 'Mrs Andrews has promised me a very specific set of instructions on how *not* to finish it.'

'Harding told me about that.'

'She did?'

'Yeah. "*And then he. Dot, dot, dot.*"'

I laugh. 'Yes, exactly.'

'No ending,' he says.

'Yes.' I pause. 'But then, most people's stories are unfinished.' My voice is scratchy with feeling, and he catches me around the waist and pulls me into him. He's still smiling, the kind of smile you rarely see. The smile of someone with a whole new page in front of them, and they can write whatever they want.

There's a future in that smile.

'If you could write your own story, what would you write?' I ask.

'This,' he says, dropping his head and kissing me. His lips taste even better than I remember. 'And this,' he adds, kissing me again.

'This is such a cliché,' I murmur, smiling. Jay lifts his head and regards me. His blue eyes are warm and glad.

I put my arms around his neck and glance through the open front door. The late afternoon has turned bleak and grey. No sunset. Just ordinary happiness and a lot to look forward to.

And then he...

Author's Note

The idea for this story really came out of nowhere. At the time I was
working as a coordinator for a weekly sit-down meal for the homeless
in my city. Sometimes those meals just didn't go smoothly, and one
night I was driving home from work, after a particularly wild evening.
I think this night there might have been a fight between two clients
with shouting, or I might have had to call the police or an ambulance.
I don't quite remember. Either way I was feeling a bit emotional as I
drove home (I was bawling over the steering wheel). I stopped at a set
of traffic lights and suddenly, quite out of nowhere, the whole story
just downloaded into my mind. Concept, plot, characters, everything.
The whole scene with Jay and Carolyn showing up at Evie's house for
the first time, dialogue and all. I rushed home and scribbled it all into
a notebook. It was such a bizarre beginning, and the fullness of that
event is probably what gave me the conviction to keep writing it to the
end. And here we are. I expect it's obvious that my life has been much
richer and more enjoyable for having Evie, Jay, and Carolyn in it.

Note: Amiton is a real substance, also known as VG. It was discovered
by a British manufacturing company in the 1950s that was looking for
new insecticides, and I used many of these details for the story (while
changing the names of course).

Acknowledgements

Big, big thank you to all the dear ones, friends, and family, who have invested in me and encouraged me. It's such a humbling thing to look back and realise you would never have made it this far without the people who chose to give time and truth and love to you. Thank you so much to Anna Stam, Danielle Redford, Niki Brown, Lynette Lenstra, Jo Shone, Andria David, Rahel Kuhn, Kristin Mason, Fran Guerry, Liz Ludlow, Renee Soutar, Hannah Dean, Sam Brown and Ben McClure. And especially to Mum, Dad and Juliette. You know what you did.

1

TUESDAY 06:54 A.M.

I wake in the darkness, still awash in the last eddy of a dream. Sunlit images slip away from behind my eyes, trailing slowly out of reach, like the wake of a boat. *Scruffy blond hair and a rakish grin. Someone who loves to laugh, with eyes full of mischief.*

Ah. I've been dreaming a new character. So clear, and so real, like I've been introduced to him in person. But too concisely: only five seconds of information.

I smile sleepily. Mmm. It's been a while since I dreamed somebody new. I rub my eyes. A new story. Good.

I can see snow falling softly onto the dark branches of the big oak outside my bedroom window, adding another ice-cold blanket to my white front yard. The quality of the darkness tells me it's probably early morning. Too early to get up, but I let myself drift toward full consciousness anyway, feeling unusually heavy and serene, and watching the snow. Hmm. Cold. Hypothermia. Such an *interesting way to go.* Depending on the amount of clothing, a person covered in snow will only survive about...

I frown. Something feels a bit off about this.

I remember now that imagining snow-packed corpses is the last thing I should be doing, with Book Sixteen well behind me. I'm also on the opposite side of the bed to the one I normally sleep on. Is that it? Or is it something else?

I hear breathing, deep and steady. Ah. Jay.

Jay.

I stifle a small gasp. *Jay is here.* He's asleep in my bed. Here. *Here.*

I hold my breath and turn toward him, careful not to yank the duvet—he sleeps lightly. My eyes have adjusted to the dark now and I can see the near-dawn tinge is etching his profile in blue. I stare in wonder. It's really him. Detective Jay Ryan, fully-grown human man. Taking up most of my bed.

I breathe out. Romance isn't my genre, but I permit myself a fifteen-second fantasy about our future together. The satisfying ups and downs of a blissfully ordinary life, taking walks, ordering pizza, falling asleep on the sofa in front of a movie. Reading books, going on holidays, being nice to our neighbours. A small life maybe, but a good life. Slowly ageing into wrinkles and retirement. Everything I've always wanted.

A happily ever after. Him and me.

I gaze at the familiar planes of his cheekbones and the straight lines of his heavy brows and am surprised to discover a hot lump in my throat. *Okay, calm down.* I'm a bit taken aback by such a rush of feelings. I guess now that I've given myself permission to love him, well, *I love him.*

It's a very nice feeling, if the word *nice* can encompass the obliterating supernova lodged in my chest. It's also terrifying, if I'm being honest. This is the real thing, *real love*, as Mrs Andrews called it. Something worth opening up (truly, fully opening up) one's heart for. Not like my last relationship with Daniel Bradley, expert box-ticker for all things 'fairytale ending' and also, world-class adulterer. Or any of my relationships, really. This is different. Jay is...Jay.

His breathing is tranquil and even. I lick my lips. His profile is shatteringly handsome in the semi-darkness, and it kind of makes me want to poke him to make sure he's real. I mean, it's been six months since he last existed, and before that, let's just say that our relationship resembled more a *dictator-to-oppressed people group*, or *warden-to-prisoner*.

Otherwise known as *writer-to-character*.

My finger is almost touching his skin when he says softly, 'Evie.' He turns his head and stares at me. His blue eyes are two dark pools. 'What are you doing?'

I whip my hand back under the blanket and clear my throat.

'You were gonna poke me?'

'I was checking,' I mutter.

'Checking?'

'That you're real. It's a legitimate concern.'

'I'm real.' He takes a deep breath and turns on his side, toward me. He's fully awake, I see. His eyes aren't sleepy at all.

'You were awake?'

'I sleep with one eye open.'

'That's not true.' I smile.

'I didn't sleep much,' he amends.

'Oh.' Well, no surprises there, I guess. Yesterday afternoon wasn't any ordinary afternoon. The supernatural return-to-reality of my two favourite people, NYPD detectives Carolyn Harding and Jay Ryan, who just happen to be—*used to be*, I remind myself—characters in my own written crime series, was anything but ordinary. I guess I wouldn't sleep that well either if I just got handed free will and released into a world where I could, theoretically at least, fulfil all my wildest dreams.

'That's because you're on my side of the bed,' I say.

'Is that right?' This forbidding comeback is delivered with a smile, and since his smiles are so rare I feel satisfied, like I just succeeded at producing gold from lead, or something equally unlikely. He reaches for me, and I think he's going to pull me in to kiss me. I have a moment's hesitation about this since my mouth feels especially gross for some reason, but instead he flips me neatly and drags me backwards into him to spoon.

Heavenly. He's warm, and most definitely real. His hand tucks me closer.

This is it, I think, making a tiny contented noise. *This is what happily ever after looks like.* Jay Ryan, an actual and everyday part of my life. Maybe we'll end up with little just-us traditions. Maybe he'll make me his mother's lasagna and maybe we're going to find ourselves using cuddly names for each other that only ever get spoken out loud here, in this bedroom. Maybe he'll bring me flowers on random anniversaries. Maybe at some point I'll get used to his kisses instead of feeling like I'm in some kind of nuclear reactor core.

I mean, will he move in? We haven't been together for that long—okay, *hours*, technically—but we've been friends for seven years. Kind of. Because until now he's also been a shadow: not quite having substance in the real world, and without the freedom to make his own choices. Which happens to be the defining features of characters generally. At least until the way I felt about him got real enough to open some kind of cosmic doorway for him and Carolyn to live and breathe reality. I'm still unsure of the actual space-time logistics of it all. That was six months ago, when I lost control of Book Sixteen and the Blade came inches-close to killing thousands of people. I had to write both Jay and Carolyn back into the story or watch Jay die. I thought then that maybe I had lost him for good, but I haven't. He's here. And now I get to spend the whole day with him.

His body is moulded to mine, and I can feel his lips on the back of my neck. I'd very much like to stay snuggled here all

day, the length of his long legs tucked into mine. But that will
never happen. Jay Ryan would never spend the whole day in bed.
Instead, he'll probably want to take a bracing morning run first
thing and then make some kind of complicated hot breakfast,
followed by a session of meticulous cleaning up. Jay doesn't do
stillness, which is ironic since he has such a sense of stillness
about him. Downtime for him means lifting weights or tinker-
ing on the engine of an old tractor (if he was visiting his parents),
or folding his clean underwear into precise squares so that his
drawer looks like a Marie Kondo showcase. Jay's idea of *relaxed* is
anyone else's idea of *military boot camp*. But maybe we could at least
stay here until it's light outside. Maybe—

I frown. That's weird. With an uncomfortable mental flick I
realise I'm fully clothed. I lift the duvet and peer in. Jeans and
camisole with a sheer black blouse. The exact clothes I was wearing last night.

'What happened last night, Evie?' Jay murmurs the question
against my skin. The sensation of his lips on the back of my neck
is *delicious* but there's enough uncertainty in his tone to pause my
breathing. A sudden, twisty regret-knot coalesces in the pit of my
stomach. Where did that come from? My fully-clothedness starts
to take on an odd hue. Because, very obviously, *nothing* happened
last night. My clothes are snuggly in a way that suggests they
haven't been recently torn off in a torrent of passion and I realise, in a slightly deafening epiphany, that *I don't remember why*. Last
night was Jay Ryan's first night ever with free will. Surely, *something* happened?

I scrabble through the pages of my memory but last night has a
hole in it. A big blank hole, where there should be a fully painted
picture of how I made it into this bed.

I remember yesterday afternoon—my neighbour Leslie disturbing Jay and I kissing in the hall, on her way out with a cup of

sugar. I remember Carolyn deciding we should go out to celebrate instead of getting takeout. I remember the hot-cold kinetic explosion of Jay brushing my hand with his as we drove somewhere. I remember...I strain...Italian food.

'Did we drink champagne?'

Jay's answer is solemn. 'Yeah.'

Gah. *What happened?*

I'm about to roll over and ask him, when instead I rip back the duvet, spring out of bed and leap right over him like a kid in a bouncy castle. I land on the floor next to the bed on his side, my hand already halfway into the gap beneath my mattress. My fingers brush the metal of the gun I have under there, my heart thumping like a kettle drum, before reason penetrates.

Okay. It's just the sound of a dog barking, loudly. So loudly it sounds like it's ricocheting through the house from an actual loudhailer, and it gave me a fright. I'm breathing like I'm at altitude and jittery as a molecule at the quantum level. But it's not a cosmic fire alarm, or the bellow of a hulking wildebeest. No need to freak out. I yank my hand back out from under the mattress.

Jay sits up and regards me. I stare back at him and remind myself that I don't need to be afraid of hulking wildebeests. There is, after all, a very capable police detective in my bed.

'Relax, Evie. It's just Ben.'

Ben? Jay's dog, Ben? A friendly black Labrador and not any kind of wildebeest.

'What's he doing here?' I gasp.

'I picked him up last night.'

Oh. What I meant was, *What is he doing here?* As in, *Here, in the real world.*

Jay flips back the duvet and slides his legs over the edge of the bed, causing me to discover that he's in pyjama bottoms—his own. He pulls me up by the elbow.

'You're jumpy.'

'No, I just...um, I'm fine.'

Not entirely true. The appearance of Jay's pyjama bottoms and a medium-sized non-fictional animal, both of which apparently appeared in the blanky part of my memories from last night, is both confusing and kind of *not fine*.

'Stay here. I'll go let him in.'

He heads downstairs. I watch him for about a millisecond before scrambling after him. Something is off, and it isn't just waking up on the wrong side of the bed.

Ben is still barking as Jay turns to give me his hand for the last few stairs, like I'm an old person or a sleepwalker. Did I stumble? I have a weird underwater feeling, like my brain is at the bottom of a swimming pool. Frowning, I brush my fingers across the comforting blue lights of my new security system keypad on my way past the front door, then slow to a stop behind Jay at the entrance to the kitchen. There's light streaming underneath the door, probably the reason for the continued barking. I can hear other noises, too, coming from inside. They're the kind of noises that, when we stop, Jay actually raises his hand and knocks.

There are different, hasty noises now, and then ten seconds later the door cracks open and Carolyn pokes her head around it. She seems to be dressed in a men's button-down shirt and little else. Her ice-blue gaze rakes us.

'Yeah?'

Jay's tone is dry. 'Mind if we come in?'

Carolyn purses her lips and grabs something off the back of the door, tossing it further into the room. Five seconds later Jack Archer, high level investigator from the New York office of the Financial Crimes Bureau, wearing nothing but my flowery printed apron, squeezes through the door and past us down the hall as I cover my eyes with both hands.

Carolyn grins smugly, unrepentant.

Jay gives her a look before heading past her into the kitchen, and over to the back door. 'Geez, Harding.'

'That was my new apron,' I say.

Carolyn shrugs. 'Yeah well, I stole his shirt. You don't cook, anyway, what do you need it for?'

'Leslie bought it for me.'

'Leslie?'

'My neighbour. You met her yesterday.'

'Oh, yeah. When we arrived.'

She says *arrived* like stepping out of fiction into a permanent existence in reality is something characters do all the time. As far as I know, it's only ever been done once before—by my writing mentor, Mrs Andrews. When Book Sixteen got out of control I discovered that Mrs Andrews wasn't just the kindly old lady who had run my writers' group for seven years, but also, impossibly, a kind of unique specialist on some supernatural aspects of writing. It was, and still is, a bit unbelievable: namely, the process of fictional characters becoming real people. She was the one who understood that it had to do with *real love*. And I guess she would know, since she married her own protagonist.

But it isn't like it happens all the time as far as I know—or *ever*, for that matter. Which makes the unfinished screenplay I started yesterday afternoon basically a wild uncharted experiment.

Carolyn grins. 'He looks good in it, don't you think? Pity your dog ruined the mood, Ryan. How'd he get here?'

Jay opens the back door and his sleek Labrador Ben rushes in with a burst of frigid air, flakes of snow speckling his black coat. Jay grabs his collar to prevent him lavishing us both with canine love. 'I picked him up last night.'

Carolyn rolls her eyes. 'I guess you stopped at the precinct and checked it out too.'

I stare at Jay. Did he? He's intensely responsible and principled. He's also a workaholic, the kind of cop who 'stops by' on weekends or after hours because he can't get a case off his mind. Did he go by the precinct to see if it was—I gulp—like I wrote it?

'All clear.' The words are low, and his body language gives nothing away. I receive this information like a silent bullet. Of course he went straight to the precinct. And it was, apparently, like I wrote it. Meaning he still has a job there. Meaning,...He turns to me. 'You were asleep.' Understatement. I must have been in a freaking coma.

Carolyn raises her eyebrows at me. 'You did drink a lot of champagne,' she says.

'I...I...' I flounder.

'She doesn't remember,' Jay says. We exchange a glance. I feel the twisty regret-knot again. Jay's look is unreadable. 'I'm gonna dry Ben off. Okay if I use one of your old towels, Evie?'

I nod, which is all I'm capable of at this moment. Jay leads Ben out by the collar, and I stare at the empty doorway for a few moments after he's gone. Well. I think this situation might call for some liquorice. Is it too early? Certainly not.

I open one of my newly renovated kitchen cupboards and paw through it, a little blindly. One of the things that happened during the Book Sixteen debacle was that about sixty per cent of my house was badly damaged by fire (thanks to a serial killer wanting to extinguish my life, et cetera), so my kitchen is almost all brand new, and I'm not used to it yet. Carolyn slides her butt onto the marble counter and scoops some ice-cream into her mouth. *My* ice-cream. Which apparently she and Jack have been eating in here, from the tub, and having a romantic moment. I glance at her. Her shapely, supermodel legs are dangling, only partially covered by the tails of Archer's shirt, and her shoulder-length blond hair, which had been styled so prettily when she got here yesterday afternoon, is mussed and very obviously the result of zero sleep and *lots* of sex. Does she realise what she's done, what the outcome of this choice she's made will be? Does she realise what Archer is feeling right now?

A phone on the counter buzzes and she picks it up.

'So, you're wearing your same clothes from last night,' she says, thumbing the screen, sounding only vaguely interested. 'And you slept in them, it looks like. What does that mean, I wonder?'

I prevent myself from muttering something about how I wish she and Jack could have taken a freaking leaf out of that book, and say instead, 'Did you want some tea?' I open another cupboard.

Carolyn says nothing, just looks up, spoon in mouth. Then she uses the spoon to point to my clearly labelled tea canister, which is in the opposite direction to the cupboard I'm ransacking. Okay, so I'm not looking for tea. Making, offering and drinking tea is my default setting. I need something stronger than tea. I abandon the cupboard and start opening drawers.

'Whose phone is that?' I ask casually, my face in the utensils.

'Mine. I just joined the Instagram community.' My search unpauses, and then continues. 'Your account is quite active, I see,' she adds. 'Lots of signings, lots of interviews. Ooh, on TV, too.'

'Lily does it,' I say. 'My new agent. She's very sweet and helpful.'

'Huh.' Carolyn frowns at me. 'What are you doing?'

'What?'

'You're making a face.'

'Am I?' I could have sworn I had some liquorice allsorts hidden away for emergencies. I don't need many. Just one. Handful. Carolyn slurps a mouthful of ice-cream.

Maybe two.

'Yeah,' says Carolyn. 'You are.'

I turn to a tiny corner cupboard and stuff myself into it. Yes. I find the bag of liquorice behind a pile of gleaming new bakeware and clutch it for a moment like a security blanket.

Carolyn jumps blithely off the counter and thumps the lid back on the ice-cream. I make an attempt to gather some coherent conscious ability and say, 'So, you and Jack Archer...'

Carolyn quirks a communicative eyebrow at me. Yes, it's clear they had a *very* memorable night. Which, apparently, is more than Jay and I did.

'Good,' I say lightly. 'Great.' I nod my head, and then several seconds later realise I'm still nodding it.

Carolyn narrows her eyes at me, looking oddly smug. 'You really passed out last night, huh?'

I clutch my liquorice tighter. *Did I?*

'Carolyn...' I push down the twisty regret-knot and aim for casual. 'I just want to make sure that you...' I clear my throat. 'That you know what you're doing.'

She rolls her eyes. 'Yeah, I do.'

'Good. Of course.' I'm nodding again. *Stop nodding.* I'm being weird.

'Quit it, Evie. You don't get to do that anymore. You're not The Writer. And you're not my mother. So relax.'

'Of course I'm not your mother.' I give a nervous laugh. Carolyn's mother lived in a fictional trailer park outside Pittsburgh. She was the kind of crushed, struggling individual who leaned heavily into victimhood and selfishness during Carolyn's early years and didn't exactly give her daughter the best start in life. She was...*was?* Or *is?* I glance involuntarily toward the back door as though a Pittsburgh trailer park might be visible through the glass. 'I'm definitely relaxed,' I say. 'I'm very relaxed. It's your life. You can do whatever you want, er, now.'

'Yeah,' Carolyn says, with a meaningful glare. 'I can.'

She stuffs the ice-cream back into the freezer and as she does I catch sight of the bunch of frozen bananas I have in there, all black and deformed. Leslie was going to teach me how to make banana bread. Funny how bananas go black in the cold.

I open the bag of liquorice.

The thing about hypothermia is that the body's core temperature only needs to drop to about twenty-eight degrees Celsius before a cardiac arrhythmia can lead to death, and even if that doesn't happen, the heart will stop beating completely at around...

'I'm going to shower,' Carolyn says cheerfully. 'Got a big day today.'

'Oh?' I say, nonchalant. 'Doing what?'

She slants a smug look back at me. 'Wouldn't you like to know.'

She sails out, and I'm left with my liquorice. 'You could try shopping for *pantsuits*,' I hiss, under my breath. 'Or any clothes that aren't mine.'

But who am I kidding? Carolyn will never wear pantsuits. She will only ever wear jeans and skirts. And short skirts at that, though admittedly 'short' in the NYPD refers to anything up to a few centimetres above the knee, so not exactly ground-breaking. But definitely shocking, for a police department. Carolyn will openly flout the real-world unspoken dress code for New York City detectives before she steps into trousers.

Oh dear, am I breathing strangely? Here I am imagining Carolyn showing up to work today with her long, abnormally breathtaking legs on show, as if she has a job here. Does she? The station I wrote—a fictional version of the Ninth Precinct—is apparently here, and functioning as smoothly as it did in fiction, according to Jay, assuming that's what he meant by *all clear*. I pour some liquorice into my hand and stuff it into my mouth.

What is Carolyn even doing here? It couldn't be because her apartment is flooded? I wrote that into the screenplay yesterday. The very first scene was her waking up to the start of a new day, the way she always does: quick shower, strong coffee, and a dart thrown accurately into a picture of her ex-husband's face from across the room. Other people practice yoga or tai chi; Carolyn keeps her reflexes precise and her focus sharp by this one small meditative act of sending a tiny weapon into Gareth's head. She keeps a stack of these darts on her bedside table, and Gareth's smiling photo pinned to the door of her wardrobe, which is where she first noticed the water leaking. Heavens. If her apartment *is* flooded then it would mean that her apartment is *also*...here.

I poke my head through the door, hoping to ask her this before she disappears down the hall and into my spare bedroom. She isn't there, but I can hear Jay's voice floating through from the living room, and I realise he's on the phone. I recognise the tone he uses with his dad, warm and intimate. It implies a lot of shared ground and good memories.

Good. He called his father. A little early for a call, but his dad is an early riser, and clearly Jay couldn't wait to check that his family is here as well. At this moment I realise I'm clutching a handful of my hair.

Jay sounds content—relieved. I, on the other hand, dump the liquorice into a bowl and inhale a second handful. Jay loves his family. He must be thrilled they're here safe and sound in reality. I try not to visualise the fact that there's a brand-new fresh-from-fiction horse farm in South Carolina with his parents on it, and a whole lot of extended Ryan family creating goodness knows what kind of reordered-reality ripples in the space-time...whatever it is.

I think I'm beginning to realise why I might have drunk so much champagne last night. I think I might know the exact combination of revelations that led to me downing a hypothetical third (or seventh) glass. I lean over and thunk my head on the bench. The new character who came this morning is still there, too, itching at the back of my mind. That carefree, laughing smile. Wanting to be written.

I palm a third handful of liquorice, grab a pad of sticky notes and write: *Christopher Murray: blond, hazel eyes. Ambidextrous. Thief?*

I don't usually go for anti-heroes. In the cops-and-robbers construction, I'm definitely with the cops. I like order triumphing over chaos. I like a strong moral compass, and innocent people going home safe to their families.

I grab Carolyn's phone, abandoned on the counter, and type *hypothermia* into the search engine, just as Jay walks into the kitchen. I slam the phone away from me. It spins too close to the sink, slippery on my new marble countertop, and I make a clumsy lunge for it.

'You found a towel?' I ask, trying to cover this awkwardness by dumping the phone into my empty fruit bowl and making a placid little sally toward the coffee machine. I flick the switch and pull down a mug from the cupboard, unruffled, calm, as if everything is normal. I might as well make Jay his normal cup of normal black espresso so he can do his normal morning ritual and drink it, because of how normal everything is.

'Yeah. Thanks.'

'Good.' I do the nodding thing again. I lift my eyebrows with mild interest. 'You called your family?'

'Yeah.'

'Everyone okay?'

'Yeah.' Such a weight of gladness in that one word. No one does *family* like the Ryans. They're the kind of close-knit, colourful, boots-and-all there-for-each-other group of people that orphans like me only dream about. For Jay, they're the place he draws all his strength and identity from, and I can see from his body language that having them here means the universe is in its right place.

'Good. Good. That's great.' I clear my throat. He comes closer to me and gently removes the container of ground coffee from my fingers. We stare at each other for a second. Into the silence I say, 'So Ben...and your apartment. And the precinct.' My voice dwindles away to a gasp. 'All here.'

'All here,' he admits. 'When I swung by my place last night I picked up some clothes.' I glance down at his pyjama bottoms, a dark green tartan flannel pair I've never seen nor imagined for him. His feet are bare, and he hasn't bothered pulling on a sweater. Jay rarely gets cold. He pauses. 'You okay?'

I swallow. Jay's gaze sweeps to the bowl of liquorice, then back to me. He puts down the coffee container, leans back against the bench and folds his arms.

'Fine. I'm fine,' I say. 'Uh, so everything is...'

'Everything is normal,' he finishes, low and distinct.

Normal. He used that phrase *all clear* with Carolyn. Like, *so far so good.* But he must realise this isn't the version of normal I was hoping for.

What have I done?

The silence stretches. All I know is that a person cannot go around rewriting the universe. Every cell in my being tells me that it's dangerous and unethical, and can only end badly.

Jay says, 'What exactly did you think was gonna happen, Evie?'

Damn. Well, he has me there. I swallow down the sick feeling in my marrow. I never considered that this much would come with them. When I started writing the screenplay yesterday, it flowed so easily, and of course I hoped I would see them, but I didn't have any thought beyond that. Mrs Andrews gave me the impression the whole wacky thing could be done in a safe way. I mean, *she* managed it. Her husband has been living here in reality for forty years.

Carolyn's phone beeps from the fruit bowl. I try not to imagine how many people she's affecting right now on freaking social media.

Jay is watching me. 'Evie,' he says, and he doesn't drop his gaze, 'is this what you want?' His tone is quiet, dispassionate. He's looking very cool and together, but as I watch, he clenches one of his folded arms into the side of his body, like he's subconsciously checking the position of his gun. It's not something I've seen Jay do before, but it's exactly the kind of tic a cop might have if he were feeling uncertain. Apprehensive. Because obviously, Jay isn't wearing his gun right now; both Glock and shoulder holster are on my bedside table and his bare torso, which looks so glaringly perfect in my warm kitchen downlights, also strikes me as kind of...vulnerable. I can see the scar over his heart where Carolyn shot him at the end of Book Sixteen, a faint, jagged patch of paler skin.

I pause. His gaze is shuttered. He knows I wrote him back from the dead at the end of my last book. So obviously I want him here. But he also knows I could write him back into my story, this screenplay I've started, as easily as picking up a pen. That I essentially hold his freedom in my hands. Deep down I feel like he might be asking me if having him here is enough to counter all the potential chaos his presence could be creating in the cosmos. And my answer is only a tenuous yes. If I'm doing some kind of eternal damage to the real world then...what? Would I write him back in?

But I want him here. I want him to have free will. I want the happily ever after I imagined this morning. Quiet contentment and peace. Doing good things in our own small world. Comfortable Sundays and family traditions. That's what I want. I think.

'Yes,' I whisper. I step forward, feeling like I'm crossing a river. His bare skin is radiating warmth, and the air begins to fizz between us. Jay responds by putting a hand very lightly on my waist. His gaze has unshuttered and the dark blue of his eyes, always so startling against his olive skin, is deep and warm.

I close the last centimetres of distance between us and put my lips tentatively to the place on his neck that I love. I put my arms around the warm skin of his waist and breathe the scent of him, trying not to be too obvious about it. This is all new, and it feels so good, and so *right*. I remind myself that Jay's existence doesn't somehow go against nature. He's here, isn't he?

His other arm comes around me.

'What about you?' I say. 'Is this what you want?'

'Yeah.' The word is rough, and clipped short, but hints at the emotion of a long romantic declaration. Not that Jay would ever say that stuff out loud.

I put my lips back on his skin. He's so normal and real and safe, and there's a tiny line on his neck, a wrinkle I never noticed before, making him somehow even more human. Like he's in better focus than ever before. And, he needs a haircut. It's reassuring. This isn't a cosmic disaster; he's too ordinary.

'You need a haircut,' I say. He smiles.

'I'm not sure if Angelo's here.'

I trace his hidden cowlick. Angelo is an old guy in Brooklyn who used to cut Jay's dad's hair. Jay is loyal like that, loves connections like that. He gently brings my wrist down and rubs his thumb over it, his eyes two smoky embers.

'There's no scar,' he says, looking at it.

He's right. This is the wrist that got broken, when everything went so wrong six months ago, and by rights there should be a scar where the bone broke the skin. But like a lot of other things, it disappeared from reality with no explanation after...after what? I still don't know how to explain what happened in that farmhouse when I wrote him—wrote sheverything—back in. All I had managed to do was scratch out a single paragraph of Chapter Three and somehow, everything that had gone wrong in reality was rewired, deleted, or edited back to normality. It was incomprehensible, unexplainable.

He examines me. 'Have you flown any helicopters lately? Disappeared from police custody? Killed any terrorists, or written yourself bulletproof?'

'No,' I say. I make a slightly strangled sound. 'I don't do that anymore.' Like I'm talking about an awkward habit I used to have, perhaps of running up to elderly nuns, tripping them over, shouting *HAHA!*, and then running away again. 'I exercise. I take vitamins. I don't want anything to do with that.' Big understatement.

He looks like he wants to laugh, and also, slightly relieved.

'I hope that's not a disappointment to you,' I say consolingly. 'But if it helps, I have been on TV a lot recently and I'm quite famous,' I add. '*Quite* famous.' The sparkle of a silent laugh moves from his eyes to his mouth. Two smiles in one day—a miracle. He dips his head like he's thinking about kissing me.

'Disappointed? That depends.'

I huff. 'Er, rude. On what?'

'On whether you're free tonight.'

My heart leaps. 'Like a date?'

'Yeah, like a date.'

Ooh. Something lights inside me. He wants to *date* me? Like, proper dates?

Jay has dipped his head further, as if he can't resist making contact with my skin. His lips hover near the corner of my mouth, and a dizzying infusion of chemicals has gone straight to my brain. He has a hand on the small of my back and the other has grazed upwards to linger on the nape of my neck. His thumb starts doing little circles in my hairline.

Okay, so I hadn't expected quite this much collateral impact. But what is two apartments and one station house full of people? And some other stuff. It's fine. Maybe it will be the best thing that's happened to this city, having Manhattan South Homicide be a reality. Maybe I've done a service for humanity.

Now I'm wondering why I'm standing here in the same rumpled clothes from last night, when I could be...we could be—

'Evie?'

'Mm?' Meeting his hot gaze is like being set alight. Hm. *Spontaneous human combustion: interesting way to go.* His skin feels *so good.*

'Evie. Do you remember what I asked you last night?'

No. And I don't care. I just want him to kiss me.

But he doesn't. He persists, 'You've never met my family.'

I blink. 'No,' I say. 'I never have.' I never wrote any scenes with them. I've never spent any time with them because I didn't need to. They were a part of Jay's backstory, not his present-day life in New York City. Just there in the background, colouring the pages of Jay's life.

'I asked you if you wanted to meet them.' His eyes are serious. 'We could go for the weekend. Or longer. Since next week is Thanksgiving.'

Now I'm the one who's still. Thanksgiving with his family. Jay's eyes are glittering with something intense, and five seconds ago I thought it was desire. Now I realise it's something much more profound. He knows what having a family means to me.

I say, 'Your mother is going to roll her eyes and say I'm too thin. She's going to look at you with this expression like, "Is this really the girl you chose to bring home?"'

Jay smiles. 'Yeah. She is.'

I imagine myself meeting his firecracker of a mother, with her red lipstick and dark curls, and her ability to simultaneously love her children unconditionally and make them feel an intense desire to be their best selves. I see myself shaking her hand, her pulling me into a hug, and my brain starts to melt.

Interesting way to go.

I feel like I've just been handed a final puzzle piece, not realising what it added up to. I try to smile back at Jay, but I don't quite manage it.

I step back. 'Sounds great,' I say cheerfully, feeling like my mouth is full of stones. Suddenly, being here with him is causing me a kind of acute ache that has nothing to do with the heat in his blue eyes. 'You know, I think I might pop upstairs and take a shower.'

Jay examines me for a moment. 'What's wrong?'

'Nothing's wrong! I just need to…I just, um.' I'm gulping air and tripping over myself as I move backwards, toward the door. 'If you want to make breakfast there's stuff in the fridge, so—' The door swings closed between us. 'Right, see you in a few minutes,' I yell.

little what I added up to. I try to smile back at Jay but I am
quite miserable.

2

Well. I've officially won the prize for world's biggest weirdo.
Which is great. And Jay has noticed, because he notices everything. Points to me for having a wonderfully clever boyfr...what-
ever we are.

I head upstairs to the bathroom, close the door and lean against
it. I'm not entirely sure why the thought of meeting Jay's mother
in the flesh has acted like some kind of existential reality-bomb.
Or why it feels like a final puzzle piece.

I don't want to get dramatic, but meeting Jay's family just feels
so final, somehow. Realising that the station house and Carolyn's apartment are now non-fiction is one thing, but Jay's family
matters. They're a part of him. Like a cup of tea: the infused tea
can't be separated from the water. It can't be *unmade*. Jay's family
make him who he is.

The situation feels irrevocable, final. If they're here, then they
have to stay. Everything has to stay. Whatever kind of mistake this
might have been, unleashing fiction here like I have, I'm going
to have to live with it. Even if that makes me a...a reality vandal.
World-wrecker? That's hyperbole, surely. Either way I'll need to
think of a catchier name for my negative self-talk. Twenty-nine

years old, can't cook but available for modern-day screwing of reality and all associated disasters.

The Butterfly Effect, it's called. I've read enough science articles to know about Chaos Theory. Does that apply to fiction/non-fiction scenarios? Are all my fictional additions to the real world causing earthquakes in Siberia right now? Or worse?

I take a few deep breaths and make a decision to take my palm off the mental panic button I'm pressing. After all, I learnt a lot about not being fearful in the last chapter of my life. Right? Before Book Sixteen I used to spend all my time hiding in my darkened writing room, afraid of everything from death to real relationships. Then I almost got blown up, and strangled, and gassed, and shot (it was a busy time). And I almost received a vertical compression fracture. Twice. Sure, it took a lot of tea and shortbread and months of Mrs Andrews' kind wisdom before I was quite myself again, but I was a different me afterwards. A stronger me.

It's fine. I tell this to my fingers which are tightened into fists against the sink. No, I hadn't expected this. It's a bit sudden, and a bit bigger than I expected, and *why can't I remember what happened last night?*

But that doesn't mean I have to lose it. Probably, I'm overreacting, and there's likely a very simple solution to all this. I've done a lot of supernatural things in the last year, and sure, I didn't enjoy any of them, but they do lead one to think that unmaking a cup of tea might not be impossible, were it necessary.

Except that in this scenario, unmaking a cup of tea would mean undoing Jay's very being.

Not quite the award-winning pep-talk I thought this was going to be.

I glance into the bathroom mirror, intending to give a hastily revised version of the pep-talk to my own reflection, but instead I melt in horror at the sight of my face. *Holy.* Maybe this is why he didn't kiss me. Maybe I'm lucky he didn't recoil and cry, 'It lives!'

My dark curls look like one of those tortured trees that grow on windy clifftops, the mangled branches all leaning in one direction. I have dark smudges where my mascara used to be, which are giving my pale green eyes an alarming intensity. This, combined with my early-morning pallor, has me looking much like a zombie revivification and not, as one would hope, like the 'just awakened' scene from Sleeping Beauty.

In fact, I realise, in a sickening rush, I look like my mother. Just like the first time I saw her after she'd been voluntarily admitted to a mental health facility in a remote village outside Shrewsbury, about nine years ago. I have the same...well, the same everything. Her eyes were brown, not green, but they had the same look in them. As if they'd lost the knack of taking reality at face value.

'Gah.' I paw through my top drawer, hoping for make-up remover pads or miracle cream, but there's nothing usable.

I am not my mother. I repeat this internally a few times. I'm just hungover. There's a difference. Champagne, geez. Who drinks, anyway? Okay, yes, I have been known to turn to alcohol in stressful situations. No need to dwell. After all, I am a more mature, capable version of myself these days.

The second drawer is equally unhelpful, so I wrench open the bottom drawer, desperate, and what I find there is about a million red toothbrushes.

'Aargh!' I slam it closed with my foot. I forgot they were there. They're all brand new, fresh in their packets. Like some maniac has been buying one (or two) every week for the last six months, and collecting them here, like an altar to colour-specific dental hygiene.

Jay must never see this.

Like, ever.

Looking down, I see the sticky note I wrote about Christopher

Murray on the floor. It must have fallen out of my pocket. I pick it up and take it through to my writing room, where I grab a pen and add: *Irish?* I'm in the process of sticking it to the screen of my computer when I feel someone behind me. Warm lips brush the back of my neck.

Relief. I smile, realising that Jay must have followed me up here. There's nothing to worry about. We're in this together, and it's going to be okay.

I turn and say, '*Aaaaaaaaargh!*'

The man standing behind me is not Jay. I leap away from him, waving some ineffectual karate-chop fingers.

Heavens. It's Christopher Murray. He has scruffy blond hair, just like I dreamed it. Like he's just stepped straight out of that dream and into my writing room. '*It's you,*' I breathe.

It's him. Like most characters, he has simply appeared, fully formed, a whole person. Unknown, as yet, but that comes over time. I stare at him in wonder, feeling the bubbling pleasure I always get at the start of new stories. The pleasure of getting to know someone, of all the unexplored possibilities. The promise of discovery.

Christopher Murray stares back. It's not the laughing, mischievous expression I saw in my dream, but I can see the faint laughter lines on his tanned face and imagine the twinkle as he smiles. His hair is tied in a messy man-bun, and he looks like he's in his thirties. He's the kind of lean that implies he stays fit doing things he likes, outdoors, like surfing or paragliding or mountain biking. He has a careless slouch and torn jeans.

He looks like trouble.

'Hello, Trouble,' he says with a grin.

TWO TIMER

OUT NOW

Dime Sheppard is a writer and former barista, waitress, Spanish teacher, vineyard labourer, bilingual interpreter, and production assistant (among other things). She has lived in Scotland, New Zealand and Argentina, has a degree in English literature, and also spent seven years working for an NGO, mostly in South America. This means she has diverse skills: she can string a sentence together, and she can also pee in the desert while fending off a baby goat, cook a delicious meal for thirty people with little more than potatoes and oregano, dig a bogged truck out of metre-deep mud with a broken teacup, and shower in cold water in the dead of winter without a murmur.*

She currently resides in Australia, the land of perfect beach days. She loves reading, swimming, and action movies. She's pretty convinced she will one day achieve a press handstand, and believes in the Curly Girl Method. She loves to laugh and never squashes spiders unless they're venomous.

* Okay fine. There was murmuring.

Visit the official Dime Sheppard website at www.dimesheppard.com or follow her on insta @dimesheppard – she loves connecting with people there.

Come find me:

Goodreads: https://bit.ly/3NQmOhM
Instagram: @dimesheppard
Email: contact@dimesheppard.com

Did you enjoy CRIME WRITER?
Please take the time to rate and/or review it on Goodreads!